wicked RULE

HEARTLESS

KINGDOM

USA TODAY BESTSELLING AUTHOR

K.I. LYNN

Wicked Rule

Copyright © K.I. Lynn

This book is a work of fiction. Names, characters, places, and incidents either are products of the author's imagination or are used fictitiously. Any resemblance to actual events or locales or persons, living or dead, is entirely coincidental.

This work is copyrighted. All rights are reserved. Apart from any use as permitted under the Copyright Act 1968, no part may be reproduced, copied, scanned, stored in a retrieval system, recorded or transmitted, in any form or by any means, without prior written permission of the author.

Cover design by Lori Jackson Designs

Editor:
Evident Ink
Marti Lynch
Danielle Leigh
Missy Borucki

Publication Date: May 17, 2021
Genre: FICTION/Romance/Contemporary
ISBN: 978-1-948284-36-3
Copyright © 2021 K.I. Lynn
All rights reserved

wicked
RULE

ATTICUS CHARLES DE LOUGHREY (1927-2020) — ELIZABETH (BARRET) DE LOUGHREY (1929-2003)

CHARLES DE LOUGHREY - VERA (ALDERIDGE) DE LOUGHREY

ATTICUS WILLIAM DE LOUGHERY (WICKED RULE)

ELIZABETH DE LOUGHREY (PRESTON) ALCOTT
 MADELINE
 BENNETT

HAMILTON DE LOUGHREY (RUTHLESS RULE)

PENELOPE DE LOUGHREY (TAINTED RULE)

GENEVIEVE DE LOUGHREY (WILD RULE)

HENRY DE LOUGHREY - VICTORIA (ROTHCHILD) DE LOUGHREY

RHYS DE LOUGHREY (LEATHAL RULE)

ADRIANNA DE LOUGHREY (DIED AT 15)

ATLAS DE LOUGHREY (DARK RULE)

SILAS DE LOUGHREY (DIRTY RULE)

GEORGIANA DE LOUGHREY (FORBIDDEN RULE)

KATHERINE (DE LOUGHREY) MONTGOMERY - WILLIAM MONTGOMERY JR.

WILLIAM MONTGOMERY III

ADELE MONTGOMERY

NATHANIEL MONTGOMERY

JAMES DE LOUGHREY
(DIED AT 27, NO CHILDREN)

HUGH DE LOUGHREY - CAROLINE (WHITNEY) DE LOUGHREY

JAMES

DANIELLA

ANNABELLE

JAQUELINE (TWIN TO JACKSON)

JAQUELINE DE LOUGHREY
(DIED AT 4 MONTHS)

SOUNDTRACK

Wow—Zara Larsson

Must Be The One—She Wants Revenge

Eyes Closed—Halsey

Blow Your Mind—Dua Lipa

Hold Me Down—Halsey

Lions Inside—Valley of Wolves

Take Me To Church—Hozier

It Was Always You—Maroon 5

Queen of Broken Hearts—blackbear

Not Afraid Anymore—Halsey

Castle—Halsey

One Thing Right—Marshmello and Kane Brown

The World We Made—Ruelle

Can't Get Enough—Jaxson Gamble

Until We Go Down—Ruelle

Stay—Rihanna (feat. Mikky Ekko)

Fallin' (Adrenaline)—Why Don't We

Where We Come Alive—Ruelle

Lonely—Benny Blanco

Don't You Want Me—Human League

Unstoppable—Sia

Fire on Fire—Sam Smith

Always Been You—Shawn Mendes

Dancing With The Devil—Demi Lavoto

Follow You—Imagine Dragons

The Business—Tiesto

Weak—AJR

The Time of Our Lives—The Venice Collection

Secrets and Lies—Ruelle

Save Your Tears—The Weekend

Monsters—Ruelle

Stay With Me—Sam Smith

Obsession—Animotion

Closer—Nine Inch Nails

Lasting Lover—Sigala

Dear reader,

Thank you so much for being here! *Wicked Rule* has been a labor of love. For those of you that follow me you know that life hasn't been easy this past winter, but I finally did it!

The Heartless Kingdom was an idea born in 2019, and I knew immediately it was going to be a multi book series. The titles were immediate, and in no time I had eight family members ready to emerge.

This book… *Wicked Rule* is long. Why? Because it sets the stage for the entire series. All eight from this massive family saga are introduced, as is much of how their world works.

It will be the longest book in the series, and the following will be shorter, but no less intricate.

If you've read *The Rulers*,
got to Chapter Six to pick up where you left off.

THEN

Ten months ago…

The woman beneath me burned. Hot and wet. Each moan from her lips, each gasp as I drove deeper into her, sent a jolt down my spine.

Finding myself looking down into the irresistible eyes of the blonde siren was not the outcome I had expected when I went out for drinks with my cousin to one of the posh clubs that he owned. I didn't pick women up often, and when I did, I certainly didn't take them home.

Well, not home exactly. To a hotel I owned.

A few hours earlier, I'd begrudgingly stepped across a threshold and into the cesspool known as a nightclub. Immediately my skin prickled, and I fought the urge to turn around and retreat to my sanctuary, but an arm dropping down onto my shoulder halted me.

"Don't even think about it, cousin," Rhys said, pulling me through the crowd and the sea of gyrating bodies.

The music thumped loudly as we passed the speakers, making my head pound in time.

"This isn't necessary," I said as we approached the velvet rope at the base of a set of stairs where a security guard kept watch.

"Good evening, Omar!" Rhys said with a jovial smile.

The guard smiled back. "Evening, Mr. de Loughrey," he replied, then unhooked the rope and moved aside. "Have a good time."

"That's the plan," Rhys called back as we ascended the stairs to the VIP section.

After a long, hard battle of a week, all I wanted to do was sink into my bed and not move for a few hours, but, as usual, my wants were never a consideration.

"Relax. We're here to enjoy the evening and maybe the company of a lady or two. Maybe three, if we're lucky."

Club rats were not my taste, but that didn't mean I couldn't enjoy the view.

We entered the private space filled with couches and a table hidden by large, heavy curtains. Shortly after, a barely dressed waitress came in and took our order.

"Would you relax?"

I narrowed my gaze at him. "Said the snake."

"To the lion. If anyone is eating anyone, it's you."

I blew out a breath and rubbed my hands across my stubble. "We need to celebrate."

"It's been six months," I argued.

He rolled his eyes. "Six months since you've been CEO, and not once have you celebrated that accomplishment."

"It's hard to celebrate something that I always knew was going to be mine."

"It's still an accomplishment. You didn't get it simply because you are the firstborn. You worked your ass off to climb to the top."

He was right. From a young age, it was drilled into me that I needed to be the best and that only the best would lead the de Loughrey legacy into the future. If I failed to rise to the top, the mantle would have been passed to whoever was worthy.

The music drew me to the railing, and I surveyed the crowd, watching the pulsing lights beat in time with the bass thumping from the speakers. It was too loud for my tastes, but Rhys was correct—I needed to celebrate.

For years I'd sacrificed everything in my climb to the top—to the point that the company was my life. Every minute of the day was spent thinking about the many workings of our near two-hundred-year-old family business. We'd come out unscathed in the battles of the Industrial Revolution, survived the Great Depression, and exploded in the Technological Age.

"Are those grey hairs I see in all that dark blond?" Rhys said, forcing me to acknowledge his close proximity.

I narrowed my gaze as I turned toward him. His grey eyes sparkled with mirth. They were the same eyes as my younger brother, Hamilton. The same as my father and uncle, as well as my grandfather.

The eyes of a predator.

An interesting observation.

My own were blue, like my mother—warm enough to draw one in, cool enough to give one pause, and calculating enough to frighten even the strongest of constitutions.

"No more than those cropping up in your dark locks. You need a haircut."

Rhys ran his hand through his hair which seemed a few weeks past the point of needing a trim. "All the better to be gripped and tugged on when I'm between a woman's thighs."

A notion he wasn't incorrect about. My scalp tingled with the desire for just that.

"I bet we could find something pretty to top your evening off with."

"It would be easier to simply call Bridget or Antonia." The two women were often called upon as dates to events or for an evening when I was in need of relief.

"Where is the fun and excitement in that? The thrill of some nimble, nubile young woman to warm your cock?"

Sadly, his mere description awakened the craving for all that he depicted.

"Where do you find the energy?"

"For starters, my brain isn't hardwired to the company twenty-four seven. Second, I don't waste *all* of my excess energy in the gym. Third, I enjoy the hunt. A hungry cock will do whatever is necessary to dive into the wet warmth of young, tight pussy."

"You do realize you're starting to sound like Hamilton."

He shrugged. "I'm not as…virile as he is. My appetite is more refined, and I don't pursue it every week. Besides, the brainless bimbos he usually beds hold little appeal to me. I prefer the chase."

"I'm here to relax."

"And nothing is more relaxing than coming into a woman's mouth up here with hundreds of bodies mere feet below."

"I'll take that under advisement."

He sighed and leaned against the rail.

"If you don't want to put forth the effort, just tell them who you are. I've had women clamoring over each other to get on my dick after they heard my last name. Everyone knows the de Loughrey name. We're a fucking American icon."

Before I could compose a retort, the waitress arrived with our drinks, and I gladly took a few hard sips of the amber liquid.

As I did, I watched as a woman with short blonde hair stepped off the dance floor and headed toward the bar. She seemed a bit out of place, which caught my eye. While most women were in tight, body-hugging, bust-enhancing scraps of fabric, the skirt of her dress fluttered behind her. It was more the dress of a garden party than a night out.

The deep navy contrasted against her pale skin, and something white danced across the fabric, breaking up the monotony.

No one followed her, and she found an empty seat at the far end of the bar. As I conversed with Rhys, I periodically glanced her way, and not a soul ever approached.

After finishing my drink, I glanced back to find her still on her own.

All of Rhys's talk of the chase—and a little relaxation from the liquor—had my mind spinning.

"I'm going to go get a refill."

His brow furrowed. "Cindy will be back in a few."

I cleared my throat as I stood. "It's fine."

He shook his head. "The bar is a mess. I wouldn't."

"I'll return," I said, not waiting for a response as I pushed through the heavy curtains and made my way down the dark hallway.

An odd thump of my heart pounded as I descended the stairs and caught a closer look at her. She seemed to be sipping a clear glass of something. Gin and tonic, perhaps?

There was something out of place about her, more than her unearthly quality. She was dressed for the evening, somewhat conservatively compared to other women, with the skirt of her dress loose and hitting mid-thigh, and her inhibitions appeared not to have been taxed by alcohol. Her attention was on the wall behind the bartender and my curiosity piqued even more, almost desperate to know what was on her mind. The curiosity drew me ever closer.

"What's the celebration?" I asked. The words were out before I even realized I'd leaned in.

She jumped and turned toward me, her brown eyes wide. I usually wasn't attracted to women with short hair, but the long pixie cut seemed to suit her. High cheekbones, large eyes, flawless skin, and perfectly pink, kissable lips were featured on her oval face.

"Forgive me. I didn't mean to startle you."

She blinked and smiled as she shook her head. "No, I'm sorry, I was spacing out. What was the question?"

"What are you celebrating?"

She sighed and attempted a smile. "It's my birthday."

I scrunched my brow. "Why do you look so down about that?"

She stared down at the glass in her hand. "Honestly, I'm questioning what the fuck I'm doing here."

I glanced around and took note of how she failed to follow, searching out no one. "Please don't say you're here alone."

She looked away and swallowed. "Everyone was busy."

I leaned back. There was something about her that drew me in closer, something that wouldn't allow me to leave her by herself—my little sea nymph, sitting on her rock all alone.

I held out my hand. "Come with me."

"What?" She looked down at my offered hand.

A chuckle left me. "I have a table. We will help you celebrate."

She shook her head. "Thanks, but I think I'm just going to go home."

"I insist." I gained the bartender's attention and called him over.

"Yes, sir. What can I do for you?"

"Can you send her drink up along with a bourbon, neat?"

"Yes, sir." He took her drink, despite her protest.

"And whatever her tab is, deal with it."

"Yes, sir."

"What are you doing?" she asked with wide eyes.

I cleared my throat and glanced down at my hand. With a huff, she took it and I reveled in the warmth of her touch as she slid off her stool, her purse tucked into her other hand. Once she was on her feet, I slipped her hand into the crook of my arm and led her away. When we reached the staircase, the music lessened as we retreated from the speakers. The bodyguard standing there gave me a nod and moved to the side to allow us up.

"What's your name?"

"Ophelia."

"Ophelia. That's a beautiful name. Mine is Atticus."

"Where are we going? The tables are down there." She pointed over her shoulder, an edge of apprehension in her tone.

Hoping to put her at ease that I had nothing nefarious up my sleeve, I gave her a warm smile, something few people ever received from me. "The VIP section."

Her lips parted and her eyes widened. We finished the climb and moved into a dimly lit walkway with large, thick curtains on one side. Once we reached the middle, I parted the curtains and ushered her through.

Rhys's gaze was wide as he eyed the woman coming into the private space.

"What's this?" he asked, his lips pulling up into a grin. I very much noticed the glint in his eye and the "I told you so" smirk that formed.

"Ophelia," she said as she held out her hand. Rhys, being as lethal as ever, took her hand in his and kissed the top.

"What did I do to be graced with such a beauty?"

She quirked a brow at him. "Does that line actually work?"

I burst out laughing, surprising both of them. "I told you, your lines are over the top, and here I am, proven correct."

"What did he say to get you up here?" he asked her, then glared at me. "And my lines warm my bed every night I desire without fail."

"He didn't say much, just to follow him."

"So direct, Atticus. It's shocking."

I narrowed my gaze at him as I sipped on the drink the waitress had set down. "I find speaking directly works."

"Ophelia, answer me this: does flattery not work on you? Atticus is quite brash and often called insensitive by women, and you have me curious."

"It wasn't really words, but I'm also not sure I understand the undercurrent of associating me with him. Yes, he convinced me to come with him, but that doesn't make me his."

Rhys leaned in closer. "Does that mean you'd be mine for the night?"

"No."

I smirked at the lack of hesitation. She wasn't falling for him. "Why not?"

"You're shady as fuck," she said without pause.

I couldn't contain my laughter again. What the hell was going on with me? Rhys's confusion at my reaction was evident in his wide-eyed stare.

"He has laughed twice now. I'm going to have to ask you to take him back down and return with the correct Atticus, but before that, why such a harsh comparison?" Rhys's wounded pride was bleeding all over the place.

"It's in your attitude. The vibe you give off."

"And by that, you trust him more than me?" Rhys was both seriously affronted and entertained. Given that I was known as the wicked king, I found it interesting that she held even an inkling of trust for me.

"She has good intuition. Lethal lawyers are shady as fuck."

He narrowed his eyes at me. "Might I remind you that it is a shadiness you have used to your advantage more than once."

I tipped my glass to him. "True. However, we aren't talking about a business venture, but the company of a woman."

"What are you boys doing up here all alone?" she asked, putting an end to our spat.

Rhys leaned back. "Trying to let loose after a hard week."

I scoffed. While Rhys was normally reserved and cutthroat, he also had a playful nature about him. He was more social than me, but I knew why he pounded back the drinks, and why he wore a façade. I saw the dark emptiness, if even just a flicker.

"What do you do, Ophelia?" I asked, curious about the little nymph beside me.

"Right now, I'm a waitress."

I'd hoped she'd be something a little more interesting to help explain her appeal. Still, it failed to tamp down my curiosity.

"Right now?" Rhys asked with a quirk of his brow.

She nodded. "I have a degree in biology and was briefly in pharmaceutical sales, but that didn't work out. I just haven't found what I want to do yet."

That was more interesting. At least she was intelligent.

"What do you do?" she asked as she looked at me. There seemed to be a current moving that I hadn't noticed before, and I quite enjoyed the simmer of heat that pulsed between us.

I glanced to Rhys, then gave her a strained smile. I didn't want to tell her. It would ruin the atmosphere. I was genuinely enjoying our time.

"I went into the family business. Boring stuff."

"Didn't have a choice?"

My jaw clenched. "Not really."

"From the day he was born, his future was set," Rhys said, covering the truth and redirecting her attention on the subject.

"And what about you? Lawyer, was it?"

Rhys grinned. "Corporate lawyer."

Nothing about his answer was untrue, just the omission of it being the family company.

"Remind me, is that better or worse than an ambulance chaser?" she asked.

Another laugh burst from me. What had gotten into me? I wasn't one to show enjoyment in anything. Something about my little nymph was drawing it out of me.

Despite what she said, she *was* mine, if even just for the night.

"You wound me, Ophelia."

She smiled and shook her head. "I doubt there is little that would wound you. What did Atticus call you? The Lethal Lawyer?"

"I do like them feisty."

She shrugged, then turned to me. "How about you?"

My heart thrummed roughly in my chest as her brown eyes bored into mine.

"Feisty or not, it makes no difference. I'm enjoying your company regardless."

She settled back against the couch, her shoulders settling under my arm. The current intensified, firing off tingles across every inch of her that rested against me.

"He wins."

Perhaps I would be taking someone home this evening.

OPHELIA

The alcohol warmed me, but not as much as the man I'd inched my way closer to over the past hour. Despite the way the evening began, I thoroughly enjoyed myself with these two gorgeous strangers in a VIP booth at Angelino.

It was one of the hottest clubs in the city, and I only came out on the invitation from my friend Jennifer.

Who then cancelled on me last minute. Whatever. We'd barely

talked over the last few years, but she saw a post on Facebook and invited me.

Still, I came, using her name, which was on the list—I guess dating a professional baseball player had its advantages—and cutting the line of people hoping to cross the threshold.

I had been two sips from walking out, ending the night early, when Atticus appeared beside me. His blue eyes held me in thrall, his voice on edge, and those were only the first two things I noticed about the man.

There was a dusting of stubble accentuating his strong jaw, and he had a straight nose, perfectly styled light brown—possibly dirty blond—hair, with similarly colored brows that shadowed his intense gaze.

His lips.

Immediately my body flamed red-hot just imagining his lips ghosting across my skin. I forced myself to look away and focus on the charcoal-colored suit that hugged his body in the most perfect way.

When I took his hand, I was pleasantly surprised by his height. At five-and-a-half feet tall, pretty close to six-feet in heels, he was still inches above me.

Two hours later, I was as entranced by his eyes, his lips, and his body as I had been when I first saw him. His voice left me wet and wanting from the beginning. I'd just returned to the VIP lounge from a trip to the bathroom, where I'd removed my thong and shoved it into the pocket of my dress, preferring the cool air to the damp sensation.

When I pushed through the heavy curtain, I was greeted by Atticus's warm smile.

"You didn't run off."

I quirked a brow at him. "Is that code for I should have left?"

He stood and stepped toward me as I moved to the railing. Rhys had disappeared while I was away, leaving us alone with the heavy crackling of attraction that pulled us together.

I swallowed hard and looked out over the crowd, trying to tamp down the lustful thoughts I was having about the gorgeous man.

My hips swayed to the beat as I let my mind go and lost myself. A gasp left me as my skin electrified, and I slowed the roll of my hips.

Atticus's strong chest was against my back, his arms on either side of me, caging me against the railing. The warmth of his body muddled my mind. The heat of his breath against my neck followed by the light brush of his lips and stubble had me pushing back into him.

"I don't do this, ever, but I have a hotel room a few blocks away. I would hate for the evening to end," he said against my ear, his voice a low, gravelly tone, deep and rich, that sent shivers down my spine.

Every word the man said held an air of power, and his voice projected confidence.

I'd never had a one-night stand, yet with the tangible chemistry between me and the man behind me, I had a feeling that was about to change.

"It would be a first for me," I said as I arched my neck and leaned back against him.

He let out a low groan before lightly nipping my neck just below my ear, sending a jolt through my system.

"Is that a yes?" He rocked his hips against my ass, and my mouth popped open at the feel of his hard length pressing against me.

I moved my hips, grinding against him for a moment before twisting to look at him. His eyes were dark, lips only a few inches away. Craning my neck, I nipped at his bottom lip, then ran my tongue against it to soothe the sting, loving the way his gaze darkened.

"Yes."

He reached up and gripped my jaw, holding me in place as his lips pressed fiercely against mine. "Let's go."

Rhys entered just as we were exiting, surprise on his face morphing into a knowing smirk.

"Have a good night," he said with a wink.

"Good night. Thanks for the fun," I said as Atticus pulled me out and down the hallway.

His demeanor was almost frenzied with the way he bulldozed through the crowd, but when we made it outside to the street, he relaxed.

"I didn't want to lose you," was all he said as he slowed to a more manageable pace.

My hand was warm in his as we walked a few blocks down to Le Magnifique, a five-star hotel that I could never afford to stay in.

His touch was forceful in a desperate sort of way, one that fueled the fire inside me with each bit of movement. He couldn't seem to let go of my hand. And the farther we walked, the tighter he gripped me. Was he afraid I was going to change my mind? As if there was a choice in the matter.

I'd never been more drawn to a man. Nor had I ever been more desperate to feel one's lips or body on mine.

Somehow, we managed not to maul each other in the elevator, but we were barely through the door when he pushed me against the wall, his lips crashing to mine. The fire that had started the moment I looked up into his sapphire eyes exploded into a raging inferno, burning every vein as my blood moved through my body.

He held my jaw tight, his thumb and fingers digging in as he devoured my mouth, his other hand fisting the back of my hair, threading through the shorter ends as he tried to possess me.

His tongue created a spiraling shock that moved through me, and I was trapped in the gravity of him too far to notice his fingers pulling at the tie on the back of my dress until the top slipped down and fabric pooled low on my hips.

A light pull at the zipper and my dress was a puddle of fabric at my feet.

"No panties?" he growled.

"I lost them."

"Lost them?"

"Yes. They were wet from being so close to you."

A groan left him and the intensity rolling off him increased. "Tell me why."

My fingers flexed against his chest and I bit down on my bottom lip. "Because every word out of your mouth goes straight to my clit."

His lips tugged up into a smug smile.

"You seem to have lost all of your clothing," he said, his gaze traveling all the way down, sending a blaze of heat across my skin as he went.

"Your fault again. I think you wanted to see me naked."

His hand slipped between my thighs, and I gasped as his fingers slid against my clit, then down until he had two fingers buried inside me. A high-pitched cry left me, my muscles tense from the sudden explosion of pleasure.

"I think you may be right. Do you want to know what I know?" he asked. My eyes glazed over, lips parting as his fingers moved in and out, sliding across my clit as he did.

"W-what's that?"

He pried my mouth open and slipped his thumb in, which I instantly lapped at, earning a strained groan. "That you will look exquisite when you come on my cock."

I reached forward and gripped his bulge, earning a low rumble from his chest and a harder drive of his fingers.

Fuck, he was thick.

He tilted my head back, his thumb slipping from my mouth just as his teeth scraped across the length of my neck.

Complete control was his, and it felt so good.

"You know what will look great as well?" I asked. Each breath reached higher in pitch as he drove me closer and closer to orgasm.

He kissed and nipped his way up to my ear before biting lightly on my earlobe. "What's that?"

I turned my head so that I could get closer to his ear, and his hand dropped down to rest lightly on my neck.

"My lips wrapped around your cock," I whispered, giving him a squeeze. He groaned, then bit down on my neck before his touch vanished from my body.

A whimper left me, but when I looked into his eyes, the predator that looked back sent a jolt of excitement through my system.

"On your knees." He removed his suit jacket before working open his belt and then his slacks. By the time my knees hit the marble floor, I was at eye level. It had been a while since I'd been up close and personal with a man, but I didn't remember ever being as in-timidated before.

My whole body flushed in anticipation, and I reached out. He was warm, heavy, and thick. I wasn't some petite little thing, but even my fingers couldn't encircle his girth. My pussy clenched in anticipa-tion of having him inside me, *filling* me, *stretching* my walls.

I looked up at his dark eyes that watched me. He reached out and gripped my jaw again before slipping his thumb into my mouth.

"Suck it, just like that," he growled before releasing me.

Leaning forward, I ran my tongue along the underside of his shaft, flicking the tip before closing my lips around the head. I worked my way down, loving each sigh and low vocalization that slipped from him.

"You're right. You are a vision with your mouth stuffed full of my cock."

I released him and dipped lower, my tongue circling one of his balls before sucking it into my mouth. Another curse hissed through clenched teeth, and I repeated the action on the other side as I pumped his length before returning to swallow as much as I could, starting at the head.

"Fuck, you're good at that." He pushed on the back of my head, and I choked, unable to go as far as he wanted.

Another low growl vibrated deep in his chest and he pulled me up to my feet. A gasp left me as he delivered a painful but pleasur-able slap to my clit before he stepped forward and grabbed my ass.

His fingers dug into my butt cheeks as he lifted me up, my legs instinctively wrapping around his waist.

"You have a fantastic ass. I'm going to enjoy fucking you from behind and watching it bounce as you take my cock."

"Promises, promises," I said before nipping his neck. A growl rumbled in his chest before I was shocked by a sting across my butt before he started walking toward the bedroom.

I felt the hot head of his cock tapping against me with each step. A few more steps, and my stomach flipped as we fell onto the bed.

His lips smashed to mine, and I was lost in the intoxicating hunger with which he possessed me.

He pulled back and I let out a whine, earning me another tap on my clit. "You are a needy little nymph," he said as he pulled at his clothes. His tie went first, followed by his vest, dress shirt, and undershirt before he finally removed everything from his lower half.

The suit that looked painted on only hid the body of a god beneath the rich fabrics. Lean, taut muscles, strong, broad chest and shoulders, defined abs, and even that heavenly, groan-inducing *V*. The man was perfection of the male species.

I reached down to pull off my heels, but his hand grasped mine, stopping me.

"Leave those on for now." He gripped my breast, drawing my nipple between his fingers and tugging, making me cry out. "Mmm, I like that sound."

He retreated again before pulling a condom from the bedside drawer and putting it on. My thighs rubbed together as I bit down on my lip, entranced by the flawless specimen before me.

I scooted back up the bed as he closed in. With strong hands, he pushed my thighs open, licking his lips as he stared down at my pussy.

He smacked his cock against my clit, making me jump and grind my hips against him as he positioned himself.

"Here's one promise for you," he said, then slammed his hips against mine. I lost all thought as he drove in, filling me in a way I didn't think I ever had been. My eyes fluttered, and my mouth fell open as he stretched me. His lips were against my ear, but I was still lost in the initial shock and pleasure. "I'm going to fuck you so hard, that you won't be able to walk when I'm done."

The pace he set up was hard and unrelenting, my back arching under his assault. His lips were fire and sin, and I burned under their touch.

"Atticus," I whimpered, my head thrown back.

"You feel so fucking good," he groaned. He lavished my neck with liquid fire, drowning me in desire while begging for more. I lost the ability to think, consumed by pleasure with every thrust as he pushed me higher and higher into ecstasy.

"Look at me," he growled. One hand gripped my jaw again, tilting my head where he wanted.

I forced my eyes open, instantly losing myself in the intensity of his gaze.

The guttural groans coming from him had me squeezing around him even harder. His thrusts became more aggressive, faster, and a scream left me as every muscle tensed, then let go.

"That's it, fucking come," he snarled.

I barely registered the last hard slams of his hips against mine, but I felt every twitch of his cock inside me.

His breath was hard and harsh against my neck, and I knew mine was the same.

Wow.

Never had a guy done to me the things Atticus had just done. For one, I came. Hard. And I felt like it was just a promise of more to come.

For another, the chemistry was off-the-charts hot.

After a few minutes, he pulled back, a relaxed grin on his face. I whimpered when he pulled out, missing the full feeling of having him inside me.

He stood and pulled off the condom before throwing it in the trash.

"Water?" he asked as he headed through the door.

"Yes, please." I rolled over in time to watch his sinful ass walk away.

Happy Birthday to me!

The night had done a complete one-eighty compared to how I thought it would go when I left my apartment.

When he returned, he handed me a bottle of water, which I greedily downed as he sat next to me. The room service menu was in his hand, and he opened it before passing it to me.

"I'm hungry. You?"

I blinked at him. "I kinda worked up an appetite."

"Get whatever you want. You'll need the calories."

A shiver zipped down my spine at the rough edge of his voice. "I will?"

He smirked. "I'm not done with you yet."

"Really?" I asked as I bit down on my lip and scanned the menu. A sigh of disappointment fell over me. "They don't have much this late."

"Whatever you want. Don't worry about the time."

"What makes you so special?" I asked, curious where his confidence came from.

"We're in the penthouse. Trust me."

It was then it really hit me—we *were* in the penthouse.

Sometime in the early morning hours, we had both succumbed to exhaustion and fallen asleep. When I woke, I found I was snuggled into Atticus's side, my head on his chest, legs wrapped with his.

Tilting my head back, I found blue eyes looking at me and felt the soft caress of fingers across my back.

"Good morning."

My face burned, and I looked away. "Good morning."

The situation felt like he would have kicked me out when done, and I would have been doing the walk of shame back to the train station, but that wasn't what happened at all. While I didn't expect, nor want, any declarations of anything, I immensely enjoyed the peace that moved between us, light and airy, while the warmth of his skin against mine settled into my affection-starved bones.

"How do you feel?" he asked, his fingers never faltering in their caress.

"A little sore, but good. You?"

"Hungry."

I looked back up and met his gaze. The brightness had dimmed, overtaken by a darkness. The intense moment was cut short by his stomach grumbling beneath my hand.

I couldn't help but laugh, and neither could he. "What do you want first?"

"Move your hand down a little more, and I think you'll figure it out."

"Bathroom first." I pulled away from him, instantly missing his warmth as I dashed to relieve myself. Once done, I found Atticus walking in, heading to the sink where he picked up a toothbrush. Looking to the other sink, I noticed a complimentary toothbrush and followed suit, giving my mouth a quick cleaning.

When he was done, he moved to the massive shower and turned it on. I couldn't keep my eyes off his cock as it bobbed about, hard and needy and completely hypnotizing, especially after the night's events.

He pulled me into the shower with him, pressing my back against the cold tiles. Just as the night before, he picked me up, my legs wrapping around him as the warm water crashed down on us. He teased me with his lips, ghosting them across mine before pulling back, a smirk greeting me. Before he could do it again, I cupped his face and pulled his lips to mine.

What started out as a languid consumption quickly escalated into a ravaging. And I loved every second. A ragged sigh left me when I felt the head of his cock push through my pussy lips, and I sank down on his length.

That seemed to morph his frenzy into a slow, sensual thrusting. "You are absolutely divine."

Though sore from our night, a slow burn grew, intensifying with each thrust.

"I want to come," he hissed, looking down to where we were connected before finding my eyes again. He reached between us and brushed his fingers across my clit. We both moaned, and his teeth clenched.

"Come, Ophelia." The pressure of his fingers increased with the speed of his thrusts. "I need you to come, baby."

My thighs shook as I clenched down around him, my head tilted back into a scream. His teeth dug into my neck, and he groaned as he pulled out, his cock pulsing as his cum shot out, landing on my breasts and stomach.

As we came down, I reached up and brought his forehead down to mine. "Where did you come from?"

He chuckled and pressed his lips to mine. "Come on, let's clean up."

Once we were washed and I was dried off, I wobbled toward the door to determine where my dress had been deposited. There was a chuckle behind me as I braced myself against the wall.

"Yeah, yeah, job well done."

He chuckled again. "I'm known for being an overachiever."

With some pain, weakness, and effort, I bent over and picked up my dress from the floor. I gasped at the feel of hands on my hips, pulling me. A groan left him as he ground against me.

"Don't show off your pussy if you don't want my cock. It just makes me want you more."

I could feel him hardening behind me. "Did you swallow a bottle of Viagra or something?"

"You are the drug. No other stimulants necessary." He thrusted his hips, groaning. "Love watching this ass."

I straightened, much to both of our disappointments, but it didn't keep his hands from wandering around my body. One hand was on a breast while the other slipped between my legs.

"Atticus," I whimpered.

"Fuck, I love the way you say my name like that."

I leaned my head back on his shoulder. "I should get going."

"Should?"

"It's already the afternoon." Well, only by a few minutes.

He dipped his fingers inside me before lifting them to my lips. I opened, taking them in and tasting myself as I licked his fingers clean.

"You are perfection," he whispered into my ear before stepping away, leaving me wobbling a bit. "Let me get you a car."

I pulled my dress up and reached back to tie the top. "It's okay. I can take the train." I didn't want to wait in an attempt to avoid the awkwardness that was growing in me, but I found my thighs didn't want to cooperate, and I fell into a nearby chair.

Atticus chuckled as he picked up his phone. "I do believe I promised to fuck you so hard you wouldn't be able to walk."

He had, and oh, how I thought he was just another asshole talking big. No, he delivered on his promise, and I felt it *everywhere*.

"Okay, so maybe I wouldn't be opposed to a taxi."

"I think I can do better than one of those cesspools."

I blinked at him. What other option was there?

"There is a car waiting for you out front whenever you're ready," he said a moment later. "I can't convince you to stay, can I?"

I shook my head. "Sorry. I have to work tonight."

He pulled me against his chest, his arms holding me close. "Thank you for a wonderful evening," Atticus said as he placed a kiss to my cheek, then to my lips.

"Thank you for a very memorable birthday. It's definitely one I will never forget," I admitted. It wasn't a night I believed could be topped.

"I never did ask how old you turned."

"Twenty-six."

"Hmm."

"Hmm, what?" I asked, unsure if the sound was good or bad.

A small smile graced his lips as he brushed my hair back. "Best night of my life spent with a woman nearly ten years younger than me. Unexpected."

"Best night?" I asked.

He nodded. "It was truly a pleasure meeting you."

"You too."

"Would it be presumptuous of me to assume you had a good enough time that you would be willing to see me again?"

I bit down on my bottom lip and smiled as I nodded. "I'd like that very much."

He pressed his lips to mine for a last searing kiss before I headed down to the lobby.

I was blissed out as I sat in the back of the black sedan Atticus sent me home in. It really had been the best night of my life, and I couldn't keep the smile from my face the entire journey home.

A few days had passed, and I hadn't heard from Atticus. I couldn't deny part of me was saddened by this, but judging based on his suit and the expensive penthouse hotel room, he was bound to be a busy man.

At least, that was the reasoning I gave myself to lessen the ache in my chest.

Once, I saw a man I thought was him, but when he turned to face me, I was wrong. The bad part was the utter embarrassment of calling out his name, only to be proven wrong.

To keep my mind off him, I dove into work. I hadn't been at 130 Degrees for very long, just under two months, but I enjoyed the atmosphere of the high-end steakhouse. One meal for a couple cost a bare minimum of two-hundred dollars, and the tips were just as good.

"Ophelia," my manager, Mitchell, called out and waved me over.

"What's up, boss?"

He led us to his office and closed the door. The action had my stomach suddenly in knots because that was a "you're being fired" kind of move.

"We have a large business meeting coming in tomorrow. Our investors will be there."

"Okay."

"I want you to take the lead."

I blinked at him, happy for the opposite of my worst thoughts. "Me? What about Chris or Megan? They've been here a lot longer. I'm still learning."

Not that I didn't appreciate it, but I was still the new girl.

"They're good, but you have the best rapport with the clients. They like you. I need your personality to shine and show these men why a plate here is so expensive."

"My smile doesn't tack on an extra hundred to the bill."

He chuckled. "No, but you are great at flavor pairing and making sure everything is perfect."

"Thank you. Really, thank you."

He grinned at me. "Tomorrow won't be easy, but you'll have help. Make me proud."

"I will. I promise."

The next morning, I made certain that the large banquet table was impeccably set.

My stomach twisted in anticipation as I readied everything. I wanted to make a good impression for both myself and the restaurant. It would be my first larger party, and I would have Drake around as a helper. He was a little bit squirrelly but friendly.

"Ophelia, they're here," Mitchell called as he stuck his head into the kitchen.

I stared up at him and nodded. My nerves kicked in, and I blew out a breath before heading out onto the floor.

The atmosphere at the table screamed money and power, and as I scanned the faces, I tried to guess their drinks. When I got to the head of the table, my mouth dropped open. He hadn't looked up, but it had only been a few days, and there was no way I would forget.

Sitting at the head of the table was none other than my one-night stand, looking devilishly handsome. When our eyes met, I caught the flash of recognition before it was covered by a look of disgust.

What is that?

I swallowed back the pain of disappointment it caused, realizing he was never going to call me, and plastered on a fake smile to cover my breaking heart. It was a stupid reaction, but I really thought we had a connection.

I was apparently the only one feeling that way. It was obvious he was out of my league, but I couldn't help but wonder. All of that was out the door, and I had to push that night from my mind. Pry my feelings away from the overwhelming sadness that came from one look as I tried to forget the best night of my life.

"Good day, gentlemen. My name is Ophelia, and I am at your service today."

NOW

ATTICUS

My grandfather is dead.

Four words I'd said to myself over and over, yet the response inside me was the same each time. There was no anguish in my emotions and little sadness in general. It was more of a relief than anything.

He was never a loving man, and I respected him, but I never loved him. Hard and harsh in every way, he'd made my life hell.

He shaped me into the man I'd become.

"Are you coming?" my brother, Hamilton, asked as I stood outside the dining room.

"I'd rather not." Nothing good was going to come from going in there.

"It's the reading of his will, and we all have to be present. Please don't torture me today by drawing it out."

I sighed before following him into the overcrowded dining room. Everyone was cloaked in black, but few mourned him. The greedy ones just wanted to know what he left them, while I was fairly certain I didn't want to hear what the old man's last jab at me would be.

All twenty of the table's chairs were taken. At the head of the table sat my father, and at the other head was the family lawyer, Alexander Corwin, with what I assumed were others from his firm to assist.

I stood against the wall next to Hamilton, with my cousin, Will, on my other side. The walls were lined with de Loughreys eagerly awaiting their take, and the gallery balcony that overlooked from the second floor was also stuffed with bodies.

"Is everyone here?" Alexander asked as he glanced around the room.

By the thickness of the legal binder in front of him, this was going to take forever, especially with a room of over seventy people.

"We are here today for the reading of the last will and testament of Atticus Charles de Loughrey."

To his brothers, my great uncles, he left money and personal items.

Unsurprisingly, money, stocks, and property, as well as a few personal items, were granted to his children—my father, Uncle Henry, Aunt Katherine, and Uncle Hugh.

Then came my turn as I was the oldest of my generation.

"To my grandson, Atticus William de Loughrey, I leave Stronghold." Alexander paused and looked around. "This residence," he added for clarification before continuing, "The position as the newest head of the de Loughrey family. He will also take over the position of CEO of de Loughrey Corporation, and with that he will inherit all my shares in the de Loughrey Corporation on his fortieth birthday."

My eyes narrowed. Why would he make me the largest shareholder?

I wasn't the only one wondering as multiple sets of eyes flickered to me. There was a catch. I just knew it.

I already knew of the impending promotion to de Loughrey family leader, patriarch of all, and that was the only non-surprise. With my father retiring, albeit slowly, the crown fell to me. There was an almost palpable shift in the air—a shift of respect and compliance.

It was the day I would be crowned.

"I apologize, Atticus. I realize you are already the CEO. This will is two years old."

"It's fine, Alexander."

"There's more."

Of course there is.

"In order to receive his shares, Stronghold, and to retain his position as CEO and head, there are two conditions which must be met. Atticus Charles has put it all into a trust with springing interest, meaning Atticus William will only gain rights to the property and shares upon fulfillment of the terms. The terms are henceforth set: If Atticus is not married upon my death, he has one year to be married or forfeit all. He also must produce an heir before his fortieth birthday. Both conditions must be met by the dates specified or he will not receive anything. If he fails to meet the requirements, the items stated will be handed to my second grandson, Rhys Geoffrey de Loughrey, whereby the same requirements will be enacted. And so on, through each male heir, until the conditions are met."

Fuck.

Fuck, fuck, fuck.

The old man got his last dig in hard.

"Comply, or lose everything I've primed you for." I could even hear the words in his voice, feel his steely gaze pinned on me.

He never liked that out of more than a dozen grandchildren, none of us were married except Elizabeth. However, he no longer considered her a de Loughrey as she was not a man and no longer held our family name. Always underestimating Elizabeth and women in general.

By the time my father had reached my age, he had multiple children already. The same for my uncles and aunt. Therefore, my grandfather believed we all should have children.

Well played, Grandfather.

I was also left with a few million dollars and some artwork. Much more money and property was given out, divided up among my siblings and cousins, and a trust was set up for eleven de Loughrey homes around the globe. It was only the tip of the iceberg, as the family owned much more than that. They were the oldest of the properties, which was why it was curious he left me Stronghold. It had been in our family since my great-great-grandfather. The original show of de Loughrey wealth to rival Vanderbilt's riches. In my eyes, it should have been the crowning property of the trust.

With every few minutes of speaking, Alexander had to take a sip of water, and by the end of hour two, his voice had become hoarse. When he finished, an elaborate symphony of paperwork was danced across the room by his assistants.

With a swipe of the pen, I accepted everything including my role, my status, and the stipulations he enacted.

I was the new ruler.

King of the de Loughreys.

"He got the final word, as usual," Hamilton said beside me as the assistant handed me my copy.

There was still more paperwork to take care of, but that would wait for another time.

"It shouldn't shock me, but I find I am surprised."

When Alexander stood, the room began to disperse, some heading home, some chatting as they awaited dinner.

As family passed I received nods and acknowledgments, as well as handshakes. However, not everyone was happy about the new power structure or distribution of my grandfather's excessive wealth.

"This isn't fair. Atticus got so much," Daniel said, making me pause.

I turned to him. "He was your great uncle. Why would he leave you more than his firstborn grandson and successor?"

He startled, not realizing I was right there. Daniel, who at twenty-five, had little pressure on him and epitomized the stereotype of families like ours by acting like a spoiled brat.

"I—"

I leaned forward, the movement cutting him off. "Isn't there a stipulation in your trust that you must maintain a job?"

"Y-yes."

Weak. So weak it made me burn with rage.

I leaned in closer to make sure he could see the displeasure in my expression and the flames behind my eyes. "Then be happy you were even here. Shut up and get out before I fire you."

His eyes widened. Pathetic. Where did this weak blood come from?

"You can't fire me."

I quirked a brow at him. Was he talking back? A low chuckle left me, and I snarled at him, "Try me."

I watched the bob of his Adam's apple as the color drained from his face. He bowed his head in submission. "I'm sorry, Atticus."

Every so often, one of the spoiled ones thought they were tough. Thought they were more than they were. Examples were made to help keep all the egos in check, and my rule had just found its first target.

Start hard to keep the insubordination down. What was asked of them all was trivial. Behave. Yet it amazed me how often someone stepped out of line.

Daniel scurried away with Petra and Phillip, thankfully heading toward the front door.

Once gone from my sight, I pulled out my phone and in one short message to cut Daniel's accounts off. The move was temporary, but his hysteria when he found he had no money would straighten out his attitude.

"Atticus," my father called.

I stuffed my phone back in my pocket and looked up. The smile on his lips coupled with the manic energy emanating from his gaze had me grinding my teeth. It hadn't been five minutes, and he was already up to something.

"Don't worry, I've got a perfect wife for you," he said as he stopped in front of me.

"Excuse me?"

"An arranged marriage. There is a girl—"

"Stop," I said, interrupting him. "Say nothing more." How many times had we had the same argument over the last decade?

His gaze hardened. "Don't be difficult, Atticus. A marriage to an influential family is a perfect solution."

"I refuse."

"Refuse?" He scoffed. "You're not really in the position to decline."

"*I* am the patriarch now. Not you," I ground out.

"How can you be a patriarch when you don't even have any children," he sneered.

"Hear me well, Father, because I will not repeat myself," I raised my voice so that all around would hear. "*I* am your king. It matters not that you are my father. I rule this family, not you. If Grandfather had died ten years ago, the responsibility would have fallen to you, but you're already entering retirement and I run the company."

"I am your *father*, and I will do what is necessary for you to succeed. You *will* marry a woman of my choosing."

"I will *never* agree to an arranged marriage, so remove that thought from your mind," I boomed out, my anger no longer tethered by a thread.

"You will come to my side of thinking."

"Stubborn old man. You need to come to my side or I will crush you."

"You're not strong enough, *son*."

"I wouldn't challenge me."

"You have no power over me." He grinned.

There was little that I could hold over him and he knew it. Charles de Loughrey was nearly untouchable and would be a constant thorn in my side.

"Your access to the de Loughrey tower has been revoked for the next week."

His eyes widened. "What?"

It wasn't much, but my ammunition was minimal at this time. I would need to become more cunning when facing him.

"For each word you say, I will add another week. You're now at two. Your little affair with one of your assistants? As of today, she is removed."

His face was red with rage, but he somehow managed to hold himself back. My lips pulled up into a smirk.

"Bow your head before I remove your maid."

His eyes widened farther.

"Oh, yes, I know about that one as well. You can't hide your indiscretions from me, Father."

His muscles were coiled right, but he managed a slight bow of his head.

"I'm glad we have reached an understanding. Now, refrain from testing me again."

I pushed past him and retrieved a drink from the bar before making my way out to the patio. I relaxed into one of the plush chairs as I swirled the amber liquid of my glass of Bowmore 1957 whiskey while overlooking the lake. The sun gleamed across the water, giving off a calming effect in addition to the drink in my hand.

It had already begun, and that outburst was only the beginning. I could feel their eyes boring into the back of my head, hear the chattering of whispers flowing in the breeze. The weight of them settled on my shoulders, oppressive as it coiled around my chest.

The expression of my status would keep many of them in line, but during the beginning, there were going to be assholes testing me. I would make examples of them, and punishments began to form in my mind for the spoiled assholes.

The Bowmore did little to settle the stress that boiled inside. Stress that I wouldn't dare show anyone. It would be seen as weakness, an avenue of exploitation.

The new head of the family. Grandfather had lived to a ripe old age, passing at the time Father began to step back in the company. That was the only thing his stipulations didn't touch. No matter what, I was the new ruler of hundreds of de Loughreys.

The king.

My word would be the last word and law.

It was a role my grandfather and my father had shared over the last two decades, but now it was all mine.

I may not have been as heavy-handed as my father, but I would still put each and every one of them in their place with no remorse. Being the head of the family was no easy task, and while my father still held some of the familial responsibility, the bulk rested on my shoulders.

The sun sparkled across the water, turning the surface into a beautiful golden orange when a hand landed on my shoulder. The dainty yet calloused fingers told me all I needed to know.

She said nothing, though I knew she had much on her mind. After the incident, my little sister had become withdrawn. The spotlight of shame was one she vowed never to enter again. It was a time in which we'd grown closer, something our nine-year age gap had not allowed before.

Of all my siblings, Penelope was the most intuitive, and the simple weight of her hand conveyed more than anyone else could comprehend.

"They're settling for dinner," she said.

I let out a sigh as I stood, taking one last look at the lake before following her inside. The table had been extended to allow room for everyone who remained and was exquisitely set. Gold trimmed china and crystal sparkled in the richly appointed table.

All eyes fell to me as they stood, waiting, and it pleased me that none were taking that moment to test me.

The heaviness that lay upon my shoulders had my spine straightening to carry the load of all in the room as I took my place at the head of the table. Once I was seated, my father followed suit before the scooting of chairs filled the silence.

While not Shakespeare's exact words, the idiom was most apt: *Heavy is the head that wears the crown.*

ATTICUS

The chatter of my family from the two-story dining room echoed in the gallery as I stared out. Small twinkling lights could be seen on the lake as fireworks boomed, sprinkling colorful bright spots against the dark sky.

The setting was familiar. I grew up in Stronghold, and now I was the lord of all I surveyed.

As long as I married.

As long as I had a child.

I knew there was no way the old man would cross over without flipping me off as he went.

The house was mine. *The* house of the de Loughrey family.

Now to find a family of my own to fill it.

That thought filled me with dread. I'd spent my life striving to be the best, to excel the business, to expand our horizons, and I was on the verge of losing it all over a fucking woman.

Lavender and linen filled my senses, and the whispered moans in the back of my mind invaded my ears. They weren't memories from either woman in whose beds I'd spent many hours. No, Bridget and Antonia were far from my thoughts. The ghostly reminder was of a woman I'd spent only one night with. A woman who tortured me weekly, and I paid her to do so.

Ophelia.

The errant thought was as mad as my behavior that evening. No, it was quite insane. The mere flash of an idea had me tilted enough I pondered if I needed to be checked out by the family physician.

Taking her home that night was one of those maneuvers I hadn't expected. Something about her beauty, the aching loneliness that almost called out to me. A siren in a sea of gyrating bodies and loud beats. Adrift with no one to save her.

Was that why I couldn't resist her? Why I continued to think of her?

"Had enough?" a familiar voice asked.

I didn't even need to look to know who it was that now leaned against the banister next to me, though I was happy to have his distraction.

"Am I that obvious?"

Rhys chuckled. "For as much as you are like Aunt Vera, you are equally like Uncle Charles."

"Except I'm not off hiding in a spare bedroom with the maid. I'm simply tired of the inane babbling."

"Are you hiding with the butler?"

I turned and narrowed my gaze on my cousin. We were the oldest of the generation, born from the oldest of the previous generation, and saddled with responsibilities that position of birth hoisted upon us.

"Simply because I'm not out fucking every slut at whatever high-end club you are currently playing at does not mean anything. My sex life is none of your concern."

"Well, it should be yours."

"Why?"

He arched a dark brow at me. "You don't have a girlfriend."

"When the fuck do I have time for something like that?"

He held up a hand. It was a conversation we'd both had, and been given, multiple times. I was tired of the constant barrage about my love life, and more than once, about the threat of an arranged marriage.

Unfortunately, all that had come to a head.

"You heard the will, same as me. The family demands an heir."

"And where is your contribution?" I asked. Rhys gave me one of his sly smirks that only devils wore. "Besides, my father seems happy to continue supplying heirs."

"They are not legitimate."

"You should know," I scoffed. Being the lethal lawyer of the company, Rhys was the one who drew up all the contracts and non-disclosure agreements for my father's philandering. Those types were not entrusted to Alexander, the family lawyer. He made certain they were ironclad and that there was no way the mother or child could ever try to extort or expose the dirty laundry.

The consequences for even the slightest infraction were dealt with swiftly.

"At this rate, our mess of siblings will have families before us, and therefore, the company."

I let out a dark chuckle. "Elizabeth has already beaten us there, and the rest of my siblings? It'll be a cold day in hell before any of them settle down. I honestly think next up will be Georgiana."

"My debutante little sister?" he asked, then seemed to ponder. "She is the second youngest of our two families, but also the purest."

"I wouldn't be surprised if she was a virgin."

He shook his head. "She lost that long ago, but I will say I don't think there have been very many suitors in her bed."

"Unlike Genevieve." The youngest of our two families was also the most unruly. She failed to fall into line and proved to be difficult to rein in.

"Genevieve is just lashing out, and you know this."

"Perhaps, but she is the biggest thorn in my side. Now this? Grandfather sure got the last laugh in."

"You expected anything less?"

"The fireworks are an odd touch."

A harsh laugh left him before he took a sip. "It's him spitting from the depths of hell."

I scoffed at that as the red sparkles glittered against the dark sky.

"Why not ask one of your playthings to fill the role?" he asked.

"Are you actually pushing marriage on me?"

"If not, you know it will move to me, and I won't be able to fulfill the requirements. It will then move to Hamilton, and if he fails, down to Silas and Atlas. I don't want the family legacy falling to ruin."

"Such faith you have in your brothers."

A sigh left him. "It's not that, and you know it. Silas…I do hate seeing him when he's…off."

"He needs to fucking find a way to keep himself calm."

"Atlas is trying. He's the only one who can get through to Silas."

The twins were brilliant when they worked together. However, in recent years Silas had been exhibiting the darker side of being a de Loughrey.

"Elizabeth would make a fine CEO."

"A woman as CEO?" Rhys's eyes widened as he looked out the window. "Look, see? There is Grandfather spewing his displeasure."

Another round of fireworks boomed.

"He's gone. We can surely change things."

"Elizabeth is the only one fit to be an executive."

"What about your sister?"

He paused and I realized I'd unwittingly hit Rhys's landmine. He quickly downed the rest of his drink and shook his head. "Georgiana is too sweet. Some days I wonder if she's a de Loughrey at all."

Crisis averted. "She's just found her niche. A way to stand out."

"Much like Genevieve, and how could we forget the Tainted Princess?"

A groan left me. "This is a problem. What am I going to do?"

He sighed. "I don't know, but whatever it is, you need to figure it out soon, or you will have no choice but to go with an arranged marriage."

My jaw clenched. "Never. If I am forced to spend my life with a woman, it will be one of my choosing, not an obligation."

He clapped his hand on my shoulder. "Start hunting."

Memories of that night flooded in again. The way she moved beneath me. The need that kept me going longer and harder than ever before.

Look at me.

Look at me… What the fuck was I thinking?

Sex was a vehicle to blow off steam, but that night I needed more. Three words that had me pleading for something I had never desired. A look into her soul as I made her come undone.

An act that had me unable to forget her.

chapter THREE

OPHELIA

A sigh left me as I stood in line, waiting to pay for yet another pair of black pants and a white button-down shirt. That was the problem with working at a high-end restaurant—the smallest amount of fading, staining, or holes of any kind, and they had to be replaced. I'd seen more than one employee sent home because of it.

I never imagined I would spend more on work clothes than I did on regular clothes, but then again, I didn't care if my everyday wares were faded or ripped or stained. Okay, I did a little, but how many pairs of jeans with blown out knees did I have? Or tees with holes that I wore until the hole was too big, and often I still would just throw a tank on underneath?

The restaurant where I worked, 130 Degrees, was a place I could never even imagine eating at and was lucky for the few scraps of leftovers I did get.

"Ophelia?" a familiar voice called.

I turned and my stomach dropped, but I put on my best smile. "Jennifer, hi. How are you?"

Once upon a time, we were roommates in college, and friends.

She hadn't changed a bit. Perfectly styled brunette waves, chocolate-brown eyes, and the posture and style of a woman who thought she was better than everyone else.

That had never been something I noticed until I left my pharmaceutical sales position. I didn't even last a year before I left. It wasn't for me, despite the money. When I became a waitress to pay the bills, I was suddenly beneath her.

"Wonderful. How are you?"

"Good."

"What are you up to these days? Still waiting tables?"

"Um, actually, I am. I work at 130 Degrees."

Her eyes widened. "Really? My fiancé and I—oh, yeah, Luthor and I got engaged!" She threw her hand out and nearly smacked me in the face with a huge assortment of diamonds.

"That's great!" I said, calling up all the fake enthusiasm I could. "Such a beautiful ring." Tacky was more like it. Cluster rings could be beautiful, but the one she was wearing was a no for me.

"Isn't it? It's three carats total." She tilted her hand back to look at it. "Anyway, we were looking at venues for our engagement party. Does 130 Degrees have a room or anything that we could hold it in?"

"How many people?" I asked.

"About fifteen. Maybe you could get a discount for a friend." She grinned.

"I think the base rate for an event like that is about two hundred and fifty dollars a head, plus any alcohol."

I took a little bit of sick pleasure watching the way her eyes bulged.

"Two-fifty a person? That's outrageous."

I shrugged. "I have one customer who comes in every week. His bill is always almost two hundred just for lunch."

"Well, I'll have to see what Luthor thinks."

I gave her the biggest, fakest smile I could. "Sure thing. If you decide to, just drop by and talk to the manager, Mitchell."

"Who comes in every week for a lunch like that?" she asked.

I knew the curiosity would get to her. The past few years had taught me that some people only cared about status symbols and money. While those were nice things to have, especially the money, there was more to life.

I was also certain that if she ever met Atticus, he would send her running out the door crying in less than five minutes. I'd seen him do it before to some high-society blonde trying to sit with him.

"Just some guy I know." By not sharing his name and coming across as having a casual relationship with a mysterious, rich guy would just eat her up. I knew her well enough that status and material things meant more to her than people.

When did I become so catty? Oh, right, when I couldn't be her friend because I was a mere waitress.

"Well, maybe I'll have to come by to meet Mr. Mysterious."

"Sure." I smiled, deciding not to tell her it was reservation only. Unless you were Atticus or some other major money player.

"It was so good to see you again, Ophelia," she said.

I waved. "Bye."

My expression fell, and I rolled my eyes. She was just too stuck up for me to handle.

I started when I found the employee running the cash register staring, wide-eyed.

"Wasn't that Luthor Anderson's fiancée?"

I sighed as I threw my items up onto the counter. "Yup." Of course, she would be recognized. Luthor, after all, was one of baseball's most shocking trades. A center fielder that just signed a three-year, twenty-million-dollar contract with the Yankees, which was why I was surprised by the ring on her finger and her balking at the price at 130 Degrees. Maybe he had her on a tight financial leash.

Then again, we were in Manhattan.

After a stop at the grocery, a train transfer, and a bus transfer, I was finally home. It seemed like half my day was spent commuting into and out of Manhattan, but there wasn't much I could do about it.

The tips I made at 130 Degrees couldn't compare to anything near me, and until I figured out what I wanted to do with my life, I was stuck with the horrid routine.

I shuffled into my studio apartment and dropped my bags of clothes on the ground before moving to the kitchen. I pulled at the refrigerator door handle and cursed when it slammed into the oven and bounced back shut.

"Shit."

I opened the door a little more gently and slid the half-gallon of milk and sandwich fixings in, then let it close. The counter was already cluttered, but by counter, I meant the six inches that surrounded the sink. It was a joke of a kitchen, but so were rent prices.

As much as it sucked, I really couldn't complain much. At least I wasn't still living with my mom and my stepdad, Lou. From the moment he came into my life, I disliked him. He brought out the worst in my mother. They were shit parents to the two girls they had together. I hated to leave Brooke and Andrea with them, but I had to get away from being afraid of a man who would smack me for the simple fact that I wasn't his child. That my mother dared have a child before he met her.

Away from the mother who blamed me for "provoking" him.

I was out of there the second I graduated from high school. I spent the summer on friends' couches while I worked, and then when college started, I lived in the dorms. Thankfully, I was able to stay there over the summer as well, giving me no reason to return home.

By the time I graduated, I was over three hundred thousand dollars in debt.

For undergrad.

It was unreal.

Thankfully, I was able to get a well-paying job right out of school, making a hundred grand my first year. I had a decent apartment, could go out with friends like Jennifer, save for the first time in my life, and live a decent, miserable life.

It didn't take long to realize I didn't have the personality for it. I hated being a pharmaceutical sales representative. I hated being the salesperson pushing something I wasn't even entirely sure I could agree with, let alone put into my body.

I also didn't care for the person I was becoming. Being that kind of salesperson colored my soul.

After eleven months and four days, I quit. Gave up my great apartment and moved into a cheaper place back in my old neighborhood.

I liked the lab work of biology and chemistry, the science side of my degree, but I applied to dozens of clinical lab technician positions in various fields that never led to any offers. In all that, I found I could use my knowledge with food, which was the beginning of my matching and pairing of different items.

The chef at 130 Degrees was great in working with me, and I helped him sculpt a few of the restaurant's signature items. It was something I enjoyed, but it wasn't a job.

Despite my meager living, I was happier than when I worked as a sales rep. Still, I was constantly applying to jobs that interested me.

Even if I didn't have any real friends, just a few people I occasionally did things with, and I only went on the occasional date, it was better. I was a loner as it was. I always had been. It wasn't like Lou would allow me to have friends over, and whatever Lou wanted, Mom went along with.

My loner status was how I ended up alone on my birthday last year, and somehow it ended up being the best birthday I'd ever had in my life. It was all due to one man.

Too bad one night didn't turn into more, but I found that Atticus in the light of day wasn't the man I spent the night in bed with.

Nearly a year later, he still haunted me. Every single week, there he was, looking as handsome as ever. Every week, those blue eyes met mine, and I got a hint of that man I met.

He was reserved and demanding; everything had to be perfect. The man had no problem complaining about the smallest thing, though it had been a few months now since my name had rolled off his tongue with the dark undercurrent that made my stomach clench in all the wrong ways.

Instead, it was those hollow eyes. Not empty, but there was something complicated in their depths. A heaviness I couldn't figure out. His dark blond brows were always crinkled in a permanent scowl, lips in a perfect Cupid's bow, straight nose, defined cheekbones, jaw clenched creating a hard line sometimes sprinkled with a light scruff, all topped with a perfectly styled head of dark blond hair.

Then there was the suit that looked like it was molded to his form, and I knew he was hiding the body of a god beneath the layers. I'd seen it. Touched it. Been with it intimately.

And down the rabbit hole I went.

That was what happened when I started thinking about Atticus. It always led to remembering his lips against mine, his body covering me as he thrust inside. An Adonis that drew me in with the promise of pleasure.

It didn't help that I hadn't been with a man since then, leaving me with nothing but a memory that no man would ever be able to compete with.

Did he ever think of me?

It was kind of a hopeless, wistful longing for a man who had the last forty-some weeks to ask me out and hadn't even hinted that he even remembered that night. He didn't crave me the way I craved him.

Well, I craved his body. His personality could use some improvement. But I supposed that was what duct tape was for.

Even then, there was something about my mysterious Atticus that drew me in, kept me thinking about him, against my better judgment.

My constant tormentor.

My teeth mashed together as I stared at the screen. Ever since the will reading, my world had been a shitshow. Whiny siblings and cousins, even aunts and uncles, all coming to me to complain that my grandfather didn't leave them more.

As if they wanted for anything.

Then there was the incessant badgering about marriage. I'd begun to lock myself away at every opportunity, hiding from relatives, which was difficult when you worked in a building with over thirty other de Loughreys, each one knowing exactly where your office was.

"Mr. de Loughrey?" my assistant called from the doorway.

"What?" I snapped, not even looking her way. I knew Holly wouldn't be affronted by my attitude. She'd dealt with it for years, but she also knew me in ways many didn't.

"Your father is on his way."

"Fuck," I hissed. My father was supposed to be retiring, but the old man couldn't keep his controlling hands out of the company. It was my turn to rule, but every time he came into my office and chided me on the way I was handling things, I felt like a little boy being scolded.

He stepped back after the fourth scandal. Not that it affected the family or the company. That wasn't something Charles de Loughrey would ever allow.

However, that did mean that I rose as the new head of the family, the ruler of numerous fuckups, stuck-up socialite bitches, and family that would sooner cut my throat to gain leverage than help me in any way. He was there to add to the drama.

"Atticus, my boy," my father's boisterous voice boomed as he entered. Charles loved an audience and to be the center of attention, and his expression fell when he saw the empty chairs—I was alone.

"Father. What brings you here?" I asked with a forced smile.

"Nothing. I was bored and wanted to see how things were going."

Lies. He saw the drop in the stock market, and I knew the will decree was going to come up. There was also the arranged marriage business that had me avoiding him as much as possible.

"The company is doing fine. The setback was due to the economy and not the company. Or did you fail to notice the dip in all stocks?"

"I did. That isn't the only reason I came to see you today. I wanted to talk to you about a personal matter."

Personal matter? Fuck me. What did the old man do now?

"Just give Holly her name and address along with the amount on your way out." I turned my attention to the phone that was buzzing on my desk.

Hamilton.

I could use him as an excuse. "I should take—"

"You're almost thirty-six," he said, pulling my attention back from my escape route. "You're closing in on the forty mark. That isn't much time to find a woman to bear a child. Not to mention you have only eleven months to marry."

"I still have time. Besides, you were still fathering into your forties. And should I even mention your fifties and sixties?"

His gaze narrowed, and that explosive anger simmered beneath the surface. "Watch your tongue."

"Then fucking keep it in your pants. You're too old to be knocking up the maids or whatever pretty young thing catches your eye. I'm tired of writing checks to pay the women off."

Somewhere in the world, there were children who had no clue the identity of their father. At least one was younger than Elizabeth's little girl, Madeline.

And they would never know. Some of the women chose to terminate their pregnancy after getting their hush money, but there were at least two alive and growing.

Never knowing what a fucking bastard their father was. At least they were saved that.

"It's your duty to clean up the mess now. You're the leader."

"Then how about fucking your wife? Or has it been so long you don't even know how to engage in conversation with the woman you've shared a bed with for forty years?"

"Vera is aware of what she married for, and it wasn't my fidelity."

Another statement that alluded to the possibility of more half-siblings somewhere in the world and closer to my age. Fucking philandering asshole.

"And you will do the same."

"The hell I will." Two weeks ago, I told him there was no way in hell I was agreeing to an arranged marriage. Now he stood in front of me trying again, but with more malice and dominance in his tone to bully me into acquiescing. He should have known by now that wouldn't work on me. I was not so weak to bend to his demands.

"I have the perfect girl lined up," he pressed.

"Don't," I ground out. Fucking thick skull refused to accept my decision.

"Amelia Harris, of Harris Hotels."

A fucking socialite? Hell, no.

The name surprised me. A third-generation hotel heiress. Something worse than what I normally encountered—gold-digging, social-ladder-climbing, self-absorbed bitches. At least the latter would suck my cock like my cum was one-hundred-dollar bills in order to get something.

I'd dealt with that enough with my family, and I didn't want it sleeping next to me in bed.

There was a reason I didn't date. A reason I had acquaintances with benefits. They sure as fuck weren't my friends.

"No," I ground out.

"It would be a great partnership and acquisition for the company."

"I told you. I will not do an arranged marriage. Ever. I thought I was quite clear on the matter."

"You will do it if you wish to remain CEO."

I rounded my desk to stand in front of him. To make him bow to *my* authority, *my* dominance. "Listen here and listen good—I refuse to take part in any arranged marriage. Stop. I have grown this company more in the last five years than you did in the twenty before."

"Your ruthless brother had a lot to do with that."

"Perhaps, but I initiated the deals. I'm not about to marry some soulless bitch who I can't even get hard for. You want an heir, I'll give you one, but I'll choose the woman."

His expression never wavered. "She'll be joining us for dinner soon."

Our eyes were locked, neither backing down. "Have fun."

"You will be there."

"Or what? I'm not a child anymore."

"But you are *my* child, Atticus. And you will remain in control of this company by any means necessary, including taking on an arranged marriage."

Ah, that was what it was about. Pride. He simply couldn't handle seeing the company fall into the hands of anyone other than his progeny.

I stepped back around my desk. "I will choose my own wife, and it won't be a marriage of obligation."

A harsh laugh sprang from his lips. "I can't wait to meet her, this unicorn you expect to find and engage in that stupid emotion called love and marry all in less than a year. When that fails, I will be here to pull your ungrateful ass from the fire, and you *will* take Amelia's hand."

With that, he left.

Every muscle in me was tense, coiled tight. I needed a release, and thus the phone sitting on my desk became a casualty of my anger when I grabbed it and slammed it against the far wall with a roar.

I was breathing heavily, anger rolling through me as I stared at the carnage of bent and broken plastic that lay scattered across the carpet.

Familia ante omnia. Growing up, I just thought it was referencing to family loyalty. That was not our family's interpretation.

Family above all. Family above your own wants and desires.

An arranged marriage was the source of many of the de Loughrey family's issues, at least within the ruling branch. Everything from cheating to children born of affairs and portraying the perfect image without the ability to understand what a functioning relationship was supposed to look like—and that was just the surface.

The younger ones were rebellious, the leash around their necks looser as attention drifted. Genevieve, my youngest sister, was a constant thorn in my side, and Penelope's strong will to be her own person was an ongoing battle because of the microscope we were always under. Gen's antics often took the pressure off other family members, like the twins. More precisely, Silas.

What I needed was more than a mere wife. More than someone to drain my cock. It was there, sitting just on the edge of my thoughts. What I wanted. What I *needed.*

A knock sounded, pulling my attention from the wreckage. "Come in."

"Everything okay, boss?" Holly asked, closing the door behind her.

"I hate him."

She pursed her lips and moved to stand in front of me. "Going to tell me?"

I blew out a breath. "Why are you my assistant?"

She shrugged. "Because I like annoying you."

"But you don't."

She blew out a breath. "Look, Att, you're my friend," she began, using the nickname I despised. "I know we have this whole boss-employee relationship tangled in there as well, but I care about you. I've put up with the whole stick-up-your-ass de Loughrey attitude for eighteen years. Pretty sure I'm the only one who can wrangle you in."

"While I'm pretty sure you're my only true friend."

She smiled and patted my cheek. "Yup. And that's why you keep me around even when I forget to order you lunch."

A chuckle left me, and I shook my head. "You get by because you're the only one who can lighten my moods."

"The curse of the gifted."

The skyline held my attention as the conversation with my father played on repeat. He wasn't one to make baseless threats. That wasn't the Charles de Loughrey way. That inkling of an idea, the stir of possibility, came back to life.

The only alternative.

I let my guard down with her more than I had with anyone in my life.

"I'm about to do something truly brilliant or epically stupid."

"I've got the parachutes packed."

"Call Jack for me, have him set up an in-house sampling of the largest diamond rings in the city as soon as possible. Nothing less than a six-carat center stone." Normally I talked with my personal assistant myself, but he and Holly had developed a great working partnership, often taking care of things without my knowledge. A good thing, as trivial matters only served to piss me off since I had little time to deal with them. For four years, Jack had been the model assistant. He perfectly handled the blend of organizing my life outside the office and rarely being seen.

She blew out a breath. "Oh, we're jumping now."

"I have just over eleven months to get married. Time is ticking."

She nodded. "I'll find a space in your schedule in the next two days. What are you going to do?"

"What else does one do when setting up a business arrangement?"

A smile lit up her face. "You see the Lethal Lawyer."

I gave her a curt nod, and she headed out the door.

For half of my life, Holly had stood beside me. Without her friendship to calm my ire, I had little doubt I would have ended up a version of my father. Perhaps Hamilton and I would have been closer, seeing as he was much like him.

I checked my calendar, then Rhys's, looking for a good time to talk. Through pure luck, we were both free, at least meeting-wise, and it seemed the best opportunity to pull him in on my plan.

"I'll be back," I said to Holly, who nodded as I headed toward the elevators. "Atticus!" Hamilton called out, stopping me in my tracks.

It wasn't that I'd been avoiding my younger brother, simply that I'd been avoiding everyone, and that was why it took great strength to turn into his office, shutting the door behind me.

As soon as I was seated, his grey eyes were narrowed at me.

"Why do I have a meeting scheduled with Harris Hotels?" Hamilton asked.

I blew out a breath. "Because our father is a conniving asshole."

Hamilton let out a groan, his jaw clenching as his hands flexed. "He wants us all to dance to his tune."

"Yes."

"I know we haven't talked much since the will reading. What are you going to do?"

"That's a question I've been asking myself for the last few weeks. If you were in my position, what would you do?" Curiosity gnawed at me. Even though he was ruthless like our father, Hamilton also hated the idea of arranged marriages.

Honestly, I wasn't sure he would ever marry because he hated infidelity just as much.

"Tell him to fuck off, look at my little black book, and figure out who I wanted to be wrapped around my dick for the next however many years. My advice? You already have Bridget and Antonia. Figure out which one you want to put a ring on and be done."

Bridget and Antonia.

Hamilton wasn't the first to mention the women I'd casually dated and fucked for years. No strings, just my dates for events and to warm my cock when I desired. They were used to the high-profile life, and they weren't interested in me solely for money. The problem was that every single time I thought about them, tried to decide which one, those fucking brown eyes covered my vision.

Look at me.

"Mother has already started planning your wedding."

I quirked a brow. "Has she?"

He nodded. "Elizabeth told me."

"Wonderful," I ground out.

"Atticus…pick someone soon. I'll stall this meeting, push it out as far as I can, but I can't hold Harris off forever. Father will stick his nose into things, and you know he will start the merger process without our consent."

"I'm the fucking CEO. Hell, you are second."

"I'm well aware. You don't have to remind me. What you have to do is ask someone, anyone, to marry you and bring them to the family dinner."

I shook my head. "He won't stop there."

"No, he won't. But make sure whomever you pick can't be bought by him."

The words were like ice to my veins. I wouldn't put it past our father to do something to thwart my desires. Familia ante omnia, after all.

After leaving Hamilton's office, I moved down a few floors to the legal department. Rhys's office was on the west side of the building with a view of the Hudson.

A little scrap of a woman stopped in front of me, her eyes wide, binders clutched tightly to her chest. With a squeak, she did a sudden snap to the left and raced away.

I stared after her in confusion before stopping at Rhys's assistant's desk. The brunette stared at her computer, blinking, with her lips parted almost in horror. There was a frozen quality about her.

Rhys had a high turnover in assistants for reasons I hadn't figured out, but I didn't care either. It was, however, annoying when I arrived and the girl sitting at the desk outside his office didn't even have a nameplate, leaving me standing there attempting to get her attention.

I cleared my throat, and her pale, fear-filled expression turned to me.

"Is he in?"

She nodded, then her brow furrowed like she was trying to figure out what to do next.

"First day?"

"Y-yes," she squeaked out.

She looked up at me with hope in her eyes that I might tell her it was all right, that she was doing well, or some shit I'd witnessed Holly do time and time again. Instead, I stared at her, wondering if she was going to make it through the day.

"If you're this flustered on day one, you should probably quit." All hope faded from her face, and her eyes began to water.

"Atticus, are you terrorizing the help again?" Rhys called, and I turned my attention to the now-open door.

"Hmph, if I remember, you were the one who used a firecracker to blow up the breakfast cart, which would make *you* the help terrorist." I stepped inside and closed the door, then settled into the plush chair across from his desk.

"Margie wouldn't come near me for years," he chuckled. "What brings you down from your perch?"

"I need a couple of contracts drawn up."

"Just send the information to Jennifer, or Jessica…what is her name?" Rhys said as he looked toward the door, then shrugged.

"It's not business. It's personal."

His brow quirked as he looked at me and leaned back in his chair. "I'm listening."

Not going to Alexander meant top secret, and Rhys loved to know all the dirty secrets to use for his advantage at a later date.

I pulled a folded-up piece of paper from my inner jacket pocket and held it out. Rhys's eyes studied me as he pulled it from my grasp and unfolded it. His forehead creased as he scanned it.

"Really, cousin?"

"Shred it when you're done."

He sighed. "I'll have a preliminary draft for you later today."

With a curt nod, I stepped out and headed back toward my office. The air on my floor was infinitely clearer. Perhaps it was due to fewer occupants on the floor, but I felt much more comfortable in my arena.

Upon rounding a corner, I bumped into a small brunette. Files dropped from her arms to the floor, exposing a glorious rack.

What was it with peons getting in my way today?

"I'm so sorry, Mr. de Loughrey. Please don't fire me," she begged as she dropped to the floor to pick everything up.

I blinked down at the small girl in front of me. Had I gained such a reputation that the poor girl trembling in front of me feared me? Was that the curse of running the de Loughrey family? I didn't know who she was, but she had been around long enough to know who I was, meaning she worked for either my father or my brother, maybe my uncle. Then again, she could have worked for me, but I didn't pay attention to any of my assistants past Holly.

"I don't understand why you think I would fire you for running into me."

I clenched my jaw, waiting for her eyes to meet mine, but became impatient when she refused. A mousy little thing, but the sight of her breasts stirred something, and I began to wonder if she'd be a perfect vehicle to relieve my pent-up frustration.

"They are two ways this can go. One, I help you gather up your files and send you back to work. The other is you following me back to my office and put those pretty pink lips…" I stopped myself. Stopped myself from divulging my desires, my need to work off some of the mounting aggression pumping through me.

She stared up at me with wide eyes, a blush blossoming on her pale cheeks. The innocent look only stoked the fire in me, awakening the wicked king all too willing to succumb to my baser needs.

I wasn't my father, and I refused to prey upon employees. The girl still staring up at me tested that resolve. I didn't like to mix business with pleasure, especially not with a young, naïve little intern, no matter how much my cock wanted it.

Instead, I glared down at her. "You shouldn't look at men like that unless you are wishing for depravity."

There was no need for a response. I simply walked away. Bridget was a brunette as well. Perhaps I'd give her a call. Ease the desire to have my cum sucked from me.

"Office. Now."

In my periphery, Holly hopped up from her chair and followed me through the door. Once she was in, I closed the door and headed over to the wet bar to pour myself a drink.

I said nothing, and Holly had been around me long enough not to ask.

"Am I really that scary?" I asked as I slammed the empty glass on the counter, then poured more before turning back to her.

"Att, you're a de Loughrey. Scary is in your blood."

I glared at her use of my nickname once again as I passed her on my way to the sofa chairs in the corner. She followed behind and took a seat across from me.

"I have high expectations."

"You also take no prisoners and have a serious case of resting bitch face."

"Seriously?"

She quirked a brow at me. "Your aura screams 'get the fuck out of my way' everywhere you go."

"It comes with the territory. I constantly feel like I'm wrangling a house full of toddlers, especially of late."

"There is a flip side to your harsh front."

I scoffed at that. "And what is that?"

"Nobody crosses you."

"Constant aggravation." The replacement phone Holly already procured and set up began ringing, but I ignored it.

"You need a vacation," she said and pulled out her phone, probably looking at my schedule.

"What's that?"

She rolled her eyes. "Time away from the office."

I shook my head and frowned. "It's not a good time." I couldn't even remember the last time I took two days off in a row.

"It's never a good time."

"Maybe it's better. Less relationships I have to manage."

"I'm just saying, sitting on a beach, drinking a mai tai would do you some good."

"Thanks, Holly."

"I've always got your back. Don't worry your pretty little head over being scary."

I glared at her. "Do you ever see me worrying about what anyone thinks of me?"

She laughed at that. "No, but I know that ego still needs fluffing from time to time."

"How is it I've never fucked you?" My phone began to buzz in my hand, my mother's name on the screen, but I ignored it.

"You're not my type."

"I'm everyone's type." Money made the world go round and women fell to their knees in front of me with their mouths wide open.

"I'm married. To a beautiful woman."

"That just says threesome to me."

She shook her head and rolled her eyes. "Do you need me to bring out the little black book?"

It was tempting, but much more of a hassle than calling Bridget. The socialites that I'd spent a night with in the past were insipid, and I couldn't stand their constant plying to gain a hold into my life.

There was only one woman who was going to accomplish that, and that was because she wasn't even trying.

"No. I do need a lunch reservation. I need out of here for an hour or two. We'll call that my vacation." Reservation was incorrect. I never needed a reservation where I was going, but it allowed Holly to inform them I was coming and to ready it.

"Table for one?"

I nodded. "The usual. And I'm going to leave my phone with you."

She blinked at me like I'd spoken a foreign language. "Leave your phone?"

"Yes."

"Why?"

The phone went off again, and I rubbed my temples. "Five fucking minutes of peace." Something I was desperate for, especially recently, with family coming out of the woodwork: third cousins I may have encountered at a family reunion, a second cousin on my mother's side, and even closer relations who wanted to ride the high of my inheritance.

After all, if I fulfilled the terms of the will, I would become the richest and most powerful de Loughery since my grandfather. I would even surpass his reign.

She gave a curt nod. "I guess lunch without your phone would be a vacation, and you'll have Damien nearby. Still, you should fly down to Haven for the weekend. Get away from the city."

Haven, our island in the Bahamas, wasn't a bad idea. I could take one of my playthings and spend the weekend fucking everything out on her. She would love the private Bahamian island, and I could get my dick sucked out on the pool edge overlooking the pristine aqua water.

The problem was that if a single member of my family found out I was going, it would no longer just be me and my playdate.

"I'll think about it," I said as I headed out the door.

My afternoon was filled with back-to-back meetings, and I picked up the pace. The longer I was there, the more time I would have to center myself before I let loose on someone. In our five-minute conversation, the phone had rung five times, and I would snap if I didn't get away. My fuse was much shorter of late.

Being free from the shackles of my phone was settling. Each step took me farther from the demands that constantly weighed me down. If there was any true emergency, Holly knew where to find me.

I stepped up to the entrance of 130 Degrees and was immediately greeted by Mitchell, the day manager.

"Good afternoon, sir. It's a pleasure seeing you again."

"Pleasantries, Mitchell?" It was a custom we had deleted from our encounters in lieu of more casual conversation.

"Sorry," he whispered as he led me back to my private booth. "We have a food critic here today, and I'm trying to make an impression.

"Wonderful to see you again, Mitchell," I replied, playing along. While 130 Degrees had been doing spectacularly well with critics, putting an exemplary perception out was a good idea.

Not that I really cared what they said, but I knew Mitchell did. He took pride in his work, and it showed.

He held the curtain back, and I slid into my booth. A sigh of relief left me when it closed, the heavy curtains dampening the sounds of the other patrons, which was aided by a small speaker playing classical remixed songs heavy on string instruments. It was a niche I completely blamed on Penelope, but I found it soothing and upbeat at the same time.

I doubted anyone who knew me would guess that.

"Good day, Atticus," my waitress said as she entered my dim sanctuary and set a brandy down in front of me.

"Ophelia," I greeted. "It may be a double today."

She nodded. "The usual? Or should I tempt you with the wagyu today?"

The usual was the healthier option, but the steak might help me get through the day. "Tempt."

"Pan-roasted fingerling potatoes with pancetta?"

"Yes."

"Broccolini?"

I nodded. "Not—"

"Charred. Yes, sir. Anything else?" she asked, meeting my gaze for the first time.

Her brown eyes were wide and met mine with respect, friendliness, and that edge of regret of missed opportunities that prevailed between us. One I was now determined to erase.

"That will be all for now."

"I will be back shortly," she said with a smile before parting the curtains and disappearing.

Ophelia had been my designated waitress at least once a week since that business meeting nearly a year ago.

I made it so.

Just so I could see her again.

I'd been having lunch at 130 Degrees for much longer than that, but not as often as when I discovered she worked here.

Before her, I'd scared more than one server out of the restaurant. Ophelia, on the other hand, caught on quickly to my habits as well as my moods. She knew me only as Atticus, as did all the staff, and the table was reserved for me and me alone.

I was certain rumors floated around about it, but the managers were told to either squash them or tell them I was an investor and it was the investors' table. The truth was—I owned it. It was a side venture of mine and run by my holding company, Aegean Rule. There were a few other businesses they managed, and all were outside the de Loughrey hold.

Not everything fell under the de Loughrey Corporation, many of us having other smaller businesses as well as charities. It was more about control than income. The money made in a year barely covered my personal staff for a few months.

Lunch wasn't my only reason for visiting 130 Degrees, but because my frequency had increased since discovering Ophelia, my presence was not out of the ordinary. However, my reason stretched beyond satiating my stomach.

It was torture every time I laid eyes on her. A desire for something I told myself I couldn't have.

When my meal was finished and after I paid the bill, I pulled out a unique business card and held it out to her.

"Come to my office. Tomorrow. Nine a.m., and don't be late."

She blinked at me, her gaze moving down to the card, then back up. "Why would I go to your office?"

I stood up and moved to stand beside her. "I need to talk to you about a private matter." There wasn't enough privacy in the restaurant to discuss my idea.

"Don't tell me you gave me something last year."

I froze and stared at her. It was the first time in a year either one of us had even alluded to that night.

I leaned in, taking note of the sweet scent of her skin. Just that small inhale calmed me in a way nothing had before. "This has nothing to do with that encounter, but if you want me to give you the same thing for your birthday I did last year, I'm more than happy to oblige." I reveled in her sharp intake of breath. "Give reception this card when you *arrive*." My lips brushed against her neck, just below her ear.

After crossing through the doors, my blood buzzed in anticipation, making my skin feel alive. The morning could not come fast enough.

chapter
FIVE

OPHELIA

"**Y**ou have got to be fucking kidding me," I hissed as I looked from the map on my phone to the building in front of me.

The butterflies kicked up in my stomach. I couldn't be in the correct place. I just couldn't. The card Atticus had given me was black with a metallic-gold inlay that held only a symbol on one side and an address on the other. But the symbol didn't match the logo etched onto the glass.

The de Loughrey building was the third tallest in the city and was completely inhabited by the de Loughrey Corporation, one of the largest companies in the world. They were so large that de Loughrey was a household name.

All night I'd worried about why Atticus wanted to see me. It was so out of the blue and had my stomach in such terrible knots that I'd barely slept.

For the last year, waiting on him every week had been torture. The looks, the attraction; they may have been one-sided, and I hated myself for that. For letting him continue to affect me. For forcing me to follow his request instead of telling him to fuck off all with one look from his beautiful blue eyes, one brush of his shoulder against mine.

Instead, I stood in front of a symbol for one of the most powerful families in the world, wondering what the fuck I was doing there. With a deep breath I stuffed the card back in my bag and entered through the glass doors.

The elevator bays were surrounded by a large desk with security scanning identification cards as people entered. It seemed a time-consuming process, and I wondered how many people were late due to early morning lines, though it seemed to be moving at a quick pace.

There was even a line at the front desk checking guests in.

As I looked around at the sharp business suits and crisp clothing, I instantly regretted my casual attire. Black leggings, ballet flats, flowy lilac tunic, and jean jacket with my ratty messenger bag stood out, and I'd received a few dubious looks.

"Can I help you, miss?"

I blinked and stepped forward to the counter. "Um, yeah, I'm here to see…" It was then I realized I didn't even know his last name.

"The name, please."

I nodded and pulled back the flap of my bag, digging for the card I'd had in my hand moments before. "He gave me a card…" In one of the pockets, I finally located the matte black card and held it out. "He said to give you this?"

It came out more as a question, but that was because of the way he looked from the card to me, then back to the card. He gently took it from me as if it held some mystical power, turned it under the light of the scanner, then held it back out.

"Identification, please."

I blinked again before reaching into my bag for my wallet and pulling it out. I grimaced as I wrestled the card from the slot and handed it over. The stare down I was getting wasn't one of animosity but more of curiosity.

After scanning my identification, he gave it back and then held out a similar black card, which was more like a hotel key card.

He leaned forward and pointed toward a single elevator. "Go

over there and scan that card. It will open and take you where you need to go."

"And where is that?"

"To Mr. de Loughrey's office. One of his assistants will be waiting for you."

I froze as I tried to decipher what he'd just said. The name weighed on me before settling in my stomach, then dropping the floor out from beneath me.

"Who did you just say?"

"Mr. Atticus de Loughrey. You better get going—he doesn't tolerate tardiness."

I gave a shaky nod while I tried to find words and managed to unintelligibly thank him as I stepped away.

De Loughrey.

Atticus was a *de Loughrey*.

For the last year that I'd known Atticus, I knew he had money. From the hotel penthouse that night to the hundreds he spent on lunch twice a week. But being a de Loughrey? I never in my life thought I would ever meet one, let alone sleep with one.

I swallowed hard, my heart hammering in my chest with each step that closed the gap between me and the looming elevator. I slipped the card into the reader, the doors immediately opened, and as I stepped into the cab, it hit me.

Oh my God, I fucked a de Loughrey!

I'd thought about that night so many times since my birthday. It was shocking when I found him sitting at the head of the table in a private dining room a week after that. The way his blue eyes widened in shock. I didn't know what to do other than to go into my greeting, and we never spoke about it. We never even hinted at it until yesterday, but I was always thinking about it.

The man I remembered was just an illusion compared to reality. At first, I thought he was just angry with a mistake I'd made, but I came to learn that he was just brash. A harsh contrast to the man I met that night.

When the elevator closed in, only slowing when it reached the top floors, did I understand. The highest floors usually correlated with the highest in the company, and the doors opened at the top.

Atticus's bad attitude came from his position. More work and responsibility went hand-in-hand with greater stress. That didn't mean his mood was excusable, it just meant I finally got why he hid away at lunch. Why the restaurant catered to making him a sanctuary.

I wasn't even a step out of the elevator when a woman appeared in front of me. She was almost my height in heels, with sleek brown hair and warm brown eyes.

"Welcome, Miss Evans. My name is Holly, I'm Mr. de Loughrey's personal assistant."

"H-hi," I stuttered. It was all really settling in.

"Follow me," she said with a reassuring smile.

My stomach was in knots as we walked, clenching and unclenching, and as we passed the placard next to a huge wooden door, I nearly threw up—Atticus de Loughrey, CEO.

Chief Executive Officer.

The highest-ranking person in the company.

Oh my God, I slept with the CEO of the de Loughrey Corporation!

It wasn't a thought of excitement, but fear and confusion. How did I not know? I tried to think back on all the magazines I'd seen with the family faces, but most of the faces that graced the covers were the women in the family, and not always for the right reasons.

She opened the door and my heart stopped at the sight of him behind a large wooden executive desk.

Holly smiled at me, but I could feel the blood draining from my face as I willed my feet to move.

"Mr. de Loughrey, Miss Evans for you."

He didn't look up, only nodded. "Thank you, Holly." A few keystrokes, and then his gaze skipped right past me to the wall behind me. "On time. Good."

"What is this all about, Mr. *de Loughrey?*" I accentuated his name. As far as I was aware, nobody at the restaurant knew who he was, other than an investor.

"Good morning, Miss Evans," he greeted, mimicking my use of his last name. "I trust you had no issues downstairs?"

"None," I said. "A little surprised, especially with all that we've been through."

"You didn't need my last name to enjoy my cock, if I remember."

I folded my arms over my chest, ignoring his gesture to the chairs in front of him. I wanted to get to the point of what this was all about.

"Is that why I'm here? My birthday is coming up, though this year I think I'll pass on your cock."

The grin that spread over his face made me shiver. "You're making me want to change your mind on that, but giving you multiple mind-blowing orgasms is not the reason I've brought you here today. I have a business proposition for you."

Business? "I'm not sure I'm inclined to listen to it."

"It involves an eight-figure payout."

I froze, my gaze stuck to the left of him, on the New York City skyline beyond that large floor-to-ceiling window.

Eight figures? For that amount of money, I could completely change my life. Get out of this hellhole of a city, away from my family, and start over. The problem was, who did he want me to kill for that amount?

Slowly I turned to meet his steely gaze that was pinned on me. "If it involves anything sexual, you can forget about it."

"What it involves would only be sexual if you want it to." His gaze roamed down my body, then back up, his lip twitching up. "I would not be opposed at all."

I narrowed my gaze. Yep, back to killing people. That was what people paid that kind of money for, right? Sex and death?

"What do you want then?"

"Sit." He gestured again to one of the button-back leather chairs that sat opposite his large executive desk. With a sigh, I sat, crossing my arms in front of me.

"Before we begin, I need you to sign this." He slid a piece of paper and a pen my way.

"What is it?"

"A non-disclosure agreement. You will never speak to anyone about what we talk about today."

My stomach clenched again. He was getting legal about a conversation? Our eyes were locked for a moment, neither moving before I leaned forward. My eyes scanned the page and found nothing amiss but a standard NDA.

With a quick swipe of a pen, my lips were sealed.

Once completed, he took a photo with his phone before turning his attention back to me. "I'm in need of a proxy."

"What is that?"

He twirled his hand in the air. "A stand-in, or in regard to this matter, a temporary."

"For what?"

"The future Mrs. de Loughrey."

I shook my head. "You're not making any sense."

"And I quite possibly won't until you agree. Right now, all you need to understand is that in exchange for five years of your life, I will give you ten million dollars. Plus clothes and food and all the necessities, of course. The ten million is your flat fee."

Ten million? "Dollars?"

"Yes, dollars."

"What do I have to do?"

"Marry me and bear me a child."

I blinked at him, trying to process what the hell was going on. Was I being punked? Was this a rich asshole practical joke? Was there some bet for a dollar between him and his brother to see if I'd fall for such an insane idea?

"You want to marry me?" It was the most screwed-up proposal I'd ever imagined and would forever go down in history as the first marriage proposal I received. I wasn't even going to touch the "bear me a child" part yet.

"Yes."

A laugh sprung from me, but his serious expression brought me to a halt. "You're joking, right?"

"I don't joke."

Fuck. He was serious.

I rolled over the basics again in my head—five years, ten million dollars, one child. Too good to be true, especially with his looks and status. What did he need some broke girl from Brooklyn for?

"What's the catch?"

"There are a few, but they aren't what you are thinking. We will be married in January, and hopefully, a year later, you will birth my first heir. If a second one happens in the timeframe, all the better. Once the five years are over, you are free to do whatever you like."

I blinked at him in complete confusion. None of it made sense. He had money, lots of it—tons—and because of that, coupled with his good looks, and he could have any woman he desired, so I was back to *why me?*

No, there was something weird going on.

"And *why* do you think I'd even contemplate agreeing to this insane idea? Buying me to be your wife?"

"Because I'm offering you a life you could only dream of and a payout that will possibly ensure you never have to work again."

"This is a heavy proposal," I said as it began to sink in.

"The fact that you are still sitting in front of me gives me hope you are entertaining the idea of becoming my wife. I will stress, this is a one-time-only offer. You will, of course, have some time to think it over, but after that, if you decide to decline, then later change your mind, it's off the table."

"How much time?"

"I'll see you back here at the same time tomorrow."

I stood, my mind whirling. "I'll see you tomorrow then."

"Before you go," he said, stopping me from walking away. "I will remind you to remain silent on this matter. Speak to no one about what we have discussed."

I nodded and swallowed. As if anyone would believe me anyway. The idea was ludicrous. So out there, even I was having difficulty believing it was real.

I also would never tell anyone because I knew the de Loughreys had the backing to sue me for all the money I would ever make in this life and the next if I broke the agreement. You didn't cross them, or you paid the price—and it wasn't always money.

A leather binder was placed in front of me, one of those legal ones that opened at the top, and pressed into the tightly bound hide was the de Loughrey logo.

"This is the preliminary contract. Look it over, and we can discuss any issues in the morning."

I numbly nodded, suddenly having a strange out-of-body experience as the weight of reality pressed down upon me. After slipping the document in my bag, I turned to leave.

"Nine sharp," he said as I gripped the door handle. I turned to look back at him, our gazes locked as I exited.

Autopilot drove me to the train station, and I stared blankly in front of me. On the one hand, I should have been insulted. On the other hand—ten million dollars.

Could I stand five years with him? He was a busy man, so technically, I wouldn't see him much, right?

Selling myself as a fake wife. Could I do it, pretend to be something I wasn't, act like a doting wife to a man like Atticus de Loughrey? *Be* a de Loughrey?

Those were the thoughts that had my heart slamming in my chest.

Atticus represented everything that was wrong with the world. Greed and privilege, patriarchy and the belief that women are nothing but holes to fuck. And I hated that, but not as much as I hated myself for wanting a taste of him again.

It would be a life most only dreamed about, but was it something I wanted? More than that, was it something I could even do?

Could I really kneel before the king?

chapter
SIX

OPHELIA

I stared across my tiny-ass studio apartment. The main room was small and barely held my day bed, sofa chair, and bistro set. The TV sat atop a cube storage unit where all twelve cubes were stuffed solid. Then, there was my joke of a kitchen where you couldn't even open the oven all the way, thanks to the fridge…which also didn't open all the way. There was no counter space, and only a sink.

Fifteen hundred a month was insane for the small space, but with no car and just enough money to get by, there was no way out. I was stuck in the vicious cycle of insane rental prices in an expensive and crowded city.

If I lived with Atticus, I had a feeling my bathroom would be larger than the room I was sitting in. Just the idea of what he was asking was insane. How could I say yes to that?

I slipped open my credit card bill and winced at the number listed, and it was only the minimum payment due.

In order to get away from my crappy home life, I was left living on pennies, and now one of the sexiest men I've ever seen was offering me freedom from all that. No more debt and money to spare for the low cost of my dignity, five years, and a baby with a man I didn't exactly like.

I didn't exactly dislike him either.

Especially late at night with my vibrator.

I might have lied about my memories of that night. They were vivid, erotic, and got me off many nights. They were also one deterrent in my dating life. What was the saying? Don't mess with perfection? I wasn't sure it could get better than the one night I spent with Atticus. Part of me didn't even want to try.

There was an attraction, one that worried me if I did decide to say yes to the insanity. I didn't want to say yes and then fall into the trap of basically being a readily available pussy who had to allow his advances because he held all the money and power. As pleasurable as it would be, I wasn't going to prostitute myself, which was how it felt.

If I was going to do it, there would be concessions, and the man who had everything but a wife was going to be making them. I would hold some power, even if it was just a small amount, solely to prove to him that I wouldn't be walked all over.

If I thought sleep had left me the night before our meeting, it was nothing compared to the night after. All night long I watched the light move across the ceiling as I went over things again and again. The answer wasn't an easy yes or no, but a multi-layer complication of emotion, attraction, and expectation.

In the harsh light of day, I took in the state in which I was living—really took it in. I was almost twenty-seven, meaning I'd be almost thirty-two when all was said and done. Plenty of time to find my forever kind of love and, thanks to the payout, I could do it in style.

Still, every step I changed my mind, back and forth. I hadn't eaten either, and it probably wasn't a good thing that I was making major life decisions with nothing in my stomach, but it was too knotted to handle anything.

The way through security went the same as the day before, and just as then, Holly greeted me with a smile when the doors opened. It was almost a knowing smile, and I wondered if she knew. She had to, right?

When I entered his office, he finished up whatever he was typing, then turned his attention to me. It was then that I remembered how the entire time I was in his presence the day before, his focus was solely on me.

With more ease than the day before, I sat down, then I took a deep breath and rolled my shoulders back in preparation for battle. Atticus was a strong man, but he wasn't going to steamroll me.

When our eyes met, he gave a small nod. I supposed it was to indicate he was ready.

"Why me?" No pleasantries, I was coming out swinging. This was a business deal, and I was going to treat it as such. By the twitch of his lip, it was a move he appreciated.

"Because you know me better than most."

I shook my head. "I know hardly anything about you. Until yesterday, I didn't even know your last name."

"If that is so, then why did you suggest the wagyu steak the other day?"

Fuck. He was right, in a way. Maybe I didn't know the particulars about him, like his last name, but over the last year, I'd become very much acquainted with his moods.

"That doesn't mean anything," I said in an attempt to brush it off. "I can guess your mood based on the depth of the crease of your brow. The deeper it is, the richer you like the flavors."

"And there is another way you know me. Intimately."

I ignored the way his tone dropped, making the hairs on my body to stand up as a shiver rolled through me. "Those memories have faded."

"Have they?" His eyes darkened, and his lip twitched. "You smell like lavender and linen with a hint of grapefruit. Your pussy is sweet and tight, and grasped my dick like it was a mold custom made for me and me alone. You swallowed my cock with expertise all the way down to the base. Your skin is soft, and your moans could make any man come just from the sound."

I swallowed and picked at the strap of my bag. I could feel the heat rise to my cheeks as it also settled between my legs, but I wasn't going to let the smug bastard know he was affecting me. "No sex."

There was no way he'd agree to such terms, giving me a way to decline.

He leaned back and folded his hands in front of him. That severe gaze of his tore into me. It was one I'd become familiar with over the last year. "How are you going to give me an heir, then?"

I waved a hand in the air as I shrugged. "Artificial insemination or something. I'm just not going to be some rich boy's sex toy. You said business, so this is business. Having money doesn't mean you have the automatic right to touch me."

"You think I'd allow my child to be created through such sterile means?"

"No. Sex."

His glare deepened, but I wasn't backing down. "Fine," he relented, but before I could celebrate my victory, he did a one-eighty on me. "Fine, but if we aren't having sex, then I'm allowed to have mistresses."

I shook my head, staying firm in my conviction. "No sex means no sex. I'm not going to be parading around on your arm only to be humiliated by everyone around me who knows you're cheating on me. Just imagine the newspaper headlines."

He clenched his teeth. "You want me to go without sex for five years?"

"If I do, you will. If you want me to fill this role, that is the price." It was a gamble, and the answer would tell me more than he would—he wanted me as his wife, above others. I was his first pick.

The solidity of his form told me he was keeping himself in check, if only by a thread. Men like Atticus were used to getting what they wanted without objection. People didn't defy him, and his aura screamed his displeasure. Every muscle was tense as I waited.

"I thought the price was ten million dollars and to live in luxury for five years, your every whim and desire met."

Tennis, then. A back and forth. Still, not immediately dismissing me and my restrictions was eye opening.

"Because I can see this for the life-changing transaction it is going to be, and I'm not talking about the money. I want to come out of this with my self-respect intact."

"There are many women who would throw self-respect out the window for what I am offering."

That wasn't a volley I was expecting. A man of his stature should have laid down an ultimatum, and his reluctance to do so let me know he wanted me in particular.

And that knowledge was powerful.

I stood. "Fine. Find one of them, then." Another gamble.

"Sit."

I jutted my chin out. "Agree, or I'm gone."

His jaw clenched so hard I thought his teeth might crack, and his eyes narrowed. "No sex," he ground out.

I gave a curt nod and sat back down while I tried not to cheer my victory or take in the realization that he truly wanted me. "Before we continue, I need some clarification."

"Go ahead."

There were a lot of variables in what he wanted. Things that could go wrong. "What happens if one of us is infertile?"

The question lifted some of the ire radiating off him, and he relaxed back into his chair. "We will pretend this never happened, but to save us both time, we will be tested for the basics before the contract is signed. Along with other health screenings."

STDs probably. Since I was from a lower class and all. The sneer in me was strong, and I had to hold back that thought.

"To add to that, what if I don't get pregnant in that time frame?"

"The second you say 'I do,' my cum will be filling you by whatever means necessary every day until you are."

Something about that sentence sent shivers through me and caused my nipples to harden as my thighs clenched. I had to clear my throat to get back on topic and away from the images threatening to take over my mind. Images of him pinning my hips down with his own hips, feeling the jerk of his tip deep inside me.

Fuck! *Get it together, Ophelia.*

"So when I have a baby and the term ends…then what?"

His brow scrunched. "What do you mean?"

"I mean, do I still get to see my child, or does my child get taken from me?"

His eyes widened, and he seemed affronted somehow. I thought it was a good, direct question. For all I knew, he planned to completely cut me off from everything as soon as the divorce papers were signed. That was a hard limit. Even though I hadn't even thought of having children yet, I knew there would be no way I would allow them to be taken from me.

"Of course you would still see them. You would simply be under no obligation to remain married to me. I would not cut off access to our children."

I nodded to the paper he was making notes on. "I want joint custody, and I want it in writing."

"You don't trust me?"

I shook my head. "No."

He released a small chuckle, his lip twitching. "Anything else?"

The knots in my stomach tightened, and I swallowed hard. Doing this, saying yes, signing a contract, I was forfeiting my life to him. Any dreams or aspirations I held were to be put on hold.

I worried my bottom lip as I scoured my mind for any last objections or concerns. The main things were covered, and as my heart thumped so hard in my chest, I had difficulty agreeing.

"My debts n—"

"Will be taken care of."

I quirked a brow at him. "You don't even know what they are."

"Three hundred thousand in school debt, two thousand on your credit card. I'll also pay off your lease."

"How…"

He quirked a brow at me. "Did you think I didn't investigate you before asking you to marry me?"

It was a shock for a few seconds, but then it made complete sense. He was the motherfucking CEO of the de Loughrey Corporation. Of course he would do his homework before offering me such a sum. "Well, you technically never asked. In those words."

"Anything else?"

I swallow hard, stalling. "What if I have skeletons in the closet?"

His hard gaze met my frightened one. I just hoped he couldn't tell how freaked out I really was. My foot tapped against the ground, and I nearly had the strap to my bag unraveled.

"Is there something I should know?"

"My stepfather…" I trailed off, unsure what to say. Was an ass? I didn't trust him? He'd hit me before? "Is a drunk bastard."

"I'm aware. However, I don't foresee him being an issue."

"Why not?"

"When was the last contact you had with him?"

I went to answer, my lips parting, then just froze. "Christmas."

"And before then?"

"August, when I dropped off my sister's birthday present."

"He may be a bastard, but I'm a bigger asshole. I have no fear of that tiny skeleton. He is inconsequential and holds no bearing in these negotiations."

Ah, negotiations. Just what I always wanted to hear when talking about getting married.

How romantic.

"Your answer, Ophelia."

I bit down on my bottom lip, my stomach turning. "You give me all that, and we have an agreement." The words slipped out, and I watched his lips creep up into a smile.

What have I done?

chapter
SEVEN

ATTICUS

She agreed.

She fucking agreed.

The moment she did, it felt like one of the large chains holding me down slid away. While tentative, she said yes, and the final draft of the contract was in motion.

We'd both spent the last few days having tests done and giving Rhys time to finalize the contract.

In front of me lay the last hurdle—our health reports. One of the most important was that we were both clean of any STDs, and we were. The second was the fertility report, which showed no obvious issues, with hormone and sperm count levels being in the normal range.

The health history and physicals didn't show anything of concern, which was good.

While her father was dead, I knew it wasn't health related. I'd done my homework before I set my plan in motion, and that included an in-depth background check. It would have been irresponsible to jump into such an arrangement without a thorough history, and I was not one to be so hasty.

Yes, I had done it a year ago, but that was due to suspicion after having her suddenly show up as my waitress after fucking her. I simply had it updated and a few questions answered.

I rubbed my eyes, the fatigue of the day wearing on me. I'd endured another visit from my father trying to set up dinner with Amelia Harris. The man was hardheaded, and I was going to have to beat Ophelia into his skull for him to understand that I would never agree to an arranged marriage.

The sun was long gone and my office was lit by only the under-cabinet lights on the credenza and the lamp atop my desk. I leaned back, my gaze glancing at the clock. It was past nine, and it was quite possible I was the only one in the office.

With a creak, my attention was pulled to the figure stepping into my office.

Well, I wasn't the last person.

"Here's your contract," Rhys said as he tossed the leather contract binder onto the desk in front of me.

I opened it and flipped through the pages. I looked toward him, watching as he sat down in the chair in front of my desk. "Ironclad?" I asked.

Rhys narrowed his eyes at me. "Really, cousin?" He clasped his hands in front of him.

"And her clause?"

"More than a few loopholes."

"Good." He stared at me for a moment, and I let out a sigh and shut the portfolio. "Spit it out."

He threw up his hands. "I'm surprised, is all. This contract is merciless, yet you've purposely left yourself room to bed her without breaking the contract."

Of course I had. There was absolutely no way I was going to go five fucking years without sex, and I was going to make certain it was her beneath me. Our children would be made by the head of my cock pressed snugly against her cervix.

"She's going to give me an heir, and I'm not letting some fucking lab do what my cock is perfectly capable of doing."

"I understand that. It's just more of a move I'd expect from your father or Hamilton."

I didn't like the comparison to my father. My entire life, I made sure to distance myself from being like him in any way that I could. "Hamilton may be a shark, but he's not a snake. You're more apt to fit that description."

"You wound me, cousin," he said with a smirk.

"They call you the Lethal Lawyer for a reason. By the way, what is it I hear about you having an intern next summer?" It was only the beginning of June, but news had already circulated.

Rhys clenched his jaw and narrowed his eyes. "Father *gifted* his alma mater a single internship. Being the only lawyer in the family besides him, it falls to me."

"The poor soul that ends up with you."

"Laugh now, but just remember you're having to buy a wife."

"I refuse to be bound to some arranged marriage like my parents. The last thing I want is some rich-bitch socialite who can't even suck my dick without getting something monetarily out of it."

He quirked a brow. "Isn't that exactly what you're doing?"

I narrowed my gaze at him. "The difference is I picked her."

"I think you need to call up one of your little playthings before this contract gets signed to work off your tension. Who knows when the next time you'll get to drain your balls in a woman again? Could be five years."

It wasn't a bad idea. Ophelia was coming by in the morning to sign the contract, giving me the evening to relieve the pressure. The problem was that it was something I'd been saying for months and had yet to do, and I fucking blamed her.

"I'll have Ophelia pinned to my bed in less than six months."

"Are we betting on it?"

"Just keep this whole business to yourself. I don't want my father finding out."

"He's going to flip anyway. She has no social standing. A waitress, for fuck's sake. Why on earth did you pick her?"

"Accessibility coupled with fuckability."

"You're really embracing your unscrupulous side. I'm proud of you."

"I don't have to behave in that manner to make this company thrive."

"And yet you are, in order to avoid an arranged marriage, and instead, marrying a woman who gets paid to wait on you."

I tapped the contract. "One I will control. She has nothing, and therefore she is more pliant when money is on the line."

"Devil's advocate—what if money isn't enough? I only remember her from the hazy night nearly a year ago, but by some of the wording you chose, she sounds like a wild horse."

"One I will break. Money is the carrot I dangle to keep her in line."

"Very wicked, cousin."

With that, he left, and I decided to do the same.

My stomach was oddly tense the next morning. I'd hardly slept, unable to take the anxiety that something would change and Ophelia would back out. Then what would I do?

Anxiety wasn't something I dealt with often. Not in my position. The level of confidence I had in all things seemed to shatter in Ophelia's presence.

Not that I could ever let her know how she affected me.

I kept the door to my office open, something that never happened, in anticipation of her arrival. My gaze flickered to the clock constantly, cursing it for only having moved seconds when it felt like minutes.

The emotions swirling inside me were absurd. Why was I so tangled up over this?

My head snapped up the second she stepped in, my eyes fixed on her, and my muscles relaxed.

She came.

"Good morning," I said. I tilted my head to Holly, who was

standing at the door. At my gesture, she closed it, leaving me alone with Ophelia.

"Good morning."

Despite my relief, my nerves still vibrated. I couldn't remember a time I'd been so desperate to have a contract signed.

As I looked her over, I took note of the dark circles around her beautiful brown eyes. It seemed perhaps I wasn't the only one losing sleep over my proposal. She looked so youthful otherwise, and she was. Ten years my junior, and so beautiful I constantly had a hard time not staring at her like some love-struck fool.

"Are you ready to become the soon-to-be Mrs. Atticus de Loughrey?"

"Ophelia de Loughrey," she whispered. It was a simple trying of the name on her tongue, but it sent a spike of heat through to my heart, making it speed up.

The name hit my core with an absolute feeling of perfection.

I cleared my throat in an attempt to get it over with so that these feelings might leave me.

I pulled the leather legal binders closer before picking one up and handing it to her. "Would you like to go over the changes?"

She nodded, then slipped back a loose lock of hair from her face. "Yes. But first, what are the consequences of breaking the contract?"

"I thought you read through it."

"I did, but can you clarify them for me."

I nodded. "If you break them you will need to repay me for any monetary loss I have incurred for things such as your debts and other expenses. If I break it, you'll have five million dollars to add to your bank account."

She chewed on her bottom lip, then nodded.

After half an hour, we'd concluded the contract revisions and I held out a pen. Her hand shook slightly as she grasped it. I watched with great interest as she set the tip down on the line over her printed name. She picked it back up again, pausing, and I swore my heart stopped, even if just for a fraction of a second.

Then with beautiful fluidity, the letters of her name appeared as the pen glided across the paper.

The process was repeated on a secondary copy, my copy, and relief washed over me.

The papers were signed, and an odd warmth filled me. Ophelia was finally mine.

Finally?

There was no time to delve into my psyche, and I honestly didn't want to. It had been on the fritz all morning anyway. What I wanted to do was make it official.

A small box sat next to my phone, almost innocuous, but it held a very important token. A hum of electricity passed between us when I took her hand in mine, drawing it up.

"And with this, we are engaged," I said as I slipped the ring onto her finger.

"Holy shit, that thing is huge." Her eyes were wide as she stared down at the diamonds that adorned her dainty fingers.

"Do you like it?" I asked, finding I was genuinely hoping she did. How odd.

She smiled at me and nodded. "It's beautiful."

It pleased me that she liked it, that I had done well at picking the nine-carat stone with its delicate circlet of smaller diamonds.

"I'm just going to pretend like it's fake, because I might shove it right back at you if I knew how much it cost."

I chuckled at that. Considering the amount I spent on it, I didn't doubt that might be the case, though she might have been the only woman I knew to make such a statement. "We have a lot to go over."

"Starting with?"

"How much your life is going to change in the next few forty-eight hours."

She stared at me blankly, much like a deer in headlights. Wasn't she anticipating the severe alteration her life was about to undertake?

"My fiancée can't be seen living in that shitbox in Brooklyn, so you will move in with me by tomorrow afternoon."

She groaned, her head falling back. "Fuck," she hissed. "Why didn't I think about that?"

We'd talked about me paying off her debts, and I clearly remember mentioning I'd pay off the remainder of her lease.

"Don't worry—you'll have plenty of room to yourself. Next, I'll have Jack set you up some appointments."

"Appointments for what? And who is Jack?"

"Jack is my personal assistant. And you'll need to look the part, not just play it."

"I thought Holly was your personal assistant."

"You're going to be learning a lot and have a lot thrown at you, so I hope you are prepared." The deer-in-headlights look resided on her face, confirming that she was completely overwhelmed. She'd thought about my proposal, read it in the contract, talked about it, but it seemed she'd missed thinking about what happened after she signed on the line. "To make it easy: Holly is office, Jack is home."

Her brow scrunched. "Please tell me you don't have an assistant that assists your life outside of work."

"We all do. For now, Jack will also act as your assistant. He can help you in any way you need."

"Is it too late to back out?" she asked as she leaned over.

"Yes." There was no way I was letting her back out now. "We both signed. You'll get used to it all—it's just a steep learning curve for you until then. Do you have a passport?"

"No."

"We need to get you one right away." I tapped on my phone, sending a message off to Jack.

"Why?"

"Because I often leave the country, and I will take you with me."

"Oh," was all she said in response. She chewed on her bottom lip, brow scrunched as she glanced down at her hand. "What now?"

"Now, go home. I have a moving crew arriving in the morning to help pack up your apartment and relocate your belongings to my condo." I paused and picked up my phone, looking over the schedule before setting it back down. "They'll be there at ten. Once that is done, you'll come here and I'll take you over."

She stared at me, already off kilter and unsure what to do. "I guess I'll get going, then. I have to get to work."

"You won't be working," I said, cutting her off.

She blinked at me. "What do you mean?"

"I mean I've already contacted your manager and told him you won't be returning."

"Why?"

"Because you don't need the money anymore."

She shook her head. "Even with you footing my food and housing and covering my debts, I still have bills."

"And they are?"

She threw her hands up in the air. "Phone, for starters." She seemed to be racking her brain trying to come up with something outside of all that I would provide, but nothing else slipped from her lips.

I picked up the phone and called Holly in.

"In regards to your phone, you will be switched to my plan," I said as Holly walked through the door, a stack of items in her arms. She set them down on the table and turned to leave. "Thank you, Holly."

On top of the stack sat her new phone and I handed it to her, enjoying the way her eyes widened.

"This isn't even on the market yet," she said in awe. Her fingers grazed mine as she slipped the phone into her hand, and warmth spread through me from the contact.

That was why I'd chosen her. Because no one had ever made me feel that kind of comfort in my life.

"Not for a month."

"How?"

I smirked at her. "The perks of being a de Loughrey."

She blew out a breath. "Trying not to freak out here."

Trying and failing. It irritated me a bit, but I calmed myself at the reminder that she'd been a de Loughrey for a whole ten minutes. A socialite would be able to handle the load with grace and without skipping a beat. A broke girl from Brooklyn was in a near completely other world. What I was thrusting upon her was alien.

If it wasn't for Holly, I wouldn't have any understanding how different it all was for Ophelia. Without that knowledge I could possibly become annoyed by the time needed for her to understand and acclimate to her new life.

Even then, I wasn't sure how she would take it all. Not in her wildest dreams would she anticipate what was coming, of that I was certain.

"What is it the game shows always say? But wait, there's more," I said, trying to calm her.

She blinked at me, her brow furrowing before lifting, a smirk forming on her kissable lips. "Did you just make a joke? I mean, it was a lame one, and that's from infomercials, but still."

"Do I look like the type to joke?" I asked. I wasn't about to reveal my failed attempt at humor.

She shook her head. "Not at all."

"Next." I held out a black credit card with her name on it.

She blinked down at it. "Seriously?"

"This is for your personal use. Whatever you need, use this." She reached out slowly, cautiously pulling the card from my fingers. "Overwhelmed?"

"A bit."

"There's more."

"Fuck," she hissed.

There was more we needed to go over, but by the paleness of her skin, I decided to wait until she was in my home before unloading the information. It would give her more time to digest what exactly she signed up for.

"We'll wait on it until tomorrow. For now, take the next few hours to say goodbye to your former life."

She nodded, the fright evident in her eyes, but there was also an edge of wonder.

"After they leave, come back here," I said, then pulled another card from the stack. "This is your card to get up here. You will no longer need to check in with the desk, just head straight to the elevator."

She nodded, her hand shaking as she took the card and slipped it into her bag along with her phone and credit card.

Most women, when handed access to unlimited funds, lit up with excitement, the dollar signs nearly visible in their eyes, but not Ophelia. I reached up and brushed a loose lock of her short hair behind her ear before my palm settled on her cheek. Blush spread across her pale skin, and I had to force myself to keep from leaning forward and kissing her—an act I'd longed for since she left my arms nearly a year ago.

I snapped back at that realization and cleared my throat, ignoring the confusion on her face.

"I'll have a car pulled up for you."

She shook her head. "No need."

"Ophelia..."

She blew out a breath and held up her hands. "Just...give me tonight to be me."

I gave a curt nod. "Have a good evening. I'll see you tomorrow."

She gave me a strained smile as she backed up, then turned. Once she reached the door, she looked back at me, then slipped away.

I thought I would settle after she signed, but something else stirred inside me: an overwhelming need to touch her that I battled to gain control over.

After Ophelia exited, Holly stepped in, closing the door behind her. There was a smirk on her face and I glared at her.

"You don't scare me, big bad wolf."

"What do you want?"

"She's beautiful. Not your normal type."

"And?"

She shrugged. "I get it."

"Get what?" I growled.

"I get why you're attracted to her."

As close as I was to Holly, I'd never told her about that night. Only Rhys knew that I'd taken Ophelia home.

"She's the only woman I've never been able to stop thinking about."

Her eyes widened, then narrowed before she swung her fist out and punched me in the arm. Thankfully, she was a tiny little thing barely over five foot, so there was no real force behind it. "Why didn't you tell me?"

"How's Becca?"

"Don't go changing the subject on me. I already figured out she was your waitress, and now it totally makes sense why you started going there more often, but there's something else."

I blew out a breath. If I didn't come clean, Holly would just keep digging. "Remember how Rhys convinced me to go out with him to Angelino last summer?"

A chuckle left her. "Yeah. It shocked the hell out of me."

"I spent the evening with Ophelia. Until long after the sun rose."

Her lips parted. "Oh, Att." There was an edge of pity in her voice.

"Don't fucking act like I'm some wounded animal for a fucking woman," I growled.

Her eyes narrowed on me. "Fine. Be an ass to me, but watch it with her. You're still not going to scare me, but that attitude will drive her away. And by the way, I'm mentally slapping the shit out of you right now."

She turned and stomped away, slamming my office door.

I grabbed hold of the leftover stack of information for Ophelia and slammed it down on my desk before dropping into my chair.

Introspection was not my strong suit, so asking myself what the fuck was wrong with me only resulted in silence. I should have been celebrating one less thing to stress about, but the worry had morphed into something else. Something that thrummed beneath the surface.

An unidentifiable emotion that I pushed down, buried deep until all that remained was the wicked king about to ruin yet another person.

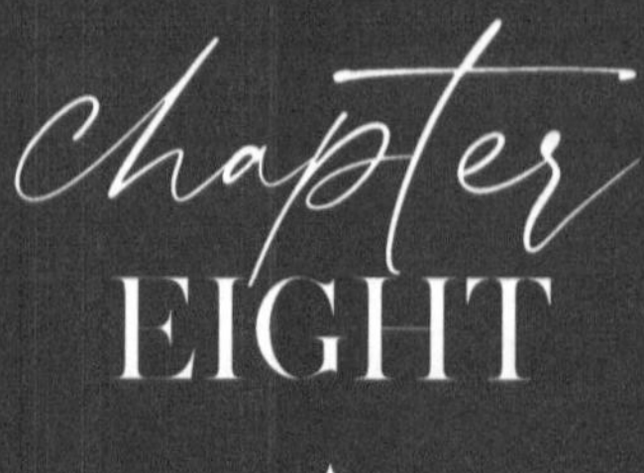

OPHELIA

Despite Atticus telling me he talked to Mitchell, I went to the restaurant anyway. Mitchell had taken a chance on me a year ago, and I hated letting him down. When our eyes met, he motioned for me to follow. Once we were both inside his office, he shut the door.

"Atticus called already," he said as soon as he sat in his chair.

"I'm so sorry, Mitchell."

A sigh left him, his body sagging. "I'm not mad. I'm not allowed to be, and if I was, it's not at you. I'm losing my best server. You're more than a waitress here, Ophelia. We're going to miss you."

"Me too." 130 Degrees had become my friends and family over the last eleven months. I couldn't believe I hadn't anticipated the move. I guess I figured I could still work, at least until closer to the wedding and maybe even after.

"What did he say?" I asked.

He shook his head. "Not much. Only that you weren't working here anymore."

"You didn't ask?"

"You don't question Atticus de Loughrey when he tells you something like that."

Every suspicion was confirmed. "So you knew who he was?"

He nodded. "Couldn't tell anyone. Still can't."

I swallowed hard. "I wish I could tell you why."

He pursed his lips. "I know, kid."

"Just know it's not a move I wanted. But you know Atticus."

He nodded. "That I do." He stood and wrapped his arms around me. "Take care, Ophelia. If something happens, come see me, okay?"

I gave him a squeeze and willed the tears in my eyes not to fall. "Will do." Knowing it was Atticus's favorite lunch spot, I had a feeling I would be returning, only sitting on the other side of the table from Atticus inside his private booth instead of serving him.

After a last goodbye to the chef, I headed out. Darkness settled inside me, and I began to wonder what I'd just done. It was as if as soon as I signed, I'd forfeited my life. Granted, that was the basis of the entire thing, I just didn't expect so much to suddenly happen.

I'd hidden the ring, slipped it into my bra so he wouldn't see. Plus, I didn't like the idea of wearing a huge-ass diamond ring on public transportation.

When I returned home, I still felt like I was in a trance. The whole ordeal felt surreal. It was like a strange dream I was going to wake from. Was I hit by a car and in a strange coma dream that latched onto Atticus and designed a weird fairytale around him?

A pinch to my arm confirmed that I was *not* in a coma. That weight on my finger was not a pulse oximeter, and it was in fact, a huge-ass diamond ring.

Why did I agree to this?

You know why. Because you never got past that night.

It was true. I hadn't been on a date or had sex since my birthday. Nearly a year of seeing him at work multiple times a week kept him constantly on my mind.

What I'd agreed to was torture for both of us, plain and simple. To be around him knowing I'd never have him between my thighs again and that I was the one that made that rule.

But I wanted there to be no illusion that he'd have anytime access to my body. Otherwise, it felt too much like I was prostituting myself. Instead, I needed to look at it for what it was—a job. My career for the next five years was to stand by his side, wear his name, and carry his child.

Wait, why did he need all that? Had I even asked before I jumped headlong into this arrangement?

Ophelia Marie Evans... You're an idiot.

I stared down at the ring on my finger, looking past the diamonds to the shackle it really was. What had I gotten myself into? I was sporting a single piece of jewelry worth more money than my student loan debt, probably quadruple the amount I owed.

An amount that I wouldn't owe in a few days.

That was the strangest part about all of this. The amount of money he was throwing around just to secure me as his fake fiancée was astronomical. It would take a long time for me to process that I now had access to some of that.

My bank account was sitting at just over two hundred dollars. I looked up the credit card he gave me online. It was one of those no-questions-asked types. You flashed it and wherever you were, they'd give you a kidney if you needed it.

That sounded too black market, when in fact it was the pinnacle of prestige.

I spent the evening devouring a large pepperoni and mushroom pizza while pulling things out of my closet and stuffing boxes left over from my last move. Thankfully I'd kept them, but I still picked up a few more, plus packing tape. Deep into the night I worked between panic attacks and waves of nausea.

I then topped it off with an entire pan of brownies for good measure.

It helped for a few seconds.

What I was embarking on was insanity, and each area of my tiny space that was packed up only made it more of a reality that I would not be spending the next night in the space that was all mine.

Around four in the morning, I crashed surrounded by a pile

of boxes, but was startled awake only a few short hours later by the traffic outside.

It didn't take long to pack up my apartment, especially not with the movers Atticus hired. In fact, the movers looked at my sad little collection of items and had them loaded into the truck in no time. Some stuff was being stored. I wasn't stupid enough to believe nothing could go wrong and I wouldn't be out the door in a week and have not even a bed to lay my head on.

Nope, wasn't having that. Still, my furniture amounted to a daybed, a chair (which I did move), a cafe set, storage cube unit, and a nightstand with a lamp.

After they left, I slipped my ring on a chain and clipped it around my neck. There was no way I was getting on the train with that on my finger. However, when I got down to the street level, there was a black car sitting out front with a man standing beside it, his hands in his pockets. He straightened when he saw me.

"Miss Evans," he called.

"Yes?" I responded cautiously.

"Your fiancé has asked me to bring you to him."

Seemed Atticus didn't like the idea of the ring on the train either. My little bit of freedom as Ophelia Evans the waitress was over. I was officially Ophelia Evans, fiancée to Atticus de Loughrey.

The driver held open the back door and I slipped in, settling into the plush leather interior. The legroom in back was deceiving from the outside, and I found myself playing with the controls on the armrest. A squeak left me when a footrest pushed against the back of my calves.

A chuckle came from the front seat, and heat flooded my face.

"So, umm, are you a personal driver for a company?" I asked, catching his reflection as he pulled away from the curb. He didn't seem much older than me, maybe mid-thirties with brown hair, green eyes, and a friendly face.

"No. I am a de Loughrey family personal driver."

"There's more than one, isn't there?" I asked, another wave of "What the fuck have you gotten yourself into?" slamming into me.

Another chuckle. "Many."

"What's your name?" I asked, catching his eye in the rearview mirror.

"Michael, Miss Evans."

"Please, call me Ophelia. It's a pleasure to meet you."

"You as well."

There was a soft string instrument coming from the speakers, and as we wove through traffic, the lack of sleep caught up to me. I was jostled awake by Michael's hand on my shoulder.

"We're here," he said as I started.

I gave him a small smile. "Thanks."

After yesterday, I no longer had to check in with the desk—I had my own keycard to the private elevator for the top floors. Three trips up had made me more confident as I walked to his office without Holly. She was still there to greet me with a smile and let me in.

"Hi," I said as I stepped into his office.

He glanced up at me, then back to his computer where he finished up his thought. Once he was done, the screen turned black and he pushed his chair back.

"Ready to go home?" he asked, his face scrunching at the oddity of the words passing his lips.

At least I wasn't the only one feeling like a fish out of water.

He pulled his suit jacket on and buttoned it before stuffing his phone into his pocket and stepping toward me. The man wore three-piece suits like lingerie, and I had a hard time not catcalling him. I didn't think that would go over well, especially with the fight I put up for the no-sex clause.

Our eyes met and the sea of awkwardness at what was happening expanded. Neither of us seemed to know what to do, even though the whole plan was his idea.

I supposed idea and execution were two different things. The plan on paper was one thing, but having to actually interact with me and pretend to be my loving fiancé was entirely different. We were both novices, and the feeling in the air was like preteens at a school dance.

He cleared his throat, and our eyes met.

Okay, maybe I was the only one feeling that way. The man before me could never be anything other than dominant and authoritative. What was I smoking? There was a slight hesitation, though, when he lifted his hand to take mine. Small, but I noticed.

I swallowed as I slipped my hand in his and tried not to melt from the electrified heat of his touch. I died just a little inside as I stuffed down the memories of the last time he took my hand.

Letting out a breath, I gave him a small smile and a nod.

Due to the early hour, we received more than a few looks on our way to the elevator. I ducked my head, not wanting to stand out when Atticus leaned in.

"Head up, shoulders back."

A simple command, but it said so much. It reminded me that I wasn't some dirty secret or paid for…well, I was being paid. The point was, I wore the ring. *His* ring. And I was going to be a de Loughrey, so I needed to learn to act the part.

I'm going to be a de Loughrey.

Another wave of nausea rippled through me.

A set of brilliant grey eyes went wide as we passed an open door. He looked familiar, and I was pretty sure he was a de Loughrey as well.

"Atticus?" he called out.

Atticus's hand flexed, squeezing mine as he stopped. "Hamilton?"

Hamilton glanced between us as he closed the gap. My stomach began flipping under his scrutiny.

"What's going on?"

"Hamilton, meet Ophelia. Ophelia, this is my younger brother, Hamilton."

I gave him a small smile. "Pleased to meet you." It was my turn to squeeze Atticus's hand.

"Ophelia?" Hamilton again looked between us. "Will you be joining us for the family dinner?"

Out of the corner of my eye, I saw Atticus's jaw clench. "She will be, as a matter of fact."

Hamilton studied me for a moment and made a scoffing sound. "You weren't going to tell me?"

At least his brother wasn't stupid—he'd caught on.

"I was, but not today. For now, we need to get home. We will talk tomorrow."

"Have a good afternoon, then."

"He didn't seem happy," I whispered as we walked away.

"Hamilton is only happy when his cock is buried in some woman's holes."

"The stereotypical rich playboy?"

"I don't know about stereotypical, but he is a rich playboy."

The elevator cab was empty, and I broke the deafening silence. "Does anybody know about me?"

"I was going to introduce you at the family dinner, but I'm now seeing that may not be the best idea."

"Better than a Facebook post."

He groaned at that. "No social media. None."

"I wasn't going to. I'm just saying, better at family dinner night than via the media."

"That is over a week away, and you're bound to run into one or two more."

"Of your siblings?"

"Siblings, cousins, aunts, uncles, parents, second cousins." He heaved a sigh. "I have homework for you until then."

"Homework? Yay." I couldn't keep the sarcastic lack of excitement from my tone.

When we arrived in the lobby, Michael was still waiting at the curb, and we loaded into the car. As the crow flies, it was a short trip, but Manhattan traffic was a different beast. When we pulled up to the skyscraper that had only in the last few years joined the New York City skyline, I was in awe.

Olympus Tower was a fitting name for the de Loughrey family to inhabit. We were greeted by the doorman, and then the concierge, upon entering. The elevators were off to the right, and I angled that way, but was pulled back by Atticus tugging on my hand. I blinked at him, but followed to the left. A large iron gate cut off an area, and past it I could see two elevators with a golden insignia of a crowned shield flanked by two lions.

As we approached, the gates opened. I didn't even have time to wait when the elevator doors slid open without even pushing a button.

"Did they do all of that?" I asked as we stepped on, noting that the buttons started at the fortieth floor.

"No. The building has sensors that pick up a unique signal from your phone combined with facial recognition."

"What kind of sorcery are you talking about?" The elevator rocketed up, making my ears pop, and I rubbed at the right one.

He chuckled at that. "It means the building is laced with technology that knows where you are."

"Does that mean it's watching you in your home?" That would seriously be creepy.

"No. Common areas only—lobby and elevator bays."

The cab decelerated and slowed to a stop on the sixty-third floor—the penthouse floor. Of course. There was a large set of double doors in front of us, and with a press of his fingers to a button near the handle, I heard a click. Upon entering, there was what appeared to be a home office or library. We turned left, and I froze.

I promised myself I wouldn't have one of those stupid jaw-dropping moments, but who was I kidding? A poor chick who was living in three hundred square feet suddenly in a condo with more square footage than the entire building I woke up in?

Yeah, that wasn't happening.

There was no keeping the awestruck expression from my face as we walked through an enormous living room that also had a huge sitting area with a door to a terrace, past a huge dining room table with what looked like a crystal waterfall chandelier, but what really got me was in the great room—a twelve-foot-high glass wall of windows with a view overlooking the Hudson. The place looked like a museum, and was as silent as one. Atticus's voice echoed on the walls as he pointed things out. It was unnerving, and I was hesitant to move from my spot, in fear of upsetting the pristine surface before me.

The kitchen was just as impressive, and I seriously wondered if the island was bigger than the apartment I came from. Maybe an exaggeration, but that was what it felt like.

"There are four bedrooms for you to choose from. All have their own en suite."

He showed me a small one that was on the same side with the view of the river, then pointed out the large door to his bedroom. It was quite a ways down a hall lined with artwork. We stopped at the next door—the room a little bit larger than the first, and south facing.

"This one," I said the second we stepped into the third option. It was a corner room, the impressive floor-to-ceiling windows curved and framed a southeast view. There was a walk-in closet and a large bathroom. Overall, it was bigger than the previous two.

"It's yours."

We continued the tour, including the fourth bedroom, which was my second choice of a room. There was a laundry room and mudroom that had access to the vestibule. We moved into the first room I saw right off the elevator. It was a cozy room compared to the rest, thanks in part to the floor-to-ceiling dark wood bookcases. There was a desk to one side, and a sitting area with a couch on the other.

He motioned for me to sit as he picked something up from his desk before taking the seat across from me.

"Homework." He patted the red leather portfolio before setting it on the coffee table between us. "This is an account of my life, to better acquaint yourself with me, the de Loughrey family, and our business. Study it well."

I took the thick binder and opened it. It was a few inches thick and my eyes strained *not* to roll at the title page—The Life and Times of Atticus William de Loughrey.

"Your phone has been integrated with the security of this building, and here are the instructions for how that works." He slid a piece of paper closer, then held out a card similar to the one he'd given me at the restaurant, only it was more credit-card like. "Keep hold of this at all times. It will show anyone that you are with the de Loughrey family."

I looked at the card, noticing how the shield with a crown flanked by lions was the same as the one I'd seen on the lobby gate. "What was with that gate? Do you own this building?"

He nodded. "There are sixty-three floors, and we occupy forty and above."

"Twenty-three floors?" Holy crap. Not only did he own the building, but his family occupied it.

He nodded. "Forty through forty-three hold family amenities."

"What does that mean?"

"Do you really think we would share anything with the rest of the building?"

Point taken. "What's on those floors?"

"There is a gym, spa, and swimming pool on forty."

"Wait," I said, holding up my hand to stop him. "There is a swimming pool in the middle of the building?"

"Yes."

"And only the de Loughreys can use it?"

He nodded. "Yes."

"Wow."

"May I continue?" he asked with a slight edge of annoyance.

I nodded as I pondered what other wonders would come out of his mouth.

"On forty-one, you will find anything for your entertainment pleasure. There is a billiards table, various other games, a movie theater, and even a small nightclub."

Night club? Though with the track record of Genevieve de Loughrey, it shouldn't have surprised me.

"Forty-two holds salons and a children's play area."

"Salons?"

"People come to us, we don't go to them. You will also find Jack's office there, as well as the other home assistants. Forty-three and above are all private residences with two condos per floor. Currently there is one family member per floor, with exception of the twins sharing a floor, and a few levels are currently empty."

"Room to grow." I couldn't think about how much money in rental they were losing by having so much empty space.

"Precisely." He cleared his throat and stood. "The movers should be here soon. Jack will help with that. I need to get back to the office, but I will see you for dinner. Until then, settle in."

I awkwardly waved goodbye, our eyes catching just as the elevator doors slid closed. It was that look, that same one that I'd seen at the restaurant—longing coupled with uncertainty. Maybe it was just me, but that was what it felt like.

I glanced up and then down the hall before choosing to head toward the family room, allowing myself to really take the space in. It was *huge*, with tons of wasted space, especially with a bachelor occupying the space. It definitely didn't feel lived in. I was certain only half of the seats had ever been sat in, and the reality was probably half of that. Marble, dark woods, and crystal. It was a beautiful marriage of modern with classic materials. Hardwoods ran throughout, creating a seamless flow.

After my solo tour, I headed to what was going to be my bedroom. The relief that flooded me when I realized I wasn't going to be sharing a bedroom with him was huge. I guess I'd just assumed, seeing as we were going to be married. Sleeping in different beds was going to go a long way in keeping me from doing something to him I swore I wouldn't allow. Something I'd made him put in the contract, and if he was abiding by it, I had to get my hormones in check when he was near.

I stood at the window looking out over the view I would have every day going forward. It was magnificent. One World Trade Center stood proudly, seeming almost close enough to touch, with Upper Bay in the background. Turning toward the bed I ran, then dove onto it face down. A groan left me as I sank into the plush mattress.

My eyes started to drift closed and what felt like seconds later, there was a knock on the door startling me awake. When I sat up, the sun had shifted and my phone showed at least an hour had passed.

"Yes?"

"Miss Ophelia, the movers are here," a male voice said.

I scooted off the bed, wiping a bit of drool from my face as I moved to greet whomever was at the door.

"Hi," I said with a smile.

He gave me a nod of his head. "Hello, Miss Ophelia, my name is Jack. I am Mr. Atticus's personal assistant. It's a pleasure to meet you."

Jack was a thin man, probably a few inches shy of six feet, with slicked-back auburn hair and pale brown eyes. He looked about my age.

"Just Ophelia, please."

He nodded. "The movers have arrived. Would you like your things in here?"

"Yes. Thank you."

Once everything, which didn't amount to much, was set against the wall, everyone disappeared and I pulled my speaker from one of the boxes and started streaming music as I got to it.

Seeing as there wasn't much, it didn't take long to unpack. I did confiscate a small three-drawer dresser from one of the vacant bedrooms to set my TV on. Once everything was done, the room didn't look that much different, and I started a list of things to get to help it feel more like *my* room.

I was halfway through when I heard voices and shuffling. I thought it was just Atticus, but there was a female voice as well. After a few minutes I made my way down the hall, listening in on the conversation.

It definitely wasn't Atticus, but I did jump when he called my name from behind.

"Ophelia?"

I spun around, eyes wide. "Hi."

"What are you doing?" he asked, having obviously been watching me creep down the hall.

"There's someone in the kitchen?" I wasn't sure if I was asking or telling.

"That is Chef Loreno."

"You have a chef?" I asked in shock. Did the de Loughreys do *anything* on their own?

"Yes. He cooks dinner."

"Who else is in there?"

"Amara, his wife. She assists him."

"Does he cook just for you?"

"No. He often cooks for the others as well, but uses my kitchen, as it's the largest. Let me introduce you." He took my hand, and I forced myself to ignore the warmth of his touch as he led me down the hall. "Good evening, Chef."

"Atticus!" He beamed. "It is so good to see you, my friend." I watched as they hugged, stunned. Then Atticus moved over to Amara and placed a kiss on each cheek. She smiled at him before her eyes went wide when she spotted me.

They began speaking in what I was pretty sure was Italian, Atticus chiming in, their gazes flickering to me before Amara walked toward me. I had no idea what was said, but I was suddenly embraced by her.

"Welcome, Miss Ophelia," she said with a warm smile. "It is so good to see Atticus in the company of a woman."

The Italian kicked up again, and by the scowl on Atticus's face, I think he took offense to something she said.

"Ophelia," Loreno said, gaining my attention. "Please, if you wouldn't mind, in the next few days, leave me a list of your favorite foods and flavors, as well as those you dislike and are allergic to. Be specific, if you could."

"Specific how?" I asked, my mind whirling.

"Atticus does not like rocket or similar other bitter greens."

"Rocket?"

He seemed to consider something. "Arugula."

Atticus perked up and turned toward us, a scowl on his face. "No weeds."

I let out a laugh at that. "Weeds?"

"Disgusting plant." He narrowed his gaze at me. "What can't you stand?"

I shrugged. "I don't like nuts. I mean, I like them on their own, but I don't like them in or on anything."

I could feel the heat of Atticus's stare, and my eyes widened. "Like peanuts and walnuts and almonds." Warmth swept through my face. "I don't like almonds but I like almond flavor, but just no to walnuts. And peanut sauce on Thai food is yummy." I kept rambling on, making my embarrassment even greater.

Atticus stepped forward and leaned in. "I do remember you liking nuts," he whispered low enough that only I could hear, his lips ghosting my ear and sending a shiver of heat down my spine. "On their own. In your mouth. The way you sucked on them, held their weight in your hand before popping them between your plump lips."

My heart sped up and I glanced at Loreno and Amara, but they're attention was fully on their task preparing our meal.

"I wasn't talking about—"

"I know," he interrupted, still whispering so not to be overheard. "But that's all I can think about. Your warm, wet tongue wrapped around my nuts. Around my cock."

My thighs clenched, and I had to take a step away to clear my throat. "What's on the menu tonight?" I asked, trying to forget the last sixty seconds.

Half an hour later, I was staring down at an empty plate wondering if I could lick it without Atticus noticing. "Loreno is a cooking god," I said with a groan. The man was beyond talented in the kitchen.

"Now you see why he's our personal chef."

"Does he do the family dinners?"

He shook his head. "Those are held at Stronghold, our family home outside the city. The house staffs multiple chefs."

Multiple? Wow. How many people were living there?

"Okay—who all comes in here, so I know?" I asked to keep from looking at the remainder of the sauce that was staring at me, daring me to just slip my finger across to wipe up as much of the goodness as I could.

"What do you mean?"

"What kind of help should I expect?" I hated saying it like that. It almost sounded as if I thought they were beneath me, when they weren't. They were here to do a job, just as I was.

"There are entire teams that keep the de Loughrey family running. Each property has a different set. We all also have assistants."

"Jack. So, you need an assistant just to keep track of your help?" I needed to find another word for them. Caretakers? Did that sound less demeaning? It seemed they all had different jobs, but I couldn't find a word to encompass them that didn't make me sound like a pompous ass.

Employees? That sounded best of them all. Household employees? That way I could distinguish them from his company.

"That's basically what Jack does. I don't have time to tell Loreno what time I might be home or what sounds good for dinner—Jack handles that."

"Does he know about us…the real us?"

"No."

"Where does he think I came from?"

Atticus blew out a breath. "He shouldn't be thinking anything."

"I'm sure he's curious."

"Perhaps, but it is none of his business."

"You're his business, ergo, I am as well."

His hand slammed down on the table, making me jump in surprise. "He doesn't need to know our history, Ophelia, only that you are now affiliated with me."

With that he stood, leaving me shaken and surprised by his reaction. I watched as he walked down the hall and into his bedroom, the door shutting with a slam, leaving me alone.

I blew out a breath and ran my hand through my hair. There went the getting-to-know-you portion of the evening. Though I wasn't sure what had set him off so suddenly, I had an inkling.

Atticus went to 130 Degrees, to a veiled booth with minimal interaction. The condo was the bigger version. My presence was bound to throw off his balance, especially with the millions of questions running through my head.

I'd rocked his peace, invaded his sanctuary, and I had a feeling he'd just gotten his first taste of having a roommate in years.

It left me to wonder one thing—had anyone ever been there that wasn't family or an employee?

ATTICUS

The first evening with Ophelia in my home didn't quite go as planned, though I wasn't sure what I had anticipated.

It wasn't like at the restaurant where our conversations were of few words. She wanted to *talk*.

Maybe I hadn't thought enough about what it would be like having her live with me. It had been an instantaneous assumption.

We get engaged equals she moves in.

Just the thought of the media hunting her down to her tiny apartment incensed me. I would not allow her to go around as if she were poor. She was going to have the finest things, no longer suffering to make ends meet.

That fucking made me sound like I was attempting to be a white knight, when it was anything but. I didn't doubt my decision based on attraction. I'd pined for her for nearly a year, something I'd never in my life done, with the exception of Delephina Monroe in my sophomore year of college—a mild crush on a beautiful girl that ended when she caught Rhys's eye.

Ophelia was the goddess I wanted to pray to, and I hadn't the slightest idea where or how that conviction had emerged. All I knew or understood was the desire to be near her, no matter what. Needing a wife only facilitated the exploration of my infatuation.

The fact that she said yes left me in a new conundrum. I didn't know how to act around her in my own home, and her questions further frustrated me

Now, there was this woman I barely knew, one that I wanted to fuck, one that I decided to marry, and she was a phantom I created that would no longer ever leave me alone. I thought I wouldn't notice her, but even without seeing her, I could feel her presence. It pulled at me, causing an upheaval in my one and only sanctuary. She wasn't like the workers that came and went as silently as possible.

And I created the situation that destroyed my peace. It was a type of change I abhorred, but one I would have to get used to, because she wasn't going anywhere. The getting used to part was difficult. Her small line of questioning had me at wits' end, and I'd snapped.

Small fingers snapped in front of my face, and I blinked to find Holly standing in front of me with a steaming mug.

"You okay?"

"Did I make a mistake?" I asked, my brow furrowed.

She leaned against my desk, the mug cupped between her hands as she took a sip. "Ruined things already?"

I sat back. "I don't think so."

"Do I think, maybe for the first time in all the years I've known you, you did something very spontaneous and very un-Atticus like with the whole not-thinking-it-through thing? Yeah."

"I thought it through," I argued.

She shook her head. "You thought the contract details through. You didn't think about having a living, breathing person now connected to you at the hip, and I'm not talking about a baby. I'm talking about that poor girl who has no clue what she's agreed to, thrust into a world she knows nothing of, with a man who she doesn't know."

"Nobody knows me."

"And whose fault is that?"

"Go away," I said with a sigh.

She set the cup she'd been sipping from down in front of me. "Here, I'll share."

I quirked a brow at her. I didn't share anything, let alone a half-drunk cup of coffee.

"It's Becca's special blend."

Or maybe I did. "Why don't you just finish that one and get me a fresh cup? Since it's obvious you brewed it here."

"Is it?" she asked in that conspiring tone of hers.

"Why do I pay you to be a thorn in my side?"

"We've discussed this a dozen times. Someone with your sharp memory should know the answer to that."

"Out. And bring me back a cup."

"Aye, aye, Capitano. Oh, by the way, Rhys called."

My brow scrunched as I glanced to my phone. "I have no missed calls."

She shook her head. "You've been ignoring a lot of people the last few weeks. He set up a lunch."

A sigh left me. "Fine."

She laughed. "You're a reclusive billionaire, Atticus. It's not hard to figure out what you're thinking when it comes to social interaction."

"I have not hit recluse status."

"Yet."

"Yet," I grumbled.

She wasn't wrong. Especially since the will reading, I'd avoided everyone and everything I could.

Once-friends from school were now acquaintances after years of little to no interaction. Friends were one of the few luxuries I couldn't afford.

Holly was one to take me by surprise. She was like a dog with a bone when we met in college, unrelenting in her quest to get to know me. Due to my upbringing, I initially thought it was because she wanted something, but that wasn't the case. She was just an exuberant person. One who could see how lonely I was and forcibly inserted herself into my personal space, despite how much I detested it.

Eventually she broke me down, proclaimed herself my best

friend, and she'd stayed beside me ever since. I paid her well to put up with me every day.

The day was filled with meetings and financial reports. Growth was slowing down, which my father attributed to the failure of my brother and I to marry someone of affluence. Still, the company was doing well. The goal was to keep it that way, to prove I didn't need to marry some hotel heiress to keep de Loughrey the leader in multiple markets.

Expansion plans for the future were in the works, but they took time and a great amount of planning.

It was after lunch when my door opened. Holly could be heard protesting, but Hamilton couldn't care less as he slammed the door in her face.

"You should apologize when we're done," I said. Holly and Hamilton had never gotten along because she didn't let him walk all over her because of his name, while Hamilton wasn't accustomed to rejection, even if the woman he approached was a lesbian.

"What the hell are you up to with the girl?" Hamilton asked as he sat across from me. Per usual, he wasted no time getting to the point.

"It's just a business proposition."

"I don't think this is a good idea."

I swore that the vein in my forehead twitched. Why did every conversation with him end up in an argument? "I don't care what you think. I'm not agreeing to an arranged marriage."

"Fine, asshole, but when this goes sideways, don't come looking for me to fix it."

I narrowed my eyes at him. "When have you ever fixed anything for me? When has anyone? I'm the one who makes the hard decisions to protect this family."

"Always taking the high and mighty road."

"Do you want to do this shit?" I snarled. "I'll gladly let you take over cleaning up Gen's messes. That alone will keep you busy and give you some taste of the shit I deal with daily. Running a company is easy compared to running this family of spoiled fuckups."

Even though the role had only officially been mine for a little less than a month, I'd been helping orchestrate the family for years in preparation. Only me. No one else was subjected to every dirty secret the de Loughreys held.

"I'm just wondering why you brought in some strange girl, and how it is any different from that girl Father picked."

"The difference is I know what it feels like to be between her thighs, and I like it." And I'd done nothing but fucking fantasize about it for nearly a year.

Hamilton let out a sigh. "This is risky. How are you doing this?"

"She moved into one of my extra bedrooms yesterday. Right now, the goal is to get her primed for the family dinner."

"Is she a good actress? Or are you going to show the family what it really is?"

His barrage of questions were irritating. "The only way I'm getting him off my back is if he thinks there are emotions, and even then, I'm unsure."

"I hope you know what you're doing, brother."

"It'll either be a spectacular idea, or a spectacular explosion. Only time will tell."

"Are you going to tell me who she is?" he asked.

I furrowed my brow as I stared at him. "Who she is?"

"Yes. What is she bringing in?"

I blinked at my brother. He understood when he saw her yesterday that she was the woman I'd chosen, but he hadn't picked up on her penniless state?

"Nothing."

He balked at me, eyes wide as he moved to the edge of his chair. "Nothing? What the hell do you mean, nothing?"

"I mean, up until yesterday she was a waitress living in a studio apartment in Brooklyn."

"Are you mad?" he asked, an incredulous edge to his tone.

"Who I picked is of no concern to you, Hamilton. She is to be *my* wife," I ground out.

"Then you better perfect that love act, brother, because he will see the cracks and pounce. Sink his teeth in until he rips her from you."

I ground my teeth together. "I will not allow it."

"He is still as strong willed as ever. That need to control and manipulate hasn't waned with age."

My lip turned up, and I let out a harsh chuckle. "Not this time. If I have to, I will waste not one second sequestering him on the other side of the globe if he tests me." The reign was passed to me. *I* ruled, and he would not control me any longer. The tides had turned, and I would do whatever was necessary to ensure Ophelia was mine.

"The problem is—how much will you let him pick and prod until you snap?"

I leaned back. "He's going to keep pushing the Harris girl no matter what, but that isn't enough."

"I still don't like this."

"You don't have to. I do. This is the path I've chosen." Silence prevailed. I could tell he wanted to argue with me more, as that was his favorite pastime, so I changed the course of the conversation. "How are the talks with Worthington going?" I asked, completely and utterly desperate to move the conversation from my fiancée.

Hamilton went silent, a rarity, which garnered my full attention. "What happened?"

"Another bidder."

"And?"

"And Donovan Trading and Investments' President of Acquisitions isn't a pushover."

"Stop speaking in roundabout ways and tell me."

"Carthwright offered them a better deal. It's going to make Donovan excel in the market."

"We still dominate the market."

Hamilton's jaw clenched. "This isn't the first time Thane Carthwright has snatched a promising addition away from us."

"You're afraid of a relatively small-time trading and investments firm?"

"At the rate they're growing and expanding, yes."

Interesting. Like Donovan, we were growing our own investment firm to go with our financial side.

"It sounds like we should have hired this Carthwright."

"We tried five years ago at the first instance of crowding, but he declined."

The phone on my desktop rang, and I reached for it. "I don't want to lose this to a lesser company. Do whatever it takes."

"Hire a hitman? Sure, you got it," he said, picking up the folio and heading out.

I shook my head and let out a small chuckle as I picked up the receiver.

OPHELIA

My eyes drifted closed before snapping back open. I shook my head and stared down at the page, the black letters blurring. I'd slept well, my bed incredibly comfortable, and it was a long, hard snooze. None of that mattered in the face of The Life and Times of Atticus William de Loughrey. After about five pages of ten-point font, eight-and-a-half by eleven sheets of white paper with small margins, I was fighting a wave of sleepiness threatening to take me under.

When Atticus handed me the leather binder, I didn't think much of it. The problem was that it read like a history textbook and had me fighting sleep in a few pages. I hated history in high school, avoided it as best I could in college. Remembering dates with events and who won what battle or who conquered what country only to give it back later or have someone else take it from them was torture to me.

This was the same. At four years old, Atticus excelled in three languages and was on his way to becoming a master in fencing.

At four.

By the time I got to twenty, was it going to talk about him becoming the supreme ruler of the Earth?

This is going to take forever.

I ruffled the pages, watching them flip by with few gaps in the solid wall of text. It was going to take me forever to work my way through. I hadn't made it past his preschool accomplishments yet, and there was another thirty plus years after that. Not to mention the history of the de Loughrey's, which started at page ninety-seven.

With a sigh of defeat, I collapsed down onto the pages. My goal of having the now-christened Binder of Doom read by the weekend was out the window. At the rate I was going, making it to page twenty would be a great accomplishment worthy of celebration.

If I made a goal of ten pages a day, I could theoretically be done in a few weeks.

That was depressing. I graduated with a 3.9 from NYU in biology, but wanted to claw my eyes out over this?

A growl of my stomach turned my attention to the clock. It was noon, giving me the perfect excuse to take a break. Afterwards, maybe I'd sit out on the veranda and trudge on.

The sun was shining when I stepped outside after I finished off a sandwich made from last night's leftovers. The air was warm with a light breeze filled with the promised heat of summer. It made me want to get out of the tower, to take a walk along the streets—some activity to fight the sleep the Binder of Doom incited.

Returning to my room, I located a small purse and filled it with the necessities, including my new phone and access card. I slipped on some sneakers, throwing the strap of my bag over my head as I walked to the elevator.

I blinked at the door, realizing it was my first time leaving since I'd arrived twenty-four hours earlier. With a turn of the handle, the door opened with little resistance, exposing the elevator bay. I pushed the call button, and within a few minutes I stepped out of the elevator and into the lobby.

Another first, and I couldn't help but look around. I felt so out of place, unsure of my steps. It felt like I was somewhere I wasn't supposed to be. As I approached the golden gates, they opened wide, just like my eyes.

"Good afternoon, Miss Evans," a man in a suit standing at the concierge desk said as I passed through into the main lobby.

"H-hi," I said, giving him a strained smile before scampering off toward the doors.

Once out of the opulent building and onto the hard, concrete streets of the city, I let out a sigh. The familiarity of the city sounds crashed down on me and calmed me. It was the first time the constant hum of the crowded streets gave me a sense of peace.

I felt incredibly out of place in Atticus's home and almost felt like I was walking on eggshells whenever he was near.

His outburst and sudden departure from the dinner table confused me, and he was gone before I woke in the morning. Granted, my lack of sleep and the comfort of the bed kept me there until well after nine.

The whole encounter started off nice, if not awkward, and ended in his blow-up. Was that how things were always going to be, or was it just our breaking-in period? I hoped it was just the break-in period. We had to get to know each other. That was the only way we were going to make it through five years.

I had no destination in mind, but the walking helped to center me. After some time, I somehow ended up in front of the de Loughrey building. It wasn't where I was intending to go and no reason to be there, but still I entered.

And got on the elevator for the top floor.

I glanced around, my heart suddenly hammering in my chest. When I reached the desks near his office, I noticed Holly's seat was empty.

"He's on a call," a woman called.

I turned to find a woman around my age, possibly. It was hard to tell. Her dark skin was flawless and completely unblemished.

"Oh," was all I could say.

"Do you want to wait?" she asked, giving me a small smile.

I leaned toward her. "Do I look as out of place as I feel?" I whispered.

She chuckled. "There is a little deer-in-headlights going on, honey."

I pursed my lips and sighed. "Why am I here?"

"Want some coffee? We have a great espresso machine," she offered.

I shook my head. "Please don't worry. I'm probably going to just go back downstairs anyway."

She reached out for my hand. "Wait. Stay. Talk to him."

I nodded and worried my bottom lip, and my stomach twisted. "I'm sorry, I didn't catch your name."

"Alexis," she said with a warm smile.

"Thanks, Alexis."

"You're welcome. Holly's chair is empty. You can sit in her seat until he's available, if you want."

I gave her a nod and moved around the half wall to where Holly resided. My hand rested on the top of the wall when the deep timbre of his voice caught my attention. There was an edge to it, much like when he was upset at the restaurant, but this was much more frightening.

"If you don't agree, Vincent, you will force my hand."

"You bastard," Vincent's voice hissed from the phone's speaker. "We had an agreement."

"You're an underhanded son-of-a—"

"Watch your next words. Carefully. I do not suffer outraged bursts of insults." The chill in his tone sent a shiver down my spine with its deadly edge. "We have a contract. I will lay waste to everything you hold dear if you do not complete the terms."

"Fucking de Loughreys. Think you can get away with—"

"We had a deal!" Atticus roared, cutting the man off and making me jump. "*You* are the one who has failed to uphold his end. I have completed the agreed-upon conditions of our bargain. Supplied you with all you requested. I am not some simpleton you can roll over. Who did you think you were getting into bed with?"

The conversation felt like a mirror image to my own situation. Who did I get into bed with?

"Do not put blame on me or my company for your inadequacies. You will find a much darker side to me if you let your ego war with mine. I guarantee you will not like the outcome."

It was a side of him I'd never witnessed. I'd seen him in a poor mood, watched him send waiters away with tears in their eyes. Experienced myself the lengths he would go to get what he wanted. Anger and annoyance, yes, but not the oppressive power with which he spoke.

The dark undercurrent full of malice in his tone was unnerving. The power, authority, and strength that radiated off him in that conversation was intense enough to send a man to his knees.

My stomach knotted, and a hollow sensation crept inside.

"You have twenty-four hours before I tear your company apart brick by brick." He gave the man on the other end no time to respond before he picked up the receiver and slammed it back down, ending the call.

"There's a button for that," Holly said, surprising me. I'd assumed she was at lunch.

"I know there's a fucking button, but that's the only fucking way my anger is getting out at the moment, unless you wish to get me yet another phone when I throw it across the room."

She sighed. "That would be two in a month. Just go down to the gym and hit the punching bag."

"Seriously?"

"Fucking de Loughreys."

"Are you just going to stand outside my door all day?" Atticus's voice floated from the open doorway.

I jumped, wondering how he knew I was there, my gaze flickering to the door.

I swallowed hard, then stepped into the opening and walked through. As I did, Holly straightened from behind him, her hands resting on his shoulders.

It was an intimate pose, not one of boss and employee, and something about it rubbed me wrong. She picked something up from his desk, her eyes trained on me as her hips swayed with each step toward me.

Her lips spread into a smile and I bristled, my hackles slightly raising. At a glance, it seemed no different than all the smiles she'd given me before, but after seeing her wrapped around Atticus, I was viewing her in a different light.

One I didn't like.

When I reached Atticus's desk, his eyes were closed, jaw set in a hard line, and he was leaning forward, his head against his hand that appeared to be massaging the stress from his temple. It wasn't working. The fire and rage vibrating from him was enough to have me scampering away, but I stayed put.

I should not have come. Whatever conversation we were about to have was bound to leave me in as foul of a mood as he was in, I just knew it.

"Ophelia," he said as he stared at me, his lip curling up in disgust as he looked me over. He picked up his phone, his fingers flying over the screen before placing it down. "We need to get you new clothes tomorrow. I can't have my fiancée looking like a fucking hobo."

I glanced down at my outfit. What was wrong with jeans, sneakers, and a T-shirt? When my attention turned back to him, the difference was night and day. Every suit Atticus wore draped his body like a work of art, perfectly tailored down to the millimeter.

It took everything in me not to lick my lips at the sight of him.

"I was just walking around and—"

"You walked here?"

I nodded. "Yes."

"No."

"No?"

"Walking down the streets of New York City with that on your hand?" He glanced at my hand, his brow furrowing. "Where is your ring?"

I stretched my fingers. "It's in my room."

"Every time you leave the house, that ring needs to be on your finger."

"Well, I wanted to talk to you, and I also wanted to get out of there for a little while, so two birds, one stone."

"No more walking around the city on your own."

"Seriously?"

"Seriously. The announcement will happen in a few weeks and once word gets out, you will be the top Google search for weeks."

"What?"

He nodded. "You're marrying me. The public will want to know who you are."

"People will be searching me?" It hit me like a punch in the gut. All because I was marrying him?

"For every little piece of information they can grasp."

"Shit." My stomach that was already in knots, tightening.

"Have you read the file I gave you?" he asked.

"You mean the history textbook on the life of Atticus William de Loughrey?"

He didn't move, but his eyes flicked up to mine. "What is that supposed to mean?"

I rolled my eyes. "It means the only way those sheets of paper could get less personal is if they were on a bullet-point timeline."

"You need to know about me."

"Yes, about you, but right now I don't need to know that you were captain of the Harvard rowing team or that you purposely failed chemistry as a social experiment in eighth grade. And who the hell is taking chemistry in eighth grade?" They were just a few points I'd noticed when flipping through the pages.

His spine straightened and he stared at me, his brow furrowed. "Those are both points of interest in my history."

"Perhaps, but they don't tell me anything about you. Not you as a person or you as a man I would find remotely attractive."

"And what would?"

I threw my hands up. "How about an actual sit down, get-to-know-you dinner date?" That was the whole reason I'd walked nearly two miles. I didn't realize it until it was out.

An evening that was two people getting to know each other. How things normally went before two people got engaged.

He blinked at me almost as if I was speaking a foreign language to him, one he couldn't identify. What was wrong with the man? How did he become so detached to personal interaction?

"We had dinner together last night."

"We *ate* together last night, then went off to different rooms. You know nothing about me, and it would be a great way to get to know me."

"I know plenty about you. From your educational background, to your father's death, and how old you were when you lost your virginity. I also know your credit score, your mounting debts, and that you are in serious need of a *good* haircut and not the five-dollar butchering you're wearing."

"Excuse m—"

"And while we're on the subject of hair, once we get someone to properly manicure that overly masculine cut, you will begin growing it out."

I slammed my hands down on his desk, gaining his attention again. "What the fuck gives you the right to tell me how to wear my hair? It's a pixie cut. Cute. Feminine. And most importantly—I like it. And that's only the first of my grievances against what you just revealed."

"Do I need to remind you again who I am? Do you think I failed to diligently research you before enacting my plan?"

It unnerved me to think he'd looked so deeply into my life. He'd only skimmed some highlights, but it was enough to realize he knew much more about me than I believed. It was naïve of me. He told me he'd done a background check, we talked about Lou, but somehow the in-depth portion didn't click.

"I'm not changing my hair."

"Yes, you are. I've arranged an appointment with my personal stylist. She has a hair and makeup crew ready, and arriving before Melanie arrives with your new wardrobe."

"Wardrobe?" I thought a few pieces, but even with as little as

I knew him, I had a feeling my closet would be stuffed by the time
Melanie left—whoever that was.

His eyes moved up and down my body. "I have a feeling your
entire outfit cost less than my lunch."

Ouch. But he probably wasn't far off.

"If you are to play the part of my wife, you also need to look the
part. You will be on my arm at charity dinners, family gatherings, and
photo sessions, and you will need to present accordingly."

I shook my head. "You are not changing how I look."

"Per the contract, I am. Or did you fail to properly read through
before signing it?"

I froze, my stomach sinking. A vague memory floated to the surface of my thoughts, a skim of a line of text that instructed I would
look the part he wanted, including all aspects of my wardrobe, hair,
and makeup.

"Shit."

"You added in a clause of no sex, and I added in control of your
appearance. If ten million dollars no longer interests you, I can bill
you for my wasted time and efforts and you can be on your way."

"You are an arrogant son of a bitch," I seethed. It was a side of
him I wasn't used to seeing—wicked in his dealings and the way he
manipulated the situation to his advantage.

"Careful, Ophelia. You will watch your tongue when cursing
out the matriarch of my family. The walls have ears, and Vera has
sharp claws that will slice through you without even touching you."

My head spun. Stupid. I was so stupid to have believed that he
was my miracle cure for all that was wrong in my shitty life. Now he
owned me, quite literally, for five years. Why didn't I realize that earlier? Was I so entranced by the man I knew that one night?

"I want a date."

"Have Holly set it up on your way out."

"You can't even do that yourself?" With all the people running
his life, it shouldn't have surprised me.

His gaze narrowed. "If I don't even have time to find a suitable
woman for a wife, do you think I have time to schedule frivolous

wastes of my time with things such as a date? Not only a date, but one with my fake fiancée?"

I flinched at the word fake. It was both true and untrue. I was legitimately his fiancée—I had the huge-ass rock to prove it. The truth portion was that I was bought and paid for. We weren't a real relationship. We were a business transaction. Still, it stung.

"Maybe not, but if you want me to be the doting piece of arm candy or trophy wife in training, you might want to warm me up to your demeanor before I decide to scratch your eyes out."

His lip twitched up, and he leaned back in his chair. "Friday night. Seven. Meet me here."

"Not going to pick me up?"

"You'll be here at seven, and not a minute late."

I rolled my eyes. "Fine."

"Michael is waiting for you outside the lobby. He'll take you home."

My fingers flexed and my jaw clenched. Instead of arguing a battle I wasn't going to win, I acquiesced and stormed out, slamming his door as I went.

Holly jumped at the sound, and I let out a growl of frustration. She gave me a small smile that for some reason heightened my suspicion. For all I knew, she spent her afternoons tucked under his desk getting him off.

What the hell had I gotten myself into?

It didn't surprise me that after Hamilton's visit to my office, the word of my engagement had spread around the family. Gossip circulated like wildfire through the ranks, but never past the family name. De Loughreys didn't talk about the family to non-de Loughreys.

"What do you mean you're engaged?" my mother screeched.

"Just as I said. She is coming to the family dinner."

There was a pause, then a sigh. "Why are you doing this, Atticus?"

"Doing what?"

"Defying everyone's wishes."

"Everyone's? I don't give a shit about everyone. I have sacrificed my life for this family, and this one act is the only thing that is mine and mine alone, and I will not have it dictated by anyone!"

"Couldn't you have picked someone like Lucinda Carmichael?"

Luci? "Aldrich's little sister? Come now, Mother. No."

"There must be someone else. Antonia? Bridget?" For my mother to be bringing them up, she must have been desperate. They were both from well-off families, though nowhere near some of the family's oldest friends, but they knew how to act at social functions.

Something I was certain Ophelia was going to have trouble with due to her upbringing.

"I have to get back to work. Goodbye." I hung up, not even waiting for a reply.

My irritation grew, and I threw my pen down onto the desk. The office was my reprieve from Ophelia, but the more people who knew, the more she invaded my work life. Even if it was just my mother on the phone, it was minutes in my office that were dedicated to my new fiancée.

My cell phone pinged at the same time as my email popped up a new message.

Rhys: You're engaged?!

The vein on my forehead throbbed, and I took a centering breath.

Atticus: You're an idiot.

Rhys: It's quite the gossip. By the way, am I doing your prenup?

While normally Alexander would handle such contracts, Rhys was the only one privy to the one I had with Ophelia, and therefore the only one capable.

Atticus: Yes. Get a preliminary draft going.

Though we had a contract for marriage and children and the payment for five years, the prenuptial agreement was a necessity.

Rhys: Am I including the 'no sex clause'?

I ground my teeth and blew out a breath.

Atticus: No.

Atticus: Add a million dollar a year alimony until she gets remarried in that in the event of divorce.

It had only been a week since I fully formed my plan, but the idea of us divorcing made my stomach clench. If after five years she couldn't stand me, I wouldn't force her to stay with me, even knowing how hard it would be to let her go. I also couldn't stand the idea of her living in some shit-box apartment again because prices were so high in the city. Could she even live off of or provide a safe place for our children with ten million?

No, I would provide that as well.

Rhys: Seriously? You're already paying her a hefty sum. What happens in the event she never remarries?

Atticus: Irrelevant. Also, child support. I am responsible for all expenses for our children, and housing in the Tower in addition to her alimony.

Rhys: You're a fucking idiot.

That was when it hit me, and I cursed, throwing the phone back down onto the desk.

I wanted to take care of her, no matter what.

I'd never even had an inkling of that desire before I met her. But there it was, in every interaction for the past year.

I made sure she was my waitress and tipped her well, all to keep her close and to make certain she was doing well. She was very good at her job, so much so I never realized what I had actually done. That I cared for her to some extent.

My computer pinged again and I turned my attention away from thoughts of Ophelia.

The email was from our in-house investigator, Hugo. He was a detective once upon a time, but after a severe injury on the job, he changed direction and we hired him on. He quickly became an essential part of our security team. Everything from business backgrounds to dates, he was paid well to find out all he could. He was who I used to get me information on Ophelia.

A groan left me at the title, and I cursed under my breath. For one fucking day could the de Loughreys behave?

```
To: de Loughrey, Atticus
From: Dennings, Hugo
Subject: Hiking the Appalachian Trail

Preston has been thinking about going hiking.
```

Short, sweet, and to the point. That was one thing I liked about our communications. I didn't have time to read the intricacies of boundless information collected. While we did need to talk in code, the messages were clear and told me all I needed to know.

My brother-in-law needed to be put in his place.


```
To: Dennings, Hugo
From: de Loughrey, Atticus
Subject: Re: Hiking the Appalachian Trail


Let me know if he sets a date so we can cancel
all plans.
```


As always, my family had impeccable timing. It was bad enough that my sanctuary was invaded, but now my brother-in-law was looking to cheat on my pregnant sister. Thankfully Hugo was always watching out for scandals. He worked solely for the de Loughrey family, and he enjoyed the detecting part without the danger.

The day called for a relaxing drink and some music, but I wouldn't have that. Ophelia's presence was more disrupting than I imagined. Simply having her near was throwing me off kilter.

We made it through the last few days fairly unscathed. I didn't think it would be difficult to have her in my space, but I found it to be tortuous. And it wasn't just her scent and the nearness of her body locked away in my home.

When I decided to have her live with me, I assumed nearly eight thousand square feet would be enough room that we wouldn't have to interact often. Everywhere I went, there she was. It had only been a few days, and she ate dinner with me, watched TV, and read books in the library while I worked.

I wasn't used to living with another person. At least not since I'd moved to the city full time a decade ago. The desire to get out of Stronghold and away from my parents and grandfather drove me to a condo not far from where we would build Olympus Tower, not to mention the need to get away from my younger siblings. Genevieve and Penelope were still in middle and high school at the time, and forty-seven-thousand square feet held no reprieve from teenage girls.

Here in the condo, I'd been forced to retreat to my bedroom

more than once to feel at peace. It was the one room Ophelia had never stepped foot in, so it wasn't filled by her.

She asked for a date, a date that was happening in a few hours, and the thought of it set me on edge. Most of my dates didn't require menial conversation, but somehow I knew Ophelia wound insist on it.

She wanted to know me, but I wasn't sure that was a good idea. I couldn't keep the darkness from her forever. It always bled through, but the wicked king had been kept at bay.

It was then that insecurities I didn't even know I had came to light—I was afraid of Ophelia getting to know me.

And hating what she saw.

TWELVE

OPHELIA

After the *enlightening* trip to Atticus's office, I'd been bombarded for days.

Melanie, Atticus's personal shopper, arrived with rack after rack of clothing. Between her and her three assistants, it was two trips to the salon level. There was a huge dressing room complete with more mirrors than needed and enough space for everything she brought and then some. Maybe it was actually a dance studio? A little while later I confirmed that was incorrect—there was also a dance studio.

Hours of going through clothes and looks and convincing me more than once that I needed something. By the end, my walk-in closet was completely stuffed and I had outfits for all occasions—though she did promise to be back, and I wasn't sure how I felt about that.

It almost sounded like a threat.

The next day was spent in the salon where my "five-dollar butchering" got an overhaul. Begrudgingly, I admitted that my hair looked better than it did before. Waxing, manicure, pedicure, facial—I felt like Sandra Bullock in that movie, only I thought I was in better shape than I apparently was.

Atticus's eyes were wide when he saw me that night. He circled me as he took in all my upgrades.

"Very nice," he said.

"Does m'lord approve?" I asked with a smirk.

His expression dropped, and he turned around and left.

A sigh left me. We would get better, it was just going to take time. I hoped our date would help with that.

The next afternoon I sat on my bed, chewing on my bottom lip, trying to decide if I wanted to call my mom.

Want? Not really. Need to before she reads about my engagement in the papers? Very much so.

Lou, my stepfather, was a worthless drunk, and I didn't want him to get wind that I was engaged to a man who had more money than the Queen of England. Hell, the de Loughreys probably had more money than at least a dozen countries combined.

The issue that pressed upon me was informing my mom of the mess I'd gotten myself into. Well, not the truth, but the lie before she found out from the news or some gossip site. We weren't on the best of terms, mostly due to my stepfather and beginning from the moment they got married over fifteen years ago.

"Hi, Mom."

"Lia? Did you change your number?"

"Um, yeah, my..." I heaved a sigh as I fought to push the next words out of my mouth. "My fiancé put me on his plan."

Silence. "Ophelia, I'm not in the mood for jokes."

"Not a joke."

"What's his name?"

"Atticus." I purposefully left off his last name. She didn't need to know. At least until it was absolutely necessary.

"And where did you meet?"

"At a club last year, then at work. It was fate," I said, lifting my tone, trying to sound happy. I swallowed hard, hoping she bought it.

"And I'm just now hearing about him?"

"It's not like we talk much." There was a bitter edge to my voice. Ever since Lou, I'd taken a back seat to him, then to my half-sisters. He was a drunk of a man who hated me because I was a physical reminder that once upon a time, my mother had loved someone other than him.

Insanely jealous, it didn't matter that my father was dead, only that I was the product of him. He pulled away my mother's attention and affection and beat me down until I couldn't take anymore and had to get away. It was why I'd been willing to suffer and struggle for the past decade.

Anything to get away from them.

Which was why I had been living in a tiny apartment in Brooklyn. At least it was all mine.

"Who's on the phone?" I heard Lou ask in the background.

"Lia."

"What does that brat want?"

I ground my teeth and waited for the non-supportive response that would fall from my mother's lips.

"Says she's getting married." There was a strange static, like she was placing her hand over the receiver, but it only muffled the next words. "But I'm not sure I believe it."

"The wedding is in January," I said. "There will be an announcement soon."

"Announcement? Such an stupid thing—why would you need to do that?" she scoffed.

I knew venomous thoughts about Atticus were dancing in her mind. Anything to try and bring me down.

"This is just a courtesy call, Mom. I wanted you to know before the news broke."

"Fine. But you'll get no help from us for this disaster. Did he knock you up?"

I pursed my lips. Of course she would think that was the only reason anyone would want to marry me.

Well, it wasn't like that was happening anyway.

"No, he didn't knock me up, and I neither want nor need anything from you."

"Okay. You know where to send the invitation."

She'd be lucky to get one. It was my anger that pushed that thought to the front, but the fact was—she was my only family. She was my mother.

Honestly, I really didn't know any more if I wanted her in my life.

The biggest problem was Lou. I couldn't stand the thought of him showing up at a de Loughrey function. I wouldn't put it past him to try and swindle some money or steal gifts.

"Bye, Mom."

"Talk to you later, hon."

"No, you won't," I whispered as I hit end and threw the phone down on the bed, then fell back next to it.

I couldn't stop the worry from knotting my stomach. It'd been months since I talked to her. Maybe Christmas? I stopped by, gave the girls some presents, and after about an hour, I left.

While I wanted my sisters there for my wedding, even if it was a contract wedding, I didn't want Lou to come, and if Mom came, Lou would be right there next to her. Even so, even though she was my mother, I didn't want her to come either. We had never been close, and as an adult, I found I never wanted more with her. My father was a different story entirely. I missed him with every breath in my body. Losing him would never be something I got over.

I wondered if I could get Atticus to commit to a very small wedding to avoid inviting my family. Like in another country. However, I had a feeling the de Loughreys would not go for something like that.

Still, I could bring it up at dinner. Speaking of…what was I going to wear? With a glance at the clock, I jumped from the bed. Somehow, I'd managed to blank out for over half an hour, and all that remained was an hour and I couldn't be late—especially with the date being my demand.

What did one even wear on a date with a billionaire? There was a ton of fancy clothes in my closet, and I caught a glimpse of a pair of white pants. I pulled them from the rack along with a soft pink peplum top.

I'd never owned white pants before, but as I looked down at the outfit laid across my bed, it was another reminder of how different my life was becoming. I found a pair of white high-heeled strappy sandals with red bottoms. I was a little worried about the red clashing, but figured nobody would notice.

Realizing I was down to less than thirty minutes, I had to acknowledge that wardrobe selection should not take thirty minutes, and promptly got my ass in gear for my first official date with my future husband.

I grabbed a chunky, sparkly necklace and bracelet, then pulled my engagement ring from its box and slipped it onto my ring finger.

Thankfully I'd had the foresight to shower and put my makeup on in procrastination of calling my mother, because I was able to do a few touch ups before I grabbed a matching purse from my closet and threw in whatever I needed before running for the door. When I reached the lobby, Michael was waiting for me and I slipped into the back of the sedan.

At 6:59, the elevator doors slid open and I rushed down the empty hall to his office.

"You were almost late," he said, his gaze trained on the clock behind me as he rested against the edge of his desk.

"Almost, but almost isn't late."

His gaze moved up and down my body. When our eyes met, I received a nod of approval before he pushed off and stepped toward me.

"Very good," he said.

Each step was almost like a lion surveying his prey, and I froze as he approached. Did he *have* to look that sexy? Between the intense smolder and the swagger in his step, I was revving up to happily let him pounce.

He circled around me, humming in approval, and I let out a breath, happy to have met his expectations at the very least.

He leaned in, and I froze again as his lips pressed softly against my cheek. "*Very* beautiful."

Heat rose to my face, and I bit down on my bottom lip.

"There's the charmer."

He scoffed, then held out his arm and I slipped mine in.

Michael waited for us at the entrance, and we slipped into the back of the car. The drive was only a few blocks, and confusion settled as we walked toward the restaurant he'd picked for dinner.

"Why are we here?" I asked as Vanessa, the hostess, held the door open for us. As familiar as he was with the place, I was surprised he didn't try to wine and dine me. Then again, I already had The Rock, as I had affectionately begun calling the huge diamond ring that adorned my finger, so there wasn't much call for wooing.

I was a front, a contracted employee with a closeness of none other. Putting energy into our relationship wasn't necessary, and possibly one reason he'd searched me out.

Still, I had to admit, getting to actually eat a meal at 130 Degrees? Yeah, I squealed inside as my mouth began to fill with saliva envisioning how *good* my meal was about to be.

"So you can see how awful your replacement is," he replied simply. In the past week I'd come to find Atticus was not much of a talker. He said what he needed to in as few words as possible. Granted, he'd been like that the whole time I was his waitress, which was nothing like how he'd been the night we met.

"Maybe you should have thought about that before you made me quit," I reminded him.

Vanessa showed us toward Atticus's table, a confused look in her eye as she watched me scoot around the booth.

"You literally have access to more money in one small account than you've made in the last three years. Why would you stay?" Atticus asked.

"What else am I going to do with my time?" I asked. It was a realization that began to weigh me down. What at first was a pleasant pseudo vacation was losing its shine as boredom set in. I was so used to doing, moving, and going that standing still was hard.

"You'll have plenty, especially when the wedding planning starts, though I'm certain my mother will be taking the reins on that. You also have a lot to learn in order to blend in."

His mother taking the reins? I supposed it wasn't the worst thing. How much energy did I really want to put into an event that emotionally meant nothing anyway?

I rolled my eyes. "One day you'll realize I'm never going to fit into your upscale world. I'll never blend in."

He quirked a brow at me, but before he could respond, the curtain opened and a wide-eyed Drake stood in front of us.

"Ophelia?" he said in surprise.

"Hi, Drake."

"H-hi." He looked from me to Atticus, then back to me. "I'm surprised to see you here. You quit so abruptly." My appearance startled him, and he lost his composure.

"Are you here to take our order or to chit-chat?" Atticus seethed. His tone made Drake straighten, his eyes wide.

"Yes, sir. Sorry, sir. What can I get you to drink?"

Atticus rolled his eyes and swore under his breath, and I knew dinner wasn't going to go well if this continued.

"Brandy, neat, for Atticus, and I'll have a glass of chardonnay. Have Mitchell help you with Atticus's order. I'll just have the six-ounce filet mignon, medium, fingerling potatoes, and the chopped salad."

He nodded and gave a quick glance to a glaring Atticus before scurrying away.

"That was annoying."

"You didn't have to be such an ass."

"I'm going to need a word with Mitchell to find out why he thought it was a good idea to send that boy in here."

As if on cue, Mitchell appeared.

"I am so sorry about that, sir. Allison is not in today, but she will be your waitress from now on."

"The redhead?" Atticus asked for clarity.

Mitchell nodded. "Yes, sir."

Atticus gave a nod in approval, just as Drake appeared with our drinks. He quickly set them down before scurrying away again.

"Besides keeping that twerp away from me, I need you to do one last thing before you go, Mitchell."

"Anything, sir."

He nodded toward me. "Tell her who I am."

Mitchell blinked at him and looked to me, pleading for some type of clarification. "Being that she is with you, I assume she knows now who you are, sir." He was careful not to speak Atticus's last name.

"In regards to this restaurant."

Mitchell turned to me. "Atticus is a generous investor."

"Not the bullshit."

Mitchell swallowed hard. "More importantly, he is the sole owner," he said in a low voice so as not to be overheard.

I snapped my head toward Atticus, and he stared at me with a slightly arched eyebrow as he sipped his drink.

"Own?"

He slowly nodded. "Bread, Mitchell."

"Right away, sir."

The formality was unusual for the two of them, and it bristled me. "Do you have to bark orders?"

"Do you not remember your first few weeks as my waitress?"

I did, which was why I felt so badly for Mitchell and Drake. Over time, I'd gotten to know his likes and dislikes, which I cataloged in my mind based on the depth of his scowl. That was how I knew the last time I'd served him that he was in need of an indulgent meal.

"Well, that explains why you were the only one who ever sat here."

"Are you surprised?"

A sigh left me. "I shouldn't be, not now, but I guess I should have known after a year of seeing you multiple times a week."

"In all that time, I was surprised you never learned my last name."

"Trust me, the thought had crossed my mind, but Mitchell was tight lipped. And unlike the rest of your family, your photograph isn't plastered all over the place."

"It was two years ago when I was announced as the new CEO, long before we met, and the news quickly disappeared in favor of juicer stories."

"You mean your sister."

He nodded. "And soon it will be your face."

My lips turned down, hating that idea. That much attention on me in an arena where I already felt like it was me versus a giant—and I didn't even have a stick to defend myself—was overwhelming.

"Why?"

"I am a de Loughrey. We are the kings and queens, the elite, the rulers of the west."

I wanted to laugh, but it was true. His family name was known across the globe.

"I need to use the restroom," I said, excusing myself and shifting toward the edge of the seat. The weight of Atticus's eyes was heavy on me as I moved through the thick curtains. Once free, I wove through the back, locating Mitchell near his office.

"Ophelia," Mitchell glanced toward the booth.

"What's going on? I've never seen you so shaken by Atticus before." Everything about the evening seemed to rub me the wrong way, but I wanted to make sure Mitchell was okay.

"Because normally Atticus is friendly to me, and we often chat when he's here for lunch, but that's only because of you."

"Me?"

"You, and since you've been gone, he's become a bit terse again. Finding a good replacement for you has been very difficult."

"It's been a week." That wasn't nearly long enough to find someone strong enough to endure Atticus's bad side and stick around.

He nodded. "A week without you to break up his day and take his stresses away. That man has the world on his shoulders, and a few days a week, all he wants is to be waited on and left alone in peace. He praised you highly for your ability to give him that reprieve. You were the only one in the last six years who was ever able to tame his ire, knowing just how to handle his moods and give him that peace he so desires."

Was that why he chose me? If it was, his abrasive nature gave none of it away. Not only that, we were in completely different territory now. A small booth was nothing compared to a penthouse condo, nor was a working me the same as casual me.

Doubts that his plan was going to work seeped in. It was that same stomach-twisting feeling every time I started a new job. Trying to find my place, figuring out the rules, and learning the ropes and what was expected of me.

I returned a few minutes later and found Atticus on his phone, his thumbs moving quickly across the screen.

"On your phone on our first official date?"

"Holly needed me," he replied without looking up.

That shut me up like nothing else could have and an awkward silence stretched between us, a tension that made further conversation stilted and difficult even after he set his phone down.

Our food arrived, and I struggled to find a topic that would allow me to get to know him in any way.

"What do you normally do on the weekends?" I asked in an attempt to break through the unease that vibrated between us.

"Work."

"Work?"

He nodded. "Running a company and family such as mine is extremely time consuming. I have time for little else."

"Do you always speak so…pompously?"

"I speak as I need to speak—with purpose and clarity. There is no room for idle chatter or gossip. What the weather is like doesn't interest me."

"How high is that stick up your ass? Come on, you have to relax at some point. You weren't like this the night we met."

"The night we met, I had ulterior motives. Since you have shut those down with a steel door, you're stuck with me as is. I don't need to impress you or romance you. Our arrangement is a transaction."

Another sting reminding me that he didn't want a real relationship, only a business one.

"We're going to be together for the next five years. Are you really going to be like this the whole time?"

"Considering I'll have blue balls for all that time, I can assure you I'll be much worse by the end."

"You were trying to be funny," I said. His expression hardened and I smiled at him, knowing I'd caught some of that warmth he kept hidden. Our interactions had taught me so. "Fine—don't admit it, but you were flashing some charisma there. I saw it."

He made a scoffing sound, but I caught the uptick of his lips.

Getting to know each other was going to be a struggle, but we had time. I had to believe that one day I'd get him to relax with me. I wanted to meet that man from a year ago.

The battle armor he wore was strong, but I was stronger. For now, I'd take every little thing I could. Even a small smirk.

OPHELIA

"**O**phelia," Atticus called out.

I was in the kitchen chowing down on dinner while talking to Amara as she washed dishes.

"In here."

He stopped at the doorway and stared at me. My brow furrowed as I tilted my head to the side. I looked all around me, trying to figure out what he was staring at. There wasn't some pile of food around the stool, or crumbs sprinkled around the counter. I glanced at Amara, who refused to acknowledge me, but there was a smile playing on her lips as she washed a pot.

"Okay, what?"

He cleared his throat, and his brain seemed to kick back into action. Weird.

"Amara," he greeted.

"Atticus."

"Why are you not at the table?" he asked.

Was that why he was so confused? "I was lonely, so I came closer to talk to Amara."

"You're interrupting her work."

I rolled my eyes. "It's just dishes." I watched his jaw clench. "Your plate is on the table." I gestured to the covered meal. "Should still be warm."

He walked over to the table and glanced back at me before picking up his plate and silverware. In a few strides he was next to me, setting his dishes down on the island counter. Amara slid a glass of wine over to him as he pulled the stool out and sat next to me.

I blinked at him and quirked a brow at Amara, who shrugged.

It was a move that reminded me of a guy I liked my freshman year of high school. I'd had a crush on him for over a year, ever since he transferred into my school. He was a popular guy, and I wasn't. One day he stopped in front of my table at lunch and asked to sit next to me. I was floored and probably bright red. Nothing ever happened past that, but I held a candle for him for the rest of high school and after.

The moment with Atticus had that same feel. Maybe that meant he was trying to meet me halfway. Yes, ten million could make a person do almost anything, but I wasn't going to let him bully me for the next five years. He asked me, so he was going to have to make concessions. Yes, I needed the money and it would make life so much easier, but it wasn't like I was going to be on the street without it.

And that was why I was determined to make him work for it.

Loreno appeared and whisked Amara away, leaving us alone. The silence was deafening, accented by the clinking of flatware against ceramic.

"How was your day?" I asked the most benign question I could think of. It was a simple, cursory question—or inane chatter and gossip that he so despised.

Maybe I'd ask him about the weather...

Nope.

A sigh left him. "It started with a large investment in a product design being completely destroyed. Then my father visited me, topping it off with Genevieve asking for more money. Hamilton is angry about our arrangement, or maybe he just needs to work some frustration out. It could go either way. Holly left halfway through the day for an appointment, leaving me with Tiana and whatever the others' names are. Therefore, Jack got my bad mood, and my usual lunch reprieve didn't happen because you weren't there." He turned to me. "How was your day?"

I was shocked by his sharing, expecting a tight lipped, "Fine," and not the torrent of information that spewed from his lips.

I bit down on my bottom lip. My day was much more laid back. "Swimming in a pool four hundred feet off the ground is really strange. The sloshing really highlights just how much the building moves. I'm sorry you had a bad day."

He scoffed at that before taking a bite. After a sip of wine, he said, "It was par for the course."

"What does that mean? I've heard it before."

"Par is a golf term, meaning the number of average strokes for a hole or total for the course. A course is a round. Therefore it was what I encounter on an average day."

"Thank you."

"For what?"

"For explaining and not talking down to me."

"Do I often talk down to you?"

"Here and there, but then I smack you down with some eloquent response." I paused a moment as that made him chuckle before I continued my point. "In all seriousness, it's not so much that you talk down to me, it's that you don't talk to me at all."

With a raise of a brow, he looked at me more intently than he had since that night at Angelino.

"Compared to some of the things you say, it was very civil."

He tossed his napkin down on the counter, his flatware crossed on his plate. I stood and reached for his plate, but he stopped me.

"The maid will get it in the morning," he said.

I sat back down and mashed my teeth together as he reached for the wine and refilled our glasses.

"I'm not above doing my own dishes."

"Will you please not fight me on this tonight?"

"Just tonight?" I asked. Having people do all the menial chores

I was used to doing every day was unnerving. I felt weird, being perfectly able to do them myself.

"I want to brief you on what to expect at dinner," Atticus said.

"The family dinner? It's dinner." How bad could it be?

"Yes, but I'm introducing you as my fiancée. Have no doubt my father will pull some stunt. He's probably invited the woman he wants me to marry."

"Wait, what? Your father already picked someone out for you? Like an arranged marriage?" It seemed archaic. I ignored the spark of unease that lit in my chest.

"Exactly. That's not what I want, and I'm not going to be stuck in some loveless marriage with a vapid woman I can't stand."

"Instead you'll be in a loveless marriage with a commoner who doesn't know her place," I bit back.

His jaw ticked. "Yes, though I have hope that one day we will no longer be in constant battle. It's exhausting."

"Relent and learn to compromise, and we won't have any problems."

He stood. "Speaking of relenting." He wrapped his arms around my waist and tugged me against his chest.

I let out a squeak of surprise as I slipped off the stool and was pressed against his chest, eyes wide as I stared up at him. My heart beat rapidly, and I felt warmth fill my cheeks. "What are you doing?"

He leaned down, his lips ghosting across mine, sending a concussive wave of electricity pulsing through me. "Kissing you."

All the memories of that night so long ago flashed through my mind, reminding me of the way he handled my body and how well we fit together. How natural we were, how at ease and affectionate.

"Why?" I asked in barely a whisper.

"Because we have to be desensitized to each other's touch, and that includes more intimate gestures." He trailed down my neck, nipping the skin and making me draw in a shuddering breath before moving back up. His lips were soft against mine, and I froze.

"Kiss me back," he groaned.

I couldn't. It would only feed the attraction I already felt for him. Feed the heat that was scorching between us already.

"Ophelia, behave."

I reached up with shaking hands and cupped his jaw, pulling him closer. The moment our tongues met, an arrow of fire shot through me, igniting my blood.

I needed to pull back, but I couldn't. Atticus's arms wrapped tighter around me, pulling me impossibly closer as he deepened the kiss. His fingers dug into my ass, his lips leaving mine, trailing kisses down my jaw until he began licking and sucking at a spot just below my ear.

Blood was replaced by fire and my breath sped up as I pressed my body into his.

At one point I'd tried to convince myself that what happened that night was a fluke, but the way my body was reacting to his, I knew it wasn't and if I didn't pull away now, I wouldn't have the will to do so in another minute.

"I think that's enough," I breathed out.

When he pulled back, there was a smirk on his lips. He knew he had me. His expression woke me up, and my lips formed a thin line.

"Happy?" I asked with an edge of venom.

"The day you're on your knees begging for my cock."

"What?"

"That's what will make me happy."

Fuck me.

All my bravado was gone, replaced by that heat. I turned around abruptly and stomped back to my room, his chuckles echoing off the walls.

Smug, hot bastard.

He was trying to break me down—I knew it—but it wasn't going to work.

I flung myself onto my bed and stared up at the ceiling, trying to ignore the heat pulsing through me. One kiss, and everything from that night flooded back. It was like no time had passed.

His lips against mine did exactly what I was afraid of.

I slipped my hand under my waistband, continuing until my fingers brushed against my clit. I drew in a sharp breath, and my nipples tightened. A little farther, and I could feel the wetness his kisses created. I slipped a finger in and then two as I focused on the sparks of his tongue against mine.

The bastard had turned me into a needy mess with one kiss. I threw my head back, a keening moan slipped between my lips as my finger tip pressed against my aching clit.

"Fuck," I hissed, my hips rocking against my fingers. My breath hitched and my other hand gripped my breast, tugging at my nipple between two fingers. I was completely lost to the pleasure, to the need to clear my hormones down to a manageable level.

"Enjoying yourself?"

I shot up, my eyes wide as my legs slammed closed. "Fuck! You can't knock?" Atticus was leaning against the wall, his arms crossed over his chest and his eyes dark.

"The door was open and you were making the most erotic sounds. If you didn't want me coming in, you should have closed it."

Crap. I'd become so accustomed to being alone that I didn't even worry about the door. Who would, with over eight thousand square feet?

"Did I get you all worked up?" he asked, his tongue peeking out to wet his lips.

"No."

"Do you need a hand?" he asked.

My pussy clenched at that idea, liking it very much. However, my anger took the front seat, reminding me that wasn't going to happen.

I narrowed my gaze. "You can get the hell out."

"No."

"No?"

"We weren't done with our conversation when you rudely ran away."

"I didn't run," I grumbled.

"Fled my presence as fast as your legs could carry you."

I rolled my eyes, hoping he would leave, but he just stood there, my hand still trapped beneath my waistband. "Can you give me a minute?"

"Why? You've already wasted ten of mine while you filled the hall with your lewd warbling."

"Fine. What is it?" I ground out, wishing to erase this moment from my memories, and more importantly, his.

"Pack an overnight bag."

"Why?"

"Because we're going outside the city. We'll spend the weekend there. I hope that will show my father that you aren't going away."

"Okay. Is that all?"

"For now. You can continue."

"Out," I growled. The moment I heard the door click I fell back against the bed.

Fuck, the weekend? Trapped with his family? Not only that, would we be sharing a bed?

If I wasn't nervous before, I was now. Dinner was one thing, but the entire weekend was another. Talk about a cold shower. Nothing could have diffused my lust quicker.

FOURTEEN

OPHELIA

The car decelerated, and I peered between the front seats. That moment in every Cinderella story when the female lead character made her way to the ball couldn't have been more accurate as a huge wrought-iron gate slowly opened in front of us, flanked by tall stone walls.

The driveway was made of pavers laid out in intricate patterns, and in the distance, past the trees, I could see a few spires reaching up against the twilight sky.

The sense of awe that filled me when I first saw from Atticus's condo paled compared to the overwhelming feeling that assaulted me. The wealth I knew he had was reinforced as I stared at the looming French-inspired chateau.

There were no words for the mansion that filled my field of view. From the window placements there were at least four floors, with the top floor probably for staff quarters.

In all my life I'd never seen such a place other than on a TV screen. The windows were dwarfed by the sheer size of the large exterior stone walls. Multiple large chimneys rose from the dark roofline.

Worried about being trapped in a house with his family? Not

in a structure that massive. Besides, glancing around the lush, manicured lawns and landscaping, I knew that if I should need to escape, I could quickly lose myself in one of the most stunning outdoor spaces I'd ever seen anywhere.

"This is your house?" I asked in complete shock. I'd only seen houses like the de Loughrey estate in movies or on *MTV Cribs*, which I used to watch as a teen.

"This is the family house."

"How many places do you have?" I'd already stayed at his Manhattan penthouse, and now I was standing in front of a fucking castle. There was no better way to describe the overpowering structure. It was a force in and of itself.

It fit the definition with its sheer size and stone adornments.

"My great grandfather built this in 1896."

"Wow. How big is it?"

"Somewhere around forty-seven thousand square feet."

"That isn't a house."

"It is for us. Up to fifteen de Loughreys have lived under this roof at one time."

The car slowed and stopped at a huge covered front door atop a small tier of steps.

After helping me from the car, he pulled me inside, leaving Michael and Damien to deal with our bags. What we stepped into was not what I would think of as a foyer but most definitely an anteroom. That fact was accentuated by the large set of wrought-iron and glass doors before us. The space that held us was at least twice the size of my apartment, and its sole purpose was to have people wait before entering the home.

Something we didn't have to do as the doors were splayed open, beckoning us through.

My mouth had been wide when I saw Atticus's condo. I was frighteningly aware that it was nothing compared to the palatial palace I found myself in. The walls were a dark, rich wood with dimension. The staircase was the same, and at least eight feet wide, if not more, with a deep red runner. It only went halfway up before splitting in half, opening the second floor to the hall below.

The central staircase and entryway were enough to let me know I was in a place beyond measure of any place I'd set foot in before. Marble, dark woods, crystal, and gold decorated every inch that laid in front of me.

What awaited me farther in? I wasn't so sure.

Atticus told me there would be resistance, that my welcome wouldn't exactly be celebrated. It wasn't reassuring, but it did prepare me for the battle to come. I wasn't going to be blindsided by insults, chased away by their laughs to cry in a corner.

Not that I would anyway. If Atticus hadn't scared me away yet, his family wasn't going to.

"Good evening, Mr. Atticus," a woman in a black dress said as we entered. She was just standing there, waiting for us. Weird, but Atticus didn't seem to think it was out of the ordinary.

"Daniella. What has Chef prepared this evening?"

"On the menu this evening is pan-seared duck breast, roasted filet, and jerk-seasoned chicken."

His eyes narrowed, and he sighed. "Gen?"

She nodded. "Miss Genevieve requested."

"What did she request?" I asked.

"Of those three, you have one guess."

"Jerk chicken?" I guess. From what little I'd heard about her, it seemed the most likely.

"You've never met her once, and you know her well already."

"Who is she calling a jerk?"

"Who isn't she, is the more apt question. It's just another one of Genevieve's plays for attention."

We took a few slow steps in, and I had to focus to keep my gaze from bouncing around and my jaw from hanging slack.

"So why did you ask what was for dinner? Are you that hungry?" It felt like more than a mild interest in what he'd be stuffing his face with.

He shook his head. "The menu informs me who is either already here or will be."

I nodded. "Jerk chicken and Genevieve."

"Precisely. She probably arrived yesterday."

"Atticus?" an older woman called out as she finished the remainder of the stairs before her. She was the picture of elegance and grace, with an aura of superiority. Her once blonde hair was streaked with white, but styled in perfect waves that framed her face. A pearl necklace filled the space between her neck and the conservative opening of her silk shirt that ended tucked into a black, knee-length fitted skirt. Naturally manicured nails adorned delicate hands each laden with a large ring, and diamonds circled her wrists. Her blue eyes were just as intense as her son's, and I could see where he got his lips and the thin-lined expression he often wore.

"Who is this?" She eyed me up and down, her lips pursed.

"Mother, this is my fiancée, Ophelia."

I held my hand out. "It's a pleasure to meet you, Mrs. de Loughrey."

Her eyes widened as she stared from my hand to her eldest son. "Fiancée?"

"Don't seem so surprised."

She looked me over again. From the sound of it, she'd been told about me, but she wasn't impressed by my looks.

"Yes, well, your father prattles on incessantly about this Harris girl. He's going to have a field day when he sees the street cat you've brought in."

I froze as the first insult hit me. Street cat. Wow.

"Mother," Atticus admonished.

She looked down her nose at me, literally, and sighed. "She's so…" She trailed off, then made a hmph sound before walking off.

"Well, that could have gone better," I mumbled.

"Actually, it went quite well."

I threw him a dubious glance. "How was that well?"

He looked down, our eyes meeting. "She at least looked at you."

"Because you already put a ring on it."

"She didn't have to acknowledge you at all. It's actually a good thing that she did."

"If you say so." I looked down at the dress I'd chosen for the night. It wasn't over the top or ostentatious, nor was it plain and overly conservative. The hem hit mid-thigh and the scoop neck wasn't too low.

A spark drew my attention as Atticus slipped his hand in mine. "Come."

My heels, which I was still getting used to, clicked against the marble flooring down the wide corridor. We passed large rooms with elegant furnishings. A parlor, maybe a drawing room, living room, possibly an office? I wasn't sure of their purposes and had only a brief second to glance inside as we flew by, but after some weaving he pulled me into a room of similar décor.

It was as elegantly appointed as every inch I'd laid eyes on since we pulled into the driveway, filled with antiques and intricately carved pieces.

A waiter came around with wine glasses and Atticus plucked two from the tray, handing me one. Voices could be heard nearby, and I knew the next battle was about to begin. I took a long sip of the red liquid, hoping it would help calm me.

"Did hell freeze over? Atticus de Loughrey with a date for a family dinner?"

Atticus's gaze narrowed at one of the few de Loughreys I recognized—Genevieve—as she passed from one of the multiple openings that led into the space. She was wearing a short dress with insanely high-heeled pumps. She looked like she was about to go to the club. Even her hair and makeup were flawless. She was gorgeous.

"Ophelia, this is my wayward sister, Genevieve. Genevieve, meet my fiancée, Ophelia."

"Oh, so this is how you're going to do it," she said as she appraised me.

"Do what?" I asked. It was beginning to feel like I was missing something. Some aspect that caused our predicament that I hadn't been made privy to.

You should have asked more questions.

"Father is going to be fuming."

"Good," a male voice said, stepping up to join the conversation. "We didn't officially meet last week. Hamilton de Loughrey." He held out his hand, and I slipped mine in.

"Ophelia Evans."

"Awe, that is such a pretty name," Gen said with a smile.

Hamilton's grey eyes studied me. I was certain it was something I was just going to have to get used to. I knew I didn't meet their standards, but that didn't mean I had to care what they thought about me. Our relationship was born from a contract and not a meaningful connection.

"Let's go get a drink, Gen. Mother's wine isn't strong enough to get me through this night."

"Okay," she smiled as she wrapped her hands around his arm.

"I'm already exhausted," I whispered to Atticus as they moved out of the room.

"Me, too."

There was a pause as I processed what he said, then a loud laugh left me.

"I don't see how my plight is entertaining to you," he grumbled.

"I'm the one trying to keep up, and you're the one who is used to this madness."

"Being used to it doesn't mean I enjoy it. With four siblings and five cousins, this house has always been chaos."

"Five cousins?"

He nodded. "As I said—family house. We lived here with my uncle and his family for many years, as well as my grandparents."

In the Binder of Doom, I hadn't even gotten to the de Loughrey family tree to see just how large and twisted it was.

"Madeline, get back here!" a woman called as a ball of fluffy brown curls in a navy and white dress went flying by.

The ball of energy giggled before stopping in front of me, her grey eyes wide. "Hi!"

"Hello."

"Are you uncle Att's girlfriend?" she asked.

I squatted down to get to her eye level. "I guess you could say that."

She tilted her head, making her curls bounce. "Say what?"

"Well, I guess you could say I'm going to be your aunt."

Her little brow furrowed. "How?"

"You're getting married?" a feminine voice said from the direction the little girl came.

I stood and took in the newest family member. Long brown hair framed her flawless skin and grey eyes. Her dress hugged her curves and when she turned to Atticus, her bumped-out stomach was visible.

"Answer me, Atticus."

"I will if you give me a moment, Elizabeth," he said as he took my hand and pulled me closer. "This is getting tiring. Meet your new soon-to-be sister-in-law."

It was a trait I'd begun to notice with Atticus before the past few weeks. When his irritation hit, he no longer cared to explain anything and expected other people to either understand or figure it out themselves. Repeating was not something he was fond of.

"Nice to meet you. I'm Ophelia." I held out my hand. Elizabeth had a calculating stare, much like Atticus. She seemed to consider my outstretched hand, then her brother. A disapproving huff left her before she walked past me.

"Come, Madeline," she said as she held her hand out.

"That was fun," I said. "Guess I didn't impress her much."

"Elizabeth will be a hard one to impress."

"How close are you two?"

He looked at me and sighed. "Just read the folio."

There it was again. How were we to get to know one another if he expected me to just read all about him? Those were facts about his life, not the man himself. It would tell me how close in age they were, sure, but not how emotionally close they were. Only Atticus could tell me that, and he was as tight lipped as ever.

"Is it so terrible that you tell me yourself?"

"Yes. I don't have the time or energy to tell you every little detail of my life. That is why I had the folio made."

I hated the thing, especially with its droning prose and sleep-inducing cadence. After over a week, I was still only to his college years. I could say the man was impressive. By the time he was twenty he spoke six languages, was Valedictorian of his prestigious high school, and there was a never-ending list of other accomplishments.

It was easy to say we would not have been friends in high school. Between the wealth gap and his obvious popularity status, the only similarities were our grades, and I was in the top one percent of my class, not number one.

"You probably dictated it."

"I'm a de Loughrey—my accomplishments and failures are kept in record and updated frequently."

"What? Even when you lost your virginity?" Some girl named Amelia Carmichael when he was seventeen.

"Vulgarity, Ophelia. You must watch your tongue," Vera said as she appeared through the doorway behind me. "*If* you are to be a de Loughrey, discreetness is a virtue you must adhere to." She let out an exasperated sigh. "Are you sure, my darling?"

"Yes, Mother."

Questioning his decision in front of me. Ouch. If my pride and ego could convey hits like skin, my body would be a mass of bruises by the end of the weekend.

She let out another sigh, then something caught her attention behind me and she stepped away, calling out for a Mary.

"Atticus, you brought a friend," a deep voice resonated. An older man entered and slowly strolled toward us with the presence of a king.

"Father, I would like to introduce you to Ophelia, my fiancée." I thought he would be upset having to repeat himself again, but when I looked at Charles de Loughrey, I understood the ferocity behind his tone.

Charles was the same height as Atticus, his hair more salt than pepper with a perfectly trimmed, matching beard. A pair of beady eyes met mine, and a zip of cold rushed down my spine. While Atticus and his sister Elizabeth held a more calculating gaze, Charles held one of a predator.

And I was the prey. The one in his way, stopping him from getting what he wanted.

"Fiancée? Interesting." He eyed me up and down, like he was taking stock but also with a lecherous edge.

Prey in multiple forms. Great.

"Charles?" a beautiful brunette beside him called, trying to pull his attention from me. She had the same air as all the de Loughreys, full of money and prestige. Every detail about her was perfect, from her hair to the set of her eyes and length of her lashes, down to her slim figure and the fabric that adorned it.

Fire red clung to her torso and hips held up by off-the-shoulder straps. It flared at the bottom above her knees in a teasing manner to catch the eye.

She was de Loughrey material, and for some reason that rubbed me wrong. Without thinking, I found I had leaned in closer to Atticus.

He didn't even grant her a once-over with his gaze.

"Ah, yes. Amelia, this is my son, Atticus."

"It is a pleasure to finally meet you," she said. Her lips pulled up into a sweet smile and she held out her hand, but it wasn't to shake. Atticus regarded it as he ignored her.

"You're being rude, son," Charles said. His eyes lost the playful edge, hardening as they locked onto Atticus. Watching the switch, I tightened my grip on Atticus's arm. He'd seen an opening to take his son down a peg.

"Hello," was all the greeting he would muster.

A bell chimed, and the room came alive as everyone stood and headed into the dining room.

Thankfully it broke the tension, and Atticus quickly pulled me around them and into the dining room.

FIFTEEN

OPHELIA

Another enormous room with large, wrought-iron windows awaited me. It had an amazing, two-story ceiling with multiple crystal chandeliers and a balcony framing the edge where the second story was.

I wasn't sure where to go or what to do, so I followed Atticus's lead and watched as everyone took what appeared to be assigned seats. They were drawn to them like it was the pattern they always adhered to. Charles on one end, with Gen on the side, Hamilton next to her, Amelia, a man I didn't know, and an empty seat before Vera at the other head. On our side was Madeline, Elizabeth, Atticus, and myself.

I was just sitting when Vera called out. "Penelope, you're late."

"Forgive me, Mother." A woman with light blonde hair and brilliant blue eyes stepped in. She was wearing an oversized sweater, leather pants, and heeled booties—a glaringly different look from Genevieve or Elizabeth.

"Atticus," she said as she sat next to me.

"Penelope."

Her blue eyes scanned me. "So, you're the desperation."

"Penny, watch it," Atticus growled.

She sighed and looked forward.

"Not to worry, Pen. He's just upset he's not lording over us," Hamilton said.

I leaned in toward Atticus. "What's he talking about?"

"I'll tell you later."

"Why not now?" Hamilton called.

Atticus was stewing beside me. "Because it isn't relevant to this dinner."

"Based on where you're sitting, it is," Gen said.

"Is the entire family here? No, therefore it is our family dinner, and parental tradition dictates."

"Again, confused."

Hamilton's jaw ticked. "He's the king, and nobody sits until the king sits."

Atticus's fist clenched on his leg, his jaw locked tightly. I reached out and covered his hand with mine, an action that seemed to calm him.

"Enough," Elizabeth hissed from the other side of him.

That solidified her as being similar in personality to Atticus.

Salads miraculously appeared in front of us. I whipped my head around trying to figure out what had happened. One second there was nothing on the plate in front of me and then suddenly, poof, there was a salad on another plate.

Everyone began eating, wine glasses were filled, drinks topped off, and it was all in a silent, seamless ballet of waitstaff.

Gen was talking while we began to eat. I tried not to salivate over the salad. I mean, who salivates over salad? But the bed of leafy greens was lightly bathed in the most delicious vinaigrette I'd ever tasted.

"Are you ever going to do anything productive?" Atticus said suddenly.

I looked up from my salad, which I was decimating much faster than everyone else, and found him glaring at his youngest sister.

She beamed at him. "Why, brother, I am single-handedly fueling the economy."

"I'm well aware."

"Everyone is aware," Charles said. "You burn through your allowance in days and then come crawling for more."

"Charles," Vera said with an admonishing tone.

Charles ignored his wife's attempt to silence him. "You've babied her too much, Vera, and if she doesn't change her course soon, she will find herself without a penny."

Vera gasped. "You wouldn't."

Genevieve simply rolled her eyes. "No, he wouldn't."

"Yes, he would," Atticus seethed beside me. "And as I am on your accounts, I can guarantee you will be shut off at the word go."

"At least I didn't get caught up in a sex tape scandal," Gen sneered.

"Enough!" Charles pounded his fist on the table, making me jump.

Based on Atticus's lack of reaction, the sex tape was not of him.

"What? It's not like she isn't going to know all the dirty little secrets. She is one, after all."

Ouch again. That was a low blow, and the hardest hit of the evening.

"Genevieve!" Atticus growled.

"Well, I've arrived at the perfect time," a voice called from the doorway. I turned, and my mouth dropped open as I stared at the man. He grinned when our gazes met. "Ah, Ophelia has joined us," Rhys said as he stepped forward and leaned down, pressing a kiss against my cheek. "Good to see you again."

I stared at him, stunned. He was a de Loughrey? How many were there? Seemed I had a lot of studying of the family tree to do.

"You know her?" Hamilton asked, his gaze narrowed.

Rhys blinked at him. "Of course. I was there the night these two lovebirds met."

The table went quiet and all eyes were on me, Charles's scrutiny burning into me. I knew my face had to be beet red. Rhys greeted Vera and others at the table before taking a seat.

"Why so quiet? Is this not a celebration? We are adding another member to our family. We could use some new blood."

"I've gone stale, I see," the man across from me said. He was holding Madeline, so I was guessing he was Elizabeth's husband. Preston?

"No offense, but you've been with Elizabeth for a decade, and I've known you since you were a child. Ophelia is truly new blood."

"Of a commoner," Charles scoffed.

The hits just kept coming. I was at the point of clenching my teeth to keep from biting back. Sadly, I didn't have anything to retaliate with. Atticus had prepared me for his father's harshness, but not for the rest of the family.

"Really, Father? What does her financial status have to do with anything?"

Charles motioned toward the socialite, who looked down her nose at me. It took everything in me to not roll my eyes at her spoiled, overdone ass.

"Amelia is new blood. Good blood."

"Good for her," Atticus said through clenched teeth.

I didn't know what possessed me to do it, but I reached out and tapped his jaw. His head swung toward me, his hard eyes swirling with so many fiery emotions. Every muscle was rigid, but when I reached up to cup his face, he relaxed into my touch.

It was all for show…right? I wanted to think so, but his reaction felt so guttural, I was having trouble believing so.

"We never found out when or how you two met," Vera said, breaking the bubble we'd unintentionally formed. "And why is it we've never heard of this relationship before?"

"Because it wasn't any of your business." Any relaxation I'd given him turned back to stone.

"My son in love is none of my business?" She turned to Rhys. "Since my son is so tight lipped, perhaps my nephew would enlighten the table?"

Nephew? That explained something.

"Aunt Vera, as Atticus's lawyer—"

She huffed and looked away. "If I didn't know you were being entirely serious, I would think you were trying to be funny."

"We met last June, on my birthday. Atticus and Rhys were at

Angelino, and invited me to join them at their table," I said, hating the way they couldn't just talk to one another. Every conversation seemed to be a constant battle. It wasn't dinner, it was a multiplayer chess match, and I may have just exposed my king.

Hamilton arched a brow. "Atticus at a club?"

"It happens. Not at the ones you frequent," Atticus explained.

"Doesn't Rhys own Angelino?" Genevieve asked.

My eyes widened, and I looked to Rhys.

"I do, and you're not allowed in," he said to his cousin.

"Why not?"

He steeled his gaze on her. "Because the last thing I need is bad press because you and your friends got shitfaced and fucked up my business."

"I woul—"

He leaned forward and held his hand up. "Let me stop you right there, little cousin. Don't even start to say you wouldn't when you *did* to Hamilton's bar."

"Do you all own bars?" I grumbled.

"No," a soft voice said from beside me. I blinked at the blonde, completely forgetting she was beside me because she'd remained so quiet. "The boys just like to have a place to play."

"What about the girls?"

"Elizabeth owns a wine bar. I have a coffee shop that features my cousin's coffee."

"Your cousin's coffee?" I asked.

Penelope gave me a slight smile. "Black Spell Brew?"

"Oh, I've heard of them."

"Will is the brains behind them, and my half-dozen cafés help spread his product in New York."

"Do you run all of your cafés?"

She shook her head. "No, they're all managed. I'm a cellist."

Given her slight figure, I expected the cello weighed more than she did.

"Do you play with an orchestra?"

"No, I make my own."

"What about you?" I turned to Atticus, who I found engaged in another heated argument with Gen.

He turned to me, his gaze still narrowed. "I'm sorry?"

"Everyone seems to own some smaller businesses. What about you?"

"You already know I own at least one restaurant."

Thankfully, once the main course was on our plates, the conversation thankfully died down, though there were still outbursts.

An hour later we were finishing dessert, and soon thereafter the room began to clear.

"That went well," Rhys said once everyone was done and we began to disperse.

I shook my head. "That was well?" All illusions I held about the richest family in the country were wiped out in minutes. Dysfunctional at best. Then again, they all held strong personalities as well as egos, with the exception of the small blonde who sat quietly beside me all evening. There was something subdued about her, a juxtaposition from the rest of her boisterous family.

"What are you even doing here, Rhys?" Atticus asked as Rhys headed toward us.

"You didn't really think I'd miss this, did you?" he asked with a sly smile and a twinkle in his eye. Even a year later, Rhys was just as slithering as I remembered.

"Why didn't I know you were cousins?" I asked. Looking between them, I could see a few similarities, but Rhys looked more like Hamilton than Atticus with his steely grey eyes and brown hair.

"Why should you have?"

I was a little taken aback by his response, but he was right. Why should I have? We were three people having drinks at a bar. They knew each other, so my assumption had been that they were friends.

"You know what they say about assumptions, Ophelia," Rhys said.

"I'm beginning to grasp the naiveté of my original assumptions, as they've come back to haunt me in unexpected ways."

Rhys grinned at me. "Yes, you'll make a fine addition." He

reached for my hand, and I involuntarily flinched when our fingers touched. "All is well, little mouse." I let him raise my hand to his lips where he placed a light kiss.

Every muscle tensed. There was something almost menacing about the gesture that was meant to hold respect and reverence.

"I must be off. See you both soon."

"You're not staying?" Atticus asked.

Rhys shook his head. "As much as I would love to watch them play with your little pet, I have to get back to the city."

Rhys gave us both a nod and a wave before heading down the hall. I kept my gaze trained on him until he was no longer in sight, having the strange feeling that if I didn't, he would strike.

"He would eat me alive at the first opportunity, wouldn't he?"

"Correct." No coddling. "Come," he said as he slipped his hand into mine.

A yawn left me as we walked down the hall that was easily the length of a football field. It was then the adrenaline of the evening and the anxiety began to crash down. Suddenly I was drained and just wanted to crawl into bed.

"That was…something. Are all your family dinners like that?"

"It was an accurate representation."

"Par for the course."

A small chuckle left him.

"Would you really cut your sister off?"

He turned to me, his expression as serious as always, and once again I wondered if the man even knew how to smile. I'd seen it a few times, but I could admit I wanted to see it more, especially with the years ahead of us.

"You come from the working class," he began. I waited until he made his point before deciding whether or not to punch him. "Tell me—if you received a quarter of a million a month to live off, with no rent because your family owns every dwelling in which you lay your head including your very own Manhattan condo, could you spend it all in five days?"

My mouth went slack as I looked at him. By the way Genevieve spoke, I thought it was maybe a few thousand dollars. "Holy shit. What does she spend that amount of money on?"

"It's not going to charity, I can tell you that."

We continued on our path, and I attempted to process what he just said. "So she gets three million dollars a year, has no rent or any other real-life bills, and on top of that ends up begging another few million out of your family, and all she does is shop and party?"

"Yes."

A harsh laugh left me. "Cut her off. Give her a taste of the poor life. She can have my old job."

Atticus's lips twitched up, and he broke out into a full laugh. It stunned me, and I stared at him in wonder. My reaction reminded me so much of Rhys's reaction to Atticus's laughter the night we met. Atticus had a beautiful smile. It was breathtaking, and when he looked at me, I got lost in the way his blue eyes sparkled.

In the week and change we'd been together, I'd only ever experienced the tight-lipped, business smile. Before me was the look of the man I let take me home a year prior.

"Hopefully that will be enough to keep you away from her."

"Keep me away?"

He nodded. "Gen always brings bad press with her. Nothing good comes from spending time with her, so stay away."

Was she really that bad?

"What was with the tense atmosphere and the Amelia chick glaring at me all night?"

He stopped, then gestured at me to follow him. We entered into a huge parlor out of earshot. "I've been honest about what I wanted from you, but not exactly the why."

I nodded in agreement. "While I've realized I was so shocked about your proposal, I didn't think to ask."

"My grandfather passed over a month ago."

My chest clenched and I reached out, my hand resting on his arm. "I'm so sorry, Atticus."

He shook his head. "Don't be. I'm not sad the bastard is gone. However, as always, he found a way to screw with my inheritance."

"How so?"

"In order to collect his company shares and this house, as well as to hold my position within the company, I have to be married within a year of his death."

"And in that time, you thought of me?" My mind spun with trying to figure out what shocked me the most—his grandfather's stipulations, or his approaching me.

"I've spent many nights thinking of you, of remembering the feeling of your tight pussy around my cock," he whispered. His breath tickled my skin while his words lit up my blood and left an ache between my legs. However, the rare glimpse of warmth and playfulness faded, hardening again. "My father has been trying to force an arranged marriage on me for over a decade, and thus far I've been able to avoid them all. With the time restriction, I was suddenly facing with delving into my options. Many suggested I marry one of the women I'd previously dated, but if I wanted to spend any time with them, I would have stayed with them. There was also the few female friends I have that often attend events with me."

"And warm your cock?" I asked.

He nodded, not surprising me. In what I'd seen, he wasn't one to spend time chasing women. Not that he'd have to with his one-two punch of sexy as fuck and money.

"Then you came to the restaurant, saw me, and thought 'she'll do'?"

"You're going to make me admit something I don't want to admit."

"Say it."

He stopped walking, turning toward me slightly, and his jaw hardened before he released a breath. "As much as I've tried, I haven't been able to stop thinking about you. And not just about how much I want to be between your thighs."

My heart fluttered in my chest, happy to know it wasn't a one-sided infatuation. "You were pissed when I suddenly popped up in front of you as your waitress."

"Yes, because I'm a paranoid asshole who thought you were after something."

I froze, my eyes wide as I stared at him in shock. "Seriously?"

"I'm a de Loughrey, Ophelia—of course seriously. When you're born with a golden spoon in your mouth, you learn to trust no one, because everyone is willing to kick you to the ground to pull that spoon from your mouth."

"What kind of daycare did you go to?"

He shook his head. "I had nannies. It is simply a hard lesson we've all learned one way or another. People will use you for what it will give them. I was afraid that was what it was, that you knew who I was, and that you were just another leech."

That was the score, why he'd approached me. The pressure he was under had to be intense.

"What made you change your mind?"

"The background check."

"How thorough was this background check?" It irritated me how detailed his knowledge of my life was without ever having asked me anything. The background check information was his version of the Binder of Doom, only I didn't know the contents, and that made me uneasy.

"Extremely."

I blanched at that. The flippant comments he'd made about knowing how old I was when I lost my virginity were true.

"When?"

"Shortly after that first lunch."

"But you still never asked me out?"

"No."

"Were you ever going to, or was that just a load of bullshit you feed women?"

He stared at me, cold and expressionless. The walls of ice returned, blocking me from more information.

"You look tired. Let me show you to your room."

"My room?"

He nodded. "It's technically Elizabeth's, but it is directly across the hall from my own."

I made a start to say something, then stopped. Being across the hall was much better than being in the same bed.

We headed to the second floor, and I was surprised when we passed the landing and continued up to the third floor and an equally long and wide hallway as the one on the main floor. The spacing between doors was almost identical and it felt like one of those halls that keeps expanding, never ending, stretching on seemingly forever. Glancing behind us, I found the other side to be equally as large.

After passing a few sets of doors, he turned the handle and ushered me inside. A four-poster bed sat against one wall across from a large fireplace. Elegant furnishings accented the room just as they had the main floor.

"Are you sure this is Elizabeth's room?" I asked. It looked like a well-made-up guest bedroom. There was nothing to identify it as a once personal space for a growing girl.

"Can't you tell?" he asked. His voice came across as serious, but when I turned, one corner of his mouth was turned up. "Most personal items moved to her home with Preston. Besides the shades of the walls and the colors of the bedding, little evidence of her twenty-some years here remains."

"Can the same be said about your room?"

He leaned in close, his breath ghosting across my skin. "Perhaps one day you will find out." He pulled back, moving to the door. "Good night, Ophelia."

I watched as he pulled the door closed but was able to call out, "Good night," before the latch clicked.

Once alone, the cool air and the emptiness of the room combined to set off goose bumps across my skin. I swallowed before stepping to the end of the bed where my bag lay and kicked off my heels. My feet ached as they flattened out against the plush area rug.

All I wanted to do was fall into the four-poster bed, but I needed out of my costume first.

Grabbing my toiletries bag, I headed into the attached bathroom.

With a flip of the light, I stared at the opulent space with a large walk-in shower and marble counter. Did each room have its own bathroom?

With the size of the mansion I was in, the answer was probably yes. I peered at my reflection, at the strange person who stared back. Despite the hours since I'd gotten ready, everything still looked flawless. My eyes showed the tiredness below, but everything else remained pristine.

I looked like I was getting ready for a fashion shoot, not just ending a family dinner. Was that how all de Loughrey events would be? Dressed to the nines?

It all needed to go. I needed a reminder of who I really was, and not the pretend woman before me.

Slowly the freckles began to reappear, breaking up the porcelain doll look with each swipe, wiping away the layers of makeup from my skin. Afterward, I managed to wrestle the zipper of my dress down and tossed it over a chair before clipping my hair back and giving my face a good scrub.

Finally, the familiarity of my imperfections eased me.

"Hi," I said, then let out a sigh.

Was ten million really worth the loss of self I was beginning to feel?

ATTICUS

A feeling of unease echoed inside me, but I couldn't figure out where the phantom feeling arose from. All I was aware of was the fact that it kept my mind and body from shutting down for the night.

I stared up at the ceiling, a hint of light from outside creating a myriad of ghostly shapes on my ceiling. As a child, they frightened me, but as an adult, they were a welcoming of my return.

However, it wasn't their haunting memories that kept me up, but the presence I felt.

Two doors and a hallway were all that separated us, and yet it felt all too close and not close enough at the same time. At least at home there was a bathroom, closet, and another bedroom that buffered my room and hers.

Her presence was necessary, but it unnerved me. I wasn't accustomed to having someone around, especially not someone like her.

Ophelia was not like most of the women I dated. Though "dating" was a loose definition of my encounters, which were generally for stress relief or arm candy for an event. I hadn't truly dated anyone since high school. There simply wasn't time, and expectations for my life were high.

Being the firstborn came with restrictions, obligations, and above all, an ironclad execution of compliance on how to behave.

If only my younger siblings had been given as strict of an upbringing, my blood pressure would be lower. Though as siblings went, there was only one true thorn in my side—Genevieve. Silas was a close second, but mild in comparison to the youngest of Charles de Loughrey's children.

She wasn't the absolute youngest. Some of Uncle Hugh's children were still in high school. Aunt Kathryn's third child was younger as well. She married a man named William Montgomery. We didn't see her family often as they lived on the West Coast, but there were three more cousins from there. There was also the extended—second, third, fourth, and fifth cousins that carried the family name.

Elizabeth, Hamilton, Rhys, and Georgiana fell right in line and caused no issues, with the exception of Elizabeth's husband, but I was going to end that nuisance. Uncle Hugh's children were young enough that he was still able to hold them in check, which helped tremendously, but soon, they too would be my responsibility.

The pit forming in my stomach told me my idea was a mistake. It was never going to work. But I needed time, a reprieve from the one aspect of my life that was a constant harassment.

One night, and I was already ready to go back to the city. However, familial obligations kept me from leaving until the following day. It had been a rough night with more backhanded insults against Ophelia than I expected.

Resistance? Yes. Full-blown disdain from more than the worst offenders was unexpected. I knew they didn't want my position, so why all the friction against the woman I chose to marry?

Ophelia was the one grand decision I'd made for my life. Ever. My single status to date was the one thing I had control of that didn't come with a leash—another reason I fought so hard against an arranged marriage.

Ophelia had already begun to turn my life upside down and

sideways. Watching her walk past me in jeans that cupped her lus-
cious ass like a second skin led me to thinking that choosing her was
the best decision I'd ever made.

And then tonight, she stood her ground with a grace that ri-
valed my mother's.

Throughout dinner, no matter what was said to or about her,
she didn't respond. She bit her tongue. Though I could feel the anger,
no one else noticed. There was also an uncanny understanding inside
her. Though I trusted Rhys, I knew he was a snake in the grass, and
that side of him was very apparent to her from the beginning. Most
women would have fallen for his charms, but she sank closer to me
every time he was near.

I should have told her about my father's plans and the stipulations of the will, but I didn't want her to turn my proposal down.
Omission was the key to everything.

The next morning I was sitting at the dining room table, enjoying
breakfast and coffee, when she entered. It was those jeans again, the
ones that molded to her skin and filled me with the urge to touch her.

"If you're going to wear jeans around here, they need to be the
ones Melanie brought you," I said as she pulled out the chair across
from me.

She halted, then glanced down. "Why? Jeans are jeans."

"Trust me. They can tell, and I don't want them looking down
their noses at you." They already did that enough. "We still have another night here."

"Does this *request* extend to home?" she asked with a hard edge.

The unpleasant twinge in my chest had my expression relaxing in an attempt to not come across as hostile. "It's our home. Wear
whatever you want."

"You mean *your* home. I may live there, but I'm nothing more
than a roomed employee. It's not my home."

There was a bite in her tone.

"It is as much your home as mine."

"No, no, it's not. At most, I'm a guest in your palace. And since
you dictate what I can and cannot wear…"

"Outside. Wear what you wish at home. Or nothing." I couldn't help the way my lips twitched up into a grin. Oh, yes, I would much enjoy her strutting around the condo naked, waiting, *begging*. "You're beautiful either way."

"Wow, did you just compliment me?"

My good mood faltered. "I know it may seem like I'm harsh at times. It's a product of the level to which I have to hold myself, and those with me."

She let out an annoyed huff just as Mary appeared beside her. Ophelia seemed like she felt out of place giving a breakfast order to her, but she would become accustomed to it in time, though I knew it grated on her to be waited on hand and foot.

"Did you enjoy your meandering?"

"My meandering?"

"I assumed you were getting the lay of the land when I could not find you this morning."

She shrugged. "It's a big place. I was heading to breakfast and got twisted around."

"Hmm."

A large plate appeared before Ophelia, and her eyes widened.

I sat down my utensils and finished off my last bite as well as the last sips of my coffee, then requested another cup be delivered to the library.

Ophelia looked up to me as I stood, her mouth full of a bite of omelet, a sausage link speared on her fork.

"I'll be in the library," I said. She gave a nod of understanding, then turned her attention back to her plate.

An hour later, I sat at one of the desks occupying a space in the opening of the two-story expanse that held the family's collection of books. It was one of the rare places in the house I found any peace.

"Where is all my stuff?" Ophelia said as she huffed into the library, pulling me from the financial report I'd been studying.

"Did you misplace your bedroom? I understand it's a large home, but I thought you'd gotten a feel for it in your exploration this morning."

"Cut the crap, Atticus."

I blew out a breath and shut my laptop before looking up to her. My heart stuttered at the fury in her eyes. She was glorious when angry, and every nerve woke up in response. I wanted nothing more than to feel her lips on mine, her body writhing beneath me as I fucked her into compliance.

"That is a crude term you really should rip from your vocabulary. If you're upset with me, simply state it."

"Fine. Enough with jabs at my intelligence. Where is all of my stuff?"

"Have you checked your bedroom?"

"Do you think I'd be asking you this question if I hadn't?"

"Then I can assure you I have no idea what you're talking about."

"Her things are in your bedroom, Atticus," my father said from the doorway. "I had them moved there earlier today."

I froze as I stared at the man who challenged me to defy him, to prove to him that my relationship with Ophelia was a ruse as he suspected.

"You what?"

I clenched my jaw as I stared down at my father. He was testing me, to see if the relationship was true. It was a business arrangement and didn't need to be brought into my only sanctuary.

"She is your fiancée and should be sleeping beside you. Get started on some grandchildren. We need more de Loughreys." I caught the challenging glint in his eye. He saw right through me, but it didn't matter. The stipulation was marriage, and I'd chosen my bride. I would be damned to let him take that from me.

Ophelia was mine.

As swiftly as he appeared, he was gone.

Ophelia stepped closer, her arms crossed over her chest. "I am not sleeping in the same bed as you," she hissed.

"Apparently, you are," I ground out, also unhappy about the arrangement.

I spent lunch with Ophelia on the terrace overlooking the lake. It was one of my favorite spots. Afterward, I took her for a quick stroll down to the dock. Honestly, it felt good to get moving and take a walk. It was a fifty-foot descent down through tiered gardens and stone walkways to reach the docks.

The Chris-Craft was lifted from the water and hidden under a canopy. Someone must have taken it out recently, otherwise it would be in the boat house.

The breeze was warm, and her face lit up when we reached the water's edge. Perhaps Ophelia would enjoy a ride around the lake.

"Fishies!" she said with a blinding smile as she pointed down at the water.

For a moment I was stunned by her giddiness at something so small, at her childlike wonder and happiness. It was a side to her I hadn't seen before, and I found it warmed my cold heart.

I followed her gaze, watching small perch and panfish swimming around the supports, popping in and out around the rocks below. She leaned forward for a better look, when her center of gravity shifted, and she began to fall. In a flash, I grabbed her arm and pulled her back against my chest, my heart pounding hard as adrenaline shot through me.

Her eyes were wide in surprise. "Whoa. Got a little dizzy there. Lost my equilibrium."

"Do you know how to swim?" I asked, still gripping her arm while the other held her tightly to me.

Her face scrunched, and I immediately stepped us back from the edge.

"I can, just not that well."

My muscles locked down around her as screams of the past filled my ears.

"Atticus?" she called out before her warm hand cupped my face.

"No more swimming by yourself at the Tower, and you will be taking swimming lessons the moment we return."

She blinked up at me. "I know how to swim, Atticus."

"But you're not strong, and I will never let you near the water until you are."

"You're dictating again?" she asked.

I narrowed my eyes at her. Didn't she understand I was trying to protect her?

"For your safety, yes."

Her eyes flicked back and forth between my own.

"Okay," she said in agreement, for once not fighting me. The incredulous tone was missing, and her voice was laced with confusion. Which meant she hadn't gotten to that part of the folio.

With a nod, I took her hand and pulled her away from the water's edge and back up to the house. I wouldn't take the chance of her near the water until I was satisfied.

Not with her.

"There you are," a sickly sweet voice called out a few hours later from the entrance to the library where I'd retreated after lunch.

The vein on my forehead throbbed as Amelia Harris walked toward me, her hips swaying with each step. It was made to entice, but stirred nothing inside me.

"Amelia." I looked back to my work, ignoring the worm my father had let loose.

In my periphery I caught her movements circling the desk, then the light touch of her fingers across my shoulders.

"Don't touch me," I hissed.

She flinched, probably in surprise.

I stood and towered over her. "I don't give a fuck what my father promised. He can try anything he likes. In the end, it's my choice, and I rule all. Just to remove any misconceptions, I assure you, you would be far down the list of possible candidates to warm my bed."

Fury rolled across her features, and she swung her arm back to strike me but I caught her wrist.

"I would not do something so foolish again. You may think you have power, that your name holds weight, but I am not someone you or your father wants to go against. Go home, tell him you failed. If you attempt to retaliate in any manner, know that I will demolish your company without a second thought."

"You don't have the power to do that."

I pulled on her arm, bringing her face closer to mine. She was putting forth strength, but I could see the fear. That fear drove me, excited my darkness for a possible challenge to tear something apart.

"Try me," I hissed, then released her.

Her lips curled up, exposing her teeth, and I could see tears filling her eyes. "You'll pay for that."

Anger coiled through me, and my gaze narrowed further on her. She dared to test me? *Me?* "One foot out of line, and I will end Harris Hotels in minutes," I said with deadly calm.

"You couldn't," she sneered. As confident as she was, I could see the fear growing inside her.

To drive my status home, I straightened. "You may have my father convinced, but remember this, Miss Harris—I rule the de Loughreys. Not him. And I have no qualms attacking if you continue to pester me or try to worm your way between Ophelia and me."

She stared at me for a moment before the look of surprise melted into a sensuous smirk. "You can attack me, just so you know. Any time. I like a dominant man. I make a great sub in the bedroom."

I stood my ground, glaring with each attempted sexualized step she took. "It seems you fail to understand me."

"Oh, I understand. But I like breaking rules. Do you want to punish me for it?"

"No. I simply want you out of my face and out of my home. Now leave before you embarrass yourself further or force my threat."

"You can bend me over. Relieve the tension inside you. She doesn't release you, I can tell." She pulled at the edge of her dress, drawing it up, exposing her bare flesh as she turned around and spread her legs. "You can take it out on me. Wherever you want."

My stomach rolled in disgust. While many men would find this flattering and get hard, it only soured my system. I had no use for easy women who behaved like whores.

"Get out," I growled.

Movement at the doorway caught my eye and I looked in time to watch Ophelia step in, then turn after glancing at the woman bent before me. The anger rose inside me toward the woman, and I was about to drag her out by her hair when Ophelia appeared before me.

With no warning, she grabbed my face and pulled my lips down to hers. Her lips parted, and I was graced with the most delicious tongue caressing mine. I gripped her waist, pulling her closer, but was left disappointed a moment later when she released me.

Her eyes were bright, cheeks flushed as we stared at each other. The link broke as she slowly turned to face Amelia, who had thankfully righted her clothing and was shooting daggers at Ophelia.

"I clearly heard him tell you to get out, so why are you still here?"

Amelia let out a shriek, her foot stomping as her hand raised clearly to strike Ophelia.

With my arm still around her waist, I turned, pulling her away as Amelia's hand struck my bicep.

The color drained from her face as she realized what she'd just done.

I released Ophelia and stepped forward, towering over Amelia. "You will be gone from this house within five minutes, or that promise I made you will be a reality within the hour."

Somehow she seemed to pale more, her eyes flitting between mine like a frightened animal before she scurried from the room.

"Are you okay?" Ophelia asked once Amelia was gone. She took my arm in her hands, moving it around in search of an injury.

"I'm fine. There was not enough force in her slap to harm me."

"Oh," she said as the heated energy that coiled around us at her kiss dissipated, and she retreated. She glanced down to the desk. "You're working."

"I am."

She reached up and swiped a loose lock behind her ear. "I'm just going to take a walk around the gardens before dinner."

I stood, frozen, as I watched her walk away. Part of me wanted to go with her, but I didn't know how to tell her that.

Instead of focusing on that, I turned my attention to the other fire raging inside me. Amelia showed many faces, but she couldn't hide her fear.

And I was going to make sure she knew to fear me.

Harris Hotels would still stand in the end, but barely, after I eviscerated them from within.

She was about to learn a hard lesson that would hopefully resonate—don't fuck with me, and, more importantly, don't fuck with my wife.

SEVENTEEN

ATTICUS

As we returned to my room for the evening, Ophelia became fidgety with each step.

"You seem nervous, my dear," I said, enjoying her discomfort more than I should have.

She started at the term of endearment and glanced up at me. It was only meant to be slightly antagonistic, but I found I liked her response. The prospect of having her soft body curled against mine overshadowed any concern for her feelings.

She swallowed before worrying her bottom lip, and picked at the hem of her shirt.

"It isn't like we haven't shared a bed before," I reminded her, which only served to remind me of what it felt like to have her wrapped around me.

"Yes, well, things were different then."

They certainly were.

Upon entering, Ophelia stood mere feet within the room. Her eyes scanned the walls and the furniture, taking stock of my childhood bedroom. Unlike Elizabeth's room, awards lined the bookshelves along with an assortment of books.

Deep navy and dark woods colored the walls. Cream tiles surrounded a long-dormant fireplace, a color that was strewn about in accent via chairs and curtains and rugs.

"And?" I asked as she perused.

"I was expecting it to be colder," she said, barely above a whisper. I was thinking of a response when she turned to me. "But it's surprisingly warm, even for its size. There are pieces of you." A small smile formed on her lips that had me transfixed.

There was something about her presence that both soothed and unnerved me. I *liked* her being there, which was odd. I didn't like anyone in my space. However, after my afternoon revelation when I called her my wife, even in my own mind, I found she was changing me, if only for her.

I turned my attention from her, desperate to shake the hold she had on me. It did not help that my body still burned from her kiss hours earlier.

As I pulled my shirt up and over my head, I reveled in the small intake of breath that slipped from Ophelia's lips. When I glanced over, she stood next to her suitcase and appeared to be stuck mid zip of her jeans, her eyes glued to me.

We stared at each other for a moment, that sweet heat circulating between us. A woman flashed her pussy at me and practically begged me to fuck her, and it did nothing to me. A simple kiss from Ophelia had my insides raging for more.

"How long has it been since you've had sex?" I asked, my voice lower in tone than normal.

She blinked at me, a beautiful pink blossoming across her pale flesh.

I quirked a brow at her as I moved to the zipper of my slacks. She turned around, pulling something from her bag and holding it close to her chest before practically running into the bathroom.

I rid myself of my slacks, socks next, leaving me solely in my boxer briefs. That was how I slept, and I wasn't going to change that simply because she was going to be lying beside me.

With a few steps, I was outside the bathroom door, leaning against the wall.

"Since your birthday, then?"

The door flew open, and a flash of hunger moved through me at the sight of her scantily clad body. Every muscle tensed as my gaze crept along the swell of her small but perfect breasts and the tight peaks of her nipples. The tank top she wore left little to the imagination, but it was the little lace panties that barely covered her mound that had me nearly reaching out for her.

Her eyes were wide, clothes draped over her arm, and she was blocked by my body from entering the room. For a moment I was trapped, warped by a lust that was overtaking me. A perfectly viable sexual partner stood before me, one I knew to be the perfect fit for my cock, and it took a concerted effort not to push her back in and take her against the shower wall.

"Move," she said, but it barely came out as a whisper. The pink was still there, enticing me to throw everything away and take her.

"When?" I snarled, barely keeping myself in check with us being so close together and very little covering her body.

She ground her teeth together before her eyes snapped to mine. Anger raged inside, but the rosy color that painted her skin still showed.

"You know when."

I stepped back, allowing her to pass, resisting the urge to grab her.

This is a bad idea.

In a few short minutes, her closeness was affecting me. Women didn't share my bed unless I was fucking them. And I'd spent nearly the last year wanting to be buried inside her again.

I entered the bathroom, emerging a few minutes later to find her tucked under the covers, lying on her side and facing away from me. Her ignoring my presence was better for us both.

After sliding in next to her, I shut off the light and closed my eyes, willing sleep to take me.

The cruel bastard sandman refused to take pity on my plight, leaving me to suffer the closeness of her skin. I could feel the heat of her body warming the air beneath the blanket. She was like a furnace, and not what I had in mind when I teased her about warming my bed.

She was so beautiful, feisty, and I was certain she hated me sometimes. Not that she knew me well, and I wondered if it was more that she hated herself for accepting my proposition. If she fought against me to shield herself.

Wasn't that what I was doing? Using her as a shield?

I'd made no promises, no declarations of feelings, though they were there. I wouldn't dare tell her. Budding and new, but I couldn't deny they were there. I wanted more from her, but held back that desire.

Because our relationship was not built on a foundation of emotions, but one of mutual benefit.

In the low light, I couldn't stop myself from turning toward her and staring. She'd rolled onto her back, arm thrown above her head, face angled my direction. The way her plush lips parted and her eyelashes fluttered when she dreamed, captured me in curiosity. What was she dreaming about?

A strand of hair fell across her forehead and I reached out to brush it aside. My fingertips tingled at the touch, and I couldn't stop myself from cupping her face and running my thumb across her bottom lip.

That beautiful bottom lip I remembered so well. Lips that haunted me. Pressed against my skin, against my lips, stretched around the girth of my cock—visions that had me swelling and aching with the need to claim.

I wanted her. Badly. My cock ached to slip inside her. To feel the wet warmth of her snug little pussy. Being so close, feeling her warmth, only aroused me further. I couldn't remember a time I'd been so turned on.

Before I realized it, I was caging her against the bed, and one leg slipped between her thighs. The heat of her pussy had my hips rocking, pressing my hardness against her. I dove down to the crook of her neck and attacked, lavishing her with teeth, lips, and tongue.

"Atticus?" her voice came out hoarse with an edge of confusion and a hint of lust.

A moan left me, and I continued attacking her neck. Running my hands up her sides, my fingers tweaked her nipples and made her draw in a breath as she arched against me.

"You're going to give in to me, and you're going to do it right fucking now," I growled against her ear. All reason had flown, driven away by the consuming desire to feel her wrapped around me.

"What are you talking about?"

I pressed into her, our eyes meeting, and the same hunger shone back at me. "Give it to me, Ophelia. I know you want it as much as I do."

Her eyes widened, and understanding crossed her features.

Blinding pain surged through me, and I cried out as I fell onto the bed beside her, cupping my cock and balls.

She sat up and backed into the headboard. "What the actual fuck? Are you serious right now? No, Atticus. Hell, fucking no," she seethed.

The agony cleared my mind, and I shook my head. I sat up, grimacing as I moved, my eyes beseeching her. "I'm sorry. I don't know what came over me."

She glared at me. "You were thinking with your dick. Don't try that shit again."

"I won't."

Bad move, old boy.

EIGHTEEN

OPHELIA

What do you do when you have unlimited funds available to you in New York?

You sit at the top of your tower and never do anything.

I'd been bombarded with so much during my first few weeks with Atticus. The life I led was flipped upside down, turned inside out, and shaken like a snow globe. Trapped in a confusing place. If I didn't have to work, what did I do with myself?

Cooking and cleaning were out—someone else took care of that.

The one upside was that I'd gotten into a great exercise routine due to sheer boredom combined with the incredible private gym that sat twenty-two floors below my eight-thousand-square-foot prison. Though, I had run into Genevieve a few times. It was almost becoming a pattern. We ran in silence next to each other on the treadmills. Even while running, she was picture perfect. I assumed all the exercise was to work off the booze from her partying.

I also spent three days a week in swim lessons. Of course, Atticus de Loughrey couldn't just find me a swim instructor or coach to improve my swimming ability. No, he hired Olympic gold medalist Rana Smith.

An Olympic gold medalist.

There was something about his insistence that I become a strong swimmer that kept me from fighting him on it, even if I did think Rana was overkill.

All the free time to myself made self-introspection a startling discovery—I was boring as fuck.

Shopping? Nope. If I needed anything, all I had to do was ask Jack or one-click it online or call Melanie. I wasn't much of a shopper anyway.

Hobbies? Once upon a time I liked crafts, but I wasn't so sure about that now. Awesome centerpieces made from things from a store where everything was a dollar would not be an appreciated item in the de Loughrey family.

I wasn't good at art or music. Maybe I could get back into video games, but that was just a brainless time suck. It would give me something to do, but it wasn't enriching in any way. Not that I needed something enriching. More that I felt like I needed something like that to keep up.

I had to look up what the other de Loughrey women did. Genevieve, well, was Genevieve. She said it best when she touted she kept the economy running. Penelope had a decent following for her music. Elizabeth was a mother as well as an entrepreneur. Georgiana was the picture of high society—grace, sophistication, and charity work.

I could probably get into charity work, but where to start with that? What kind of charity? What was I even passionate about?

All I knew was that I needed to figure out what I was going to do with my life. Until then, I would continue my studies on how to be part of the one percent of the one percent.

That was a staggering thought, but the more I researched the de Loughrey family, the deeper the money well went. They had at least forty properties around the world, including a private Caribbean island with its own landing strip and customs.

I'd resorted to using Google to learn about the de Loughreys because I couldn't take the soul-sucking monotony of the Binder of Doom any longer. The internet was a much easier place to learn about the family then that damn binder. It was the bane of my existence, and I had fantasies of setting it on fire. I'd be damned if Atticus thought that I was going to learn about my future husband from a fucking book with bullet points.

The amount of Wikipedia articles was insane, and nearly as knot tying as the binder. Births, deaths, names repeating—it was all a blur. I tried to soak up as much as I could, but if it wasn't a name I'd heard before, it didn't stick. And I didn't know that many names. Basically whomever lived in the Tower, which was Atticus's family and Rhys's.

Finally, I took a walk to the nearest bookstore, much to Michael's horror, and perused the shelves, settling on a biography of the family—*The de Loughreys: America's royalty.*

The amount of books about the family on the shelves was insane. The amount online was astronomical, and once again had me wondering what the hell I'd gotten myself into. I knew he was rich, I knew the de Loughreys were huge, but I never comprehended just how enormous the numbers were or how extensively the family was integrated into people's daily lives. Every American owned a de Loughrey product, whether they knew it or not.

Private yachts, private planes, and access to anything they desired.

A few weeks ago, all I desired was to have enough money that I wasn't constantly pinching pennies. All the what-ifs when I'd thought in the past about winning the lottery paled in comparison to the life I was now living. My dreams were trivial compared to the wealth I was surrounded by.

And again, I was stuck in the same position—what was I going to do with my life?

Being the wife of Atticus de Loughrey was going to be a job in itself, but outside of that, what would I do to pass the hours?

Once we had a baby, things would be different and filled with someone to take care of.

That thought stopped me.

In as little as a year and a half, I could be a mother. How could I forget that? That it wasn't just five years, but also having a baby? My only guess was the fact that I'd been so consumed with my whole life switch.

Maybe making a baby together could be fun instead of clinical.

Really, Ophelia? After what he attempted in his family's home I shouldn't have been thinking things like that, but I also couldn't deny that even as mad as I was that he was trying to have sex with me, I was also incredibly turned on.

The weight of his body pressing into mine. The warm, wet pressure of his tongue was divine against my skin. His touch.

Why did I have to want it all so much? It took everything in me to raise my knee into his groin. I hated doing it, but I also knew it was the only way to stop what would soon become the inevitable.

We continued to struggle with interaction, but I knew that would fade with time.

He had a softer side. I'd seen it. I just had a feeling he didn't know how to handle me. I wasn't like the other women he'd known in his life. I actually expected things of him that weren't monetary, and that threw him off.

I had a lot of time to ponder Atticus as a person, since the amount of time I spent alone while he worked was staggering and the days passed in an endless cycle of boredom and more boredom.

As my birthday crept closer, I pondered what to do. One of my favorite activities was going to the casino in Queens, but I had a feeling Atticus wouldn't like me doing that. I was sure that he would be working, but the thought of another day spent alone didn't sound the least bit appealing and yet, I had no one in my life except him.

If I'd learned anything in my study of the de Loughreys, it was that being a de Loughrey may seem glamorous from the outside, but the price was freedom, trust, and love.

I was marrying into a large family, but I'd never felt so lonely. Did they all feel the same?

I woke up like it was any other day of my never-ending cycle of boredom, but it wasn't exactly the same. At least not for me.

It was my twenty-seventh birthday and the official one-year marker since I'd met Atticus.

After having a small bit of breakfast, I headed down for a workout. Because, why not?

When I walked into the gym, Genevieve was already there on one of the ellipticals looking as cover-model ready as ever. Had the woman ever had a pimple in her life? A rogue hair growing out of some strange spot? Something, anything, about her that wasn't flawless?

"Morning," I said as I climbed onto the treadmill.

The high-energy music that thumped through the speakers lowered in volume. She then did something that shocked me.

"Happy birthday," she said between panting breaths, surprising me more than the fact that she spoke to me.

I turned to look at her and smiled. "Thank you." My brow scrunched. "How did you know?"

She held up her phone. "Family calendar. All important dates and events are programmed in. Your phone should have it too."

My phone.

I let out a little laugh. "I kinda forget I have that half the time."

"Forget you have what?"

"A phone." Nobody ever calls me, and I used my laptop for internet surfing. Sometimes I used the phone, but most of the time it sat in my bedroom.

Gen's eyes widened, and her pace slowed as she stared at me like I was some strange creature.

"*Forget?*"

"Yeah." I felt uneasy under her scrutiny. I hadn't noticed it before, but despite her reputation, Genevieve had just as calculating of a gaze as Atticus did. "I mean, I don't really have many friends, and I talk to my mom as little as possible."

She shook her head and sighed. "Maybe you two are perfect for each other. How old did you turn today?"

"Perfect for each other? What do you mean?"

"I mean Atticus has few friends, and even fewer people he trusts. Not surprising, really, but I think that kind of loneliness attracts loneliness. Maybe it's a good thing. God knows we need something to release that stick from his ass."

I couldn't help but laugh at that, and she laughed right along with me. It felt good to talk to her in a normal conversational fashion.

"I turned twenty-seven today."

"Plenty of time to pop out five kids."

I tripped, but caught myself, lowering my speed as I stared at her, wide-eyed. "Five kids?"

She nodded. "De Loughreys are prolific in the child area. Father is one of five. Well, technically six, but one died as a baby. There are five of us, five from Uncle Henry, five from Uncle Hugh—Aunt Katherine only has three, though, and Uncle James died shortly before he was to be married."

See, was it really that hard? In mere seconds, Genevieve had relayed to me much of the de Loughrey family tree—at least two generations' worth—in an understandable way that wasn't a graph on a piece of paper. She gave life to names I'd read. Made them real instead of just a jumble of letters inked onto processed tree pulp.

"Thanks."

She quirked a brow at me. "For?"

"Explaining something to me like I'm a human being."

She scoffed. "Atticus isn't the most personable."

"No, he is not. It makes me wonder how he's so good at what he does."

"You don't have to necessarily be good at something to excel at it."

"What do you mean?"

"He's not the most cutthroat, but he has other qualities that make up for it."

"What is it about him, then?"

"He's the most driven. Doing whatever it takes to get what he wants, what he needs."

Her words sliced at me, though she didn't mean to. I wasn't the subject she was thinking of, but it still struck a chord. He knew my weaknesses and exploited them to get me to agree. Offered me financial freedom and even acquiesced to my no-sex demands.

Did he even care about me as a person in the least?

"The wicked king."

I snapped my head toward her. "What did you say?"

"That's what people call him. The wicked king. No one dares to defy him for fear of awakening the wicked king. He can topple empires in hours."

The conversation I'd overheard weeks ago immediately came to mind, confirming what she said. He used the brute strength of the de Loughrey power.

Genevieve slowed down before stepping down and patting her face with a towel.

"Same time tomorrow?" she asked with a friendly smile.

My lips parted before turning up into a smile. "I'd like that."

"Have a good rest of your birthday!" she called with a wave.

A smile crept onto my face as I sped the treadmill up. It was the first time any of the de Loughreys had talked to me like I was a person and not the trash beneath their shoe. Gen had been aloof, but less abrasive than the others. Our conversation really opened a door between us. The more I thought about her, the more I began to wonder why Atticus had such a low opinion of his sister.

The wicked king. A fitting title for such an imposing man.

The slam of a door startled me awake. I wasn't sure when I'd fallen asleep, but by the angle of the sun and the time on my clock, I'd taken a decent-sized siesta after lunch.

The clack of hard soles against the wood floors grew closer, and I sat up in time to watch Atticus step through my doorway. My brow scrunched as I looked to the clock—it wasn't even five.

"Hi," he said, then pulled a beautiful bouquet of calla lilies from behind him.

I gasped and stood, closing in on the soft white petals that held a violet center and were surrounded by sprigs of lavender.

"Happy birthday," he said.

I looked up, our eyes meeting. "Thank you."

I was floored. The bouquet in my hand was so simple, yet so elegantly beautiful. How did he know I loved calla lilies?

He held out his hand. "Come, let's go find a vase to put those in."

"Did you pick these out yourself?" I asked as I slipped my hand in his and attempted to ignore the way my skin lit up. While mentally we were still walled off from each other, or rather he was walled off from me, physically, we'd become more relaxed.

"I did."

When we entered the kitchen, Loreno and Amara were bustling around.

"Happy birthday!" Amara shouted, a huge smile on her face as she skipped over to me and wrapped me in her arms.

"Thank you," I said, surprised, but it still warmed my heart.

When she pulled back, she took note of the flowers in my hand and jumped into action, pulling a vase down from one of the cabinets.

"Come, come," she called, waving me over to one of the sinks. She filled the vase up, then took the flowers from me, snipping the ends before setting them inside.

As she set them on the table, I couldn't help but smile as I thought about how they warmed the space up, giving life to a beautiful but cold room.

When I turned back toward the kitchen, my mouth opened, but I was silenced by a smiling Loreno pushing a cake forward across the island.

"For me?" I stared down at the layered cake. The colors were just like my flowers, with purple at the bottom transitioning to white at the top. The hue of the purple lightened with each little ruffle of frosting that circled the cake. "It's beautiful."

Amara smiled. "Atticus picked the flavors. Chocolate with a hint of lavender, and Swiss meringue buttercream frosting. On top, there are candied violet petals."

I turned back to him. "Really?"

He gave a nod, his expression soft, making my heart speed up.

Amara began singing, Loreno jumping in, and near the end I could hear the deep timbre of Atticus beside me.

I couldn't remember the last time anyone had sung to me, and I smiled at the warmth that filled me.

Once they were done, Loreno cut into the cake and handed me a slice.

A moan left me at the first bite. The cake was moist and rich, and the hint of lavender in the frosting was a wonderful hit of fragrance. In no time I had devoured the whole piece.

"That was so good. Thank you."

"Our pleasure," Loreno said before turning back to his task of preparing dinner.

"I'm going to go change," Atticus said. "Why don't you sit on the balcony and I'll be there in a few minutes?"

I nodded. "All right."

Grabbing a glass of wine, I moved out to the balcony and took in the skyline and the peek of the Hudson River. It was the most relaxing space in the entire condo, and I would miss it when the weather cooled.

Atticus came out with the wine bottle and a glass of his own before sitting in the chair beside me. "I didn't know what to get you as a gift."

"You've given me so much lately, there is no need. Besides, you've also given me access to buy just about anything I could want."

"True, but those were necessities for your new life. Though there is one thing I could give you that money can't buy."

I blinked at him and watched his lips pull up into a smirk, his eyebrows rising.

A groan left me, and my head fell back. "I can buy a little friend to help me with that."

"But skin on skin is so much more enjoyable. Plus, you have the ability to have it now and not wait for delivery."

"Did that kick to the balls not get through that ego of yours?" I asked. That was the problem with all the touching—it created the desire for more touching.

He shrugged. "I'm just offering a solution to your problem."

"Aren't you helpful."

"Quite."

"What's for dinner?" I asked, pulling the subject away from sex.

He took a sip of his drink before responding. "You didn't want to go out, so I had Chef prepare your favorite."

My favorite? Did I even have one? I did love salmon. Really just about anything Loreno made was incredible.

Also, I didn't exactly say I didn't want to go out. Days before, he asked if I wanted a repeat of last year, and I said no. Then he was offering up again tonight.

My body begged me to say yes. A craving that grew deeper every day. It made me regret kissing him when we were at his family home. I was only doing it to get that bitch away, but it set something off and containing it was getting even more difficult.

When I declined, he dropped the subject entirely. Did I *want* to go out? It was a toss-up. On one hand, it was my birthday and I was engaged to the hottest bachelor in the country. On the other, it was my birthday and I was engaged to the hottest bachelor in the country.

Party and have fun, versus lots of people all clamoring for my date. A conundrum to be sure.

What did I want to do for my birthday? Even I didn't know the answer to that. All of my needs were met, desire for anything I wanted fulfilled, and none of the stuff I used to do in my old life was acceptable in my new life.

"Why do you call him Chef and not Loreno?" I asked as I picked at my plate an hour later.

"Because that is his title. It was hard earned, and he deserves the respect it entails." He stopped eating and stared at my plate. "Do you not like it?"

I shrugged. "It's fine. I just…never mind."

He let out a harsh sigh and leaned back. "If you tell me 'never mind,' I will do just that. Seeing as it is your birthday, I will press for more."

"It's good, it's just…" I let out a sigh. "It's my birthday, and you know what I really want? Pizza. A good old New York-style, fold-in-half, slice of pepperoni pizza with mushrooms. And a beer. Some crappy, piss-water beer. And then after I've had my fill and am about to explode, I want a sundae with all the fixings except nuts. And somewhere in there, I want to celebrate with some shots of peach schnapps while playing a game of pool."

He blinked at me. "That is oddly…specific."

I shrugged. "That's what you get when you ask a question about me or about what I want—an answer that you'll probably turn your nose up at."

He was ignoring me, his attention down on his screen.

"Of course you're ignoring me," I said, defeat swallowing me up. The one day of the year I wanted to feel important to somebody, and there was nobody. I swallowed and blinked back the tears threatening to spill. Was this loneliness all I had to look forward to?

"I'm not ignoring you, but the sooner I contact people, the sooner we will have access to all that you described."

"W-what?" I stuttered.

"It's your birthday. If you want a hundred dollars of crap, then you'll get it. Now, this shitty beer—do you prefer bottle, can, or tap?" He looked at me expectantly. That same expression he always wore that was devoid of emotion.

I missed his smile.

Or really, any warmth he directed at me.

But I couldn't stop the warmth that blossomed at his effort to make me happy.

"Bottle."

An hour later, Loreno's wonderfully prepared dinner was in containers in the fridge and a huge pizza box covered the table. My mouth watered at the aroma of freshly cooked dough, gooey cheese, and the slight tang of sauce and pepperoni along with the light earthiness of mushroom.

Jack arrived at the same time with his arms full of ice-cold beer, my schnapps, and a smorgasbord assortment of sundae toppings and flavors.

A low moan left me after my first bite of pizza in *weeks*, which was weeks too long in my book. Atticus regarded me dubiously after my reaction and stared down at the pie.

"Please tell me you've had pizza before."

"In Italy." He pointed down to the box, almost eyeing it like it was some sort of monstrosity. "This is not Italian pizza."

"No, this is New York pizza." I shook my head. "You're a born-and-bred New Yorker, but you really don't act like it a lot of the time."

"How is one supposed to act?"

"Like you don't care about…wait, you have that part down." I racked my brain before embarrassment rose. "Well, I don't know, but you should know staples of your region and this"—I held up my folded slice and took a bite—"is New York pizza." My full mouth mumbled the words, but he understood.

He sighed and lifted a slice, then took a tentative bite. Once he was done, he nodded. "It's not terrible," he conceded.

"It's the best. I think you just don't like to be proven wrong."

"Nobody does. And who says I was wrong?"

"You stuck your nose up at it. That is the same as you saying you thought it was disgusting."

"Did the words leave my lips?"

"No."

"Then I have not been proven wrong."

"You were thinking it, though. Admit it," I goaded him.

His gaze narrowed. "If and when I am ever proven to be incorrect on a topic, I assure you I will own up to it."

I rolled my eyes at him. A man admit he was wrong? Yeah, right. Especially when that man led the largest company in the country.

How did I end up his fiancée again?

While we hadn't been together long, what time we were in the same space was often spent in quiet solitude.

After a few slices, I relaxed back in my chair.

"Had your fill?" he asked.

I took a sip of beer as I rubbed my stomach. "Oh yeah."

He gave a curt nod and then stood. For a moment, I thought maybe that was the end of that and he was going to run away again to his room, but his hand hung in the air between us. I looked from it to his eyes, and he quirked a brow.

"I believe a round of pool with peach schnapps was next on the list."

My chest clenched, and I slid my hand in his as I stood. Why was it that on my birthday he could be caring and put forth effort, but no other day?

As we passed by the counter, he grabbed the bottle and then stopped at the cabinets to pull down some glasses, which he handed to me.

"Where are we going?" I asked, trying to ignore the warmth of his hand.

"I thought you'd explored all the common floors?"

I nodded. I had, and that was when it clicked. It had only been a glance into the game area in those first few days, but in the center there was a beautifully carved pool table. Once off the elevator, he pulled me through the large double doors, and there it was.

Large lion heads were carved into the dark-stained wooden legs, and on the side, in the middle, was the de Loughrey family crest. Deep red felt covered the top, and along a nearby wall sat a rack full of cues.

On a nearby table, Atticus sat the bottle of schnapps down and I followed with the glasses. He released my hand, and I hated the immediate disappointment of missing his touch. After pouring two glasses, he handed me one.

"I know this birthday is very different from your last, but I am pleased to be spending it in your company once again." He held up his glass. Our eyes met, and I sucked in a breath at the intensity in his blue depths. His expression was as stoic as ever, but inside him was a fire that I longed to feel. "Happy birthday, Ophelia."

I smiled at him before tipping my glass back. The burn of the schnapps raced down my throat while the peach flavoring tingled on my tongue.

Atticus's face scrunched up and he gave the bottle a very, "What the fuck is this shit," look that made me laugh before pouring more.

"It gets better," I said as I handed him a full glass again.

"I highly doubt that. Are you certain this is okay for human consumption? Should there be a poison warning on it somewhere?"

That made me throw my head back in laughter. "Hey, I lived off this stuff."

"I definitely need to introduce you to some good spirits."

My whole body warmed, and I couldn't keep the smile from

my face as I turned to the table. Atticus pulled me over to the wall to pick a cue.

"Eight ball? Nine ball? One-pocket?" he asked as he rubbed the chalk block on the tip.

"Huh?"

"What game are we playing?"

My eyes widened. Was there more than one? "Umm....solids and stripes?"

"That would be eight ball."

"I'm about to get my ass handed to me, aren't I?"

A chuckle left him. "Have another drink. Maybe that will help."

"It helps in darts!"

His eyes widened in horror. "Drunk with a sharp object being thrown? No matter how much you plead, I will decline."

"Spoilsport."

"You would hit me out of spite."

"Maybe."

I followed his idea and poured another drink while he racked up the balls.

"Birthday girl is first," he said with a bow, his arm extended toward the table.

I blew out a breath as I leaned over the edge of the table with my arm extended, the neck of the cue resting on my fingers with my pointer finger looped over the top as I lined it up with the cue ball.

"It's been a while," I said as I began to wonder why I thought it was a good idea.

I pulled back on the cue, then pushed it forward. The cue ball rocketed forward, surprising me as it slammed into the tip of the pyramid and sent balls scattering across the felt. The satisfying thunk of the red seven ball against the edge before falling into the pocket had me cheering.

"Solids!" I threw my hands up in the air, laughter pouring from me. It was infectious, and a smile crossed Atticus's normally stern, handsome features.

"Just because it is your birthday, don't expect me to go easy one you."

"I don't think backing down from a challenge is even in your DNA."

"Probably not."

With that, he proceeded to kick my ass. He won, with me only sinking three balls. The next game we made a wager—one shot for every ball your opponent sinks.

When he scored two at once on his first shot he declared half shots, or as he said, I wasn't going to make it to the end of the game.

Again, he won.

"You cheat," I said.

"It's a good thing you ate a lot of pizza, otherwise you would be on your ass instead of lazily smiling at me."

I shrugged. "Happy drunk."

He tucked a lock of hair behind my ear. "I like it."

If my cheeks weren't already nice and rosy from the alcohol, they were after his intimate touch. We were still so far apart, but I felt that the night was bringing us closer together.

"Come. I want to show you something I think you might enjoy."

I slipped my hand in his, warmth spreading through me at the simple touch. It made me realize I'd begun to miss that natural connection, and I tightened my hold to soak it in for as long as I could.

It wasn't the first time he'd taken my hand, but it was the first time when my barriers were down and I allowed myself to feel him, if even just for a few short hours.

"I don't know if you've seen this are yet, but I thought you might like this," he said.

He pulled me into the theater, another area I'd just poked my head into simply because I didn't know how it worked. Inside was a stadium-seating layout with a row of beautiful black leather tufted recliners in a one-two-one setting, creating a loveseat in the middle.

He pulled a tablet off the wall as I plopped down into one of the seats.

"This tablet controls everything in this room from the lights to the sound. It also shows you everything that is available to view, which is pretty much everything."

I looked at the screen, my mouth dropping open at the "New Releases" tab and the summer blockbusters that hadn't even been released yet.

"This is amazing. Do you really have that?" I asked, pointing to one of the newest Marvel movies. It didn't come out for two more months.

"Yes."

"How?"

He caught my eye. "We're de Loughreys."

"So you just get everything beforehand?"

He nodded. "At least when it comes to movies. It helps that we own a few studios."

"Seriously?"

He sighed and shook his head. "Are you ever going to finish the folio?"

I glared up at him, but then began laughing, my face planting into the side of his arm. "I've tried, it's just so boring. And even with all that I've read, I've retained so little because have I mentioned how boring it is?"

"My life and family are boring?"

"Oh no, your family is…some kind of soap-opera drama, but that thing is so dry."

"What have you learned?"

"That you need a better recorder of your history."

"Besides that."

"Oh, well…that you're kind of amazing. You have more accomplishments before the age of six than I've had in my entire life," I said, my high wearing off as that fact sunk in. "After my dad died, I was really lost. Then my mom married Lou, and I spent my time just trying to get out of there and stay away from him."

"Stay away from him?"

I nodded. "Lou drinks. A lot. Way more than I did tonight, and he's not a happy drunk. He never liked me, but get some booze in him and he hated the sight of me."

Atticus's jaw clenched, and I reached up to smooth the tightness away.

"I learned fast. Mom told me, she warned me, that if I didn't want to get hit, to stay away when he was like that. If I messed up and he hit me, Mom told me it was my fault. That I should have noticed and known to keep from his view."

"Your *mother* said that to you? Rather than keep you safe, she blamed you for upsetting her husband? Her own daughter?" There was so much anger pouring out of him that all I could do was nod. I sucked in a breath at the feel of his fingers against my cheek. "You never have to worry about him or being struck again. I promise you that."

I shook my head. "You can't promise that."

He gripped my chin and tilted my head back until our eyes met. "I will protect you, Ophelia. You are mine."

A heat enveloped me when he called me his with the slight gravel in his voice.

Being all alone with him, saying such things, only seemed to heighten the attraction, the pull that always seemed to circulate between us. I reached up and ran my fingers against his lips, then pressed them to my own as an indirect kiss that pooled the warmth of desire between my thighs. When I moved my gaze from his lips to his eyes, the fire inside me roared to life.

Why did I say no sex? It was something I was sorely regretting at that moment. It would be an act I would regret in the morning, but right then, all I wanted was for him to touch me.

Suddenly he turned his head and stood, leaving me staring up at him.

He held out his hand. "Come. There are still ice cream sundaes to be made."

Despite his sudden cool attitude, the heat of his hand soothed me.

"Oh, my God, I have a great idea," I said as we walked to the elevators.

"And what is that, my dear?"

"Put the peach schnapps *into* the ice cream."

"I think that would be a terrible idea," he said with a chuckle, a small smile playing on his lips.

"You're so pretty when you smile," I said with a dreamy sigh.

"Pretty, huh?"

I nodded, then my brow furrowed. "You're so unbelievably...I can't say pretty again, but the words are gone, but you are so pretty."

"And I think you've had enough of that awful peach stuff."

We returned back up to the penthouse, and I looked over all the goodies Jack had procured. All sorts of candies and cookies, chocolate, fruit, and caramel sauces, maraschino cherries, whipped cream, fresh fruit slices, and even some marshmallow fluff.

I sat down on one of the stools, salivating as Atticus pulled the ice cream out of the freezer and grabbed a few bowls and spoons. It was quite possibly the first time I'd ever seen him do anything in the kitchen other than eat, so I was a little shocked he knew where anything was.

I bit down on my lip in an effort to contain my smile as I watched him scoop large globs into the bowls before handing one to me. The assortment of toppings was so extensive I didn't know if I would be able to decide, so I broke the bowl up into three sections. On one, I added in cookie bits and chocolate, a little marshmallow. On another, some fruit sauce, fresh fruits, and chocolate shavings. The third consisted of every type of candy, whipped cream, and a cherry on top.

He chuckled as he looked at my bowl.

"I couldn't decide," I said defensively, then dove into my concoction.

It was kinda the best of worlds, though when I got near the end, the sections had melted together and left a strange combination of bites. Not bad, just not exactly the best.

When we were done, he set our bowls in the sink and when he returned, I threw my arms around his shoulders and pressed my face into his neck. He seemed a bit confused and hesitated to wrap his arms around me, but finally did, and I sank into his warmth.

"Thank you for tonight. I know it wasn't much, but it was exactly what I wanted and needed."

His arms flexed, pulling me tighter against him. "You're welcome. Happy birthday."

The longer I stayed in his arms the more the electricity charged between us. Slowly I pulled away, my lips slipping across his jaw as I leaned back. Our eyes met, and my fingers flexed while the attraction grew, burning deep inside me.

My inhibitions were subdued by the drinks, and all I wanted was to feel his lips against mine, his skin to mine.

His lips ghosted mine, and then he let out a groan as he stepped back, my arms slipping from him. "Goodnight, Ophelia."

"Atticus?"

His jaw flexed, and he shook his head. "No sex," he hissed. "Your condition."

The warmth was gone, replaced by a steaming anger beneath the surface. Then he disappeared down the hall, leaving me standing alone in the kitchen. I jumped at the slamming of his door and slumped back down onto the stool.

Despite the abrupt ending, it had been the most fun I'd had in a year. A harsh laugh left me at the thought.

Atticus de Loughrey—pain in my ass 364 days a year, knight in shining armor one day a year. The evening wasn't some grand revelation. Our interactions weren't going to change, but I appreciated the one night where we weren't constantly dancing around each other.

The one night I could just be me.

TWENTY

OPHELIA

Almost a month had passed since we signed the contract, and the announcement was everywhere. One of the world's most eligible bachelors, Atticus de Loughrey, CEO of the de Loughrey Corporation, was off the market.

And I was freaking the fuck out.

After my birthday, Atticus returned to his MO of minimal interaction and keeping me at arm's length as much as he could. Even more so, it felt like.

Which was why I was stomping back and forth in front of the muted television screen that held our faces. Pictures from our engagement session, my college ID, photos from who knows where. They were already digging into my life and my past for a tabloid news story.

"Why are you second guessing yourself?" Atticus asked, his jaw twitching in annoyance.

I paced back and forth in front of him. He sat in the middle of the sofa in lounge pants and a white undershirt—a level of dressed down I never thought I'd see him in, and I had to admit I liked it. Then again, it was his house, and it was seven in the morning on a Sunday.

"Because it's out there now. My little bubble of nobody knowing or caring who the hell I am is shattered. They're going to be digging into my life." They already had.

"And?"

"And what if they find something?"

His lips formed a thin line, and he sighed. "Ophelia, I've been through your history. Thoroughly. There is nothing there that is scandalous."

"There could be."

One of his eyebrows lifted. "Is there something I missed?"

I threw my hands up in the air. "I don't know!"

He stood and walked past me into the kitchen. "This is annoying and not worth my time."

"That's what you have to say about my concerns?" I asked, following him.

"If I felt they were valid."

"Great. Nice to know my emotions are invalid," I seethed. The whole situation was his idea, so I felt he could at least reassure me, but instead he was spoiling for a fight. It could be the lack of coffee.

He rubbed his forehead. "Was being your emotional support part of the contract?"

Oh, how I wanted to slap him. "Is being a decent human being to the woman you dragged into this that difficult for you?"

"You weren't kicking and screaming when I slipped that ring on your finger."

It wasn't the reaction I was expecting. Maybe he woke up on the wrong side of the bed. That was the morning vibe, and I hated it.

Though not as much as I hated myself for still wanting a taste of him. And fuck, I liked his anger because all I could imagine was him directing that energy into pinning me against the wall and fucking me until I couldn't walk.

He had reduced me to a quivering mess when he was near. A mess that wanted nothing more than to feel him stretching me. Not good.

"You are such a fucking asshole!" I growled, both in frustration at him and myself for letting my hormones take over for a moment.

"So I'm told. Look, I warned you, Ophelia, that this would happen.

For the last month you've been safely concealed, but that is gone. You must accept it and learn to live with it, because this is your life."

"For the next five years," I grumbled.

"No. For life."

I blinked up at him. "What?"

"You think when we divorce they will suddenly leave you alone? You haven't even begun to live under their scrutiny yet. This was just a tidbit. It will ebb and flow like the tide, but when we divorce, a tsunami will crash upon the shores just as it is now. Their curiosity will be reignited."

"Why do they care?"

"I don't know. All I do know is that they will follow you, bait you, but you must remain calm and reserved. Don't give them any fodder. There is a reason I don't go out often."

"A reason for a curtained-off booth." I was beginning to understand his desire for seclusion.

"Exactly. From now on, you are not to ever leave without Michael or one of the others driving you. This will calm down, but it will take time. For now, be on guard. And for all that is holy, don't do anything stupid."

I spent the rest of the day stupidly surfing the internet, reading articles and watching videos. The warped way people chose to view me was unnerving. They knew nothing about me.

Eventually I fell asleep on the couch, the TV playing in the background and my laptop open with the headline: DE LOUGHREY HEAD TO WED WAITRESS.

When I awoke the next morning, silence greeted me. Atticus had probably turned the TV off, and he was already gone. Not that there was really a way to tell. He came and went as he pleased, saying nothing, though there was a blanket laid over me that wasn't there before.

My muscles were sore and stiff from the couch, and I decided the best cure was a run to work it all out. When I arrived after some breakfast, the gym was empty. It wasn't often that I found another de Loughrey working out, and ninety-nine percent of the time it was Gen—we seemed to be on the same schedule.

Though one time as I was walking in, my shoulder slammed into the arm of Hamilton, who simply sneered at me before continuing to the elevators. Once when I left the pool, I caught a glimpse of what I assumed were the twins—Silas and Atlas.

I'd barely gotten the treadmill going when the door opened and Gen stepped in.

"Morning," I said with a smile, happy to not be alone. It was then that it hit me just how lonely I'd become if *any* interaction was welcomed. That, and I was actually really starting to like Genevieve.

"Morning. How is it living in the limelight?" she asked with a grin.

My expression dropped. "Terrible. Is your brother always such an elusive asshole?"

"Yes."

We both laughed at that, and it felt good after my strained days with Atticus.

After a thirty-minute run, we moved over to the Pilates reformers and completed a one-hour online class. I hadn't felt that strong or that in shape in my life. My already-straight figure was still straight, but I was gaining some tone in my muscles.

And my ass was popping.

Maybe I'd find some way to flaunt it in front of Atticus since I remembered how much he liked it.

"You want to come up for lunch?"

"Not if he's there."

"He's not. He was gone when I woke, and I didn't see him after the morning yesterday. I really think he just wanted to get away from me."

"Things are going that well?"

I shrugged. "I don't know what I was thinking when I said yes." It felt good to be able to talk to someone about how I felt after staying silent for so long. I'd confided in her that Atticus and I were basically a marriage of convenience, but I didn't tell her about the contract.

"That he's worth a whole lot of money?"

I shook my head. "I don't care about the money."

She reached for my arm and halted my steps. "Be real with me.

You do care about the money. Everyone does. The question is—what does it mean to you?"

Thinking about it, she was right. As much as I wanted to say I didn't care about the money, I obviously did, as I thought about how ten million dollars would change my life. But that was five years out. I didn't expect the amount of money Atticus was spending on me to prepare me to stand beside him. Just the weight of my student debt no longer hanging around my neck was a relief our agreement afforded.

"I care about it in that it got me out of my crappy situation. That I wouldn't have to worry about scraping by anymore. That maybe I could have a breather and figure out what I want to do."

"So he was a lifeline."

"I guess."

"It's okay to admit it."

"I just don't want people to think I'm with him just for the money." It was more than the money, right? It was the ghost of a single night that had me imagining fantasies of what life with him *could* be.

"Why do you care?"

"It's bad enough people are already saying so much shit about me." I'd turned it off that morning for fear of smashing it when they played the song "Gold Digger" behind their snarky remarks.

"And?"

I scrunched my brow. "Don't you care what people think about you?"

She shook her head. "I make them think what I want them to think. That way if I do something wild, they just shrug."

"And here I thought you were just a spoiled little bitch."

"Meow, little kitty. And you would think right—I am a spoiled little bitch, and I own it."

I smiled at her. "You're also the nicest person in your family."

"Can't be the hostess if you're not friendly. Then nobody would come party."

Oddly, she had a point.

"Tell you what—I'm going to take a shower, and then I'll come up and we'll order some lunch and chill on that veranda he has."

I nodded. "That sounds good. I'm going to do the same. I'll leave the door unlocked so you can come on in."

After a shower, I slid on a pair of shorts and a tank top, ready to see if we had anything for lunch. While I waited for Gen, my phone went off.

My mom's number flashed across the screen, and I answered without a pause.

"Hi, Mom."

"Not your mom," Lou's gruff voice replied.

I froze and thought about hanging up. "What do you want?"

"What you owe me."

"I don't owe you anything, Lou," I spat.

His breath was harsh through the phone. "Listen here, you little bitch. You're going to get me fifty grand, or I go to the press."

In the background, I heard my mother's voice say, "A hundred grand."

I ground my teeth together as the last thread to my mother frayed before snapping. Any relationship we might have had was dead. She was as shitty as her worthless husband.

"A hundred grand," he said, his tone loud as he tried to inflect force into it.

"Go to the press with what?" I asked with little inflection. He was out of his fucking mind if he thought I was going to play his game. He wasn't getting a dime, and I wasn't going to allow him to bully me.

"The media would eat up little miss goody-goody's past. It's filled with all sorts of scandalous things."

"You're full of shit."

"Maybe, but they don't fact check that shit. They'll eat it up, especially with all the photographs I have of you. Especially this one of you kissing your high school boyfriend, Jimmy Varetti. Wasn't he just convicted of murder? He's not going to marry you with that kinda bloody baggage tainting his pristine image."

The blood drained from my face.

"By your silence, I'm guessing we have an understanding. Now, be a good little bitch and be useful for something."

The line went dead, and I slammed my phone onto the bed as I let out a scream. It bounced, hitting the headboard before settling at the base of my pillow.

Tears filled my eyes as dread settled in my stomach. There were no skeletons in my closet, Atticus even said there weren't, but there were. Did he just think they didn't matter?

The move wasn't surprising from Lou, but it was from my mom. I was done with her.

It all crashed down on me—the anxiety, the loss, and the fear—and tears fell from my eyes as it washed over me. I fell back down onto the bed and curled up in the middle as I let out a sob.

"Are you okay?" Gen asked as she stood in front of me.

I didn't know how long I'd been crying, but it started to abate. I sniffled and wiped away the tears. "No."

"Do you need a drink?"

I let out a laugh. "Fuck, yes."

"Good. It's a deal, then."

"Wait, deal? What kind of deal?"

She disappeared into my closet. "Gen?"

A moment later she popped out, a Cheshire grin on her face. "Drinks and dancing, just what the doctor ordered."

I tilted my head and shook it slightly. "I don't know about that. It's three in the afternoon. Besides, Attic—"

"Atticus can go fuck himself," she said, cutting me off. "Besides, he isn't here, and even if he was, he wouldn't be able to help. By the time we get ready, it's going to be at least six. Booze and letting loose for once will help tremendously. Your spirits will be lifted in no time, and you will forget all about whatever has caused the waterworks pouring from your eyes."

Atticus had steered me away from getting close to Gen, but she was right—I did need to let loose. I needed a break on the outside from being the perfect little de Loughrey in training, and away from the reminder of the shit parents I'd had for the last twenty years.

"Grab whatever you need, and let's go to my place. There is nothing in that closet for you, but there is plenty in mine."

The moment we were in Gen's condo, she headed straight into the master bedroom and into the massive closet. I was in a bit of shock about her place, thinking it might be a mess, but it was in perfect order and pristine shape.

Gen reappeared after a few minutes in her closet and tossed a small scrap of clothing at me. "Here, wear this."

I stared down at the dress. It was skimpier than anything I'd ever wear. It was short, and had a cutout, asymmetrical one-shoulder design with an envelope hem. It was a coral color, not my usual.

And I kinda liked it.

The music was ear splitting, but it quieted my thoughts. For the first time since my birthday, I was genuinely happy and enjoying myself. The drinks were strong, and my inhibitions lowered as worry flew out the window. I quickly found that I actually liked my future sister-in-law as a person. She came across as a spoiled party princess, but she possessed so much more under that tough exterior, and now I'd started to figure her out.

It didn't matter that I knew none of her friends—they welcomed me. More than one handed me a drink, and as my hips swayed to the beat, I felt a body press against mine.

Time had no meaning as I lost myself.

To the music.

To the drinks.

To the sway of the beat.

I was free and flying and smiling.

Then I felt it. The intensity of a gaze I knew very well.

I stopped dancing and opened my eyes, the smile fading from my face as an angry god stared me down.

Atticus was wickedly gorgeous in his fury.

TWENTY-ONE

ATTICUS

I shook with rage at the photo that showed up on my phone. A photo of Ophelia dancing with Gen in a dress that was too short and too tight, with some asshole's arm around her waist, had me on my feet and racing toward the elevator.

I studied it to keep from punching the wall as the cab descended. She held a drink in her hand, her hair matted against her glistening face, eyes unfocused.

I told her to stay away from Genevieve, and on today of all days when the world was hyper-focused on her, she did the worst thing possible. For all the tamping down I'd done, for all the information I'd had hidden or erased, and it was all for naught.

She would be scrutinized even harder, dissected, and labeled in the same category as Genevieve.

Damien was waiting for me at the front door with the car running.

"Go," I said as soon as I slammed the door shut.

There was no need to say more. He was the one who forwarded me the photo, after all.

Ten minutes later, we pulled up to the front of the club.

"Meet me around back."

"What about security?"

"Jason is in there, correct?" I asked, needing verification that Genevieve's bodyguard was where he was supposed to be.

He nodded. "Michael is also in the background."

"Pull him when I get her out."

"Yes, sir."

I exited the car and strode toward the entrance. The bouncer didn't even attempt to slow my pace, giving me a nod as he held the door open. Lights flashing, music thumping, and a crowd going wild—everything I hated about clubs.

Luckily, finding my sister and my fiancée wouldn't be difficult—look for the largest group of people. Genevieve better be hiding from me.

Anger rolled through me, a fire raging as I pushed my way through the crowd. When I made my way past the barrier, I found my Ophelia dancing with a blinding smile, in a dress that left little to the imagination, with a strange man grinding against her.

I wanted to hate-fuck the hell out of her. Turned on and angry were a bad combination. It was bad enough my anger was at explosive levels. I knew what would happen when I let it out.

She stopped, her eyes finding mine. The smile faded, and her alcohol fuzzy eyes widened.

"Atticus," she said, my name rolling off her tongue in a delicious way. It only made my need to possess her greater.

I stepped forward, glaring down at her. Fuck! In that moment, I hated her for what I was going to be forced to do.

My attention shot to the imbecile behind her and his hand that rested on her hip.

"Get your fucking hand off my fiancée before I break it."

His eyes widened, and he stepped back. She never even glanced back at him, what little awareness she held remained focused on me.

Looming over her, I grabbed hold of her arm. "What the fuck do you think you're doing?" I seethed, not waiting for an answer as I turned and pulled her through the throng of people.

"I was just spending time with Gen," she said as she tried to free her arm from my grip—a grip I was trying desperately to tame in as my anger was at the point of exploding.

Desperation to hit the man who dared to lay a finger on her burned in my veins. I wanted to wipe him from her skin and imprint my touch until she collapsed from exhaustion.

A moment later, we crashed through the back door where Damien was waiting.

"Atticus, you're hurting me."

I spun toward her and pulled her close. "I don't fucking care." I roughly pushed her into the back of the car and climbed in after her before the car sped off toward home.

"Ow," she whined as she rubbed at her arm. There were dark imprints from my hand, and a wave of guilt rushed through me. I tamped it down before it became anything more than a fleeting notion. She needed to learn, and I was going to make tonight the example.

Fuck her for making me.

The ride from the club to home lasted an eternity as my rage simmered. I clenched and unclenched my fists to keep my tightly wound muscles calm and my mouth from expelling the vile vitriol that was to come.

When we arrived in the parking garage, she got out and followed behind me. I'd already exploded in public once, and I was not about to make that mistake again. Once we were home, she tipsily walked down toward the great room, but I grabbed her again and spun her, pinning her against the wall.

"Explain."

Her eyes were wide but unfocused as she stared up at me, her lips parted. "I was just blowing off some steam with Gen."

"Any phrase that includes you being with Gen needs to be ripped from your vocabulary. You are *never* to go out with her again. Do you understand me?"

Her brow scrunched, and she pushed at my chest. "No, I don't. Why is it bad that I spend time with her? She's your sister."

"Because Gen brings nothing but bad press, and tomorrow morning your photo is going to be plastered all over the tabloid and gossip columns. That *my* fiancée was letting loose with the de Loughrey bad girl, and I guarantee it will be the worst photograph you have ever taken. Your image is my image, and I cannot and will not have it mixed up with Gen more than it already is."

"Oh," was all she said, her gaze drifting to my mouth. She reached up and unsteadily dragged her fingertips down my lips. "You know, you're sexy when you're angry."

My lip curled up. "As much as I might want to take some of my anger out on your pussy right now, you're drunk." Grabbing her arm again, I hauled her to her room. "Drink some water and go to bed."

Once she was inside and the door was closed, I entered my office, heading straight for the bar. I poured myself a scotch and swallowed it down in two large gulps, then refilled the glass and repeated.

I'd told her to stay away from Gen. It baffled me that she even went out with her. I was going to be spending the next morning trying to cover up this disaster. If she'd just been one of Gen's friends, it wouldn't be an issue. The problem was that her finger held my ring we had been announced, and the vultures were looking for any vulnerability to attack.

And she'd presented her jugular.

Now I was going to be forced to show her why I was called the wicked king.

"Fuck," I hissed.

I knew our arrangement was difficult for her to acclimate to, but I'd kept myself at arm's length on purpose.

Every day with her weakened me more and more, and I'd begun to regret my decision. Every encounter made me want her more. She'd opened up a part of me I never knew was there—the crack that started the night we met. The one she squeezed her way into.

And in the morning, I was going to kill any notion in her mind that I was a person she could care about.

No, in the morning she would be treated like any de Loughrey who screwed up.

And she would hate me.

A heaviness settled in my chest.

I should have chosen Bridget or Antonia to avoid all this. They were upper class and were familiar with the world in which I circulated.

I wouldn't have to be the bad guy to Ophelia. I could have kept my longing at a distance without her ever knowing she affected me, and in return, she would never be hurt by me.

Things were already in motion, and I needed another set of eyes. After throwing back the rest of my drink, I dialed Hugo's number.

After talking to Hugo, I went to bed but only slept about two hours when my phone started pinging with notifications, pulling me from the warmth of my bed.

"Fuck," I hissed as I glanced over the screen. "Guess I'm getting up."

The damage was already filtering in. As I suspected, they found the worst representation of her as they could—hair wild, eyes drooped, drink in hand, mouth open, at an angle, some douche behind her, and her fucking ring front and center.

After a shower and dressing, I headed down the hall.

Upon entering the kitchen, I was surprised to find Ophelia up and sitting casually at the island, sipping from a mug and chatting with a maid who was putting away dishes.

"Leave," I told the maid, who didn't hesitate to set down what she was doing and walk to the elevator.

"Good morning," Ophelia said. Her tone held a repentant edge, but I couldn't let it sway me.

I couldn't look at her. I hated myself for what I was about to do, and I hated her for making me do it.

The next words out of my mouth were filled with a venom edge that sat like a stone in my stomach. "You're not to leave the building."

Out of the corner of my eye, I caught her jump off the stool. "What? Why?"

I turned on her. "Because I said so." I stepped forward, towering over her. "You forget that I am the head of this family, and that includes you. Last night, you fucked up, and now you have to pay the price."

"But—"

"No fucking buts, Ophelia! Just as I told you last night, if you can even remember, your face is plastered all over every gossip website, magazine, and news show. You were even on this morning's news. I fucking had to fire the producer who put that through."

She blinked at me. "What?"

"We own the news station who plastered your drunken face. A station that knows any bad press against the de Loughreys is strictly forbidden. Five people in total lost their jobs today. Because of you. And they won't be the only ones."

Her face paled, eyes wide as she sat down. "I didn't know."

"No, you didn't, because you've never fucking done the *one* thing I told you to do—read the binder. It's not just me in there, but the history of the family as well as every business we own, and at the back is a fucking basic code of public conduct."

Fuck! Why did she have to make me be an asshole to her?

"Actions have consequences, and when you're a de Loughrey, it's other people who are hurt the most."

"You didn't have to fi—"

"*Yes*, I did." My voice boomed out, echoing around the walls. She flinched at the sound and shrunk back. "You need to absorb the fact that you are no longer some girl from Brooklyn. You will never be her again. Even after this is all over, wherever you go, you will still be a de Loughrey."

Her eyes were filled with tears, and it tore at me. I fucking hated that it affected me so. That she had me caring so much for her to feel guilt and anguish. But feel them I did and it sliced at my heart, an organ I wasn't sure I even possessed. Nevertheless, if I had learned anything, it was not to discount the effect Ophelia had on me, undermining my hard-won control and revealing a tender center, even if only to me.

Looking at her right now, into her large, wide doe eyes that beseeched me, I knew that I had to keep it that way.

"Now fucking do as you're told and stay put so that I can do damage control."

With that, I turned and headed back down the hall. I heard the scrape of the stool against the floor as she followed after me.

"Atticus," she called out.

I stopped, but didn't turn. "What?"

"He threatened me."

I snapped around to look at her. The tears that filled her eyes flowed freely down her cheeks, and she looked completely distraught.

"Who?" I asked as the darkness came to the surface even more. Whomever threatened her was going to regret it.

"Lou. My stepfather."

"What did he want?"

"A hundred thousand dollars."

I gave a curt nod. "Done." I continued on.

"Done? What do you mean, 'done'?" she asked, her feet tapping on the wood floors as she chased after me.

"Meaning he will get his trivial money and keep his fucking mouth shut."

"He won't! You don't know him. He'll say it's done, but he'll just keep coming back."

"He will."

"Attic—"

I turned to her, jaw clenched tight. "He will, because if he steps even the tiniest bit out of line, if he even breathes your name, he will wish he never met your mother."

"What do you mean?"

I stepped closer, my gaze connecting to hers. "You still have no understanding what lengths I take in order to safeguard the de Loughrey family name. The lives I've ruined. I have a reputation as the wicked king for a reason. By any means necessary, I *destroy*."

"Destroy?"

I loomed over her to drive my point home, my glare never leaving her eyes. "I tear things apart bit by bit. Leave the corpse bleeding on the ground as they beg me for help, but I take the knife and continue to shred until there is nothing left. And if I am especially angry, I move on to the family and reputation. You do not cross me, Ophelia."

Her lips parted, and if it hadn't happened earlier, it was happening before me now. I watched the switch in the way she looked upon me. The fear and confusion in regard to the man before her. A man she thought she knew at least a little.

Any attachment to me broke. Any positive emotions she bestowed upon me leached out, leaving me cold and empty.

There was no reason to wait for a verbal response that would alter the emotional one that just took place. It wasn't going to come.

The elevator pinged, and I stepped into the cab.

"Don't leave. I'll be back later."

The doors slid closed, but her eyes never found mine.

TWENTY-TWO

OPHELIA

It felt like the world stopped spinning and everything came to a screeching halt.

I wasn't sure how long I stared at the elevator doors after they closed. A numbness had spread through me, and the feeling of a large stone sat heavy in my stomach. I was frozen, unable to move, unable to think.

The man that left me standing there after him—*that* was the real Atticus de Loughrey.

I knew he could be cold, harsh, but I thought I'd gotten to know him over the last month. I was dead wrong. That was the kid-gloves version, but the man I woke to was the wicked king.

A remorseless man with a dangerous tongue.

A dark ruler striking down any opponent.

I stared at my reflection in the shiny steel doors, wondering how I'd gotten there. To that exact moment.

What the fuck had I gotten myself into? While it was a question I'd been asking myself for over a month, it never rang as true as it did right at that moment.

When he spoke, it was like a siren was going off inside, begging me not to proceed. The cold rolling off him surrounded me, but what froze me was the dangerous flare of anger that simmered below the surface waiting to break free. The target wasn't me, but that eruption would engulf, spreading like fire until the surface was burned to ash.

My chest clenched at the sudden loss, but I wasn't sure what the loss was. Of the man I thought I knew? Of the life I thought I was living?

One thing was abundantly clear—the situation was not what I signed up for, and I had to get away. I couldn't be with that man, with the one who just left me standing there feeling cold and more alone than I ever did before I met him.

I couldn't live like that. I wouldn't.

Running to my room, I pulled out my suitcase and an old duffle bag. In them I began to toss in *my* clothes, leaving anything he had purchased where they were. I continued on, doing the same with my shoes and jewelry, toiletries and anything else I could fit in the bags.

Anything given to me by Atticus was left in place. Every article of clothing, makeup, piece of jewelry, shoes—all of it was left, along with whatever I couldn't fit in my bags.

It didn't matter. All that mattered was that I left the gilded halls of his palace. I didn't belong. I knew I didn't belong, yet still I tried. For him.

But it was all a waste.

I went in blind and naive, but I would leave with the rose-colored glasses shattered and the longing for him tattered on the ground.

Agreeing was a mistake, one that I would rectify by doing what I did best—leaving as quickly as possible.

My stomach twisted as I entered the kitchen. Many of the few good memories of him were there, including my birthday. I shook my head to clear my mind and continued with my goal of grabbing some bottles of water and a few snacks. It would get me by for a little while until I found a place to stay.

That thought stopped me in my tracks.

What was I going to do? Where was I going to go? I had nothing that wasn't from Atticus, my old bank account emptied and gone.

Was my life really filled with so little? No friends to count on, no family, and no job. For a brief moment I considered hopping on a bus down to my grandfather's house in Florida, but I didn't even know where he lived.

Or even if he was still alive.

My mother cut off all contact with my father's family after the funeral, refusing to let me see them or even talk to them, to the point they eventually stopped trying.

The only option I had was to pull some money off the credit card and use it to find a cash-only hotel. That would be the only thing I took from Atticus.

And my phone. I considered leaving it, but then remembered I probably wouldn't be able to get out of the building without it, thanks to the tracking tech within the walls.

With one last glance around, I let out a sigh and then headed for the elevator with my arms crammed with bags—my rolling suitcase, backpack, and two duffels.

The lobby was my next hurdle. There was always someone at the concierge desk.

"Good morning, Miss Evans," Amy said with a smile. At least, I thought her name was Amy.

I gave a tight-lipped smile and a nod before continuing on.

"Would you like me to call Michael for you?"

"No," I said a little too forcefully. "Thank you, though."

Once outside, the familiar hum of the city settled me and I headed quickly across the street and as far away from Olympus Tower as I could get. A few blocks away, I pulled out a few thousand dollars in cash—enough to help me along before I could find a place. I then pulled out the sim card from my phone, threw it on the ground, and stomped on it. Minutes later, I was struggling down the steps to the subway and boarding the first train that arrived.

The destination didn't matter. The only important thing was distancing myself from the rule of the wicked king.

TWENTY-THREE

ATTICUS

The hoops and contracts every single employee had to go through were simple compared to those pertaining to people brought into the family. We hadn't even gotten to the complexity of our prenuptial agreement, but I'd already worked most of it out with Rhys.

Now, I was forced to make it even more complicated. I'd been so giving, wanting to protect her, but there had to be consequences. She had to know.

A slew of photos and video were scattered across my monitors. Hugo and Damien had the IT security team working on getting rid of all they could, but the damage was done.

We hadn't even had our first public appearance, and now we would be entering society with a stigma.

"How did it go?" Rhys asked as he entered my office unannounced.

I glared up at him. "How do you think it went?"

He settled into one of the chairs in front of my desk. "She hates you, then?"

"She would have eventually anyway. I was stupid to think I could keep her from seeing that side of me."

"The wicked king strikes again. Breaking hearts and lives."

"I shouldn't have chosen her."

"No, you shouldn't have," Hamilton said as he entered, taking the chair next to Rhys.

"What is this?" I asked, surprised to see my little brother joining the conversation.

"Do you actually have feelings for her?" he asked.

"If I didn't, I would have gone the obvious route." At least Bridget and Antonia knew how to behave. But while I might not verbally acknowledge my feelings for Ophelia yet, I couldn't deny them. I was a good poker player, and everyone had a tell. If anyone knew mine, Rhys did, and he wouldn't waste a single second calling me out, especially with Hamilton being the only audience.

"She was too much trouble from the beginning. Just let her go."

Rhys remained quiet, seemingly interested in our volley.

I clenched my fingers into a fist. "I can't."

"Can't, or won't?"

I narrowed my gaze at Hamilton. "Both."

Rhys shook his head. "You never should have taken her to bed that night."

"It was only supposed to be one night. Maybe two."

"But then she became your waitress," Rhys said with a smirk.

Hamilton looked between us. "Waitress? What?"

"You didn't notice him suddenly going to 130 Degrees multiple times a week for lunch on his own?" Rhys asked.

Hamilton shook his head. "Why do I care where he goes to lunch?"

"Well, he went there to see her."

I quirked a brow at Rhys. "Since when do you know so much of my business?"

"Since I asked Hugo for information about the girl I was writing a contract for."

I shook my head. "Fucking Hugo. He shouldn't have."

"He doesn't just work for you, cousin. Besides, I was curious why her name suddenly came back up after so long."

"At this point, you should just let her go," Hamilton said with a wave of his hand.

"Why the hell are you so dead set against her, Hamilton? Are you conspiring with Father? Trying to push me to Amelia Harris?" Though I'd managed to kill that avenue. Amelia nor her father had contacted Hamilton or me since I threw her out of Stronghold.

Granted, I had managed to convince many of their suppliers to discontinue working with them. And six of their eight hotels in the works were all stopped dead mid construction all in a matter of hours, and weeks later they were still shut down.

Hamilton's eyes shot wide, and he shook his head. "No. Nothing like that. It's just...she's beneath you."

"Not yet, she isn't," Rhys snickered.

I arched a brow at my cousin. "Really?"

He shrugged. "That's part of why it got to this so quickly, isn't it?"

"No." My anger began to flare again. "If Genevieve hadn't run into her, this wouldn't have happened."

"It would have eventually," Hamilton countered. "She knows nothing of our world. It's like you've brought a toddler into the family."

Rhys narrowed his gaze on Hamilton. "She's rough around the edges, I'll agree there, but toddler?"

"Madeline is better behaved than her," Hamilton argued as he loosened his tie.

Rhys shook his head. "Do you not remember the family dinner at all?"

Hamilton unknotted his tie, his aggravation growing, and pulled it from his neck before undoing the top buttons of his dress shirt. It was a tell of his—the tie was the first to go. He didn't like Ophelia, but I had yet to discern the real reason.

"Yes, but you weren't there for the rest of the weekend, Rhys."

"She was nervous and unsure of herself," I cut in. I refused to let Hamilton cut into her any longer. "None of you but Pen gave her a very warm welcome, and even that was a little frosty. But, she held herself in check despite the insults being thrown at her."

Hamilton shook his head. "Dress her up all you want, she's still a square peg trying to fit in a round hole, and she always will be."

"Maybe I like that." My voice was barely over a whisper.

Hamilton's eyes narrowed on me. "Are you serious?"

I blew out a breath and relaxed back into my chair. "It doesn't matter anyway. What does matter is a man named Lou Milner."

"Who is Lou Milner?" they asked in unison.

"Someone I need to pay off and ruin."

Hamilton's lip twitched up, and excitement filled his eyes. The shark smelled blood. "What can we do?"

"Pay him, then bury him in legal action."

Rhys perked up at that, excited for a challenge. "Who is he that I get to make him bleed?"

"Ophelia's stepfather. He threatened her, so I will end him. The mother is a piece of work as well, but he is the focus."

"Won't that be more bad light shed on your bride-to-be?" Rhys asked.

I shook my head. "Not when he is arrested for extortion of his stepdaughter. Paint him as a monster."

Rhys quirked a brow. "And you as her knight in shining armor?"

I nodded. "It will help tame the public opinion."

"Why do we care about that again?" Hamilton asked with a groan.

"Because gods only hold power because their subjects pay tribute to them," I said.

"Even if we were all hit with bad press, it will hardly make a dent in the company," Hamilton argued.

"True, but I refuse to let the de Loughrey name fall like others. Names that are known to all, but have disappeared." It was a common problem in those that rose in the industrial age—shirtsleeves to shirtsleeves in three generations.

"Through mistreatment of wealth," Rhys pointed out.

Hamilton nodded in agreement. "We are constantly growing and evolving. A little shadow can't hurt that. Look to Genevieve as an example."

"She's the exception," I pointed out. "She's trained them over the years to the point that the only way to truly get her to straighten up is by revoking access to her trust."

"I wield the pen and you wield the power, cousin." Rhys grinned a little too large for my liking, though I didn't disagree with his excitement. "Simply speak the words, and it will be done."

I sat back. "Let Father handle her for the time being. Right now, I need to concentrate on destroying my soon-to-be stepfather-in-law."

"We will leave you to it," Rhys said as he stood.

Hamilton didn't move, gaining our attention. "How did he threaten her? You said he threatened her? What did he have on her?"

That piqued Rhys's interest, and he looked back to me.

"I'm not sure, but I've always suspected it might come to this."

Hamilton gripped his tie in one hand as he stood. "I may not like her, but whatever you need, I'm here. She's yours, and that makes her a de Loughrey. Nobody threatens us."

My lip twitched. "Thank you."

He gave a nod before turning. "Call me."

"You know where to find me," Rhys said as he followed Hamilton out.

While it aggravated me that Hamilton didn't approve of Ophelia due to her upbringing and status, he was still willing to fight for her. Then again, he also loved a fight.

None of that mattered. What mattered was their support in helping me rid the world of a cockroach.

From the background check, I'd always known in my gut Lou Milner was going to be a disturbance in my plan. Born of blue collar. A drunk.

Amy Milner, Ophelia's mother, wasn't much better.

I combed over the information I had and pondered how different Ophelia's life would have been if her father had not died. Divorce papers had been filed, and in them he was asking for full custody of his daughter.

It didn't get to judgment before a hit and run left him for dead.

Something about that rubbed me wrong, and before I could stop myself, I'd texted Hugo to look into it. The police report called it an accident, but with the new development with Lou Milner, and knowing he married Amy only a few short months later, there was something that didn't sit right.

My hunches often worked out, and if I was correct, Lou Milner was about to be an easy one to bury.

No one threatens a de Loughrey.

There was silence when I stepped off the elevator. That wasn't unusual, even with Ophelia sharing the space. We needed to talk, and instead of heading to my bedroom, I stepped across the hall into the library. After depositing my jacket, I moved to the bar and popped the top from the decanter before pouring a few fingers of whiskey. My neck ached from the tightness it held through the day, and I craned it from side to side in an attempt to loosen it.

Once I had enough to take the edge off, I removed my tie, popped the top buttons of my shirt, and headed down the hall. The silence continued as I drew closer to her bedroom. While I was prepared to be civil and knock, the door to her room was open.

My brow scrunched as I stepped in. "Ophelia?" I called out.

She wasn't there, nor was she in her bathroom. There was also something off about her room, but I brushed it aside as I moved out of the bedroom and in search of her in the main living areas.

"Ophelia?" I called out again. Once again, there was nothing. Each room was the same—not a speck of evidence she was there.

Anger boiled inside when I got to the last space and found it empty.

I told her to stay. I told her not to leave. Yet she defied me?

Perhaps she was in the common levels? It was a solid idea, but that feeling of something amiss crawled in and I rushed back to her bedroom.

Quickly, I pulled out my phone and began a search for her. My stomach sank when the tracker couldn't find a signal in the building. My chest tightened when the last ping signaled over eight hours before.

"What the fuck?"

A zing of cold zipped down my spine, and I rushed back to her bedroom.

I scanned the room, and nothing seemed out of place until I checked the bathroom. While makeup and perfume remained, the room was devoid of toiletries. In her closet, the dress she wore the night we met was missing. Her dresser was the true tell—her drawers were mostly empty. Drawers that had been filled with many of her clothes before we met, including her jeans, were empty, leaving behind only the designer ones Melanie had brought her.

She left me?

Anger rolled off me. I knew she was upset, but to the point of leaving before we could talk? My emotions oscillated, and I hated the swing that enveloped me.

She needed to be found. Returned.

She couldn't leave me. I owned her.

Yes, that was why. Not the lie that I desperately wanted her. That my heart ached for her.

The thought that maybe someone could ever care about me was a lie to soothe my wretched soul.

But I refused to give up on her.

A single button on my phone was pressed, and after one ring, a deep voice answered.

"Hugo, I need you to track down someone," I said.

"Sure thing. Who am I looking for?"

"Ophelia Evans."

There was a pause. "Last seen?"

"Penthouse, Olympus Tower, seven this morning."

There was the click of fingers on a keyboard. "Have you tracked her phone with yours?"

"I tried, but it cut out a few blocks away and I don't know why."

There was a small pause that felt like hours, but only mere seconds passed. "Looks like she pulled a couple grand off her credit card at a bank on Broadway."

A couple grand? What would she be doing with that kind of money? Did someone force her to do it, then kidnap her? Her stepfather?

The panic that set off inside my chest had me gripping the edge of the counter, my knuckles turning white from the force.

"Find her. Now."

"Yes, sir."

I hung up the phone and rubbed at my chest as harsh breaths left me.

And then the wicked king fell, consumed by his grief from a situation he created.

Almost poetic, but nothing about my life created such beauty. No, I was a destroyer. A conqueror.

A king.

But without my queen…

Ophelia had taken over my heart without me even noticing, and my oversight was costing me and causing a pain I'd never encountered before.

All night long I tossed and turned, the worst possible scenarios coming to mind. Closing in on twenty-four hours and she still hadn't returned, nor had she been found.

What had I done? It was my fault. I showed her, and that pushed her away. Who would want to be with a man like me anyway? I wasn't some nice guy she could ever have feelings for, even if I couldn't understand my own. Love in any form was not a nurtured emotion in the de Loughrey household.

All I could comprehend was that I wanted Ophelia in a way I had never wanted another woman in my life. She pulled at something inside me, deep in my chest, that I wanted her near. The problem was that once she was, I had no clue what to do. Affection was for the weak, or so I had been told my entire childhood.

Competition was cultivated from birth, and only winners were praised. That level of expectation of winning wasn't just in peer competition, but also pertained to sibling and cousin rivalry.

It was a cycle I hated, because all it did was push me further and further away from people. The absolute *need* to be the best, to prove my worth, had me cutting off friend and foe at the knees. There was no room for failure. No room for second best.

And I craved the win. Not to gloat, but for the small, fleeting praise bestowed upon me. The more accolades I garnered, the more praise I received. It wasn't until Ophelia that I began to understand that praise did not equal love.

I sat up, unable to take staring at the ceiling any longer, and rubbed my face.

"What are you doing, Atticus? What do you want from her?"

Her smile, the little smirk she would give, flashed into my mind. There was a light to her, and she drew me in, a moth to her flame, desperate to feel the warmth only she could provide.

I wasn't getting any more sleep, and I pulled the covers from my body before settling my feet on the floor. There was no notification light blinking on my phone, and I'd been awake enough that the smallest vibration would have had me grabbing for it. None of that was enough to satiate the need for something to suddenly pop up, and when I woke the screen up, I was greeted with nothing.

What made my nerves ramp into overdrive was not that she had run away from me—a reaction I could have predicted if I'd wished to indulge my worry instead of focusing on destroying her stepfather—it was that the signal from her phone had disappeared.

That was what had my hands shaking. Me. The wicked king, supreme ruler of the heartless kingdom, was consumed with the fear that my fake fiancée was hurt and needed me.

For all my fucking resources, they couldn't find her after nearly twenty-four hours.

After a shower and still no notice, I dressed in simple slacks and a button-down with the sleeves rolled up. It was then I noted how my wardrobe consisted of mostly suits. With summer coming in and with Ophelia in my life, more trips to the Hamptons would be had, and I would require more casual dress. I tasked Jack with contacting Melanie about a summer wardrobe.

An odd thing to do at that moment, but for those few seconds, my mind wandered from the anxiety that vibrated through me.

TWENTY-FOUR

OPHELIA

What the hell are you going to do?

It was the question that buzzed around in my brain, but no answers came.

I ran away.

It was an act of desperation, of sheer need to be away from anything de Loughrey related…away from *him*. My mind was a whirlwind, and all I knew was that I couldn't stay. I had to go.

So I did. I withdrew an amount that was pretty much pocket change to him and destroyed the sim card in my phone. I needed space away from him, and I wasn't going to get it if he knew exactly where I was. To make it harder, I boarded the train and rode into the Bronx.

But after many hours of sitting in some budget motel in a sketchy part of town, the adrenaline long ago having worn off, I began to question my rash plan of action. I couldn't hide forever, especially not in New York. He would find me in a heartbeat.

If he was even looking.

My chest clenched at that thought. What if, after my disappearance, he gave up on me? But didn't I want that?

My mind was a massive rat's nest of contradictory confusion.

Was that due to the feelings I had for him? The more space between us, the more I began to realize that as much as I was angry at him, it was my own fear that thrust me out the door.

I was a flighty personality when things got too heavy, whether that was from an overbearing fear of a drunk, or the emotional upheaval of being thrust into a spotlight. There was no real preparation for it, just a general warning of things that would happen.

How could he be so blasé over firing others? He was like ice when he dictated that not only would they be fired, but it was my fault entirely. While I knew my actions at the club were on no one's shoulders but my own, I couldn't reconcile the thought that I'd never again be allowed out for a little breather… some fun.

I should have predicted Lou's response to the announcement. His eyes were probably shining with dollar signs when he'd watched the news and concocted his plan. The amount wasn't much in the de Loughrey world, but to Lou, it was riches beyond his dreams and all he had to do was threaten me.

When I grasped at straws before signing the contract with Atticus and mentioned skeletons, it was a true air grab. Anything to postpone the inevitable, but I didn't believe there was anything. My life had been standard, with the only thing hanging in the air being the identity of whomever killed my father. It was a mystery that was still unsolved two decades later.

I suppose I could have declined his proposal, but there was something that stopped me from saying no, from just flipping him off and storming out.

Yes, the money was part of it, but there was more. The promise of different, of not having to worry about so much, of spending time with Atticus.

But the shiny had worn off, and I found that the life of the rich was harder than it looked. Rules and etiquette and an aching loneliness prevailed.

I fell back down on the bed, my stomach choosing that moment to rumble—no surprise since I hadn't eaten since I'd grabbed a sandwich before checking into the hotel. Since then, I'd lived off the snacks I snagged from his penthouse condo when I left. The problem I faced was that I finished off the last bottle of water, and *had* to leave the security of the crappy walls that surrounded me.

The temperature was near ninety out, so I slipped on some shorts and a tank top, then my flip-flops. My identity was out there all over the place, so I'd made sure to conceal my face beneath a hat and sunglasses. Even if someone thought I looked familiar, nobody would suspect a future de Loughrey would be caught dead in an area like this dressed the way I was.

After picking up a gyro and fries, I dipped into a corner bodega for drinks and an abundance of soul-nourishing chocolate.

And a pint of Ben and Jerry's.

When I was done, I rushed out and back down the street.

In and out. Avoid all people. Just walk. Get back to the hotel. Hurry.

"Hey, lady, got any change?" a man asked.

The hairs on the back of my neck rose.

Ignore. Get back.

"Hey, sweetheart, I'm talkin' to you." His voice lost its friendly edge.

I picked up the pace, hoping the guy would move on to the next person.

"Listen, bitch," he sneered.

My arm was yanked, throwing off my balance and halting me, my leg kicked out to stop my fall. I was met with dark eyes that seemed to glow with anger, his pupils blown from whatever drugs he was on.

"Let go," I said through clenched teeth. There were people everywhere, but nobody seemed to take notice of us.

"Gimme your money and maybe I will."

I was just about to laugh at him when I heard the distinctive *schnick* of a switchblade. My stomach dropped, and my eyes peered around trying to catch anyone's glance.

"Ain't nobody gonna help you. Not here."

Fuck this. Fuck him. Fuck all the men who think they can control me and walk all over me.

"I said leave me alone!" I cried out, pulling my arm to wrench it from his grip, not caring if I was cut in the process.

Suddenly I flew back, my arm free. I stumbled briefly but regained my balance in time to watch as a man slammed his fist into the druggie's face again and again until the man lay groaning on the ground. There was a small wave of applause, but everyone ignored the man lying in an outcome of his own making.

I watched the heaving back of the man who saved me, a chill running down my spine. He turned, his blue eyes lit with anger, but also an edge of panic as he raked his gaze across my skin. My heart thumped wildly in my chest. He came. He actually came, and I wasn't sure what scared me the most—the fact that I was bound to be in trouble, or the relief I felt that he found me.

Glancing away, I fought my desire to flee and clenched my jaw to keep the tears at bay.

"What are you doing here?" I demanded while steadfastly refusing to look at him.

It wasn't something Atticus would allow. Of course he wouldn't. Atticus would always be the one in the position of power, and he proved nothing had changed when his thumb and finger gripped my chin and simultaneously tilted my head back, while his other pulled my sunglasses off.

"You left. I followed."

I pulled away from him. "Go away, Atticus."

He arched a brow. "And leave you here, in this shithole?" His comment was as blasé as always and only further solidified that my decision to leave was the right one.

"I understand this place more than I will ever understand your home," I said before stomping away.

"Am I that awful that you would prefer to be threatened by a drugged-up thief than sleep next to me in safety?"

I stopped in my tracks.

"Yes." *Because nothing about you is safe.*

My eyelids closed at the warmth that filled me, the electricity that continued to pass between us even now at his chest pressed to my back.

"You really want to break the contract?"

My eyes snapped open. Yes.

No.

Fuck, I hated that contract.

"Well, considering I'm pretty sure my addition was loopholed the fuck out, yes, I do. If I have to work three jobs to pay you back, I will, but I'm not going back with you."

"You know, then."

I spun in his arms to face him, anger leaking out at being correct. "It became pretty fucking obvious the day you pinned me to your childhood bed. I'm sure there are all sorts of wicked ways you schemed to have sex with me without breaking the contract."

His gaze hardened, as did his jaw. After glancing around, he took hold of my arm and walked me down the sidewalk toward my hotel.

"Let's talk about this in private."

I rolled my eyes. "Whatever."

When we entered my room, I set my bags down, lamenting the ruin of my appetite despite the vicinity of my delicious gyro.

"Pack your things. We're going home."

I snapped around to him, noting the sour expression of his downturned mouth while he scanned the room, careful not to touch anything.

"Excuse me? No."

"No?"

"You heard me."

"And why not?"

Tears welled in my eyes, and I fought them back by clenching my jaw. "I can't go back to that. I can't! Why would I *want* to go back?"

"I have ten million reasons."

I threw my hands up in the air. "Screw the money."

That seemed to startle him, and he blinked at me. "What?"

"I said screw the money. No amount of money would ever be

reason enough to put up with that life or with you. I'm not built for it. You chose wrong."

He shook his head. "No, I didn't."

"I'm telling you, you did."

"Why do you think that?"

"Because I'm not de Loughrey material."

"And who said this? The media? The trash simply loves gossip, and right now you are the juiciest bit to cross their desks. All will calm down soon."

"It may, but it will never be like it was."

His lips formed a thin line. "No. You're associated now. Even if you…leave me, they'll come for you."

I hated the strain in the deep timbre of his voice and the way it tugged at my heart. "Why can't you just let me be?"

My gaze was glued to the floor, and in a few seconds the shiny surface of his crocodile-embossed loafers came into view. He gripped my chin, forcing me to look up at him. Forcing me to see the tortured twist of his beautiful features.

"I'm different with you than I am with other people," he said lowly.

"If you're saying I got to see the good version of you…wow, *you need some improvement.*" I kept the hard edge, not relenting. I wasn't someone he could just walk all over. "We obviously learned two different versions of the word *good* in school."

"You didn't see the bad," he stated, releasing my chin and stepping away. "I went from having lunch there once a month to twice a week when you started working there."

I gasped at that. I'd always assumed it was normal. No one at the restaurant told me differently. But to go there so much just to see me?

"I didn't just pick you at random, Ophelia. You must understand that by now."

After his dismissal of any knowledge of that night, I'd assumed I'd just been another notch in his very expensive bed post.

Then he asked me to marry him, but I still could never reconcile the two men I knew him to be.

"I don't know who you are, Atticus," I said in a whisper. "Are you friend or foe?"

He paused, thinking it over, his head dropping before his spine straightened. "I'm both. As the head of the de Loughreys, I don't have the luxury to choose one or the other."

That was a sad revelation, but fit with what I'd witnessed. "Were you…" I trailed off, my nerve to ask him the one question I'd wondered for over a year. It wasn't the first time I asked, but I needed an answer. "Were you ever going to call me, or was that just a flippant remark you tell all the girls?"

He shook his head, and I bit back a tear. "You act like I take every woman I meet to bed, when that is far from the truth. With regard to the first part of your question, the easy answer is yes. Yes, I had every intention of calling you. However, after you left that morning, I was thrown back into work, with many meetings the following week. When I was sitting at that table with all those men, it was in celebration of an eight-hundred-million-dollar acquisition of a sports team. The moment I saw you greeting us, I began to doubt the sheer coincidence of meeting you. By the time I'd dug far enough into your history, weeks had passed."

"And?"

"And how was I supposed to ingratiate myself to you with the attitude I'd shown?"

"I figured your ego wouldn't stop you."

"Hmm, perhaps if I was Rhys or Hamilton. With the way I treated you those weeks, I felt there was no going back. Why would you want to deal with me?"

"I didn't think you had any insecurities."

"Only one," he responded with a sad smile—one that if I didn't know better would be taken as a grimace—while our gazes remained locked. "Only you."

"And yet, after our arrangement and living together, you continued to push me away when I can see what you hide from everyone else."

"And what is it you think you see?" he asked.

"That you're lonely. That you're dying for any sort of affection, but have no idea how to ask for it." He stayed frozen in front of me. "And you've made me lonely with you. All alone in that huge home, and the only person I have is you. But you ignore me, because why?"

"Because…" He let out a frustrated sigh. "There is no dark beast lurking in the shadows. It's just me, in broad daylight, standing in front of the cameras with a look of strength while I wipe the dirt from my hands. You have no idea the burdens of my position."

"You're right. I don't. But that doesn't mean I don't see the strain it puts on you. You don't have to shoulder it all."

"As the head of this family, yes, I do. I will be the final say in all regards. The king of the de Loughreys left to rot in the makings of my birthright."

It was the most open he'd ever been by miles, and my heart hurt for the anguish in his voice. Had he ever done anything for himself? "Even kings have advisors."

"Is that what you want to be? My advisor?"

"All I know is that I want to be more than I am. Being treated like a person and not like an object."

"What if I'm not capable of that?" he asked. The insecurity he spoke of was on full display. He felt for me, but didn't know what to do about it.

"But you are. I know you are."

"How?"

"Because for one night, I couldn't stop looking at the most wonderful man I'd ever met. I still feel like that was a dream, but I know he was real. And he's in you, somewhere, buried under all the duty and loneliness." I pursed my lips and tilted my head as I stared at him. "Have you ever been happy, Atticus?" His brow furrowed, and he remained silent. "It just seems sad to go through life never being happy."

"Work fulfills me."

"Do you even enjoy it or is that just the de Loughrey brainwashing in effect?"

His silence held so much. The weight upon him was crushing, piling up around him so he couldn't move.

"I was happy once," he says after a few minutes, his voice so low and almost reverent. I cringed against the emotion, because it was obvious she touched him. "For one night, I had happiness and peace and fun."

"Just one night?"

The furrow of his brow deepened. "That was all we had." His eyes met mine, and shock rocked me.

I was the one who touched him. Our one night was the same.

"You weren't chosen at random, Ophelia. You were chosen because I couldn't stop thinking about you. About that night. The one night in my life I felt like a regular man and not the head of a five-hundred-billion-dollar company. With you, I wasn't a de Loughrey. That was why I forbid anyone to tell you my last name, and why my credit card held no name at all."

That was something I'd always wondered. I'd only ever seen prepaid credit cards like that, not personal ones. But it always went through, so there was no need to know, and Mitchell told me he was one of the investors.

"I wanted you to see me as a man, even if it was from the other side of the table. Even if I couldn't bring myself to even attempt to undo the damage of my silence and contempt. What would I have said to you? I felt like a schoolboy nursing a crush and unable to act upon it. You weaken me."

"Emotion isn't a crippling thing. It should set you free, not weigh you down. Your obligations to your family do that enough. Even if we're never anything more than a contract, I want you to find an ally in me. Someone to lean on. I'm not made to be a doll; I'm built to be a warrior."

"I don't know if I can open up like that."

I reached up and cupped his face. "It won't be easy at first, but once you let go, like you did then, it will flow from you with ease."

"You'll come back?" he asked, a hopeful edge lacing his words.

Would I? I was so vehement about it earlier, but then he opened up. My loneliness embraced his loneliness and bonded. For a few brief moments, he'd been so honest with me. More honest than I think he'd ever been with himself, and that was worth sticking around to see more of.

I nodded. "If you promise to try, I promise to be on my best de Loughrey impersonator behavior."

"Outside the home."

My lips curled up into a smile, liking that I still had freedom in our little haven in the sky. "Outside the home. As long as you agree that inside the home, we can be more than strangers."

He reached out and enveloped my hand with his. "I think I'd like that very much."

"Good. We're in agreement."

"One last thing."

I rolled my eyes. "Of course there is."

"Don't run again."

I blinked at him, my gaze flicking between his eyes and taking in the deep sorrow and pain reflected there. Without my thinking, I threw my arms around his shoulders and pulled him close. "I'm sorry."

"You should be apologizing for scaring me like that." He pulled back and cupped my cheek, his thumb lightly stroking the skin beneath. "I'm sorry that I had to show you that side of me. I tried to shield you, hoping to not make you hate me."

"I don't hate you, Atticus. We'll get past this. Just take it one day at a time."

He held out his hand. "Come on, let's go home."

I smiled up at him and slipped my hand into his. "Okay."

chapter
TWENTY-FIVE

OPHELIA

Atticus kept sneaking a peek at me, his gaze flipping toward me all through breakfast. I'd returned with him days ago, and his behavior had been similar since I'd taken his hand—always watching like he thinks I'm going to disappear.

"What?"

His brow furrowed. "You promise that you'll stay? That if you leave, it is with Michael and you will return with him?"

I reached out and placed my hand on his, giving him a comforting smile. "I promise."

I bit down on my bottom lip as he returned to reading something on his tablet. With as closed off as he was emotionally, I had to admit I liked seeing the almost desperate desire for me.

Maybe not the kind of desire that set me on fire, but the desire for me on another level, one that would make the next five years a lot easier on us both if it continued.

More than just strangers with an arrangement, but a true relationship of sorts.

I jumped at the sound that suddenly sprang from the speakers, my eyes widening while I froze.

"Last weekend Atticus de Loughrey, head of the de Loughrey Corporation, was seen pulling his fiancée, Ophelia Evans, from the night-club Stratus. Eyewitnesses recount the wild behavior of the soon-to-be wife caught drunk and partying with Atticus's sister, Genevieve. Since the event, the de Loughrey family has remained silent, and there has been no sight of Ophelia."

I glared at him, wondering why, for a brief moment, I was content. "Turn it off," I grumbled.

He arched a perfect brow at me and turned the screen toward me. "You need thicker skin."

I looked away from the awful photo of me. And there I was, almost thinking he was sweet and a marshmallow on the inside. There was a softness there buried deep inside, but it wasn't sugary.

"Well, probably not going to happen."

"A reminder, then. Behave how you want within these floors, but out there, you are a representative of my family now. Even if by name you aren't yet, you *are* a de Loughrey."

"Are you trying to scare me off again?"

"No, I'm simply trying to be more transparent. From now on, we need to be a united front."

I nodded in agreement.

He grabbed my hand and raised it to his mouth to place a kiss on it and topped it off with a lick. The atmosphere had thickened, and so had Atticus's touch. I loved seeing the different flashes in his eyes, and the darkness that was taking over excited me. It wasn't the cold detachment I'd seen so often.

"Be a good girl, and perhaps I'll reward you," he said as he stood.

"What kind of treat do I get?" I asked.

"Why does that matter?"

"Because I need to know if it's worth it."

"Let's just say it's long and thick." The corner of his mouth ticked.

My gaze narrowed, and I shook my head. "Not happening."

"I thought you wanted a, what was it called...pool noodle?"

I froze for a second and straightened. "Well, yes. But I have a feeling we're talking about two totally different things." I was surprised he remembered my offhand comment about one of those.

"Are we?"

"By the near lecherous expression you're wearing, yes."

He poured himself another cup of coffee and headed back my way, giving me a full view of his grey sweatpants and white T-shirt. Everything he wore fit him with perfection, and added with his natural swagger and confidence and with the authoritative vibe that rolled off him, it was amazing women weren't constantly clinging to him like a koala. I knew I wanted to.

Suddenly I was shocked out of my imaginings by a swath of skin appearing in front of me. Almost innocently, Atticus inspected something on the hem of his shirt, drawing it up and exposing his abs—something that I hadn't seen in a year.

The unabashed sexiness in front of me was blinding.

The clearing of a throat caught my attention, and my gaze snapped to his. A smirk played on his lips, and he had that look, that one that said, "Got you."

"Who has the lecherous expression now?"

Heat flamed my face. "You did that on purpose."

He stepped up next to me and reached out, his fingertips lightly caressing my collarbone, sending a shiver down my spine and causing heat to settle between my thighs. "Of course. If I'm to suffer, you should burn with me."

Once he was done torturing me, he took his seat again. My plate was clean with the exception of a few crumbs, but I wasn't ready to leave his presence.

Since my return, we'd settled into a different pattern than before. One where we actually spent time together.

I found I liked it. It wasn't as lonely as before. The atmosphere had been intimidating with the museum-like stillness and pristine cleanliness. Somehow, since I'd returned, even with its large size, it had become a little more homey.

Maybe I was relaxing a bit since his confession, but I enjoyed our simple times together.

In order to continue our growth and to keep his walls from coming back up, I began texting him throughout the day. Responses weren't always prompt, but I didn't expect that they would be, so it made me appreciate when he did. Not in a badgering way, but simple, innocuous things.

Today was not one of those days.

Ophelia: Survey says?

I was pleasantly surprised when his reply came moments later.

Atticus: What survey?

Ophelia: *sigh* never mind.

Atticus: Are you referring to the plans regarding your stepfather.

Okay, now he's playing with me.

Atticus had glossed over what he was going to do to Lou, not wanting me to worry, but how could I not? Lou had tried to blackmail me, and it would have worked under normal circumstances if my fiancé wasn't the wicked king.

The king bowed to no man, and he was determined to make Lou feel his wrath.

Ophelia: You did say there would be a meeting this morning. What happened?

Atticus: Meet me for lunch at noon. You know where.

I rolled my eyes. I guessed after a year of eating there multiple times a week, it was a hard habit to break.

Being that it was already ten, I moved to the closet to find an ensemble that was de Loughrey-worthy while being cool. It was supposed to be in the upper nineties.

There was so much in my closet, but I finally located an odd but pretty silk scarf wrap top in gold and blues that looked kind of like a halter but wasn't, some *Versace* pleated shorts, and my strappy *Louboutins*.

The designers names were something I *never* thought I would own, let alone feel comfortable enough going into a store to browse, knowing full well I couldn't buy anything. Even with everything, it was nice to be pampered.

And have someone coordinate your outfits, because there was no way I was up to the task. Some of the stuff Melanie brought was so out there and baggy in design that I couldn't believe it was considered fashionable. In the end none of them stayed, thankfully, because she said they didn't meet the image someone in my position needed.

At the time, I didn't understand what she meant, but I began to learn. I learned more about fashion and designers. Since I didn't go out much, I would create outfits with occasions in mind.

Once dressed and ready, I headed down to the lobby. Atticus had a new sim card created for my phone, glaring at me the whole time it was replaced, which was necessary to navigate the overly teched-out building.

When I arrived in the lobby, there was an immediate, rigid response from the concierge and security. I blinked over at them, an oppressive aura that seemed to be made up of fear and worry emanated from them.

"Good morning, Miss Evans. Shall I call Michael for you?" Amy asked, giving me a forced smile.

I gave her a small nod. "Thank you."

My response sent a wave of relief through her, and her smile brightened considerably.

When the sedan pulled up to the pickup location, Michael got out and held open the door for me.

"Thank you," I said as I slid into the back seat.

Even his demeanor was strained, not relaxed like usual. "We will be stopping to pick up Mr. de Loughrey today."

I nodded. "Is everything all right?"

"Shouldn't it be?"

"Everyone seems weird today."

"Perhaps it's because you ran away from Atticus de Loughrey." His steely eyes met mine in the rearview mirror. "He is normally friendly even in his curt attitude, but you released his dark side on the staff."

My mouth dropped open. When I left, it was for my own self-ish reasons. I didn't really grasp what he'd said that morning—my actions have consequences for those around me.

"I'm sorry."

He let out a sigh. "I'm the only one that saw where you came from. The change has had to be difficult for you, so I understand *why* you left after that night."

"How can I make it up to everyone?" I asked. The guilt of having his rage directed at all the different employees didn't sit well.

"Don't leave him again."

I nodded before turning to stare out the window. A few minutes later, the car slowed to a stop. The door clicked open, and I watched as Atticus slid into the seat beside me. He froze before he could close the door, his eyes glued to my legs.

Heat from his gaze licked at my skin as he moved up to my shorts, then shirt, then meeting my eyes. Something deep and deliciously dark burned inside him, and I found it affecting me in an unexpected way. My nipples tightened and my thighs clenched, rubbing against each other.

I didn't even notice the slamming of the door or the acceleration of the car. He'd ensnared me, trapped me in an overpowering confusion of lust. I drew in a sharp breath when his hand rested against my thigh, his fingers drawing lazy circles.

"What are you wearing?" he asked, his tone deeper than normal. Between that and his overpowering presence, I felt overwhelmed by him.

"Shorts?"

"Hmm," was his only response.

My mind was completely focused on the light touches. I wasn't used to it, used to that level of affection, especially not from him.

The car once again slowed to a stop, and I blinked at the familiar building in front of us.

"Why are we here?" I asked as we got out of the car.

Atticus held out his hand, waiting for mine. "Because I like the privacy. You should know that by now." Once again, his eyes raked over me.

After all the gazes and whispers as we entered, I did understand to a degree.

As we sat waiting for our drinks from his new waitress, Allison, to arrive, we went over the menu, his hand once again landing on my thigh.

Warmth flooded my face. "Why do you keep doing that?"

"Hmm? I can't touch you?"

"You can, but, just…do you have to do it so intimately?"

"How would you prefer I touch you? Especially when dressed like that." His hand left, and I blew out a breath. "It suits you, though, even if I believe it's too short. Fashionable, but not overtly sexual."

"You mean not like Gen."

"I mean a dignified level of restraint while still being so alluring I am having difficulty refraining from feeling your skin beneath my fingers."

Butterflies kicked up in a torrent in my stomach. I wasn't used to this version of him. Had he been restraining himself the whole time?

Our confusing relationship only grew more and more confusing. Not friends, not lovers, not even an odd employee/employer affinity. What *were* we, besides engaged?

When I left, something snapped in Atticus. Well, maybe not snapped, but he definitely acknowledged something. His confession affected me as well. That, coupled with touches of genuine affection, and it was becoming harder and harder to resist him.

"Have you picked out a dress for this weekend?"

I blinked at him. "Dress?"

"For the charity gala."

All the blood drained from my face. "A charity function with no notice?"

He froze, giving me the most frightening side eye that sent a shiver down my spine. "If you had checked the calendar Jack has set up, it wouldn't be a surprise."

Oh, that. "What's it for?"

"If you'd read the folio, you would have seen all the charities we are involved with. Most important are at the top."

I rolled my eyes. "If you'd read the folio," I mocked back at him, earning a glare that didn't affect me the same way it used to. No, the heat flashing through my body was definitely new.

Even with his emerging softer side, he was still a hardheaded, overbearing ass at times.

"It is our first official event out in society as a couple," he said as he grabbed the glass Allison set down and took a sip, waving her off to come back for our order.

"And?" I asked as I took a large sip of my wine.

"And there are things you need to know. We need to come back from that debacle with Genevieve, therefore you will be on your best behavior." His aggravation grew as he spoke, the level of his voice growing as well.

"Take that tone down a notch." We'd spent the last few days without the wicked king coming out, and I intended to keep him away.

His jaw clenched, and he let out a growl of frustration. "It was a PR disaster, and it is your duty to change the public's opinion of you. You will dress appropriately, and will present yourself with grace and elegance. You will be on my arm with your head held high and give them no reason to tear you down."

"Yes, master."

His fist slammed onto the table. "This is a serious matter, Ophelia."

I blew out a breath. "I understand that, but put some warmth into your voice. You're like a fucking robot sometimes. I thought we pushed through this crap."

He ground his teeth together. "I'm trying, but you can't expect me to literally change overnight. I am simply trying to convey—"

"How I will look and act at our first public function," I said, cutting him off. "I get it. I won't embarrass you. I will stand by your side like a good little prized pony, all primped and proper." Anger coursed through me, hating that he felt he needed to talk down to me like I was a child.

He reached across the table and took my hand in his. "I don't want to give them a reason to hurt you."

The sincerity in his tone completely deflated me. "See? Was that so hard?"

"Yes," he said, but his lip twitched up and he let out a sigh as he relaxed back into his seat. "Be patient with me."

I grabbed his thumb with my own. "Just keep admitting you were wrong and petting me, and we'll be good."

His lips pulled up into a grin, and I blanched at the sight of the hunter staring at his prey.

"Petting? Do I get to *pet* you now? I assure you, that will make me much more agreeable."

Heat rose to my face, and I looked away. "You know, you tricked me with our contract," I said, pulling our attention away from the flames that grew around us.

"Did I?"

I shook my head. "Don't play stupid. You dangled ten million in my face and gave me only twenty-four hours to decide if it was worth it to marry you."

"And have my child," he added.

I tried to ignore the silky smooth and sinful undercurrent, but it was almost impossible when all of his attention was centered on me. Something about the way he said it made my thighs clench and squeeze together. He was completely unraveling me.

I cleared my throat. "That was shady. You knew I'd take it."

He shook his head and opened his mouth to speak, then closed it.

"Out with it," I said, prompting him to come clean. He hated when I did it, because he hated showing weakness, and somehow any affection toward me was a weakness?

His jaw jutted forward, and he looked to the ceiling before that dispassionate glare was aimed at me. "You have a wildness about you. It was something that attracted me to you. That aspect sprinkled doubt. If you hadn't agreed, I didn't know what to do, therefore I gave you whatever you wanted so you'd agree. But until your name was scrawled across the bottom, part of me believed you would turn me down."

"You're blaming your insecurity on me and twisted it to gain a deceitful hand?"

"Correct."

I pulled back and crossed my arms in front of me. "Is this a tactic you use a lot?"

"Quite often."

"The deceit?"

He let out a humming sound. "No. I do whatever is necessary to get what I want."

"As long as it doesn't involve emotions."

"I'm not above making concessions, but I knew then that spending five years next to you, there would be nothing to tame my thirst for you. In order to keep our agreement and still be able to feel your thighs clenching around my hips as you shatter around me, alternative wording was created."

"And those would be?"

He leaned forward, his lips drawing up into a smirk, the intensity in his gaze making me squirm in my seat. "It would be a waste to share them with you, since you have no intent to allow me to utilize them."

I blinked at him.

He took my stunned silence as an opening to lean in and run his lips against the column of my neck.

"And you wouldn't want me to utilize them, would you?"

Thankfully that was the moment Allison parted the curtain to take our order, though I could tell my face was flushed. At least it got him to back up before he touched me more.

In the end, he never did tell me what he did to Lou, and I think that was exactly what he wanted.

TWENTY-SIX

ATTICUS

Of all the clothes in her closet, *why* did she have to choose something that would affect me so? I was behaving in a completely uncouth way.

I also needed to speak to Melanie about *why* she brought shorts that showed off nearly every inch of her flawless legs.

My attraction to her had never dwindled, and with the changes in our relationship, it had become even more difficult to keep my hands off her. Such as the situation I found myself in. My ability to rein my desire in had come loose. The wall of decorum was crumbling.

The new waitress, Allison, was growing on me. She was more competent than that worm, whatever his name was. Still, she was nowhere as good as Ophelia, and I regretted every day I came that I made her quit.

At the same time, I quite enjoyed having her sitting next to me in the half-circle booth, even if everything about her was driving me to distraction.

Her brow was knitted as she stared down at her glass of wine. "What?" I asked, wondering what was amiss with her drink. She blinked at me. "What, what?"

"You have a look on your face."

"I was just thinking."

"Expand, please."

"De Loughrey Pharmaceuticals."

I set my phone down and focused all of my attention on her. "Yes."

"Did you know I worked for them?"

I gave her a slow nod. "Your resume was one of the many background check items."

"Do you have to keep doing that?" she asked with a huff. I quirked a brow as I stared back at her. "I know you dug into me, but do you have to remind me that you dissected my life before you got to know me as a human being? Can we have a conversation where you don't have to hammer that fact out yet again? If you know something, just agree."

A harsh chuckle left me, and I nodded. "Forgive me, my dear. You are correct. I will do better."

She straightened, though I did see her nose crinkle at the pet name I threw out. "Good."

"De Loughrey Pharmaceuticals?"

"Oh, right."

I couldn't help but chuckle when she was reminded about what she was thinking about.

"Do you think I could work there again?"

I froze as I attempted to process her thought path that brought her to that point, and was once again thwarted. "Why would you?"

She shrugged. "I don't know. Something to do."

"What about wedding planning?"

"Your mom has that covered, right?" she asked.

"You don't want to give any input at all into our celebration?"

"Some, but..." She heaved a sigh.

"My mother is a very intense presence."

"You all are. I have no clue what she's already done, and I kinda feel like it's a sham wedding and so what do I care?"

I drew in a sharp breath. "Sham?"

She rolled her eyes. "When I envisioned getting married, it was to a man I wanted to spend the rest of my life with and who thought the world of me. Not some contract."

My chest constricted at her description. Love and marriage did not always coincide in my family, therefore, I had difficulty imagining needing one for the other. I could admit that it wounded me hearing her talk about us in such a harsh manner. No, we weren't some doe-eyed couple in love, but...

Five years wasn't going to be enough for me. I wanted Ophelia in ways I'd never wanted *anyone*. She filled something missing inside me.

When she left me, I'd become a shell of a person again. A robot.

"Even if we don't have that kind of relationship, it doesn't mean the day can't be special. Make it what you want. Whatever dream you have. Whatever dress you want. With regard to my mother, if you want your opinion heard, you need to state it loudly. Assert yourself, or she'll walk all over you."

She blinked at me, pink spreading across her cheeks before nodding. "Okay." She returned her attention to her plate. "Grr, you distracted me. I want to work. I don't want to be some rich housewife like on those shows. I'm not a socialite by any means."

That wasn't where I thought the conversation was going. "Good. I hate socialites." I tolerated them. After growing up surrounded by them, Ophelia was a refreshing breeze. "What about when we have a baby?" I reminded her.

"I could stop then and reassess, but until then, I'm tired of being bored out of my mind around here. I want to work, use my degree. I know I don't have a doctorate, and I refuse to be a rep again, but there must be something somewhere I can work within some de Loughrey company. It doesn't have to be in pharmaceuticals, just somewhere."

I thought it over. In a way, I wanted to hold her up at the top of the tower forever, but I knew I couldn't do that. I also knew what she was asking would not go the way she envisioned it.

"You will be judged. Whispered about."

She pursed her lips. "I know. Trust me, I understand."

"I'm not against it. The last thing I want is for you to be miserable."

"Really?" She seemed surprised.

"Really." However, I would be engaging in other avenues to pull her into. Perhaps calling Georgiana was in order.

"Wow. I thought you'd be against it."

"Why would I be against it?" I asked. Had she seen through me?

"I don't know. We didn't talk about it during the contract phase, and I've spent the last few months in a de Loughrey crash course of what not to do, which is everything I've ever done in my life."

"There is a position I know of."

"Yeah?"

I nodded, my lips drawing up. She stiffened and narrowed her gaze at me.

"I've always wanted a personal cock warmer."

Her head fell to the side with the most exaggerated eye roll I'd ever witnessed.

"How do you say no in Italian?"

"No."

"Exactly."

Her eyes sparkled, and I got lost in their warmth. Reaching out, I placed my hand on hers, my fingers wrapping around as I brushed my thumb across her knuckles. The light died down, but not in a bad way. My touch had replaced it with another emotion I quite enjoyed.

"I like this," I said.

Her fingers squeezed mine. "Me, too."

The waiter, whatever his name was, arrived and set our food down, disrupting our moment.

"Thank you, Drake," Ophelia said, giving him a warm smile.

Where did Allison go? I hated the twerp.

As soon as the curtain closed, she reached over and pulled the broccolini from my plate, replacing it with her sautéed green beans.

"Don't," was all she said as she did it.

The dark marks on the green stems showed me what the issue

was. They were heavily charred, and she knew I disliked that. "If it wasn't correct, it should be fixed."

"Give the guy a break," she huffed.

I quirked a brow at her. "Do I look as though I'm about to spit fire at him?"

"He's scared enough of you as it is."

Good.

"That is his problem, not mine."

"You could try smiling at him," she said as she cut her steak. It was an odd choice for her, a divergence from her normal salmon addiction.

"If I expose my teeth, he may believe I'm threatening him."

She coughed on her bite, attempting not to laugh but failing utterly. "Maybe, but scowling at him constantly isn't doing any good."

"He's not up to my standards."

"Nobody is."

"You were."

She looked up from her plate, and when our eyes met, all I wanted was to close the space between us and press my lips to hers.

"And now?" she asked, her voice barely above a whisper.

The tension in the air heightened, and I kept glancing between her lips and her eyes that were drawing me in.

"Now I find I may be below your standards."

"Not possible."

"How so?"

"Because there is no man that has ever come close to you."

A confession. A validation that I wasn't the only one being pulled in more and more with each day.

In a fraction of a second, I held her head in my hands as my lips crashed to hers. The table clattered, drinks spilled, and glass broke as she fell down to the booth, taking me with her, but I only cared about the woman whose tongue was caressing mine while soft mewls vibrated beneath my hands.

A tug on my back pulled me closer to her. A groan left me as I palmed her bare thigh, the overwhelming need to taste her, to have her, taking over my senses.

"How is every—" a voice called, and I snapped my gaze over to the curtain, scowling at the girl standing there.

"Out!" I snarled.

Ophelia's slight fingers brushed against my jaw, drawing my attention back to her. Delicious pink painted her skin, her eyes dark and lips swollen, and I wanted nothing more than to rip our clothes off and take her right there.

"Our lunch is getting cold," was all she said in response, lips brushing against mine. The interruption wasn't enough to tamp down the fire that burned brightly between us.

"I could give you a trial run today as my personal cock warmer. As soon as we're done with lunch."

She bit down on her lip, stifling a small moan, but I heard it nonetheless. "No sex."

A groan left me, and I pressed my lips softly to hers. "Yes, my dear."

Making it through the remainder of lunch was going to be difficult with a stiff dick and a woman who continued to tease me in unexpected ways.

TWENTY-SEVEN

OPHELIA

It was amazing the amount of "friends" that came crawling out of the woodwork with the announcement that you were marrying the country's most eligible bachelor—a statistic I didn't even know about until the announcement came out.

My social media, which I'd blanched and scrubbed the hell out of weeks before the announcement came out, was awash with notifications. People I hadn't had contact with in years except for social media exchanges—which I didn't consider contact, really—had been bombarding my social media.

The one good thing was that they didn't have my new number, which some of them noted as they'd tried to call, but it had been so long since we'd hung out or really talked, I felt like it was a feeler post. Like they were throwing out a line to see if I'd take it.

What surprised me the most was when an unknown number called and I actually answered it almost on instinct, knowing the person on the other end was someone of importance. Probably because so few people had my new number.

"Hello?"

"Lia?"

I blinked as the voice was familiar, and the nickname…"Brooke?"

"And Andrea!" a high pitched voice called out.

A smile spread on my face, and I leaned back against my bed. "How are you calling me?" I asked. Last I knew, she was stomping around throwing a tantrum about how she asked for a phone for Christmas and didn't get one. She was the *only* one in her class that didn't have one.

"I used my part-time job to get a phone. Mom couldn't say anything about it. So save the number, okay?"

"You got it. How are you? How's school?" It had been so long since I'd gotten to talk to her that I cherished every word. Talking at their house was always stunted, careful not to say the wrong thing, always guarded.

"Lia, we miss you," Andrea said with a whine. "Why don't you visit anymore?"

"You know why," Brooke hissed.

Did they know? Really know? Brooke was obviously in her teenage rebellious phase, but I also believed that gave her an insight she didn't understand before. At least that was the vibe I got from her phone comment.

"What did Mom say?" I asked, the curiosity too great to withstand.

"She just says you're busy. When I asked why you never call, she said 'why would she want to talk to her two bratty sisters?'"

My stomach sank, and I pulled my legs up against my chest. Such a horrible mother. "You know that's a lie, right?"

"Of course!" Brooke cried. "If it were the truth, you wouldn't still give us gifts and hugs and smiles and come to school functions, though it's been a while on that."

"I'm sorry about that." I hated that their own parents didn't attend recitals and events, and went when I could. "I started a job where I often worked late into the night, and getting any info from Mom was impossible."

"Dad says it's 'cause you don't like us. That you're an uptight, ungrateful… ummm…" Andrea trailed off before her voice dipped into a whisper. "B-word."

"That doesn't surprise me," I grumbled.

"Lia, when can we come see you?" Andrea asked in that pitiful tone. She was fourteen and still sounded like she was eight half the time. I'd long wondered if it was a defense mechanism.

"Why do you want to see where I live?" I asked. Their response would be a huge tell, because as happy as I was to hear from them, I still doubted their intent.

"Mom says you probably live at the top of a tower like a princess," Andrea squealed.

She may have been a teenager, but she'd never outgrown her princess obsession.

"It's not that kinda tower, Dee," Brooke said with an exasperated sigh.

"How do you know?"

"Because it's a condo, not a castle," Brooke argued. "Anyway, yeah, Mom said you were living in a tower in Manhattan. She and Dad…"

"What?" I prodded her to continue.

"They keep saying bad things about you, Lia."

"Do you believe them?"

"No," Brooke said with more confidence than I expected. "You've always been nice, and I know Dad has never been nice to you." Maybe Brooke really was coming into her own and seeing things as they were.

"Mom said you don't come around anymore because you don't want to see us," Andrea said, her sad little tone breaking my heart. We'd come back around to this, which made me realize how much my absence had hurt my little sisters, even though I hadn't lived with them in nearly a decade.

"It's not that, little Dee."

"It's Dad," Brooke said, a bit of venom lacing her tone. "He's a stupid drunk. I hate living with him."

"Ssh! Don't say that. What if he hears you?" Andrea said with a whimper.

Fuck, was he hitting them now, too?

"Why do you say it like that?"

"He gets mad and yells really, really loud."

"Does he hurt you?"

"Yes," Brooke growled, but then her voice broke. "He's so much bigger and stronger."

"What does he do?"

"He grabbed Dee the other day and threw her against the wall. There are bruises on her arm and a knot on her forehead."

My fists clenched, and my anger fought against the tears that threatened to fall. "You shouldn't have to stay with him."

"Can we come live with you?"

My chest clenched. I had to tell Atticus. There was no way they could stay there, and I knew he'd be able to help them. Things between us were not stable enough to add two teenage girls, but maybe they could stay with Aunt Stacey, Mom's sister. She was always sweet and loving, and I knew she'd fought for us before.

Somehow, some way, I was getting them out of there and into a loving environment. They were innocents who deserved more. No matter what, they were going to be safe.

"I'll get you out of there."

"Really?"

"I don't know how or when or where, but I'll get you somewhere safe."

"Anywhere is better than here," Brooke whispered, and I could hear her break out into a sob. She'd been showing such strength for Andrea, but the hope of being free broke her resolve.

I could hear Andrea in the background. "It's okay, sissy. Lia's gonna make it better, see? I told you. Lia will help."

What had he done to Brooke to make her break down like that?

"Text or call whenever you need something, but make sure to erase the messages so he doesn't see, okay? Hold tight. I love you both."

"Love you, Lia."

"Stay strong."

My hands were shaking as I hung up. Guilt wrecked me. I'd fled, leaving them alone with that monster. All of her daughters had suffered at her husband's hands, even his blood daughters, and yet our mother did nothing.

Once again, I was ecstatic that I didn't take after her.

Letting out a shaky breath helped to steady me, and my fingers flew across the screen.

Ophelia: I need my sisters away from Lou. Now.

I closed my eyes and wondered if we couldn't bring them here. What would he think of that?

Atticus: Done.

I blinked down at the screen. For one thing, I didn't expect such a prompt reply, as busy as he was, and I also wasn't expecting such a blanket response. It was similar to when I said Lou wanted a hundred grand.

Ophelia: That's it? You don't want to know why?

Atticus: If your concern is so great you use the word now as a single sentence, that tells me all I need to know.

Ophelia: Thank you.

I'd just hit send when the phone rang.

"H-hello?"

"This is too much to type," Atticus's voice hummed across the line. There was someone talking in the background, but I couldn't make it out. "Until the business with Lou Milner is settled, I'll have them sent to your aunt. We've already been in contact with her, and she is prepared for whatever is necessary."

"What do you mean, you've contacted her?"

"After he threatened you, I started preparations to remove your sisters."

"You did?" Tears welled in my eyes, and I covered my mouth to hold my sob in.

"That man will only get what he deserves from you and me and nothing more. CPS will remove them by tomorrow night, and Lou and Amy will have no knowledge of their whereabouts."

"But Stacey is in New Haven."

"Do not worry. I'll be home in a few hours. We'll talk more then."

I nodded, not that he could see. "Okay. See you when you get here."

However, I couldn't do as he asked, and I'd worried my thumb nails down to the quick. The sound of the door and footsteps against the hardwoods had my gaze snapping to the doorway of the family room where I'd moved hours before.

Atticus's broad chest and perfect posture, along with his always standoffish demeanor, crossed the threshold into the room. The second his eyes met mine, I leapt from the couch and ran to him. I stopped in front of him, my hopeful gaze trained on him.

I blinked at the feel of his fingers brushing lightly across my jaw, tickling my neck and sending a shiver through me. He tilted his head as he observed me.

"You seem expectant."

I swallowed and nodded. "I'm worried."

"Hmm." He straightened, his warm touch leaving me. "Didn't I tell you not to worry?"

"How can I not? He's hurting them."

"Not anymore."

I flicked my gaze between his eyes. "You mean…"

"They were pulled from the house thirty minutes ago and are on their way to New Haven."

Without thought or reservation, I threw my arms around his shoulders and pulled him close. "Thank you!" I cried. Tears streamed down my face, and I choked back a sob.

His arms wrapped around my waist as he held me tightly against him.

"I didn't know."

"It's okay," he said as he rubbed his hand up and down my back.

The wicked king was taking his anger out on Lou, but there was another side to him. The side that would tear a man's world apart to protect me. He'd set into motion so many things that I had no idea about. What else had he done?

What else had he prepared for?

OPHELIA

Early Saturday afternoon, Jack called me down to the salon for my first event makeover. It was unnerving seeing the team of people in the salon waiting for me.

Penelope sat in one of the chairs, her large blue eyes meeting mine in her reflection.

"Hello," she said as I sat in the chair next to her.

"Hi. Are you going to the event tonight?"

She nodded. "We all are."

"All."

"Mm-hmm."

I tried to rack my brain about the night's fundraiser, and I couldn't seem to reconcile water safety with something that would call all the de Loughreys out. I'd only glanced at the invitation and it was obvious I needed to learn more, because I was evidently wrong about something. Right?

I opened my mouth to ask something when someone grabbed my chin and started wiping something across my face. I blinked rapidly, realizing it was a facial cleansing cloth. Another person tugged at my hair, while a third held up different foundations against my

skin, and even a fourth started on my nails. I was poked and prodded, different types of brushes flying everywhere. By the time I got
my thoughts back, Penelope was gone.

After an hour, I was moved from my seat to the dressing room
where I was stripped of my clothing and slipped into a dress Melanie
had picked out. It had some weight to it, thanks to the overwhelming amount of sapphire sequins that adorned it.

The fabric draped over one shoulder with a cutout from the middle going from my shoulder to my cleavage. It wasn't enough to show
anything off, but a little tease of skin and relief from the abundance
of sequins. At the top, the fabric from the back slipped through the
cutout and knotted at the top, a sash of fabric falling past my waist
that gave it a very Grecian look. A thigh-high slit topped off the look
and gave a subtle sexiness.

Overall, it was a combination of elegance with a dash of mod-
esty and sleek allure.

I stared at my reflection and the stranger that stared back. Maybe
one day I would get used to it, but for now, I remained amazed.

My hair wasn't in my usual style of straight or textured curls.
It was voluminous and sleek. The makeup was stunning, even if I
hardly recognized myself.

"For your first event, you need to be perfection," Atticus said,
startling me as he stared at me via the mirror. I turned toward him,
and a small smile drew up on his lips. "And you have attained it. You
look gorgeous, my dear."

I took in his navy three-piece suit with a light blue tie. The colors made his eyes almost glow, and I was entranced by them.

I shook my head to clear my mind. "Damn suits are like lingerie,"
I mumbled as I stepped away to pick up my clutch. It was an under-
stated, flat-black color so as not to detract from The Rock.

He held out his arm, and I slipped mine in as we headed out.

"I heard the whole family will be there," I said as Michael closed
the door to the sedan. Another man I wasn't familiar with sat in the
passenger seat.

"Yes."

"For water safety?"

"It provides swimming lessons for hundreds of thousands of people across the world, and also teaches about safety when in larger bodies of water."

Well, that made me understand a little more about why he pulled me away from the lake's edge like he did. Also the insistence of swim lessons. But where did the passion come from?

"And this is a de Loughrey charity?"

He nodded. "Georgiana is one of the organizers."

"So, I'll meet her tonight?"

"Meet? Possibly. See? Definitely."

"What does that mean?"

"It means she'll be hitting up big donors that are outside the family, and will avoid us. Not out of spite, but that time is limited. She will give a speech, though."

"But I'll meet the twins at least, right?"

He closed his eyes and let out a breath. "Shhhh."

I blinked at him, unsure of whether to be annoyed or not, but decided to drop it. I knew my constant questions grated on him and he'd probably hit his fill for the moment.

The rest of the drive was left in silence, giving my nerves time to ramp up. I'd never been to anything like what I was about to walk into, I was certain of that.

I blew out a deep breath when we pulled in front of the venue. People trickled by, everyone decked out like they were going to a wedding or grand ball. It reminded me of my senior prom, though Atticus was a much more attractive date than Jeff Russell.

I looped my arm into his as we made our way in.

"Spine straight, shoulders back," he whispered into my ear, sending a shiver down my spine.

I nodded and adjusted my posture to match his.

My eyes were wide as I looked around at all the different shades of blue created by lights coupled with draped fabrics. There were tables set up everywhere with more of the beautiful blues coupled with silver and gold, a stage at one end, and a bar on the other.

A banner held large, bold letters—The Adrianna de Loughrey Foundation.

Adrianna? I wanted to ask Atticus who Adrianna was, because her name wasn't familiar, but I knew his answer—read the folio.

One day I was going to set fire to the Binder of Doom and laugh gleefully as it became a pile of ash.

"Now what?" I whispered.

He let out a sigh. "Now, we be sociable."

"Do we have to?"

A deep chuckle resonated in his chest, barely perceptible over the music thumping from the speakers and the dull roar of chatter.

"Come, let's get a drink."

He pulled us toward the bar, but we were stopped by a familiar face. While I'd only met her once, there was no way I could forget Elizabeth.

She smiled broadly at her brother. "Atticus!"

"Good evening," he said before leaning in and placing a kiss on her cheek.

"I thought you would end up being fashionably late as usual."

I narrowed my gaze at him, which completely unaffected him. "We could have been late?"

"No."

"He could. You couldn't after that little upheaval." Elizabeth looked me up and then down before meeting my eyes. "You look very nice," she said, and knowing her frankness, it was genuine.

I smiled. "Thank you. You as well."

She pursed her lips and looked down to her stomach, which had grown quite a bit since I'd seen her at the family dinner. "As well as one can look while imitating a whale."

"When are you due?" I asked. I'd asked Atticus, but he'd only stared back at me with a blank look.

"Not soon enough. Just wait until it's your turn, and you'll understand."

My turn. My turn that wasn't so far into the future. Though I was happy for the candid conversation, Elizabeth didn't scowl at me before ignoring me like last time.

"Boy or girl?"

"Boy." She rubbed her stomach and smiled. "My little baby Bennett."

"*Our* little baby Bennett," Preston said as he wrapped his arms around his wife, a huge smile on his face. "Atticus. Ophelia. How are you?"

"Ophelia was just telling me how she can't wait to be pregnant," Elizabeth said.

I did? I glanced at Atticus, a small smirk playing on his lips.

"You're going to seal our fate with this man in charge?" Preston said with a groan.

"Well, when he asked, I figured why not. Sorry."

That got Preston to full-out laugh while Elizabeth shook her head and rolled her eyes.

A flash of red caught my eye, and I turned to find Genevieve walking toward us in the most revealing and outrageous dress made of red lace and red straps, while a few patches of cloth holding the skirt section together left little to the imagination. In fact, if she wasn't wearing panties, you'd be seeing all of her. The flat-panel front barely held her nipples from view out of stripes of lace.

"What the fuck are you wearing, Genevieve?" Atticus growled.

A smile brightened her face, and she held her arms out before doing a little twirl, catching more than a few eyes.

"Do you like it?" she asked, clearly happy with the reception she was getting from her brother.

"I believe there are crucial elements missing. It is not appropriate for tonight."

She pursed her lips and straightened her spine. "Mother said that the hem of my dress had to be to the floor, and it is."

For all the time I'd spent with Genevieve, I hadn't really gotten to experience what made her earn the title of the wild princess, but between the dress and her obstinate behavior, I was beginning to see it.

Atticus's hand rested on my hip and he pulled me in closer, like he didn't want me getting too close to Genevieve. That, or he was extremely happy my soon-to-be sister-in-law didn't help pick out my outfit. The skin under his touch resonated with warmth.

"Genevieve," a deep voice boomed out, catching everyone's attention.

I looked at her just in time to see the smirk form on her lips before she turned. "Yes, Father?"

Charles and Vera appeared, oddly arm in arm. It occurred to me then that I'd never seen them actually standing together, but even now, there was nothing in their touch more than formality.

They both looked regal, like royalty. The whole family looked so, but their posture was more rigid, and the air around them radiated with regality,

Charles's gaze flashed to me, and the intensity of disgust that was aimed at me nearly had my knees giving out. I blinked at him and leaned in closer to Atticus.

He seemed to understand, his grip tightening. "Father."

The unbearable weight of his scrutiny fell away as he regarded his son. "Atticus."

"Refrain yourself from looking at my fiancée like that."

Charles's eyes widened, and his muscles locked down while all the blood rushed to his face. An explosion felt imminent.

"Ophelia, dear, we must get together soon to talk about the wedding," Vera said, ignoring the temper tantrum the man beside her seemed to be gearing up for.

I gave her the best friendly smile that I could attempt under the pressure of Charles's mood. "That would be wonderful. Please, contact me at any time."

She gave me a polite smile before tugging on her husband's arm. "Come, Charles. I find I am quite thirsty."

"Well, he seemed even more lovely today," I said as I watched them walk away.

"He's angry with me," Atticus said.

I turned back to look at him. "For?"

"For completely derailing his plan to bring Harris Hotels into the family."

Harris. It had been weeks since I'd even thought of Amelia Harris and her hopeless tricks.

"I'm surprised he's held a grudge this long."

"He's a de Loughrey. He can hold a grudge forever."

"He'll never like me, will he?" Though I wasn't sure I wanted something like that.

"Trust me, it's better that way. Because if he does like you, he'll try to bed you, and I am not interested in jail time."

"Jail time?"

He grabbed my chin and tilted my head back. "Do you really think I'd let him touch what's mine?"

He leaned down, his lips ghosting mine.

"Ugh, could you please not do that, I might throw up."

We turned to find Hamilton glaring at us.

"Do you *have* to start off the evening being a ruthless asshole?" Gen asked.

"Do you have to start off the evening looking like a whore?"

"Excuse me?"

"Come," Atticus whispered into my ear, pulling me away from his siblings.

"Why is he always so hateful toward me? I mean, I get disinterested, but Hamilton seems to have a deep dislike of me." Every time I went to the office he glared at me, and at the family dinner he had some of the hard hits.

"I long ago stopped trying to understand Hamilton's pride."

"You think it's pride?" I asked.

"Atticus, my boy, it's been a while," a man said, drawing my attention. His brown eyes were honed in on me, and I didn't miss his perusal of my body. He was decent looking, with dark hair and a strong nose, but something about him bothered me and I felt Atticus tense.

Atticus's jaw clenched, and his grip on my hip tightened as he pulled me closer. It wasn't the first time, and I wondered if he would ever let go of me, but I had to admit that I liked it.

"Whitaker."

He looked from me to Atticus. "Well, aren't you going to introduce me to this beautiful morsel on your arm?"

Atticus gave a tight smile. "Ophelia, this is my old friend,
Whitaker James. Whitaker, my fiancée, Ophelia."

"Ophelia, what a lovely name," he said as he reached for my hand.
He drew it up and placed a kiss to the back of my hand. "Pleasure."

Atticus's fingers flexed and his jaw clenched as he glared at his
friend. He did use that word, but the look of fury on his face told a
different story.

"No date tonight?"

He glanced my way before meeting Atticus's gaze. "I was thinking of picking up something tasty tonight."

"Hmph. Well, we wouldn't want to hinder your search. If you
will excuse us, I need to speak to Rhys."

Whitaker nodded and smiled, and I shuddered as he looked me
over again. "I will await seeing you again."

Atticus pulled me away, heading straight for Rhys who was
standing on the edge of the mass of people.

"I'm not a criminal lawyer, so wipe that look off your face," Rhys
said as we approached.

I glanced up and blinked in surprise at the dark expression that
had overtaken Atticus's handsome features.

"I thought he was your friend," I said in confusion. He'd been on
the defensive from the moment he'd heard that man's voice.

"Who?" Rhys asked.

"Whitaker," Atticus bit out.

Rhys's eyes widened, then a smirk drew his lips up. "Ah, I see
now."

"See what?" I asked.

Rhys's gaze met mine. "Whitaker is a bit of a ladies' man. Known
to make women stray from their husbands."

"Therefore, I don't trust him within a ten-foot radius of you,"
Atticus grumbled.

Oh, so he was a player who had a penchant for taken women.

"Do you think I'm so gullible and pliable?" I asked.

"You agreed to marry me with little thought, so yes," Atticus said.

I rolled my eyes. "That was different."

"How so?"

I reached up and cupped his cheek. "Once upon a time, you showed me a wonderful evening, and I wanted to meet that man again."

Rhys let out a laugh. "Then you shouldn't have insisted on… you know."

I narrowed my gaze on Rhys before wrapping my arm around Atticus's and pulling. "Away, ye snake."

That lightened Atticus's mood, and a chuckle left him. A glance back showed Rhys's amusement as well. While the lethal lawyer had always made me edgy, he was also the only one to be nice to me from the moment we'd met.

"I wouldn't do that, you know," I said.

Atticus stopped and looked down at me. "Do what?"

"Cheat. I know our relationship isn't conventional, but still. I'm… yours," I said, feeling my cheeks suddenly flame.

I hadn't meant for it to come out like that, but it did, and I refused to look anywhere near him for fear I'd embarrass myself more.

His warm hand cupped my jaw and tilted my head back to look at him. The softness in his eyes caught me off guard.

"Just as I am yours."

My heart began beating wildly in my chest, and it felt like I was going to explode. Leaning down, his lips brushed lightly against mine before pressing down, adding a heat that seeped into me. It coiled and flowed, invading every inch of me.

When he pulled back, what felt like minutes had only been seconds, and I followed his lips, searching for more.

"Come."

We continued our circuit around the space, Atticus introducing me to so many people I couldn't keep track. It was hard enough with the de Loughreys that were everywhere we turned. Anyone else from the evening was in one ear and out the other.

An hour later, I glanced around and spotted Rhys arguing with the twins. He looked thoroughly sloshed.

"Damn it," Atticus grumbled, obviously seeing the same thing. "Stay here. I'll be back."

With each step from me, my inadequacies grew louder and louder that I didn't belong. I stood out, earning my attention, and I no longer had the shield that Atticus's larger-than-life reputation afforded.

I watched as he approached Rhys. Something about Rhys's behavior struck me, and not in the rage-fueled drunkenness of Lou kind of way. There was a darkness in Rhys, a pain so deep that leached out when his walls were down.

Most people were preoccupied, too stuck in their own bubble to notice, but a few caught a glimpse. I tried to seem inconspicuous, but it was difficult when I had no idea how to act and knew hardly anyone. Gen was the only one I was even remotely close to, but if I went near her, I'd face the wrath of Atticus.

And I really didn't want to disappoint him again.

"You seem out of place," a deep voice called, and I turned to find a stunning man with blond hair and the face of a god.

Why did everyone in this world have to be so beautiful?

"Hello," I said. An awkward feeling rolled in my stomach. I was certain Atticus would know who he was, and I desperately wished he'd return.

"I'm not sure I've seen you at one of these gatherings. You look out of place, and I feel it is my duty to make sure you are well taken care of."

"She is." The deep timbre of Atticus's voice sent a shiver down my spine that was electrified when his hand rested on my hip and he pulled me back into him.

The man blinked. "Mr. de Loughrey, what a pleasure it is to see you tonight."

"Go away, you toad, before I have you thrown out."

He nodded, then sauntered away.

I turned in his arms and was met by that dark look again. My brow furrowed as I reached up and poked his cheek, his gaze angled down, directing his glare at me.

"That's scary. I like how you called him a toad, though."

"Why was he over here?"

I shrugged. "He just appeared."

"Next time, turn and walk away."

I furrowed my brow. "That would be rude."

"Then be rude."

"Is that proper de Loughrey behavior?"

The crease in his brow deepened and he scowled at me.

"That look is definitely not de Loughrey approved." A small laugh left me, but as he looked at me with that overbearing intensity it died away. Why would he look at me like that?

"Are you…jealous?"

His gaze narrowed, and I would truly be frightened of the expression he wore if I didn't sense that my intuition was correct.

"You are, aren't you?"

He looked away, refusing to answer. "Come, we need to find our table."

"What was that about with Rhys? He looked like he was hurt."

"Rhys has his demons, like we all do. He just hides his very well until he can't anymore."

A gasp left me. While Atticus's description left much out, it told me all I needed to know.

There was so much to each member of the family that it would take years to understand them all.

As we approached our table, a familiar blonde was heading toward us.

Penelope and Elizabeth were the siblings I'd seen the least of. She held a quietness about her, but that silence wasn't due to shyness. She had a confidence and air along with a wall, much like her brother. The long-sleeved, high-neck, short black dress covered in rhinestones with knee high boots was another indication of her bold fashion sense.

"Pen," Atticus said as he leaned down and kissed her cheek.

"Att."

Att? It wasn't the first time I'd ever heard a nickname for Atticus—little Madeline had called him that, but I assumed that was due to her young age. The name felt weird. And very informal for a man like him.

"Your dress seems short."

She gave him the same neutral expression he wore. "My boots are tall."

"Have you seen Gen?"

She nodded. "And when she tried to throw a fit, I pointed out that I was showing far less skin than she. Even Mother couldn't complain."

"Hmm."

"Yes?"

"It's very you."

She gave her brother a slight smile. "Thank you."

Most of the time a smile so small would seem disingenuous, but the reserved air that surrounded Penelope made it a beaming expression. It made me curious what had stunted the younger de Loughrey. Was she always so silent in her presence? Or, did it have to do with the title I'd heard—the tainted princess?

None of my research had pointed out why or how she received such a brand. Then again, the Binder of Doom was focused on Atticus.

Another beautiful creature with dark hair and a soft, glowing smile stepped in our direction. She wore a mermaid-style dress covered in a smattering of blue, green, and gold that reminded me of the ocean. The blue in her dress made her matching eyes almost glow.

"Georgiana, you are looking stunning, as always," Atticus said, earning the sweetest, most beautiful smile I'd ever seen.

"So kind of you, Atticus." She turned her stunning blue eyes to me, nearly knocking me over.

Atticus was regal like a lion, but Georgiana was regal like a goddess.

"And you must be Ophelia. It's a pleasure to finally meet you." She took my hand in hers. "Are you enjoying yourselves?"

I nodded. "Very much. You've done a beautiful job on everything."

"It isn't all me. I'm merely the face. There are dozens of volunteers that put in tireless hours to our cause." She turned on a laser beam of a smile, a conspiratorial glint in her eye. It was the look of a salesman hooking their next target. "You know, we are always looking for volunteers if you're interested."

My mouth popped open, and I blinked at her. It was an idea I'd had, and this was my perfect opportunity.

"Yes, I would be." I glanced to Atticus and blinked at the confusion etched across his face. "Would that be okay?" I asked, doubting myself.

He swallowed and nodded, pulling my hand up to his lips. "I think that would be wonderful."

My reaction seemed to make him happy, and that made me happy. Plus, it would give me something to do other than waiting for the hours to pass.

"Wonderful," Georgiana said with that dazzling smile.

Once again, a de Loughrey I didn't understand. Her expression seemed completely pure, so unless she was a top-rate actress, Georgiana really was happy about me joining.

"Oh, there is my cue. Excuse me," she said before popping away.

"She is…perfect," I said to Atticus after she stepped away.

Atticus chuckled. "Georgiana, our little debutante. The *only* one that doesn't cause me problems."

I opened my mouth to say something, then quickly closed it.

"You were going to say something along the lines of they can't all be that bad, weren't you?"

"How did you know?"

A chuckle left him. "Your naiveté of my family amuses me."

"It's just a very different type of family than I'm used to." My expression fell, and in that brief fraction of a second, my dad's face popped into my mind. I missed him and the family I was cut off from when he died.

"They're your family now as well, you know."

Dozens of de Loughrey names and faces tumbled in my mind, burying me. From a family of five to one of nearly five hundred with all the cousins? It would definitely be an adjustment. But, at the same time, I kind of liked it. They were dysfunctional, and all had issues, but they were Atticus's, and now mine.

He pulled out my chair before taking the one beside me.

"I'm looking forward to getting involved with this charity and others," I said, smiling at him. It was the truth. If I was going to be part of the family, I couldn't be sitting on the sidelines, hiding at the top of the tower with Atticus.

"Knowing that something this important to me matters to you. Thank you," he said, his voice gruff. It held emotion that I wasn't used to, and I loved every single speck he showed to me. I loved even more that they were coming out more and more frequently.

"Thank you all so very much for being here and to support our cause." Georgiana's voice floated through the speakers. "As you all may know, this charity is close to all de Loughrey hearts after the tragic death of my sister Adrianna. Accidental drowning takes thousands of lives a year. For every person we educate and encourage, it's the chance of one less family having to go through what we were forced to face."

Once again, I tried to recall where I'd seen or heard about her before. Her name sparked a memory, but I couldn't understand why. In all my reading of the family, had I only seen it in passing? Such a tragic event would have been highlighted, but maybe I hadn't gotten to it.

"Your cousin drowned?" I whispered to Atticus.

He only nodded, a solemn expression clouding his handsome features. I didn't press for more. I couldn't. I felt like it would only push him away, and that was the last thing we needed. For now, I would let it rest. For now.

TWENTY-NINE

ATTICUS

The charity dinner was a success, and not just for the foundation. Ophelia was seen as more than what was portrayed on her night out with Gen. I was proud of her.

Shutting myself away had only created a friction that held her back from accepting my family, but I felt like she had opened up. The disconnect faded away as our connection tightened.

Being in a relationship, even one as undefined as ours, took more effort that I imagined, but somehow, with her, it almost felt effortless.

The more time we spent together, the more attached to her I became, to the point she had me texting her, just to keep a connection throughout the day.

Atticus : I'm going to be about an hour late. Will you wait and have dinner with me?

Ophelia : What do I get in return?

Atticus : I didn't realize this was a negotiating request.

Ophelia : I mean, foot rub? Watch a movie with me? Maybe, just maybe, sit next to me on the couch?

A small chuckle left me. If that was what she wanted, I'd give it all to her.

Not that I would tell her that.

Atticus : That's asking an awful lot.

Ophelia : No, asking a lot would be for me to ask you to cuddle me against your body while we watch a movie. But don't worry, I won't request your strong arms to hold me tight. I wouldn't want to ask the wicked king for affection.

She topped it off with the kissy face emoji, but I ignored her sarcastic flirtation.

We'd been getting closer since she came back. I enjoyed our dinners together, and every day I found myself even more entranced by her than I was the day before.

Sitting on the couch with her as we talk about our days had become the highlight of my evenings. Simple, yet comforting in a way I had never experienced before.

Over the last few weeks, I had enjoyed our breakfasts together. She didn't have to get up with me as it was often as the sun crested the horizon, but it warmed me to see her smiling face over the mug of coffee her hands were always wrapped around.

The nectar of the gods, she called it.

When I entered the great room the night before, I'd faltered in my step, struck by the smile on her face. It was so large and genuine and lit up her face.

My cold, dead heart thawed a little more each time she looked at me like that.

"You're in an uncharacteristically good mood," Holly said with narrowed eyes as she stared me down.

I schooled my expression to my negative neutral position. "I don't know what you're talking about."

She rolled her eyes at me before hopping onto the edge of my desk. "Things are going better, huh?"

"With?"

She rolled her eyes. "Do I *have* to play dentist with you? Just admit to me you have feelings for her."

"And I should admit that to you because?"

"Because I'm Holly."

"And that gets you special favors?"

"Come on, Att," she whined and stomped her feet.

A small chuckle left me. "Fine. I want her. Truly want her. Is that what you wanted to hear?"

She hemmed and hawed before giving me a stink eye. "What I wanted was to hear you say how much you're in love with her and how you want her forever and ever."

I stared at her and her twinkling, hopeful, expression. "No."

The elation fell from her face, and she grabbed my shoulders and gave me a light shake. "Why do you have to be such a suck?"

"Because what is between Ophelia and myself is between us."

"But I'm me!"

"Yes, and if one day I have the feelings you spoke of, I will tell her before anyone else."

"You're a party pooper, Atticus de Loughrey."

"Am I supposed to be offended by that?"

A sigh left her. "By the way, your ten o'clock is here."

I glanced to the clock—it was ten after. Normally it would have angered me if an appointment was late to start, but I didn't mind for him.

"You're just now telling me?"

She smiled and nodded. "I'm letting him stew."

"Why are you doing that?"

"Because he's in trouble."

I narrowed my eyes on her. "How do you know that?"

"Because unless it is Hamilton, Rhys, Elizabeth, or your father, they've done something wrong and are about to get their ass handed to them by their king."

I scoffed at that. She wasn't wrong. Not often did a member of the family come to me for anything other than to be reprimanded in some form.

"Show him in."

"You got it, boss," she said as she pushed off the edge of my desk.

My jaw twitched, and I was not looking forward to having to deal with this bullshit.

Hugo had gotten another indication that Preston was looking to have a rendezvous with a woman that wasn't his wife. Elizabeth could take care of herself, but I didn't want to see her hurt because her husband was attempting to fuck another woman. Knowing her, what I was about to say to him would be a walk in the park compared to what she would do.

"Atticus, how are you today?" Preston said with a smile as he stepped in.

I refused to even look up from my desk, letting his discomfort continue to climb. "I would like to remind you of your vows to my sister," I said, wasting not a precious second with frivolities getting to the point. There was no time for dancing around issues.

His expression was hidden due to my ignoring his presence, but his silence spoke volumes.

"I don't know if you've broken them yet, but do know your hotel reservation has been canceled."

"Atticus, I—"

My gaze snapped to him and he froze, his brown eyes widening at my expression. "Not another word," I seethed. "Don't forget, *brother*, there are consequences for certain actions. I'm giving you this one warning. There will not be another before I rip your wife and children from you and ruin every single person in your family. You are not to speak to this girl again. Her name and number have already been stripped from your phone."

"Atticus."

I stopped him. "Don't. Go home and spend some time with your pregnant wife."

"I'm not under your control!" he shouted. "You have *no right* to interfere with my life."

I narrowed my gaze at him, taking note of how he froze again, and the fight drained from him, his throat bobbing in a hard swallow. Preston held the confidence of most aristocrats. The thought that he could get away with whatever he wanted and was untouchable. To be told what to do went against every fiber of his being.

It made no difference that he was not a de Loughrey by name

or blood. He married into the family. The blood of the de Loughreys ran through his children's veins.

"Do not speak to me with that self-righteous indignation. Did you think, because I am not my grandfather or father, that because we have been friends our whole life, that I will not cut you down? You married into this family. It was explained to you that actions have consequences. We are not some family that lets frivolous egos run rampant."

"You're a bunch of stuck-up, cold bastards," he spat back. His hits had so little force, his will was easy to bend.

"And you're a spoiled little boy. Man the fuck up, and take responsibility for your family. Do one more thing out of line, and I will destroy you," I seethed in warning. I would not forgive another outburst.

His teeth mashed together, but he remained silent. Rage shook in his hands, but it seemed his brain was holding back his ego before the consequences became dire.

"Have you fallen out of love with your wife? Is that why you seek comfort in a younger pussy?"

"No."

"Good. Then either seek that comfort with your wife or use your fucking hand until she's ready, but do not make the mistake again of looking for something outside of your marriage. I'm always watching, Preston. Never forget that."

He gave a curt nod, anger radiating off him, but he swallowed his defeat and fled from my presence.

With a sigh, I threw my pen down and rocked back in the chair. Elizabeth would be devastated if she knew, but she was never going to know her husband was even looking at another woman. My way was also better for Preston in the long run because I knew my sister, especially in her current state, would have no issue castrating him.

I spent the next few hours in a string of meetings and conference calls. It was late in the afternoon when Damien, my head of security, called.

"Damien?"

"So the Milner guy."

"Yes?"

"In jail for extortion and various other infractions."

A small sense of relief shed some of the tension from my body. "Good. And?"

"And he's been fired from his job. Bail has been set, but I made sure it was high enough to be a hurdle."

I'd kept Ophelia as far away from her stepfather as best I could, even going so far as to make sure there was no way he could get in contact with her. She'd expressed her trepidation when her sisters called, thinking they might have been put up to it by their parents since I'd blocked their numbers, but she said her youngest sister couldn't fake the fear she heard in her voice.

The moment she said that, I knew he'd found a new target for his anger, and I ripped those children from his care. Ophelia's happiness over her sisters being safely away from that piece of shit had flowed out of her. That level of relief told me one thing—I was going to bury the man.

It wasn't something she talked about, but more than once she'd told me he'd hit her before, and my investigation revealed it wasn't an uncommon thing. She was too strong to be broken, especially by a weak drunk of a man, but still, it fractured her. Knowing your mother chose a man over her own child had to be devastating, but she'd persevered.

My own mother may not have had a high degree of affection, but she'd put the five of us above everything. Even with all the nannies, she'd been highly devoted to her children, even if her expression of love was different than most.

I didn't want our children to have either of our upbringings. I was going to shower them with affection and show their mother the same care. They would learn what love was from the moment they came into the world, even if their father was still learning himself.

THIRTY

OPHELIA

I stared down at my buzzing phone and the name that flashed across the screen. Panic shot through me and I quickly fumbled with the phone to answer, then drew in a deep breath to settle myself.

"Hello?" I answered, hoping I came across as calm and collected when I was a bundle of knots.

"As reluctant as I am that my son has chosen you, it does not change the fact that in seven short months, you will be married," Vera said. Her tone was just as terse and clipped as when we'd first met, and I wondered if that was just a de Loughrey trait. "That being said, I have already reserved venues."

"Already? But I haven't even gotten to look at any." In truth, the wedding had been far from my mind.

"There are few places that can hold an event of this size, so options are limited."

"Of what size?" The largest wedding I'd ever attended was around two hundred.

"A thousand."

I choked on my sip of water, nearly spitting it out all over my computer. I coughed to clear my throat, my voice coming out coarse and stunted. "A thousand?"

"Over three hundred are de Loughreys."

"Three hundred?"

"Honestly, Ophelia, must you parrot everything I say?"

"I'm sorry. I'm just stunned. I didn't think we'd even have three hundred total."

An amused laugh danced across the line. She was laughing at me, at my naiveté.

"Sadly outside of a horrid sports arena, our options are limited, and nothing will hold the current total. I have no idea how I'm to cull the list down to only five hundred."

Only. I was flabbergasted. I knew we were getting married, I just hadn't thought about the actual wedding. Atticus said January and I thought nothing more of it, but it was obvious by her call she wanted some input.

Or to tell me what my colors were going to be. With her take-charge attitude on the event, that was a possibility.

"And where is this enormous ceremony being held?"

"Atticus didn't tell you?"

"No."

She made a hmph sound. "Not surprising. The Plaza, dear. We've reserved the entire hotel."

"Like all their spaces."

"No. The entire hotel."

My mouth dropped open. "You can do that?"

"Of course we can. We're de Loughreys. All I had to do was reserve every room for wedding guests as well as utilize the grand ball-room and all the other rentable spaces."

"What happened to the people who had reservations already?"

Another scoffing sound. "They were compensated."

"Why?" I asked. Why would she do all of that for just a wedding?

"The head of the family will only marry once. It will be the grandest occasion the city has seen in decades. An event to rival the weddings of British royals in people's minds. My son is, after all, the king of our family, and the de Loughreys are US royalty."

My mind skipped over the second part of what she said, instead sticking on the first.

The head of the family will only marry once.

"I'm sending you some papers to look over for your opinion. We will talk later," she said before the line went dead.

The head of the family will only marry once.

It echoed in my mind, repeating over and over. A sudden burst of desperation had me clawing for my laptop. I pulled up the internet and typed in my question.

Have any de Loughreys divorced?

I clicked on the first article. It was a history of the family.

The family is known for a low divorce rate. Only three divorces have happened since the first in 1965. None of the divorces happened within those in the upper echelon of the company and family. It is said that divorce is forbidden in the core group, especially the head of the family.

Forbidden? What did that mean, then?

"I'm home, my dear," Atticus called out as I was sitting on the couch, scrolling through wedding ideas.

I wasn't hating it as much as before, probably due to my growing affection for the brooding man.

I glared at him as he rounded the corner, earning a smirk. He knew I couldn't stand his overly proper and sardonic pet name.

"Do you do that just to see my eye twitch?"

"Do what?" he asked with the most innocent expression I'd ever seen on his face. His eyes were wide, eyebrows raised, but he had trouble hiding his mirth.

My lips formed a thin line, and I rolled my eyes.

He surprised me by sitting on the couch, and even more so when he leaned over and grabbed my ankle. I cried out, my eyes wide as I watched him pull my leg out from under me until I'd twisted from my position with my legs out straight and sitting on his lap.

I blinked at him in stunned silence. Not only did he pull an affectionate move, but *he* put my *feet* on his expensive suit. They were clean and all, as I hadn't done anything but walk around the condo after my shower and the maids made certain there wasn't a speck of dirt or dust anywhere, let alone on the floors.

It was more than a small victory.

A hum rumbled in his chest and he closed his eyes, his thumb making small circles on my ankle. After a few deep breaths, he looked over to me.

"Better?"

I felt the heat rise in my cheeks, and I nodded. My text had been a half joke thinking he would never do any of it, and he did. What I think surprised us both was the obvious effect it had on him.

"Better?" I asked in return.

His other hand ran up my bare leg just past my knee, leaving a trail of heat as his hand rested on my thigh.

A groan left him. "You and fucking shorts."

"What? It's summer and hot as hell out there."

"You are in a perfectly climate-controlled interior."

I shrugged. "I like shorts."

He ran his hand higher, dipping between my thighs on his way back to my knee, making me gasp at the electricity that zipped through me.

"I appreciate your shorts as well. Especially these little cotton things that are easily discarded."

"Meaning?"

His lip twitched. "Are you not following my mood?" he asked as his fingers skimmed the inside of my thigh again.

"You'd destroy my clothing?"

He grinned, and I was forced to swat his hand away before I began squirming and giving away how much he was affecting me.

"Your mother called me today." As I said the word "mother" with regard to Vera, I suddenly understood why her children opted for the more formal title over the simple "Mom." If there was a motherly bone in her body, I hadn't seen even the slightest hint of it. Then again, she was a de Loughrey, and Atticus's mother. They seemed similar in many regards.

That seemed to be a cold water equivalent, and the heat that encircled us receded. "Are you to begin working on the wedding?"

"Did you ask her to call me?"

He shook his head. "Why would I thrust you into such a position?"

"To give me something to do, since you blew off my work request."

"I agreed, didn't I?"

"And yet, no calls or contacts."

"Do you want the position due to my name or your own merit?" he asked.

My lips formed a thin line. "My own, of course."

"Then apply as everyone else does."

"Fine," I huffed. I really did want to do it the hard way, but I also knew one word from Atticus and I could be working as early as next week.

"What did she say?" he asked. His posture had stiffened since I mentioned she'd called and he almost seemed frozen, as if he were on guard.

"That we're getting married at the Plaza and you should have told me."

He hummed, some of the tension leaving him. "I suppose I failed to convey that information. She had it set weeks before our contract."

"Seriously?"

He nodded. "I think my mother is in desperate need for something new and exciting."

"She told me some things."

"Things?"

"Why did you…" I trailed off, trying to form my thoughts into a coherent question. "Why did you agree to divorce me if the head of the family is forbidden to divorce?"

He arched a brow at me. "No one forbids me anything."

"Except me."

He nodded and squeezed my ankle. "Except you."

"I was just reading something, and it said—"

"It's nothing more than conjecture mixed with the knowledge that no head of the de Loughrey family has ever divorced. It's not forbidden, it simply isn't done."

"Your mom said that the head of the family will only marry once."

"Because lasting marriages have preceded."

"Will you marry again after we divorce?" Even saying that word in conjecture to my relationship with Atticus felt wrong on every level. Even if my head knew that we were a contract, a business agreement, my heart still felt more for him than I was willing to acknowledge.

His gaze met mine, and I could feel him shutting down on me. The lazy touch was gone, and his jaw was clenched tight.

"No."

"Why?"

He glared at me. "Before we're even married, you want to talk about me marrying someone else?"

"It's just that you seem so set on it. Once I'm gone, you'll be free to find someone to love."

"Once you're gone, you'll still be here!" he roared.

I pulled back in surprise. "What do you mean?"

"What I mean is that you will have a condo in this building. Our children will remain close to me. No matter what, you will still always be there, haunting me."

His voice broke on the last words, and a vice gripped my chest. I reached out, but he pulled away before I could touch him. There was no way I was going to let that go so easily and I straddled his legs, trapping him in place, not letting him run from me again.

I cupped his face as he pulled away and snarled at me, his eyes focusing on anywhere but me.

"Hey, calm down. It's okay. It's okay," I said lowly as I smoothed my thumbs against his cheeks. It was like trying to soothe a wounded animal. Fear and a lack of trust had him lashing out against me. Exposing his emotions was difficult and left him feeling open and vulnerable.

He glared viciously at me, and I couldn't help but smile, then laugh, before leaning in and pressing my lips to his.

It had been a move born purely from instinct. A moment where we were both relaxed with our walls down. Our flaws laid out.

For a moment, it was just Ophelia and Atticus. A man and a woman.

His arms wrapped around me as the kiss deepened, pulling me as close as possible. Maybe he was as reluctant for me to leave one day as I was.

Maybe one day, we could be bound by more than signatures on a contract.

THIRTY-ONE

ATTICUS

"Tis is torture! Inhumane!"

I pinched the bridge of my nose. "I'm hanging up now, Gen."

"Seriously? How can you do this?" she whined.

Not surprisingly, Genevieve's bank account was near empty, depleted of her monthly allowance. Her issue was that she'd just been informed that she would not be getting her usual deposit, meaning she was forced to subsist on what she had for another month.

"How? Because per usual, you were only thinking about yourself. The media backlash against Ophelia for that night is egregious. She was fresh meat, and you threw her to the wolves." Genevieve had gotten away with much more in her life than most. Partly because she was the salutatorian of her high school class, and she graduated from Yale with a 3.87, but I knew she never got the praise she was searching for. None of us did.

"I didn't mean for that to happen. I was just trying to help."

"Help?"

"She was so upset about something, and lonely. I like her, and I didn't want to see her like that so I thought going out would cheer her up," she said, her voice lowering. I could hear the sincerity in her tone. There was nothing malicious about her intent, but in the end, someone was hurt.

"Cheer her up? Do you even know why she was upset?" I asked. Despite the care she had for Ophelia, I could not back down due to that.

"Because of the rush of fame, I think."

"Because her stepfather was blackmailing her. And then you ruined her public image just as she was exposed to the world as my fiancée."

"I didn't think—"

"No, you didn't," I said, cutting her off. "And therein lies the problem. I'm being generous because you were accepting of her, but you are not absolved from punishment."

"But six weeks?"

"Nothing. And all family members have been advised not to give you a single penny, or else I will come after them next."

"Atticus," she whined.

"You want two months?"

If she was in front of me, I could just imagine the spoiled little stomp of her foot.

"Also, stay away from her."

"But…"

"I mean it. Repairing her image is going to take time. The charity for Adrianna helped, but right now, I don't need her associated with you in any way."

"I really do like her." Her voice was low, repentant.

"I know, but for now, go back to ignoring her like everyone else."

Ophelia had been told not to interact with Genevieve, and after that night, she was falling into line there. It helped that things were improving between us.

"Be good."

"Yeah, right," she said, her boisterous voice returning. "I'm the wild princess, remember?"

"I still remember when you were on the Dean's list."

"Don't ruin my image."

A chuckle left me. "If you gave me any harder of a time, I was going to kick you out of the tower and put you up in Ophelia's old apartment."

A sharp gasp left her. "Fine. I'll deal with it. It's not like I have any other choice."

"I'm sure with as smart as you are, you can come up with some way to make money on your own."

"Whatever. Bye," she said, clearly sulking before the line went dead.

The conversation went better than I'd anticipated, but I could hear the guilt in her voice. She really was trying to be Ophelia's friend, but that was the problem, wasn't it? Did any of us even know *how* to be friends with anyone?

Ophelia wasn't after Genevieve's status or money. Only her company.

That was the refreshing part about her. Despite how much money I spent on her, what she wanted was my time. It was a foreign concept to me, but I was beginning to understand her desire for it.

A longing to be near her had settled inside me. She was infecting my thoughts and had me racing home to spend time with her. Being around her was calming, and that calmness was like a drug in my system, making me itch for more and more every day.

I didn't ever want to part from her.

The door to my office slammed open, and I groaned as I wondered why the fuck I was paying to have assistants if they couldn't stop people from barging in. My father's larger-than-life ego waltzed in.

"How is it dealing with a fiancée that embarrasses the entire family?" he asked. Nearly two weeks had passed, and I had fought off interacting with him so not to deal with his bullshit.

I ground my teeth together. "I don't know. Perhaps I shall speak with Mother, since you embarrass her often."

The usual quick temper had anger rolling through him and fire sparked in his eyes. "Watch how you speak to me, son."

Once upon a time, his overbearing presence kept me in line, afraid of his ire.

But I wasn't a child any longer, and he still had not come to accept that I had surpassed him. His anger no longer had me freezing and trying to please him in hopes of praise.

Those were emotional hang-ups I no longer had with him. They'd long been gone. No, now his anger served to stoke my own. His ego forgot who was in charge.

I am the king.

"What power do you hold over me that I should tuck my tail for you?" I asked.

"I'm your father," he boomed.

"That only gets you so far. The issue has been dealt with, the punishment administered."

"Do you even have it in you to punish the girl?" he asked, speaking about Ophelia.

"Are you testing my ability to lead? I can assure you, if you continue to attempt to throw heiresses at me, I will make certain to show you how apt I am at controlling and administering punishments."

"You should have taken the Harris girl."

"I do not wish to continue speaking of that piece-of-trash whore."

His eyes widened.

"You told her to throw herself at me, didn't you?" I asked, already knowing the answer. It had been confirmed by Harris himself as he'd begged me to stop destroying his company.

"She was a better match."

"By whose standards? Ophelia is the best match for me. All aspects of me."

"She's making you weak."

"On the contrary, she is making me stronger. Now, if you wish to continue bashing my fiancée, get the fuck out. If you have business to speak of, then use your words for that, because I will not tolerate any further verbal griping or attacks against Ophelia."

Once I was done, silence stretched between us as electricity crackled. He didn't want to give up the power, even though it was already done.

"Atticus, have you seen—" Elizabeth stepped in, her thought ended as she blinked at the tense situation before her. Her expression flattened into one of disdain mixed with disinterest, often described as the de Loughrey default setting. "With this tense atmosphere, I take it that Ophelia is the subject."

"You should talk some sense into your brother, Eliza."

She folded her arms across her chest, which had them resting awkwardly on her baby bump. "The one who needs sense knocked into them is you, Father. You seem to be lacking that in spades."

"Excuse me? I taught you to have more respect than what you are both showing."

"Respect is earned, and you lost ours ages ago. If you'd like to regain some, accept Ophelia into the family with open arms. She has quite a sunny disposition—an asset to this family."

"She is an albatross around this family's neck. You're just too blinded by pussy to see it."

The anger rose up in me like a tidal wave, fierce and fast and ready to destroy everything in its path.

"Go home, Father. Back to Stronghold. And stay there. If you say one more fucking word at this moment, I will not be held responsible for my actions against you."

His eyes widened, and finally, for the first time, I could see the spark of acceptance. The sharp edge of his gaze flicked from Elizabeth, then back to me. His posture was rigid, unwilling to back down, but he knew he'd pushed me too far and wasn't prepared to fight back.

With a reluctant nod, he headed for the door, slamming it as he went.

"You showed great restraint," Elizabeth said once he was gone.

"At a time I shouldn't have," I seethed, my muscles coiled tightly, desperate for an outlet.

"Perhaps, but you were able to exert your dominance without bashing his face in. That in and of itself is a massive accomplishment."

With a whip of my hand, I picked the phone up from my desk

and slammed it against the wall with a roar. The explosion of plastic shattered the red from my vision and settled the burning need to smash his face in to a manageable level.

"Why does he test me so?" I growled.

Elizabeth took my hand in hers. "Because he is greedy for control. Losing the responsibility of being the head of the family took a burden from his shoulders, but I don't think he anticipated the complete loss of power, control, and obedience. We are not in his court any longer. We are in yours."

"You are much more diplomatic than I am."

She gave me a slight smile. "Not that much. I simply use my temper with a piercing tongue instead of a brash fist."

"I appreciate your praise of Ophelia. Thank you."

Her smile spread, and her gaze softened. It was almost nostalgic. I hadn't seen a look like that cross her face in years.

"She's good for you. I could see that plainly at the charity dinner. I know I wasn't the most receptive toward her at the family dinner, but perceptions change. Anything that is good for you is good for us all." She stepped forward and stretched up to place a kiss to my cheek. "Open your heart to her. Don't keep yourself locked away."

"When did you become so wise?"

"What are you talking about? I was always wise, you're just a stubborn man."

A chuckle left me, and I leaned down to kiss her cheek. "I will heed your advice, counselor."

"Good. Now, I'm going to waddle back to my office and put my feet up."

"You know you can take maternity leave at any time."

Her nose scrunched at that thought. "I prefer to keep busy."

"You should go down to Haven for a week or two to relax before the baby comes."

A hum left her. "That's not a bad idea. Have a good rest of your day."

"You as well."

As I sat, I was surprised to note how calm I was. After a normal visit from my father, I was a fuming disaster of bottled anger, but after letting off a small bit of steam, Elizabeth's presence and backing of Ophelia tamed me. True, I had lost it for a moment, but normally I would still be stewing. Instead, I opened up my phone to read a missed text from Ophelia.

Ophelia: I was sitting on the patio when this little friend came to visit.

Attached was a photo with a wide-eyed, huge-smile selfie of Ophelia pointing over her shoulder to a small black and white bird with a bright yellow head sitting on the chair's back.

I couldn't help but smile at the childlike giddiness of her expression. It was just as I'd seen on the dock with the fish. A different kind of warmth spread through me as I looked at her. It wasn't the intense desire that I was accustomed to, but a burning ember deep in my chest.

A groan left me as I glanced up at the clock. I'd lost track of time again, and it had gotten past six. There was still work to be done, but I could get to it at home after dinner.

It was nearly seven when I entered the condo. Loreno and Amara could be heard in the kitchen, but no other sound. The great room was empty, and from my vantage point I could tell the terrace was as well. Turning back down the hall, I headed toward Ophelia's bedroom, but it was also vacant. I stopped by my bedroom to drop off my jacket, tie, and cufflinks, leaving my vest on and rolling up my sleeves.

I'd noticed the way she stared just a bit longer when my forearms were exposed. Continuing on my circuitous path to the kitchen, I entered to find Loreno and Amara, but still no Ophelia.

"Ah, my friend, how are you?"

"Well, and you?"

"Good, good."

"Have you seen Ophelia?" I asked.

Amara looked to her husband, then back to me. "No. She didn't greet us when we arrived."

I furrowed my brow. "She greets you?"

Amara smiled. "Oh, yes. Nearly every day. Such a sweet woman."

I ground my teeth together as a nagging sensation settled in my chest. It was akin to the panic I'd felt when I realized she'd left me weeks ago. I swallowed it down and pulled up my phone to locate hers.

A wave of relief moved through me. She was twenty-two stories below me in the theater room.

The tech team had managed to link the phone-finding application with the building's internal location system. It didn't matter what floor she was on. If the phone hadn't exited the building, it was still there.

"She's downstairs. I'll go collect her for dinner," I said before turning and heading back toward the elevator.

"Dinner will be ready in thirty minutes," Amara called after me.

After I'd shown her the theater room on her birthday and the excitement she exhibited, I'd expected to find her down there more often, but it was the first time. It was very possible that she spent time there during the day, but I was curious what had captured her so much that she was still down there.

The sounds of something playing hit my ears as I slid through the doors. Even the clunk of the door couldn't pull her attention from the screen, and she failed to notice me.

I was completely enamored watching her screen-highlighted features that I had paid no attention to anything other than her. The recliner legs were up, exposing the way her tight-clad hips were grinding against the leather.

My gaze flicked to the screen, and I was shocked watching a man grab the back of a woman's neck and turn her back to him. They were naked in a shower, and it surprised me to see her so captivated by such a film, but soon realized it was not one of a pornographic nature.

A groan left me, thinking about how she was grinding against her seat, and my cock began to harden, desperate to fill her ache.

I moved toward her and the movement caught her eye, causing her head to snap toward me. She froze as she stared at me while I took the seat next to her.

An alluring siren drawing me in without even realizing it. The pink of her cheeks and the way she clenched and rubbed her thighs was coiling me tighter and tighter. She was a delectable snack, and I wanted a taste.

I leaned forward, my lips ghosting her ear, and I grinned at her shuddered intake of breath.

"That feeling you have right now? The fire in your blood and the heat between your thighs? That's lust."

She turned to me, our lips almost touching. Her wide eyes met my lust-laden ones. I perused her body, noting how close her hand had gotten to her clit between her thighs. Her pert nipples were next, followed by those sinful lips I'd dreamt about stretching around my cock for over a year.

"Take off your shirt," I ordered.

"N-no."

"Your nipples are already stretching against the fabric in such a lewd manner." I flicked my fingers across the small bumps, earning a sharp moan that moved straight to my dick. "Show me how aroused you are."

THIRTY-TWO

OPHELIA

"**S**how me how aroused you are."

Atticus had shown up so suddenly that I was still trying to process what was going on. When did he get home? What time was it? All questions that should have been burning through my mind, but instead, all I couldn't think about were his lips and hands.

The movie had pulled me in, and I'd lost track of all senses except for the heat pooling between my thighs.

"Do you want help?"

My heart jumped, and I stared at him.

Yes.

Yes.

I wanted him to touch me so badly, but I'd made the rule in the contract. At that moment, I didn't care. I *needed* him to touch me.

And touching wasn't sex.

"Yes," I whispered, my breath hitching.

A low rumble of approval resonated in his chest, and he moved to loom over me. The anticipation only amped up my desire. Inches apart, and I could feel the soft tickle of his breath against my neck before I jumped at the sudden electric shock of his touch on my thigh.

A low chuckle left him as he slowly moved his fingers inward until they were running along the seam of my leggings.

"Such heat," he whispered as he pressed his fingertips in.

My heartbeat sped up and a moan ripped through me. It was the first time in a year that anyone had touched me, and the blood in my veins seemed to explode upon contact, even with the cloth barrier between us.

"Hmm, I like that sound." His touch remained strong as he moved up to my waistband. Our eyes locked as his fingers slipped between the waistband and my skin.

It was incredibly hard to keep myself from grabbing hold of him, because I knew if I did, I would give in. My eyelids drifted closed as he skimmed my clit and down to my lips.

"You're incredibly wet, my dear. Just what kind of movie is this, hmm?"

Uncontrollably, my hips moved against his hand, and I stared up at the ceiling, lost in the feel of his fingers curled inside me. I fisted the arm of the chair, my body moving against the one spot he was touching.

"Look at me," he said lowly.

A shudder rolled through me at his words and the commanding tone. It was the same tone from that night, the one that I'd recalled over and over. When our eyes met, every muscle clenched. The powerful darkness of his eyes drew me in, and I cursed as my body begged to break.

Just a little more.

"What are you doing to me?" he whispered against my lips.

"Aren't I the one that's supposed to be asking that?"

That earned me a growl and the palm of his hand to rub my clit harder, his fingers curled in the perfect spot. A whimper fled from me and I grabbed onto his arm, resisting the urge to take hold of his shoulders.

A sudden tug on my waistband with his free hand drew my

attention, watching as he pushed my leggings down my hips, then down my thighs. I didn't even protest, my body so needy for his touch.

"Spread your legs."

Electricity pulsed everywhere he touched me, and even a single glance set me on fire. I stood no chance, and my legs, still tangled in my leggings, drew up as my thighs opened, exposing where his fingers were still buried.

A groan left him and he pulled his fingers out, spreading my juices across my skin. My hips rocked, and a whimper left me. When did I become such a desperate woman driven by her pussy?

"Look at that beautiful pussy," he said, his tone low and gravelly, sending a shiver down my spine. He was entranced, watching his fingers move in and out. "You have no idea how much I want to be buried inside you."

Something about the desperation in his tone and the way the words slipped from his lips made me come undone. I needed them as much as I needed his eyes burning into my soul, as much as his touch scorching every inch of my skin.

"Look at me," he growled. His hand gripped my jaw, just like it had that night, and forced my gaze to meet him. The fingers inside me began to move deeper and harder, chasing a purpose, while his grip tightened.

My back arched, unable to handle his onslaught, every muscle locking down. His lips ghosted mine as he began snarling, his force growing.

I could do nothing but feel him, his desire and lust that he held by a fraying cord ready to snap at the slightest. His lips crashed to mine and a whimper left me as my lips parted, his tongue brushing against mine, pushing me into the cushion of my chair.

The grip on my jaw released, and he took hold of my hand and pulled it to him, pressing my palm against the hard, hot outline of his cock.

"Tell me you want it."

I locked my jaw down so that my mouth wouldn't betray me and shook my head.

"Tell me, and I'll let you come. Beg for my cock."

My mouth fell open, a scream leaving me as my body convulsed against the recliner, gripping his arm as I held his hand in place, riding out my orgasm.

I collapsed down, aftershocks rocking my body as nerves fired off.

I was faced with the terrifying fact that Atticus had given me the hardest orgasm I'd had since the last time he touched me like that over a year before. A shock rocked through me as his fingers slipped out.

I glanced up in time to watch as his tongue lapped at his fingers, licking up my juices. My face flamed as my senses began to return, and I was ready to bolt when his knee settled between my thighs.

Startled by the intensity in which he stared at me, I'd forgotten that my hand was still softly stroking him through his slacks.

"My turn," he said as he pulled the zipper down.

Deftly, he freed himself by simply pulling his length through the hole his zipper made. I stared at it, having forgotten how large he was. My pussy pulsed in longing, wanting to feel him fill me again.

I wrapped my hand around him, lost in the reality of what my fantasies could not do justice to. His low moans were a sweet symphony of longing and desire I knew all too well. He watched silently on as I caressed him, slowly jerking him off.

The urge to take him into my mouth, to feel the hot, silky weight of his cock on my tongue was so strong. But I knew if I did that, it would no longer be a period of mutual masturbation and would cross the line, blurring them until they were gone altogether.

He caged me against the recliner, hands on either side of me locked down onto the frame while his hips rolled his cock through my hands.

With yet another sexy sound, he ripped my shirt up so that it rested above my breasts. I wasn't wearing a bra.

"Push them together," he instructed in that tone that left no room for argument.

My breasts were not very big, quite small actually, and I had to use my fingers to bridge across the top. I loved the deep groan that resonated in his chest and the clouded look in his eyes as he thrust between my breasts.

Without warning, I felt a warm splash beneath my jaw before a deep growl left him and another splash hit my chin and bottom lip. More warm ropes of cum landed on my chest and pooled at my collarbone and the hollow of my throat before a final flex of his hips and the last drops released.

He was breathing heavily as he pulled back. Reaching up, he swiped the droplets that landed on my lips away before leaning in for a kiss.

"Dinner should be ready by now."

I blinked at him. After all that, those were his next words?

"That's it?"

His brow arched. "What would you have me say?"

"I'm covered in your cum. Doesn't that evoke some response?"

"I forgot how soft your skin felt. If you find yourself in this state of arousal again, please don't hesitate to ask me for my assistance."

I narrowed my eyes at him and glared.

His lips drew up into a smirk and he pressed another kiss to my lips.

"Thank you for the spirited welcome home, my dear."

I pushed him away and sat up. "Yeah, that's not happening again." I felt the cooling liquid start to slide and I pulled my shirt off to catch it before it was everywhere. However, when I was done, it hit me. "Ah…crap."

I glanced at him, just then noticing his rolled-up sleeves, my gaze stopping at them. *Why* did the man have to look that good in a suit?

After he finished tucking himself away, he glanced over. He began to undo the buttons to his vest before sliding it off his shoulders and onto mine.

"Too big."

He helped me pull my arms through, then buttoned it up the front. "It will do until you get back upstairs."

With a swipe to the tablet, the movie stopped and the lights came on. He set it back in its charging spot and held out his hand.

"Come."

"I think I just did," I said as I slipped my hand in his.

A moan slipped past his lips. "Are you sure I ca—"

"No sex," I said, cutting off what I knew was going to be another attempt to convince me.

"Yes, my dear," he replied as we walked toward the elevator and back up to our floor.

From then on, I decided not to watch anymore sexy romance movies right before he got home. I couldn't take a repeat, because I knew another encounter would break my clause in the contract.

I wouldn't be able to hold back the need to feel him inside me again. The tenuous thread of my desire would snap, and I would give everything to him.

THIRTY-THREE

OPHELIA

Staring out across the buildings at the river, I focused on my reflection, my fingers running across my lips. I could still feel the tingle, the overpowering explosion of his lips on mine.

Ever since his fingers were inside of me, I'd thought of nothing more than having him between my thighs, filling me with his cock.

How many times had I rocked on my vibrator until I passed out over the last few days? I was constantly chasing that high he gave me, but always unable to get there and I knew why.

It was all Atticus.

It wasn't just lust and attraction that drove us together—that was just a catalyst. My *need* for him grew every day, and not just physically. Emotionally, I'd become attached. I enjoyed our time together, even if it was just spent lounging on the couch or having dinner. We didn't often go out together, but I found I didn't mind that, even though cabin fever was becoming a real problem.

In fact, I couldn't stay there another minute. I had to get out, because working out or masturbating wasn't helping to calm the overpowering itch anymore. A vicious vibration pulsed through my veins.

It was a cross between anxiety and craving. A withdrawal symptom that begged for just one more touch, one more kiss.

"*Look at me.*"

A shudder rolled through me.

When he said that, I was transported back to that night and nearly lost all sense of self-control.

I wanted to see him. Outside of the condo. Outside of family matters and events. I wanted to go out with him. He was my fiancé, after all. What stopped me from going to his office and pulling him away for lunch?

We'd gotten closer and proven there was more between us than attraction. I no longer felt like we were strangers, but two people trying to make something more concrete work. A real relationship was in the realm of possibility. All we had to do was make a conscious effort to give it a shot. If it didn't work, we still had the contract to fall back on.

As much as the wicked king had frightened me, that wasn't all there was to Atticus. He was multifaceted and hard to understand, but he wasn't the cold man I thought him to be, and I wanted to know all sides of him.

Including physically.

Maybe that was my out-of-control hormones, but couldn't we be more? Be real? Did we have to be the type of relationship drawn up in the contract that was written up when we were strangers?

We didn't have to have a test-tube baby. I hadn't really wanted that then, and I didn't now. It was the only card I held, and I used it to keep a small increment of power in a heavily weighted arena.

First order of business when it came to entering the de Loughrey Tower was my battle armor. To be with Atticus, any time I exited the building I had to exude confidence and elegance, even if I was shaking in self-doubt on the inside.

But I was learning to be both myself and a de Loughrey. It was all about balance. In order to not lose myself entirely, I was absolutely and completely me as soon as I entered the condo. T-shirt, shorts, tank tops, leggings, no makeup, shoes optional, hair maybe brushed—relaxed Ophelia.

De Loughrey Ophelia was decked out in high-end *everything*. Even all my makeup was thrown away and replaced. Nothing could even look like it had the possibility of any wear on it unless it was made that way.

Once my hair and makeup were done, I pulled on a white pair of capris and a sky-blue flutter-sleeved top. All of the pieces came together and were crowned by The Rock.

As I gave myself a once-over in the mirror, I was halted by my reflection. Evolution stared back at me. It was no longer a painted-on mask, but a new part of me. I recognized the woman that stared back, even if I did think she was outclassing me.

With each step out of the building toward the waiting car, my confidence grew. I understood the steps, no longer floundering around, stumbling like a newborn calf knocking things over.

The feeling coursing through me continued as I made my way across the lobby of the de Loughrey Tower, stopping at the private executive elevator. When I arrived at the top floor, the purposeful, confident strides slowed as I grew closer to his closed door. Holly's chair was empty. The door was closed. Another glance at Holly's empty seat and my stomach sank as wild imaginations began to fly around.

After that look she'd given me the last time, I'd been on edge about what their relationship entailed. They seemed too close, and a sudden shot of anger and jealousy pierced my chest.

None of the other assistants batted an eye at me, and I didn't even bother knocking as I wrapped my hand around the knob. I drew in a deep breath to steel myself, then turned the handle and stepped through the threshold into his office.

While none of my wild imaginings of Holly draped over his desk naked appeared before me, I wasn't fond of the way she was draped over his shoulder. He turned to smile at her, neither noticing the door had opened, their lips mere inches from each other.

It was intimate, much too intimate for a subordinate. One I'd witnessed before.

A spark of anger ignited in my chest, and my teeth mashed together as I glared at them. Just what was going on between them?

"Ophelia?" Atticus called, breaking me away from my turbulent emotions.

I caught Holly's eye and she straightened, taking a file with her. "I'll get this sent out with the noon courier."

He nodded. "Remind me later—"

"To talk to Silas about the Harrington integration. You got it, Att."

I flinched at the nickname, my fists clenching at my side.

Holly smiled at me as she approached. "You look beautiful today, Ophelia." Her smile faltered at my glare as she passed.

Once the door was closed, it was just the two of us. That powerful need to have him touch me was replaced by the equally powerful urge to punch something. Preferably him.

"I wasn't expecting you."

My gaze snapped to him. "What the fuck is going on, Atticus?"

His brow scrunched. "Whatever do you mean?"

I stomped forward and stopped in front of his desk. "What is going on with you and Holly? Are you fucking her?"

His gaze narrowed and the warmth seeped from him, replaced with the coldness of the wicked king.

"I'm not fucking my assistant, Ophelia. If anyone was to have an affair with Holly, it would be you."

"Me?"

He nodded. "You're more her type."

My jaw dropped open as understanding flooded in. "Oh."

"Do my ears detect jealousy?" he asked as he smirked at me.

"Jealousy? No. I'm protecting my image." I knew he totally saw through my cover-up.

"Hmm, are you sure that's it? You barged into my office on a rampage to accuse me of fucking outside of our arrangement, didn't you?"

I chewed on my bottom lip. Crap, was that why I was so worked up? "You aren't fucking anybody."

"Only you, my dear."

"Exactly," I agreed, then blinked at him. "What? I mean, no. Nobody."

His tongue slid out between his lips as he stared at me with an intensity that caused the hair on my neck to stand up and my nipples to harden. I swallowed hard and adjusted my arm to try to hide my reaction, but he caught the movement. His lip twitched up.

"Is that all, my dear?"

I glared at him, hating that stupid term of endearment that held no real emotion to it. "Yes." I turned to stomp back out. Whatever my motive was for seeking him out had been completely ruined by both my accusation and the lingering anger, even though nothing was going on. Maybe I was jealous, because Holly got to see a side of Atticus that I dreamed of and hoped one day I would meet.

"I'd think you'd want me breaking the contract."

I ground to a stop, nearly losing my balance at the force as I whipped around to look at him again.

"What I want is to come out of this with my reputation intact."

"And a lot of money."

"Of course."

"That's all you're here for anyway."

I didn't like the venom in his tone, and I headed back over to him. Each anger-filled step amped up the tension in the air. What the hell was with the sudden attitude?

"Isn't that what this is? A *business* arrangement? You pay me to be the dutiful wife and mother of your child?"

"You're lacking in your dutiful wife responsibilities."

"How so?"

He stepped closer, and I noticed how hard we were both breathing. I also took in the spice of his cologne, hating the way it made me want to lean forward and lick his neck. We were so close together and every muscle was tight, ready and waiting for something to happen, but I didn't know what that was.

"Why don't you get on your knees and I'll show you?" he spat.

My eyes widened before narrowing. "Sorry, no sex, remember?"

"No vaginal sex," he leaned forward as I froze. "It never specified no oral sex." His hands took hold of my waist and pulled me tightly against him.

A gasp left me as I felt the hard line of his cock pressed against my abdomen. My thighs squeezed together, and I blinked up at him.

"I'd settle for setting you on my desk and rutting against your covered pussy for now."

The sound of a slap resonated around the walls, and it wasn't until it settled that I realized my arm had swung out and connected with the side of his face.

His eyes were slits, and my stomach dropped at the realization of what I'd done. In one quick movement one of his hands cupped my jaw, his fingers pulling at the back of my neck as his lips crashed to mine.

A squeak left me, and a shock tore through me as he held me tight. I pushed against his chest until there was some amount of space between us before whipping my hand across his face again.

His eyes darkened and he backed me up, pinning me to the wall. "Stop doing that," he growled.

A shudder rolled through me, but what surprised me most was that it wasn't from fear, but lust. It didn't matter that I'd risked waking the wicked king, because I realized how intoxicating that destructive energy was, seductive and alluring as I imagined how he would touch me when he was so worked up.

His lips met mine again, and his thumb pulled at my jaw. My lips parted and when his tongue brushed against mine, I was overwhelmed by the electric shocks that pulsed through me.

There was no stopping my moans of pleasure, or the way I bowed into him as I wrapped my arms around his shoulders. He groaned and reached down, grabbing my ass as he lifted me up. The move had my legs around his waist and pulling him closer.

A groan left him, and he deepened the kiss.

This was what I needed.

His lips attacked my neck, and I felt him chuckle against my skin. "If this is how you react, I should make you jealous more often."

"Jerk."

His hips flexed, pressing his hard length against my clit. A low keening slipped out as his lips ghosted mine.

"Only for you, Ophelia. All of me is only for you."

My heart beat wildly and my eyes pricked with tears. The man before me reminded me so much of the way he was the night we met. I was hanging at a dangerous precipice.

"Asshole," I whimpered as I pressed my forehead to his.

A deep chuckle vibrated as his piercing blue eyes tore into my soul. One hand slipped under my shirt as he continued to rock his hips. A wake of electric fire ignited upon every inch of skin he came in contact with.

"You are mine, Ophelia, and I—"

The door suddenly clicked open. "Are you ready yet?" Hamilton asked as he stormed in.

I froze, my eyes locked with Atticus's as I watched them morph from a smoldering lust into a flame of anger.

"Oh. She's here."

Atticus's muscles tensed and he retreated from me, slowly lowering me until my feet were stable on the ground.

"Yes, my fiancée came to see me, and we were in the middle of something, so what do you want?"

"We have a meeting, remember? Stop messing with your little pet. We'll be late."

"Do you mind?"

"Yes, I mind," he sneered, his predatory eyes locked on me. "You're fucking around with that alley cat who shouldn't even be here."

Atticus swept me behind him with his arm. "Family or not, you will not talk to her that way."

I put my hand on Atticus's chest and stepped in front of him. "It's okay. I don't need you to shield me from him."

I locked eyes with Hamilton to show him that his attitude didn't affect me.

"In our life, women come and go. You're just here for the moment, and I can't wait until you're gone," Hamilton said. His glare was almost as frightening as Atticus's, but if I was going to be part of this family, I wasn't about to let Hamilton bully me.

"I don't know, five years is a pretty long moment, and I gotta say—I'm settling in nicely," I said. My spine was straight and my eyes were locked with his, making certain he understood I wasn't going anywhere.

Atticus's hands rested on my hips before yanking me back to him, his arms wrapping around me as he placed a kiss to my neck. "Very nicely."

"I don't know what your problem is, Hamilton, but I do believe in karma. I'll be sitting here with popcorn waiting for the day you eat those words."

"Then you'll be waiting until you're in your grave," he spat.

"Go ahead to the meeting," Atticus said. He gripped my chin and turned my head back to him. "I wasn't finished playing yet."

Hamilton tsked, his teeth flashing before turning and stomping out of the room. I barely heard the door click because Atticus's lips were firmly pressed to mine and he was devouring me again.

I could get used to this. The strong, possessive grip and overflowing desire that poured out of him was intoxicating. I wanted to drink more of it until I was entirely consumed by him.

When did his lips against mine become so natural? So perfectly right?

A low groan rumbled in his chest. "Keep teasing me like this, and I won't be held responsible for my actions."

"No. Sex."

He bit down on my bottom lip and pulled. "You're entirely too infuriating. I'll be in a rage all afternoon, and it's your fault." He turned me in his arms. "Are you ever going to tell me why you came by?"

I bit down on my lip. "Well, I was thinking of taking a reprieve from my busy schedule and taking my fiancé to lunch."

His lips twitched. "Lunch, huh? I have not eaten today. Where were you thinking?"

"A special little place I know. I'm in good with the owner, so we'll have no problem getting in."

His lips brushed against the column of my neck, leaving a low humming vibration against my skin. "I heard the owner was a little *frustrated* right now. Perhaps a dark, secluded hiding spot isn't the best. I'm hungry, Ophelia, and food will not satiate me."

"Then I guess I should be heading back. I don't want to tempt you too much."

"You should take responsibility for the state I'm in. After all, you barged into my office and accused me of cheating, remember?"

No, I didn't, because every single thought in my brain had been completely overridden by him. His touch, his scent, his domination—all things that set me on fire and had me craving for more.

OPHELIA

"We're having an engagement party?" I asked, my eyes wide as I stared at Atticus.

"Yes. Next month."

We were sitting on the couch when he dropped that bomb on me. Though over the last few weeks, our position had gone from my feet on his lap and worked my way up. Currently my head was resting on his lap while his fingers made slow circles around my exposed midriff.

And I really liked it.

"Here's a question that has been bugging me for a while now—if there is a time limit on when you need to be married by, why is there such a long wait? Why didn't we just elope?"

The word "elope" felt weird to say. Even though I was marrying Atticus, elopement always seemed like a rash execution of love by need due to either opposition or heightened emotions.

"Because things have to be done in a certain order. First was the announcement, now the engagement party. You should have adapted enough to know that our wedding will be highly publicized."

"You mean *your* wedding. I'm just the girl in the white dress. They don't care about me."

"Perhaps. Still, they will all want to know the woman who tamed me. Don't you want them all to see who I belong to?"

That was the second time he mentioned him belonging to me this week, and I liked it.

"Do I get any say in this engagement party?"

"Of course. Mother will talk with you more about it this weekend while dress shopping. She's thinking either at Stronghold or the Asylum."

"Asylum? The Hamptons house, right?"

I received a rare smile. "Yes. Our reprieve from the city."

"Ah. I was…never mind."

He seemed to sense my reason for hesitation. "It was a fair bit of wordplay on Elizabeth's part, no?"

"Elizabeth named it?"

He nodded. "A name that encompassed both the inhabitants and the reprieve from the city. She was twelve. We started calling it that and it stuck so much that it is now commonplace."

"I can't wait to see it one day."

"I'll take you wherever you want to go," he said. My gaze found his, and a shiver rolled through me. It had been happening more and more when we were together—a growing desire every time when he was close.

I tilted my head. "Do you even take vacations?"

His brow furrowed. "Not really. Long weekends to Haven on occasion, but besides the New York properties, that's about it."

Haven.

I'd seen the photos of the de Loughrey private island in the Bahamas, complete with its own airstrip and customs that would come out to them. I'd never been much outside of New York, and not that far afield. New Haven, Connecticut for my aunt and grandparents, Jersey because of friends, but outside of that, I'd never left that couple-hundred-mile radius.

Would he have time off that we could go? I'd gotten to be a better swimmer, stronger, so we could, right?

I froze when it hit me. I wasn't thinking about *me* going and spending a few days, but of *us* together.

Atticus and I alone in paradise.

My face flamed, and I covered my face in my hands.

"What are you hiding from me?" Atticus asked as he pulled my hands away.

His blue eyes pinned me down. "N-nothing."

"By the enticing blush that is spreading across your beautiful skin, it isn't nothing."

"I was just thinking about Haven."

"What about it?"

"You and me. Alone. Together. In paradise."

He chuckled as he leaned down and grasped my jaw, pulling me closer. "What did I say before about enticing me? I won't be held accountable." He pressed his lips to mine before pulling back.

The heat in my face burned hotter. "So, engagement party?"

"Yes. You're dress shopping this week with my mother, correct?"

I nodded. "Yes."

"I know that our marriage is a contract, but I hope you're looking forward to the wedding, because I know I am. That being said, don't let Vera steamroll you. This is your wedding, and you have the right to say yes or no. But I will also say that society at this level is new to you, please listen to what Mother suggests. If it is something you are adamantly against, I will support you." His lips twitched and his eyes narrowed. "Drinking with Gen aside."

I reached up and cupped his cheek. "Thank you."

The truth was that I hadn't let myself get excited about the wedding. How could I? Yes, I'd given Vera my opinion on many things, but I had failed to let my inner child dreaming of her wedding to Prince Charming run wild. Atticus was a prince, but charming was up for debate. He also hadn't fallen for me after one night.

That thought stopped me, and I froze.

But in a way, he had, hadn't he? We had one fairy-tale night, but afterward, he wasn't walking around the streets of New York carrying a glass slipper. He was, however, carrying longing and regret.

For a year, he searched me out multiple times a week, and when he needed a wife, he said all he could see was me beside him.

So why was I reserved—cautious almost—in my excitement to be walking down the aisle to him?

"You've gone far away," he said as he brushed a lock of hair from my forehead.

"Do you want to marry me? Are you excited?"

He cupped my face and leaned down to press his lips to mine. "There is no other I want to call my wife."

"Not even Bridget or Antonia?" I asked, my jealousy flaring up. For years he'd seen them. Even if it was casually, I still worried that he might want them.

"I have no feelings for them."

"You've had sex with them."

"Attraction is different. They've been on my arm for many events, but they were just convenient decoration." His hand moved farther up under my shirt, and his eyes locked with mine. "Look at me."

It felt like a bolt of lightning had come down from the heavens and struck me. I jolted in his arms.

"There it is."

"W-what?"

"Why I could not even consider them. Never once have I wanted a woman to look at me like that. Only you."

I blinked at him, my heart thumping wildly in my chest.

"If you keep that expression, I'm going to try to do very bad things to you." His hand moved farther up until his fingertips skimmed the underside of my breasts, then brushed across my nipples.

I drew in a ragged, shuddered breath, my nipples hardening and sending jolts of pleasure straight to my clit.

"No sex," I said, but even I could hear my lack of conviction.

He leaned down and pressed his lips to mine. "Your weakness is showing."

He was absolutely right, because *he* was my weakness, and my resolve was crumbling to pieces.

"Stand up straight, Ophelia," Vera said in her sharp tone, leaving no room for argument.

Spending the day with my soon-to-be mother-in-law was not in my top one hundred things I wanted to do at any time, but I had no choice. Almost two months had passed, and I had done very little for my upcoming wedding.

A wedding Vera had planned for January before she even knew about me. One she had already hired caterers for and sent out announcements. Granted, it was for her oldest son, but so far it was very much Vera's wedding and not mine.

Things were changing between me and Atticus, and I was starting to come around to the idea that we weren't just a business contract. That we could be more. And that actually made me more interested in our upcoming nuptials, but I was steamrolled at every turn.

Not that I let her walk all over me, but I'd shown so little interest in the first month or so that she'd done whatever she wanted.

I blew a stray curl from my face. Vera scrutinized my appearance the moment she stepped foot into our home. While the outfit I chose was passable, she balked at my hair. What was with the de Loughreys and my hair?

I ended up in the salon with some frazzled-looking woman huffing as she attempted to catch her breath. It looked like she'd run from wherever she'd been. There was sweat beaded on her forehead, but she still managed to give me a smile, even if it was a bit strained.

And that was how my normally straight blonde hair, that was almost to the top of my shoulders, was now curly and pissing me off.

My hand felt heavy due to not being used to the weight of the hunk of rock that sat on my finger. It was over the top, much like everything the de Loughreys touched, but even so, it was gorgeous.

Yes, I loved The Rock, but why did it have to weigh so much?

My phone went off, which was odd. My phone hardly ever went off.

Atticus : Just remember to breathe and make sure to get what YOU want.

I stared down at the screen, my chest clenching as I read the words. He was worried about me. Soothing me from afar. How did he know I needed him?

Ophelia : Thank you. I needed that.

Atticus : I know.

It felt like a very Han Solo response, but still, him responding, him even thinking about texting me, was a hard hit to my emotions, and I had to blink back tears. Being with Atticus was overwhelming in itself, but falling for him was worse. It was all-encompassing and frightening.

The car slowed to a stop outside of a large building.

"Why didn't we just do this at the Tower?" I asked, to which Vera scoffed.

"There simply isn't enough room in that tiny dressing room."

Tiny? It easily held half a dozen racks of clothing, a personal shopper and her two assistants, me, and there was still plenty of room.

"Besides, we are only gauging style, designer, and fabric. It will then be tailored to our design preferences down to the stitch."

You mean your *design preferences.*

"That didn't answer my question."

Her steely eyes narrowed on me. "Ophelia, your wedding is *the* wedding of the century. More than any royalty, the world will be looking at *you* standing next to my son. I think you forget at times just whom you are marrying. Atticus isn't some common CEO. He is CEO of the de Loughrey Corporation, one of the largest, wealthiest companies in the world. He is the leader of one of the wealthiest families in the world. Your children will one day take his place. You will be the mother to the wealthiest child ever *born*. And I still haven't the slightest clue as to why my son chose you."

My eyes were wide as I took in everything she said. A cold strike of fear rushed through me.

It seemed so simple on paper that I never really took into consideration the depth of the pool I was jumping into. I'd seen bits of it after the announcement, and Atticus had mentioned it before, but it wasn't until Vera put it into perspective that I really started to understand *why* there had to be a wedding.

Vera huffed and wrapped one of her talons around my wrist, dragging me into the building. "Come."

As soon as we stepped in, we were ushered into a private room. The building was empty, and even the doors were locked after us.

I was going to ask what was going on, but then I remembered who I was with.

It was a de Loughrey thing. People threw out the red carpet for them.

Maybe royalty wasn't a bad description.

"Hello, Mrs. de Loughrey, we are so pleased to be graced with your presence," a flamboyant man said as he entered. For a moment, I was envious of him because he had way more style than I ever would have, no matter what Melanie put in my closet.

"While flattery is appreciated, it is wasting time." Vera turned to me. "Philip, this is my son's fiancée, Ophelia."

He aimed his beaming smile at me and reached for my hand. "Ophelia, what a pleasure. Come, let's have a look at you."

I slipped my hand in his and he raised it, using it to twirl me around in circles.

"Did you receive the letter with some of the specifications?"

He turned his attention back to her. "Yes, and I have a large selection ready, but after seeing her figure, some styles will have to be weeded out. We need something to make it appear that her boyish figure has hips."

I twitched at that and looked down. Was that why my closet was filled with a lot of peplum tops? To give some dimension to my straight-up-and-down figure?

"You have no hips or breasts," Vera said in agreement. "What does he see in your curve-less body?"

"He likes my ass," I said, then slapped my hand over my mouth.

Vera's stern eyes widened, and she tilted her head to look behind me. "Well, at least you're curvy somewhere."

Philip disappeared into another room while we were seated, then came back and handed me a glass of what I thought was orange juice, but I quickly found it to be a mimosa.

My phone went off, and I pulled it from my purse to find another message from Atticus.

Atticus : Take photos of the dresses.

I smiled, my chest filling with warmth.

Ophelia : You know the groom isn't supposed to see the dress before the wedding.

Atticus : Then send photos without the dresses on. ;)

Ophelia : Are you encouraging me to send nudes? *shocked*

Atticus : Not at all, my dear.

Ophelia : Cheeky bastard.

"Are you talking to my son?" Vera asked.

I straightened and focused on the room again. "Yes. Sorry."

"No need to apologize if you're wearing that expression while thinking of him."

"Oh."

"I'm a bit envious, to tell the truth."

"Of?"

"You. That look. I married out of obligation. An arranged marriage like his father was trying to thrust upon him. At the will reading when he stood up to Charles and refused an arranged marriage, I'm not sure I had ever been that proud before."

"Then you ended up with me instead."

Her expression fell. "Yes, well." She fluffed up her hair and continued staring straight ahead. "I can make something of you. You have spirit and strength, and with a lot of guidance, I believe you will make a fine matriarch of the family."

For a moment I was filled with happiness, but then she dropped a bomb on me.

"Matriarch?"

She turned to me. "Ophelia, you are marrying our ruler, our king.

Despite his age, he is the patriarch of the family. That is why there is such discord between him and his father. You are to be his queen, and therefore, mother to all."

I slumped down, hiding my face in my hands. *Mother to all?*

For months I'd studied the Binder of Doom, multiple books written on the family, gone through the extensive family tree and was lucky enough to remember Atticus Charles de Loughrey's descendants, but to be mother to all de Loughreys?

I signed up, quite literally, to be the mother of one. One child. How did I not foresee this?

The first model walked out, pulling me from the weight settling in my chest, forcing me to focus on the task at hand.

What I thought would be hours of trying on dresses turned into hours of looking at dresses. Model after model came out, and Vera took notes. She immediately dismissed some, and others she kept to the side.

It was overwhelming, and I had a hard time saying much more than "I like that." Perhaps because it wasn't on me? There were aspects I liked about the different dresses, and all of them were so regal and elegant that I felt undeserving of wearing such beauty.

Is this really my life?

Finally, I was taken back and was stuffed into undergarments and the first dress I'd see on myself. When I stepped out, Vera's eyes widened and she straightened as she watched me walk in. I stepped onto the platform and took in my reflection in the large mirrors.

It was an A-line gown with a deep sweetheart neckline and scalloped, cap-sleeved detail. The skirt was full and flared out. There was embroidery and beading coupled with tulle and satin.

It fit and accentuated my body perfectly. I felt like a princess.

"That is what we will build on," Vera said. "What do you think?"

"It's beautiful," I answered honestly.

And it was. Tears pooled in my eyes, and I had to bite them back. I never thought I would wear something so beautiful, and I couldn't wait to see the expression on Atticus's face when he saw me.

OPHELIA

Once again, I was wearing more money in my outfit than I probably made in a year. Scratch that—with The Rock on, I constantly surpassed that. Even without The Rock, even taking out the other jewelry that was on loan, I knew I was wearing at least six months' rent of my old apartment just between the dress, shoes, and purse alone.

The metallic black and gold seemed to almost flow with every movement. I was entranced by the mirror when Atticus's voice called out. I turned just as he walked into the dressing room.

His eyes raked over me, his fingers brushing against his lips as a groan slipped out. "You need to stop looking more beautiful every time I see you. I don't think I can handle much more."

I blinked at him. It didn't happen often, but when he told me I was beautiful, I got embarrassed. My face flamed, and I had to look away from him.

In a few steps, he was in front of me and he gripped my chin, tilting my head back. "Don't hide yourself from me."

"See, I knew that charmer was in you somewhere."

With his hands on my hips, he pulled me closer. "You bring it out in me." He leaned in closer and pressed his lips to mine. "And you know I only say what I mean."

We headed out to my second-ever charity event, and I was about as nervous as I was at the first. The difference was the calm that moved through me from his touch. Knowing he was beside me set me at ease.

The charity dinner for the Adrianna de Loughrey Foundation seemed almost small in comparison to the event we walked into. Maybe the atmosphere was just different, but the first I went to was all I had to draw on for comparison.

It felt like we were walking into a wedding reception with the dim lighting and sparkles, not to mention the music. The room was already at a steady hum of conversation. I was overwhelmed, and we'd just walked in the door.

"Remember: spine straight, shoulders back. Hold your head high, and remember who you belong to."

His last words had my abdomen tightening and caused heat to flush my cheeks. They reminded me of the other night, his fingers deep in my pussy as he held me close, driving me at lightning speed to an orgasm.

I was his. My orgasms were his. "You belong to *me*," he'd growled, sending me over the edge, shaking in his arms.

A small chuckle brushed against my ear.

"Did I say something to…disturb you?"

I rolled my shoulders back and held myself as straight as I could. "Not at all."

He leaned in again. "Your nipples say otherwise."

I glanced down and sure enough, straining against the liquid-looking black and gold metallic fabric were my nipples. A gasp left me and I abruptly turned into him, hiding myself from the prying eyes of the room. "Oh, my God."

With no bra, there was nothing to even attempt to hold them back. In fact, I wasn't wearing *any* undergarments because the fabric picked up any hitch, and even though the dress flared out at the waist, I wasn't taking any chances. Unfortunately I wasn't thinking about what happened if my fiancée decided to turn me on in the middle of a very upscale party.

His chest rumbled beneath my hand, and I gave him a small smack against his pec. "Not funny."

"Yes, it is, but I also don't want anyone seeing them. I'm having a hard enough time not slipping my fingers over them."

They tightened again, stiffer than ever, pressing against him. "Stop," I begged, embarrassment coloring my face.

"I quite like seeing you so flustered. It's adorable."

"It is *not* adorable at a ten-thousand-a-plate charity dinner for children," I hissed.

He hummed. "I suppose you're correct."

"I know I am."

"Georgiana," Atticus called out to the brunette approaching us. Her hair was pinned back in dark waves, and her blue eyes sparkled as much as the diamonds circling her neck and adorning her ears.

A wide smile spread across her face. "Atticus." She held her hand out and he took it, drawing it to his lips and placing a kiss.

"You look absolutely beautiful, as always."

She glanced to me and smiled. "Good to see you again, Ophelia." Her demeanor was as gentle and soothing with the air of a princess as the last time I saw her.

She was entirely too nice, and had been the warmest welcome I'd received from any of the de Loughrey family.

"So good to see you again." I smiled back and held out my hand. She took it and started to say something, but her eyes widened as she stared at my chest.

"Oh, my."

Insecurity surged through me, and I turned into Atticus again.

"Really, cousin?" she said to Atticus. My brow furrowed as I looked up to him, but the puzzled expression he wore told me he was as clueless as I was. Georgiana sighed, then caught my eye. "Men. They just don't understand these things." She held out her hand and beckoned me with her fingers. "Come, let's see what we can do about that."

I pulled away and reached for her, using my other arm to try and cover myself. A groan left Atticus. "Wait," he called. I turned back to him, watching as he pulled his jacket from his shoulders. "Since I am partially to blame." He grinned as he wrapped the jacket around my shoulders.

"Thanks."

He leaned down and pressed his lips to my forehead, giving my hand a squeeze before I stepped away.

"That was…interesting," Georgiana said once we were out of earshot.

"Interesting good, or interesting bad?" I asked before glancing back to Atticus.

"Oh, it was very good, trust me. I simply never expected the king to bow to a commoner."

I flinched at the term. It wasn't the first time I'd been called that, but it still stung.

She noticed and patted my hand. "I'm sorry, I didn't mean that in offense. By your reaction, my cousins, aunt, and uncle have probably used those terms or worse."

"You would be correct."

"I'm afraid if I say anything more, I will only make you feel worse, and that isn't what I want to do. What I will say is that in my entire life, I have never seen Atticus that relaxed, charming, or considerate of another person."

"Really?"

"He would never admit it to any of us, but I know his position is incredibly lonely. He comes across as hard and brash because he has to. In order to be the king, sacrifices are made, and he's made many."

What she said wasn't anything I hadn't already observed myself. The air around Atticus, the look I sometimes caught in his eyes, was nothing short of cold, dark loneliness.

We entered the bathroom, earning a few wide-eyed looks as we entered. Georgiana pulled me into one of the large stalls. Once the door was locked, she rifled through her small clutch and pulled out something slim wrapped in plastic.

"I usually carry a spare set with me. This isn't what I normally use, but it will help. May I?" she asked, motioning to my dress.

I held out my hand. "I can do it."

She sighed and smiled at me. "Please, Ophelia. We're both women."

I swallowed and turned, pulling Atticus's jacket from my shoulders and placing it on the hook. Her delicate fingers were cool against my skin as she dragged the zipper down.

"Turn around."

I held onto the front of my dress as I shimmied back around. Gently she tugged at the straps, and I let it fall until my breasts were exposed.

"Awkward," I said as I looked anywhere but at Georgiana.

"Think of it as bonding time." She giggled. "Ah." Her voice caught, and I looked down to find her a bit embarrassed. It was odd; she said we were both women, then I noticed the dark kiss mark on my breast Atticus had left the other day.

All of my blood filled my face, and I couldn't even look at her.

"I'm glad to see you two are getting along," she said in a gentle but serious tone.

It did me in, and my embarrassment turned to laughter that she joined in on. Once we settled down, she stuck round disks over my nipples, pushing them back down.

"The things we girls do to make these dresses look fabulous boys just don't understand." She smiled and helped pull my dress back up.

"They aren't the only ones," I said as I looked down. "Thank you."

"You're more than welcome."

"I mean for more than just this."

She squeezed my arm. "We're a lot to take in, but I promise not everyone is a complete jerk."

"I'll take your word for it."

"Besides, it doesn't matter what any of us thinks. Only what Atticus does."

I grabbed Atticus's jacket, and we stepped out of the bathroom.

As we did, Georgiana's phone went off. She glanced down at it, then to me.

"I'm sorry, Ophelia, do you think you can find your way back to Atticus?"

"I'm sure I can."

"I'll see you soon."

I nodded and waved as she headed off in the opposite direction. The path we took was obscured thanks to the growing crowd, so I meandered through, searching the faces for anyone familiar, though there was just one I was looking for.

I found Atticus on the outside of the crowd. I expected him to be mingling with his people, but when he pushed off the wall and his eyes met mine, I realized he was waiting for me.

"Better?" he asked when I approached.

I held my arms out and he gave a nod.

"I think I have a girl crush on your cousin," I said as I handed him back his jacket.

His eyes widened. "Really?"

"I'm also pretty sure she is the best person of all of you."

"I'm beginning to think you may like her more than me," he said in a teasing tone.

I leaned forward, my breath hot against his neck. "You have something she never will."

When I pulled back, his eyes had darkened. "You shouldn't say such tempting things to me."

"Were my six little words tempting? I thought they were quite innocent."

"Say the word, my dear, and you will have what she never will. I will drag you from the building across the street to the same hotel I dragged you to a year ago and do the same unspeakable things as then. With my very large something she will never have."

I let out a shaky breath. It was tempting. Very tempting. There was nobody near us. It would be nothing to slip out the exit door just feet from us and disappear into the night.

The problem was that I hadn't given in yet, hadn't given him the one thing I knew we were both desperate for. I had to step back to cool us both off, or I knew I'd be the one dragging him.

"Atticus?" a feminine voice called out, breaking us from our heated bubble. When his eyes left mine, the heat flooded away as a cold bucket of ice chilled the air around us.

"Antonia. Bridget. Lovely to see you two."

The women before me were everything one thought of when talking about high-society women. Antonia's skin was a light brown/olive coloration, with black hair and brilliant crystal green-grey eyes. Beautiful wasn't a strong enough word to describe her. She was unearthly.

Bridget had the poise and grace of someone born to money, much like Georgiana, with perfect features: piercing light brown eyes, and long brunette waves that cascaded down her back.

They didn't seem to either notice or care, I wasn't sure which, that I was standing next to him. It seemed I was invisible to them.

"It's been many months, Atticus darling. I've missed you," Bridget said seductively as she reached out and placed her hand on his chest.

Antonia stepped forward and settled herself into his side, wrapping her arm around his waist. "It's been too long since we've spent time together."

I stiffened next to him as I watched them drape themselves over my fiancé. These were the women I compared myself to. The ones that were his acquaintances with benefits. The women that graced his arm when he needed it and tended to his cock when he wanted it.

Atticus shifted, his hand wrapping around Antonia's arm, pushing her from him before doing the same to Bridget. He stepped back and wrapped his arm around my waist and pulled me into his side.

"Didn't you read the papers? I'm engaged."

Both sets of eyes dialed in on me, and I straightened my spine.

"Her? Atticus, baby, you can't be serious."

"Very serious," he said. His tone was like ice, and both women stared at him in shock.

They seemed completely confused that he was pushing them away both literally and figuratively.

Antonia's lip quivered, her jaw tight. "After everything, you chose a nobody over me?"

"You suck cock very well, Antonia, but I need more than a human vacuum that will take it up the ass."

Antonia's mouth dropped open, her body shaking, looking like she was ready to slap him, but something held her back. Then again, I supposed hitting a de Loughrey was not a wise idea, no matter how distasteful his comment was.

"I've known you since I was twelve," Bridget screeched. "We've been sleeping together for a decade, and some *waitress* gets the ring? The *help?*"

The aura coming off Atticus grew even colder and darker. I couldn't decide if it scared me or turned me on, but it was strong.

"I made neither of you a single promise. You both knew the stakes. I told you both, multiple times, that I didn't want a relationship with you. I kept you around for events and to warm my cock. Our relationship was nothing more than an exchange of goods and service. Nothing more."

The indignation that boiled up in both of them was entertaining to watch. Basically referring to them as high-class whores. For a moment I thought at least one of them would explode, but with the cold glare Atticus was giving them, neither woman seemed inclined to incur his wrath. It was ice and it froze them in place.

"You did your job, but my *wife* will fulfill my needs from now on."

My heart thumped hard when he called me his wife. I knew that was what was going to happen, it was the deal we made, but the way he said it made me swoon. If I was just a contract, he would have been more accommodating to them, but the way he shut them down and laid claim to me left no room for hope.

Somehow, I felt vindicated. All of the buried insecurities involving them was brushed away. *He* removed them with his firm words and dark aura.

With a squeeze to my hip we pulled away, leaving them wallowing in their misery together.

"Wife, huh?"

His eyes were dark when they met mine. "Fiancée doesn't sound as resolute. Wife is sound."

"Your father doesn't think so. A wedding ring doesn't stop people from cheating."

He stopped and turned me to him. "I don't cheat."

"You wanted to have mistresses."

His gaze narrowed on me. "That was when you didn't want me to touch you, and I wanted you to relent."

Wait… "So, you tried to threaten me with them in order to get me to forget my clause?"

"Yes, but it backfired."

I couldn't decide if I wanted to slap him or kiss him. He didn't care about them, only me, even when he made me think he'd stay with them.

"You've never talked to them since the contract, have you?"

"And months before that. I was consumed by another woman. One that was stubborn and strong willed."

It wasn't until he revealed how long it had been since he'd even had contact with them that I realized I'd assumed he'd slept with one of them before we signed. That jealousy had been sitting so close to the surface over women I didn't even know. Was it because of the binder? That I saw their names within the pages, giving them some sort of significance, some permanence, in his life?

"You've burned all bridges with them. I don't think they'll take you back in five years," I said as I berated myself for the passive-aggressive comment. While he erected a steel wall with his words, there was still that doubt.

I knew why.

I just wasn't ready to admit it.

He tilted my chin back, his eyes dark as they locked onto mine. "I don't want them. Not today, not in five years."

"What do you want?" I asked in a whisper.

"What are you fishing for, Ophelia?"

I blinked and swallowed, backing up. My insecurity was the cause of my timid questioning. Atticus was direct, and he expected everyone else to be direct as well, even if I didn't feel he was being the most direct at that moment.

I tried to calm my racing heart as I formed words for the heaviness in my chest. There was only one thing I wanted to know. "Will you want me in five years?"

The magnetism between us kicked up a hundredfold and my breath sped up as he pulled me until we were chest to chest. No words passed as he cupped my face, his finger deftly sliding down my neck, resting on my collarbone before sliding down to my shoulder.

The fire in his eyes died down to a smolder as he released me. "We should get to our table."

Disappointment shot through me and I swallowed, looking down as I turned from him. I had to blink back a tear. For a moment I'd been so sure he was going to say yes, but it was fleeting.

Still, I knew he had difficulty with expressing his emotions, even with the progress he'd made. My own realizations only highlighted that I was the same. I'd been protecting myself from him for over a year, and suddenly I was laid bare before him, my chest open, heart beating, begging for a connection.

With each step, I stuffed my emotions down, released my insecurities as his voice rang in my head: "Spine straight, shoulders back." I was chosen to be his wife above all others. That knowledge brought strength, and I exuded it, refusing to falter again.

We drew closer to the tables, Atticus greeting many people as we went. It amazed me how he knew everyone's name. Occasionally that professional smile, the one that didn't reach his eyes, popped up, but it was all a polite mask for the sake of business—it wasn't real.

A real smile was special, reserved, and precious.

And all mine.

"You must be Ophelia. It's a pleasure to meet you, dear," an older woman with a kind smile said.

I returned her smile, realizing I'd spaced out at her name. "Thank you so much. The pleasure is all mine."

She looked to Atticus with a smile. "She's so sweet. However did *you* manage such a fine creature?"

"The words that wish to pass my lips are not suited for your delicate ears, Miriam."

A blush spread across her cheeks. "Oh, my."

He gave a nod. "Have a good evening," he said, leaving the poor old woman to stare at us.

"What perverted thoughts did you put into her mind?" I asked once we were clear of her.

He smirked at me. "Only whatever her imagination conjured."

Laughter cascaded from a few feet away, a sound I was very familiar with.

"Oh, fuck," I hissed low.

"What is it?"

Jennifer.

It'd been months since I'd run into her while shopping, but after years of friendship, I'd recognize that sound anywhere. Suddenly her brown eyes lifted. The shock when she recognized me was unmistakable. She pulled at her fiancé Luthor's hand, their skin in contrast.

"Well, hey, Ophelia, how are you doing?" Luthor asked with a big, genuine smile.

I returned his friendliness, remembering why I liked him more than the woman on his arm. "Very well. How's the season going?"

He nodded and opened his mouth to speak, but was cut off.

"Ophelia, I'm so surprised to see you here. Are you working?" Jennifer asked.

My teeth clenched together, but I had to keep my cool. Come on, didn't she even look at me, or was I just so inferior to her that she refused to acknowledge anything about me.

I put on my best de Loughrey fraudulent smile. "No. I'm not waitressing anymore."

"What are you doing, then?" she asked as she scanned my attire, her eyes widening. "Is that a Givenchy?"

I looked down, smoothing the dress, then met her eyes. "I'm honestly not sure."

"You were wearing a Givenchy t-shirt the other day, so it's entirely possible," Atticus said, his hand squeezing my waist.

That small gesture was more reassuring than any words ever could be.

"Oh, yeah," I said, remembering the T-shirt I'd been wearing. It was such a basic white that I didn't think anything about the name printed across the fabric.

"A Givenchy T-shirt costs hundreds of dollars. Where did *you* get that kind of money?" she seethed. Luthor leaned back from his fiancée, shock written in the furrow of his brow as he stared at her.

I turned to Atticus. "Hundreds for a T-shirt?"

He gave a small shrug. "The shopping bill was a few hundred thousand. I just paid it."

Before I could question him more, Jennifer grabbed my hand, pulling it to her. "Oh, my God." She turned my ring in the light. "Is this real?"

Atticus scoffed. "For nearly a million dollars, it would be an impressive fake."

Jennifer's eyes were wide, and for the first time she seemed to notice the man beside me who was throwing out enormous numbers. Which was odd for him. Atticus didn't talk about the cost of anything, except Genevieve's allowance, so the only thing I could think of was that he was doing it for my benefit.

"I told you I didn't want to know how much it cost!" I cried out, trying to forget what he just said about The Rock.

He shrugged, and that calculating gaze was locked on Jennifer. Her face was frozen. That was when I understood why. He saw Jennifer for what she really was, and he wanted to destroy her like any other foe that attacked me.

He was standing up for me, beside me, ready to set fire and lay waste to anyone. The wicked king was at play, and he wouldn't let anyone hurt his queen in any way.

"This has to be at least six carats," Jennifer said, her hand shaking against mine.

"Nine-carat cushion cut," Atticus clarified.

Jennifer's jaw clenched. "What the hell is going on, Ophelia?"

Her anger was amusing. The fire in her eyes showed me that

our friendship was only of convenience. She liked feeling that she was better than me. I was beneath her. On my birthday that fateful night, she probably decided she didn't want to associate with me, and that was why she didn't come.

I should have thanked her for that, because her dismissal of me was an opening for Atticus to approach me. Without that, we might not have spent that night together, leading us to where we were now.

"I'm sorry, I forgot to introduce you to my fiancé." By the way she was acting, I had to wonder if she was so self-absorbed she didn't see the news or any of the announcements. Then again, even if she did, it was possible she didn't notice or recognize me. She probably never thought of me except when she needed to feel better about herself.

Atticus held out his hand. "Atticus de Loughrey. Pleasure, Miss…"

Jennifer paled, her eyes wide as she stared at him in disbelief, then gaped back at me.

Luthor took his hand. "Pleased to meet you, Mr. de Loughrey. Or should I just call you boss?" he asked with a chuckle then turned to me. "Small world, huh?"

"How so?" I asked.

"Your fiancé owns the team I play for."

Atticus smiled back. "You're very talented, Luthor, and I'm excited to see what you'll do for us for a full season."

A groan left me. "You own the team?"

A chuckle left him, and he leaned in. "Read the binder, Ophelia."

I turned, our lips ghosting. "I have, my dear. There's just a lot of information to remember."

A high-pitched screech broke through our friendly conversation, and we all stopped to stare at Jennifer, as did anyone within a fifteen-foot radius.

Her eyes were wide, and anger twisted her features as she shook with fists clenched.

"I can't believe you would use such underhanded means to get a man. Are you that good of a fuck?"

"Jennifer…" Luthor trailed off.

"No!" she screeched. "It's not supposed to be this way." She glared at me, teeth bared while tears filled her eyes. "You're nothing but a—"

"That's enough," Atticus said. The volume was the same, but the power backing his words shut her down quickly. "You seem to be under the impression Ophelia cheated her way into my life by using unscrupulous persuasion."

"How else?" Jennifer seethed.

Atticus stepped forward and leaned in, a smirk on his lips. "That wicked deed belongs solely to me. *I* am the one who used everything at my disposal to make her mine. I don't take kindly to those who try to belittle my precious flower."

Jennifer was shaking with anger, and by Luthor's wide eyes, he'd never seen his fiancée in such an ugly state. She may have been gorgeous on the outside, but inside was a very different matter. With a tight expression and pursed lips, she turned away and stomped off.

"I'm sorry about all this, Mr. de Loughrey. Ophelia," Luthor said before turning and following after her.

"You were a bit brutal there," I said as we took our seats.

"Are you saying she didn't deserve to be put into her place? I could read the writing on the wall, Ophelia. She thought she was better than you because you were a waitress."

"You think you're better than everyone."

"Because I am, that doesn't mean I treat those below me with blatant disrespect because of an unearned ego."

"You do have an ego." I couldn't say much about the disrespect part, because for the most part, he was very respectful of those who worked for him. Sure, he was hard and harsh to deal with, but I'd seen him with Jack and Loreno and Holly, not to mention countless other staff. He was a demanding boss, but there was no revolving door of personal employees. There was a loyalty to him that was only earned through respect.

"But not an unearned one."

"Why do you have to be so devilishly handsome, incredibly rich, and have a big cock?"

He chuckled. "Simply blessed."

An hour later, dinner had been concluded and the presentation had been conducted. All that was left was the silent auction and more socializing. The social aspect had worn off, and I found myself at the silent auction display.

My head spun at the collection of items I could never even think of bidding on. Being part of the de Loughreys meant anything was within my grasp, but it was something I had never really utilized myself. Up for bid were a wide assortment of trips, antiques, and fragile-looking things.

"See anything interesting?" a familiar voice said.

I jumped at the closeness, my hand flying to my chest as I turned. "You scared me, Gen."

She giggled at that. "Sorry, it was too easy."

She appeared more refined than her normal party-girl attitude, and I wondered if it wasn't a de Loughrey decree that she actually followed.

"I didn't know you would be here."

She glanced around the room. "Yeah, but with so many people, it's impossible to see everyone. But I did catch a glimpse of you two earlier. You look so happy with him. Way different from last time."

I paused as I pondered her words. Happy? Actually, I was. The night had been wonderful in so many different ways, and I felt closer to Atticus than I had when the night began.

"I am."

"Except for the damn folio."

I blanched and stared at her. "He didn't."

"Oh yes, he fucking did."

I shook my head, and we both began to laugh.

"What has you two so amused over here?"

I waved my hand in front of my face in an attempt to dry the tears. "Nothing. It's nothing at all."

"Hmm." He pulled me back into his chest and stepped away. "Genevieve."

"Atticus."

"I'm taking my fiancée home."

"Bed her well."

We both froze and stared at her.

"What? It's obvious you two are finally sleeping together."

Heat rose in my cheeks, and I looked away.

"We will see you another time," Atticus said as he spun me around so that my face was buried in his chest. "Goodnight."

The evening was not what I expected it to be. Boring, mind numbingly so, with rich assholes flaunting their wealth. And while there were some of those, one evening opened my eyes to so much about my fiancé. If I hadn't already been falling in love with him, I would have been now.

Fears of his ex-lovers were buried, catty ex-friends were humbled, de Loughreys were nicer, and my connection with Atticus had grown stronger. We were a true couple throughout the night. His hands rarely left my body, and when they did, moments later I was soothed by his touch again.

At first I thought he was simply trying to calm my nerves, but halfway through, I realized it was also me calming him.

OPHELIA

The tension in the air was thick as we rode the elevator up to the penthouse. After a night of affection, we were on opposite sides of the elevator. Not out of anger, but out of something else that was crawling and swirling around us. Something strong. A force that was pulling us closer together, and if we collided, the explosion would be earth shattering.

"Stop looking at me like that."

"Like what?"

"I'll eat you up, Ophelia."

The elevator doors slid open, and we headed out and down the hall.

I swallowed hard as we reached my room, his blue eyes meeting mine before I stepped into my bedroom and closed the door behind me. I slumped back against the hard wood as I stared up at the ceiling, willing my blood to calm down.

The tension between us grew heavier every day, and despite the hiccups of the night, despite feeling inferior to every woman we encountered, including the two that knew him more intimately than I did, all I wanted were his hands all over me.

The question was, did I jump, or did I hold on to the butterflies in my stomach with everything I had. If I didn't succumb tonight, when would I?

It was inevitable. I knew it, and so did he. My skin begged for him, my pussy ached for him, and my heart yearned for him.

I'd already come to the conclusion that I was going to cave, so why, after such a wonderful night, was I hesitating? I wanted him.

I debated showing up to his room naked, but then realized I had the perfect excuse to walk to his bedroom. First, I kicked off my heels, and peeled the pasties from my nipples—I wasn't letting anything hinder finally getting what I'd been wanting for so long.

My dress swished against the wood floors as I padded down the hall. When I reached his door, I took a deep breath before knocking.

A moment later, Atticus stood before me. I'd caught him in a half undressed state, and it took a ton of effort to not just reach forward and tear open his shirt.

"Yes?" he asked, his voice deeper than usual.

I stepped in past him, entering his room for the first time, and glanced over my shoulder. "Can you help me?"

There was a flash in his eyes, and his nostrils flared. I could feel the heat radiating off him, feel the static charge that was building between us with each inch of space that dissolved between us. His gaze boring into me was so strong, but nothing compared to the soft caress of his fingers against my skin.

I drew in a breath, and goose bumps erupted across my flesh. He gripped the zipper and slowly drew it down. Each inch felt like a supercharged heat that grew as he went. His fingers caressed as he went, sending a trail of fire across my skin.

He stepped closer, and when the zipper couldn't move farther, my back was against his chest. The warmth of his breath swept across my neck. I couldn't move, completely trapped in his gravity.

His lips pressed against my shoulder, and a small moan left me. One arm wrapped around me, tugging me until there was no air between us.

"You're playing with fire, Ophelia."

"I know."

He pushed the straps of the dress over the edge of my shoulders, the weight of the dress causing it to slide until the straps caught on my bent arms. A low moan escaped me at the feel of his warm hand running along the exposed skin.

Hands that I'd longed for swept across my skin; one cupped my breast and tweaked my nipple making me cry out.

"Tell me what you want," he whispered against my ear.

"I-I want you."

"Beg for it."

"What?"

"You wanted to know the loopholes." His fingers flexed against my skin. "Beg for me to fuck you," he growled.

Even though I was throwing myself at him, he was still lucid enough to think about the contract. I could feel how strong his desire was pressed against my backside, but he refrained.

So I threw his words back at him from that night at Stronghold. "Give in to me," I said, then turned in his arms. His eyes were darker than I'd ever seen them. "Please fuck me. I need you to fuck me."

His lip curled up into a snarl and he leaned down, his lips crashing to mine. I melted into the possessiveness of his tongue, bent to the will of his greed. My veins flamed, fire moving through me with each frantic beat of my heart.

He released me to pull his shirt off, followed by his belt and slacks. I relaxed my arms, freeing the straps and allowing the weight of the fabric to pull it to the ground.

A groan left him as I stood naked before him, a smirk on my lips as I dropped to my knees before him. His abs tensed as my fingers slipped beneath the waistband of his boxer briefs.

I wanted to tease him. To make him beg as he made me.

My movements were slow, precise, slowly exposing skin until the head of his cock appeared. It was resting near his hip bone and I leaned in, wrapping my mouth around it. He cursed as I ran my tongue around the sensitive tip. I continued exposing little by little, taking more and more.

His fingers fisted my hair and pulled me back. Dark eyes glared down at me.

"Quit playing and suck."

I made sure to keep my eyes locked on his as I leaned forward again and ran my tongue up the underside.

"Are you sure my mouth is where you want to come this time?" I closed my lips around the tip.

A growl vibrated in his chest, and I pushed his underwear the rest of the way off. His cock was heavy as it slapped against my face. I turned and continued my tease with my mouth.

"I'm not coming until you are exactly where you are supposed to be."

"And where is that?"

I gasped in surprise as he pulled me from the floor and grabbed hold of my waist. He stepped forward, and my feet left the floor. The sudden flip of my center of gravity confused me until I fell against the softness of his bed. He climbed up, his arms caged me in while his hips pinned me down.

"Right here. In my bed with your thighs open and waiting."

I drew in a sharp breath that quickly morphed into a low moan at the feel of his hard length pressing against my core.

"Mmm, the symphony of your pleasure is my favorite music of all. I've waited over a year to be inside you again. I'm not waiting a moment longer." With that, he slammed into me.

I cried out as a delirious pleasure ripped through me. My head fell back against the bed, my legs clenching around his hips, drawing him deeper. Low moans left him as he pressed all the way in.

"Fuck. So good," he hissed. "So tight and wet wrapped around me."

His words send a wave of electric excitement through me. He set up a slow, steady pace of long, hard strokes. Every one of them filled me, flaming the electric sparks that went off with each thrust.

I rocked my hips with his, driving myself closer and closer to ecstasy.

"Look at me."

My vision focused, and the lust-heavy gaze that I met only served to excite me more.

"Harder," I whispered.

His lips crashed to mine as his hips pulled back and slammed in, making me cry out. It was no longer slow and sensual, but mind-numbing euphoria. My body tensed, focused on the mounting pleasure that filled me until I fell.

I couldn't tear my gaze away from him as I came in his arms, my body shaking, my pussy pulsing around him.

I hadn't even come down when he pulled out, a cry of protest leaving me at the sudden emptiness. He flipped my lax body over and pulled my ass up.

I cried out as he slammed all the way in. He let out a hiss, his fingers digging into my flesh. The new angle allowed him to get deeper, and each time he bottomed out, my mind lost all thought.

He cupped my throat and pulled back, forcing my back to arch, his other hand sliding across my torso to rest on top of my breast, holding me in place.

"I'm going to fill your pussy with my cum," he said into my ear, his voice gruff. My body lit up again, tightening around him. "My first time ever raw. Remember it. Crave it, because I'll never fuck you any other way again."

His thrusts became harder and faster, amping me up for another orgasm primed to rip from me, forcing my body to respond to his.

"You are mine," he growled into my ear. "Your pussy is mine."

"Yes," I cried out as my muscles shook. A high-pitched whine left me as I clenched around him

"Mine," he yelled out as his hips slammed against me for one last thrust. I could feel him twitching inside me, letting his cum out deep within nestled against my cervix.

He fell back to his haunches, still holding me to him, my head resting on his shoulder. After a moment he pulled out, groaning as he stared at me.

"There is something highly primal and erotic about that view."

He lay down next to me and pulled me into his arms, his chest heaving as he regained his breath.

Wow.

That night a year ago paled in comparison to this one. There was no going back to how things had been, because I was going to crave him constantly.

We lay there for a few minutes, calming down, nestled in each other's warmth. Basking in the shift of our relationship.

"And that is how we're going to make our children," he said. It startled me, and I realized I'd begun to doze off.

"Okay," I replied, my head falling back to look at him, a smile on my lips.

I was stunned at the smile that met me, at the softness in his eyes that I'd never seen before. His hand slipped up to cup my face, his thumb tracing my bottom lip.

"You are so beautiful that I can't look away."

"Who said you had to?"

He gripped my jaw and pulled me closer until our lips met. "How do you feel?"

"Boneless," I said with a giggle. "You?"

"I wish this moment would never end. And invigorated."

I blinked at him. "Invigorated?" I glanced down and drew in a sharp breath at the sight of his hard cock resting against his abdomen. "Already?"

He bit down on my shoulder, and I let out a moan from the electric shock that pulsed through me.

"You've teased me for more than a year. I find myself with a lot of pent-up hunger, and once will not satisfy me."

I wrapped my arms around his shoulders and pulled him down to me. "Then have your fill."

THIRTY-SEVEN

ATTICUS

Pulling myself out from underneath Ophelia's warmth as the sun crested the horizon was torture. All I wanted to do was spend the day in bed exploring every inch of her body, finding every erogenous zone, every spot that heated her up, and every millimeter that drove her wild.

Duty and obligation pulled me from her arms. Responsibilities that I couldn't put off. The acquisition of a major South Korean electronics company would ensure our growth for more years to come. They would only entertain our offer in a face-to-face meeting, which put me on a plane instead of between her thighs.

After a shower, I slipped on a pair of slacks and a polo before slipping on some loafers. For an over fifteen-hour flight, I wanted a little more comfort.

When I stepped out of the bathroom, a groan left me at the sight on my bed. Ophelia had turned, the sheet slipping down exposing her perfect breast, the nipple tight from the cooler air.

Never had a woman slept in my bed, and I'd never wanted nor allowed it. I wasn't counting my bed at Stronghold. Ophelia looked like she belonged there, wrapped in my scent, naked. A goddess for me to worship.

One that I had to leave.

Leaning down, I pressed my lips to her forehead. "I'll see you soon, my dear," I whispered. I brushed a lock of hair from her face, completely mesmerized as I stared at her. "How do you do this to me?"

I was unable to resist kissing her, to resist the need to feel her lips against mine before I would be without for days. As I did, her arms wrapped around me, pulling me closer. It was a shock, and I drank in the warmth she enveloped me with. Her eyes fluttered open, a small smile on her lips before her grip lessened and released as she returned to sleep.

I resisted the urge to play with her teasing nipple and covered it back up with the sheet before reluctantly heading for the door. With a last glance, I memorized the sight before me to keep me company until I returned.

A quick stop to my office allowed me to slip my laptop into my briefcase, along with a few files. When I got into the elevator, I waited for one last sound that maybe she was up, but I was met with silence.

In moments I was on the rooftop, walking out into the warm summer air.

"Good morning, Mr. de Loughrey," Carlo greeted as I neared the helicopter.

"Good morning, Carlo." I held out my hand and gave him a smile. "Who do you have with you today?"

"Vincent. We should have you to the airport in ten minutes. They already have the jet ready and waiting for you."

"Thank you." He shut the door, and we took off. I hated watching the building grow farther away, knowing soon she would wake up and I wouldn't be there.

Minutes later, we landed and I was ushered into the hanger where on the other side, one of the smaller of our aircraft waited. The de Loughrey Aviation Express seated ten and held a bed at the rear. Being the only one going on the trip, it was the perfect size for the journey.

"Morning, sir," Damien said as he stepped up beside me.

"Should be an easy few days," I said. "How is she doing?"

"Well, thank you. And thank you for the in-home help, sir."

"The least I can do for stealing you away when your wife is in need of extra care." Damien was my personal guard, and his wife had just undergone surgery to fix a broken leg. While normally another guard could easily take his place on a trip, Damien was fluent in Korean. The only one on our security team who was, and it was a huge asset. Most thought the six-foot-four burly man was all brawn, instead of the most intelligent member in the guard and fluent in multiple languages.

"Good morning, Mr. de Loughrey. Damien."

"Brandy. How are you today?" I greeted with a smile as I entered, placing my bag on one of the seats before dropping into the one across from it. Damien stowed his bag before selecting the seat up one and across the aisle from my location.

"I'm well, sir. How about you?" she asked.

"Tired."

"Would you like me to get the bedroom ready for once we reach cruising altitude?"

"I've got some work to do, but eventually, yes."

She nodded. "Coffee?"

"Please."

"Atticus, good morning," John smiled as he exited the cockpit.

"Captain. How are the kids?"

"Teenagers are a handful." He chuckled to say that explained it all. "Just to let you know, we will be stopping in Anchorage for a refueling today, but we've adjusted the course and it should only add about half an hour onto our flight time."

"It's going to be a long flight either way."

"It sure is. We're just finishing up the preflight checklist and will be on our way shortly."

"Thank you."

Brandy set the coffee down next to me just as he headed back to the front.

"Is there anything else I can get you right now?"

"No. Thank you, Brandy."

"Jack selected a few options for meals, and he put your suitcase in the closet."

I gave her a curt nod, then turned my attention to the phone in my hands to dial one of the many pains in my ass.

"It's Sunday. What do you want?" Hamilton growled into the phone.

"Had a fabulous night, did you?"

Hamilton groaned. "She's still here."

"Did you take someone home last night?" Taking a one-night stand, or anyone, to the Tower was an almost unheard-of move.

"Hell, no. I took her to the hotel." His voice lowered. "But she's still fucking here."

"Just leave."

"I'm thinking about it. I'm also thinking about having her suck me off one last time. Mouth like a fucking Hoover."

Images of last night, of Ophelia's lips stretched around the head of my cock filled my mind, stirring my dick.

"Did you take anyone home last night?"

"Ophelia."

A grumble came over the line. "She doesn't count. You're not fucking her."

I wasn't about to divulge to Hamilton or anyone else what had transpired the night before. "Well, she is the only one I will be taking home for a long time."

"Why did you call?"

"I'm on the plane getting ready to take off, and I wanted to make sure you had the offer ready by the time I land."

"I sent the information to Rhys on Wednesday. Check your email."

"I haven't checked it since I left the office on Friday, so it could be there."

"I'm doing a little more research, but I want to make sure you

get a good look at their R and D section before you have them sign.
The information was vague and threw up some red flags."

"I'll make sure."

"How long will I be graced with silence?" he asked, a hint of
amusement in his tone.

"I should be back on Wednesday or Thursday. But don't think
there will be silence. With my absence, you know he will be in the
office more often."

There was a groan on the line. "Didn't he get a new assistant?
Shouldn't he be off fucking her or something?"

"He's probably going to pressure you on some other heiress up
his sleeve again."

"Just marry one of his girls and end my suffering, okay?"

"So I should suffer the rest of my life?" I asked.

"Better than the sexless marriage you're going to have."

"Hmm. Debatable. Besides, I put the fear of God into him, so
he should be behaving, even if he does meddle."

Brandy caught my eye as she closed and latched the door.

"Time to go," I said.

"Let me know when you land."

"Hamilton, do I detect an ounce of care for my well-being?"

He scoffed. "Yes, because I've decided I don't want to be king.
I'm happy being a prince, so come back."

A chuckle left me, and I hung up.

Normally, my conversations with Hamilton were not filled with
idle chatter because I didn't have time for it. Since Ophelia had entered my life, I found myself opening up to my siblings a bit more.
She was right—I didn't know them. Genevieve and I had more than
a decade that separated us, causing our rift. Even the five-year gap
with Hamilton kept us from getting close.

Elizabeth was the only sibling I was close with, and even then,
I was closer to Rhys. Then again, Rhys and I were only separated by
a year and a half and grew up running down the halls of Stronghold
together.

As the jet rocketed down the runway, my mind returned to the beautiful blonde I was leaving behind. It was only for a few days, but with the progress we'd made, I didn't want to risk fucking it up.

Everything changed last night. No longer did we dance around each other, fighting the attraction that constantly overwhelmed the space we occupied.

I was reminded why I chose her. Every reason I couldn't get her off my mind for a year was exponentially clear. The taste of her skin, each sound that passed through her lips. Her body was a temple I wanted to worship for the rest of my life.

I couldn't answer her last night, because it wasn't until this moment that I understood.

I wouldn't just want her in five years. I knew I would want her at ten and twenty, thirty and forty. Until my last breath, I would want her.

It's always been her.

None other.

The center of my chest burned. Emotions I'd never experienced bombarded me. What started out as a contract, a way to get closer to her, had morphed into a feeling I couldn't put into words.

In my entire life, I'd never felt the overwhelming need to be with someone that I did with Ophelia.

I wanted to be with her forever.

THIRTY-EIGHT

OPHELIA

My eyes strained against the sunlight, fighting to stay closed and to return to the comfort of sleep. In my half-awake state, memories of the night flooded in, and I smiled. From the words that spilled from his lips, to his hands that excited every inch of my skin and his gaze that possessed my soul.

The culmination of months burned bright in the night. Forever altered and owned by him. It wasn't just physical. My whole heart and soul had been captured by the wicked king.

After months of strife and struggle, my wish from a year ago had become a reality. While those initial dreams were of a man I knew little about, not even his last name, that feeling of possibility had nagged at me relentlessly.

When he first told me he wanted me to marry him, those dreams came back to me. But dreams and reality were two totally different worlds. The real Atticus was emotionally sealed until he cracked and his affection came spilling out of him unrestrained. That affection was the manifestation of emotions he had difficulty processing and forming words for.

The depth of blue in his eyes was endless like the ocean with its rough seas, calm waves, and tsunamis. Powerful, alluring, and impossible to control—that was Atticus.

A smile spread and I reached for him, but as I woke more and comprehended my surroundings, I found myself alone.

The sheets were cold.

"Atticus?" I called out and waited, but not a single sound resonated.

I sat up and took in the room. The view out of the large windows was almost the same as from my own, but the size was stunningly larger. Straining my hearing, I listened for any hint of him, but I was met with nothing but silence.

He left the room without waking me? It was Sunday. I expected to wake up in his arms with him holding me close before he filled me again. A shower, then food, then again on the island or table, taking our fill of each other after months of resisting.

Instead, silence surrounded me. Emptiness invaded me.

My chest clenched, and I swallowed before slipping my feet over the edge of the bed. I ran my hand through my hair, working out some knots.

Flashes of the night before danced across my mind. I'd forgotten how possessive his touch was, how demanding. His lips were intoxicating as he kissed me like he was trying to devour me, my name a litany that fell from his lips like a prayer.

Maybe he was in the kitchen?

I moved to stand and fell back to the bed, my legs giving out on me. It took another try to get my legs under me, but my steps were unsteady.

My body throbbed in the best way. Atticus wasn't the only man I'd been with, but none before had ever left me so completely satisfied. A perfect synchronicity as if we'd been together for years instead of one night long ago.

He read me in ways that never ceased to amaze me. Something I couldn't ever let my husband-to-be ever know, because he already had a god complex. There was no need to increase his ego further.

A smile drew up on my face. He really did a number on me.

I put my hand on the door handle to open it but stopped. Looking down, I was completely naked, and while I would normally walk around my home in whatever state I wanted to, that was because I was always alone. That was not the case in the Tower. There were always people popping in and out without notice, silent and stealthy like ninjas, which was why I couldn't be sure there wasn't anyone right outside of the door.

Our clothes were still strewn about the floor, and I picked up Atticus's dress shirt, slipping it on, and buttoned it up. It was long enough that it covered everything.

Tentatively, I opened the door and moved down the hall, paying attention for the slightest sign of life. Each room I encountered was empty. As I passed my bedroom, I grabbed my phone but there were no notifications.

My brow furrowed, and I made my way back to the kitchen. Nothing was out of place. Not even a coffee cup sat in the sink.

The clack of shoes echoed in the hall and I turned, the excitement in finding him filling me.

But it wasn't a scowling, tall, brooding blond that entered the kitchen.

Jack stopped as he entered and saw me. "Good morning, Ophelia," he said with a friendly smile.

"Jack? Have you seen Atticus?"

"Atticus is on a plane right now."

I blinked at him as I tried to remember him talking about a trip. "A plane?" I asked, completely confused.

"Yes, he has a meeting in Seoul on Monday."

Seoul? He was going to South Korea?

Why didn't he tell me? More importantly, why didn't he say goodbye?

"He asked me to give this to you," he said as he handed an envelope over.

My brows scrunched as I took it from him. "What's this?" I asked.

"He didn't say." He turned to leave. "I'll be downstairs if you need anything."

"Thank you," I said, watching him leave.

The envelope was thick, and my brow furrowed deeper as I slipped my finger under the edge. I froze, feeling the familiar edge of a stack of bills. I pulled a few out, noting the denomination—one-hundred dollar bills. There had to be forty or fifty of them.

"What…is…this?"

My stomach dropped, and a wave of nausea washed through me.

Was it a payment? What I'd earned for the night?

The envelope slipped from my fingers, bills spilling out across the floor as my worst fear seemingly came true.

I really was just a whore.

He won. Got what he wanted. He didn't really want me—just sex.

Because if he did, he would have stayed, and even if he couldn't stay, he would have woken me up. But no, he'd just left.

It didn't mean anything to him.

I didn't mean anything to him. At least not past our contract.

"So stupid, Ophelia." My face scrunched up as the pain in my chest threatened to erupt in a sob.

Every insecurity toppled me and the urge to run screamed inside my head while my heart began to crumble. I promised Atticus I wouldn't run again, but the urge was growing in intensity. When I made that promise I never thought I would find myself in this position.

I believed he had feelings for me—convinced myself that maybe we could be a real couple—but it seemed those emotions were completely one-sided. He only considered me a doll to stand prettily next to him and warm his bed. To warm his cock.

Oh, God. Just as he'd said to me when we met before the contract was signed.

I'd always been a runner. To protect myself, I ran from that which caused me pain. My flight response was strong. That was why I lived in dorms from the first moment I could, to get away from Lou.

Months ago, I tried to leave Atticus, and the pain in my chest told me I should have kept going, but he pulled me back in.

And I fell even harder for the man. So hard it silenced the warnings, subdued my gut instinct, and overrode my fears with empty promises.

It was time to run again. To save my heart from more of the pain that was overwhelming my system.

This time I needed help. Things had changed, and I couldn't just run like I had before.

I entered my room and slipped on some leggings before grabbing my phone again and getting onto the elevator. After a few floors, the doors opened and I slammed on the door to Genevieve's condo.

"Ophelia?" she said, her eyes wide as she stared at me.

Did I look that pitiful? "I need your help."

"What's going on?" she asked as she let me in.

I choked on a sob, fresh tears streaming down my cheeks. "I can't stay here. I can't stay with him."

"Calm down and tell me what happened."

It all spilled out as the tears fell, releasing my pain and sharing my struggle. Cathartic at the core, but when I was done, my confidant wasn't as convinced that I'd been duped.

I'd never seen Genevieve so contemplative, worried almost. What was she afraid of?

"Are you sure that was a payment?"

"What else could he have meant?"

"It's just…" She trailed off.

"What?"

She gave me a sad smile, an uncommon sight for the notorious party princess. "We've all noticed the difference, especially last night. I think Atticus really does care for you. I'm not so sure it means what you think it means. A couple grand is like lunch money to us. Maybe he just wanted to make sure you were taken care of while he was away."

"You are defending him?" I asked incredulously.

"Don't get me wrong. Atticus is harsh, hard, and cold, but I also know how lonely he's been."

"You do?"

She gave me a sad smile. "It's a family trait."

Gen had always been so full of life, but as I looked at her, I saw the most surprising thing—the same darkness that often shadowed Atticus's eyes clouded hers.

"Why don't you call him?"

I shook my head. "He's on a plane."

She made a humming sound as she tapped her finger against her bottom lip. "Okay, I have an idea. Leave him."

"Isn't that what I said?"

She waved her hand in front of her. "Your flight response is incredibly strong, so use that, but don't leave him, not really. Just…go on a personal vacation. Don't contact him. Disappear. His reaction when he gets back will tell you everything you need to know."

"And if it's not the right reaction?"

"Then I'll help you get away from him for good."

Her words sliced at my chest. Away from him for good? The thought alone brought the tears back.

"Go get your stuff and meet me back here when you're done. I've got to arrange a ride, and we'll go."

"Go where?"

"Leave it to me."

I nodded before heading toward the elevator. "Thank you. I know we haven't talked much lately, but…"

"Atticus. Trust me, I get it."

When I returned to the penthouse, I began packing up my bags. Just like last time, I took only my things, because despite what Genevieve said, there was a chance I wasn't returning.

Anything de Loughrey purchased was left except for the clothes I was wearing. I didn't want to tip off the front desk or security. The bags would be enough of a giveaway, but with Genevieve beside me, hopefully they wouldn't scrutinize me too hard.

"Don't leave him again." Michael had said that, and I was going against it.

I needed the break to think. To get my emotions in check because they were all over the place. Even with Gen's assurance, I couldn't trust it.

I couldn't trust him.

I clenched my jaw to hold back more tears. What was wrong with me?

You know the answer to that, Ophelia.

You're in love with him.

That was why I had to go. I wouldn't be a convenient pussy for him.

I was numb as I set the de Loughrey cards from my wallet onto the kitchen island, also setting The Rock beside them. They were a sign, a symbol, that I wasn't there and that if he wanted me, he needed to find me.

I did the one thing I shouldn't have—I fell in love with him. There was no way I could spend the next five years with him not reciprocating. It would kill my soul to be beside the man I loved, only to be his contract wife.

At that moment, I really hated our contract.

It felt wrong to say goodbye as the elevator doors closed, and I felt sick when I knocked on Genevieve's door.

Deep in my core, I prayed that it was all a misunderstanding, that Gen was correct, but until he returned, I needed to be away from the Tower.

When she answered, she was ready to go, her hand held out. "Leave your phone."

"Why?" I asked as I handed it to her.

"He can track you in no time. They're all linked. In minutes, he'll find you."

I knew that for a fact, but didn't I want him to once he returned?

"Make him chase you."

"I don't know," I said as I chewed on my bottom lip.

"You want him to prove himself, right? Why not try?"

"Because I'm scared that every fear is truth." I didn't really want to leave him.

"Use this time to get away from him. A much needed Ophelia break. Time to think with a clear head and no de Loughrey influence, because you'll never get it here. Even now, I'm influencing you."

It was better than just running away entirely, but still, my hands shook as anxiety ran rampant through my system. A breather. An escape from the heavy atmosphere of the Tower and to center myself.

"Let's go," Gen said, grabbing one of my bags and heading to the elevator. "Time to hide you."

ATTICUS

Four days.

Eight hours.

Thirty-six minutes.

That was how long it had been since I'd left Ophelia in my bed. Since I used every ounce of strength to pull away from her warm, soft skin. Away from the only thing in the world that I had ever wanted to cherish.

That amount of time was also the last time I had any contact whatsoever with my fiancée.

By day three, I'd employed Hugo to check in on her, but I had yet to hear any positive news. There was a cold dread that had settled over me with each unanswered text or straight-to-voicemail call.

"Where is she?" I asked the moment Hugo's name flashed on my screen.

"I don't know."

I froze and threw my head back against the headrest. "What do you mean, you don't know?"

"We've just confirmed a few places she's not. We're going to go over and check out the penthouse and talk with the staff."

"Keep me informed. We're still a few hours out."

My heart was beating hard in my chest, and my foot wouldn't stop tapping. The anxiety was to a level I'd never experienced. Every dastardly scenario my brain could come up with swirled around, making me nearly choke at made-up horrors.

I knew nothing, but that didn't stop my imagination from running rampant.

Was she kidnapped? Is someone torturing her? Hurting her?

I never should have left her. It didn't feel right, and I should have trusted my gut. Now, I had no idea where she was or if she was all right. Was she hurt? Calling for help and nobody was there? Taken off the street and nobody noticed?

All the worry confirmed one thing—I was never leaving her again. On any and all future trips, she would be sitting next to me on the plane.

"Mr. de Loughrey, the captain wanted me to let you know we will be landing in thirty minutes and that there is a helicopter standing by to transport you to Olympus Tower."

"Thank you, Brandy."

There was no pause. The moment we were on the ground and the door was opened, I was running for the chopper. Seconds later, we were back in the air.

We'd barely gotten off the ground when a call came through. "Hugo, what do you have?"

"You're not going to like it," he said.

The cold seeped in deeper, taking over every inch of me. "What?"

"Everything points to her still being at the Tower, but she's not there."

I clenched my fist to keep my hand from shaking. "She has to be."

"I'm sorry, boss, she's not. Me and three guys and Jack checked every corner. Concierge hasn't seen her since you got back from the charity dinner."

"Was her phone there?" I asked as my mind tried to understand, to process.

"No. Funny thing is, it shows it in the building, but we haven't been able to locate it."

"Have you checked the common floors?"

"Inside and out."

"I'm in the heli now. I'll be there in ten."

"Want me to meet you?" he asked.

"No. Keep digging. She has to be somewhere."

"Right, boss. Damien's heading down to the garage to be at the ready at a moment's notice."

"Thank you."

Please, Ophelia, where are you?

The metal steps clanged beneath my feet as I ran to the elevator. Every second I wasn't moving was another second she was missing.

"Ophelia!" I called out as soon as I entered. I threw my laptop bag into the office before running around.

There was nothing but dead silence. A stillness that was familiar, but also foreign. It had only been a few months, but in those months I'd gotten used to having her near, used to not being alone. Used to her warmth and light that radiated off her.

I ran through the rooms, but nothing. There was no sign of a single thing out of place.

In her room, a sense of déjà vu took over. Again, nothing was amiss, but there was a lack of Ophelia in the room. Did Hugo notice as well? Or did he even think anything was amiss?

In my room everything was in place, the maid having cleaned at some point after she left.

Upon entering the kitchen, nothing looked out of place but something sitting on the island caught my eye. Lying in contrast against the white granite counter were two square black items. I cautiously approached, recognizing the first one as her de Loughrey black credit card and directly beneath it the black card with the de Loughrey family crest.

My hands shook as I picked up the small black box, and when I popped the button, her engagement ring was nestled inside.

She left me.

Again.

I doubled over from the pain. A soul-crushing yell burst from my lungs. The pain unlike anything I'd felt in my life.

Why? What happened? What did I do that would make her run from me again?

And how did she get out of the building?

I pulled up the locator app for her phone. The last ping was five flights down.

Genevieve.

In seconds I was in the elevator, and a minute later my fist was slamming on her door.

"Open up!" I growled. The anger coursing through my veins was at destructive levels. I would set the city on fire to find her, and my sister was in on it.

It took a few minutes, but eventually a bed-headed Genevieve opened the door. I pushed past her, my eyes searching.

"Where is she?"

"Calm down, Atticus."

I turned on her. "Tell me. Where the fuck is she?" I was shaking, barely hanging on by a thread.

She swallowed hard. "I don't know."

"Fucking lies," I spat at her and made sure her eyes were on mine. "Her phone is here, Gen."

Her eyes widened, knowing I'd caught her in a lie.

"You know it's here. Tell me this instant where she is, or I swear I will cut you off without a penny to your name and revoke access to every single de Loughrey property."

There was no time for negotiation. If Genevieve continued to withhold information from me, in five minutes she would be without her trust fund and other accounts or access to any de Loughrey properties, including the one she was standing in, for years to come.

She swallowed. "Le Magnifique," she whispered.

"How long?"

She shook her head and shrugged. "A couple of hours after you left? I don't know." She leaned forward, her eyes beseeching me. "She was a wreck, Atticus. I couldn't stand to see her like that."

"What right did you have to interfere with our relationship?" I seethed.

"I was just trying to help her."

"Help her? Why the fuck would she need your help? Did you encourage her to leave me?"

Her eyes were to the floor. "You disappeared without a word, leaving a stack of cash like a payment. She thought you were paying her for sex."

Cash? The money for her sisters? Was that how things suddenly became so fucked up?

"We made love. And then I had to get on a plane. Not sex. Not fucking," I growled, hearing the broken edge in my tone.

She heard it as well, regret evident in her expression. "The room is under my name. I don't think she's left it."

I spun and headed back to the elevator, leaving her staring after me.

In the elevator, I texted Damien that I was on my way down. By the time I made it to the garage level, Michael was jumping out of the passenger's seat of a sedan to hold open the door. I glared at him as I slid in. She was his responsibility, and he'd lost her. After the first time, I didn't think he would fail again, but he did.

"Le Magnifique," I barked.

My knee bounced with excess energy and anxiety. Until I saw her, held her in my arms, nothing would calm me. Until then, my murderous intent was on the surface.

The car had barely rocked back to a stop when I burst from the backseat, Michael hot on my heels as I ran up the steps and through the doors held by the doorman. There were people all over the lobby, and I wove my way to the check-in desk.

"Mr. de Loughrey, what a pleasure it is to—"

"What room is Genevieve in?" I asked, cutting her off.

She blinked, then looked down at the screen. "She is, umm…"

"1208, sir," Tomas, the manager, said before stepping around the desk. "Let me show you up."

I gave a curt nod, following him to the elevator bay.

The seconds ticking by itched my skin with their slow movement. It would have been better if I'd taken the stairs than waited in the elevator.

I reined in my anger as we approached her door. I didn't trust myself, so I had Tomas knock for me.

We waited but were greeted by nothing but silence. Not a single sound resonated inside.

The anger in my veins morphed into anxiety with each second. Until I saw her, I wouldn't be able to calm down.

"Open it," I growled once there was no response, my mind unable to handle the images circulating.

Tomas wasted no time unlocking the door. As soon as it was open, I rushed in but was once again me with nothing but silence. The room was filled with Ophelia's bags, but completely empty otherwise.

She wasn't there.

I walked toward her things to find her bags open, her toiletries case on top with a laundry bag, a single change of clothes inside of it. The only other signs of life were her laptop and its bag strewn all over the bed, the power cord stretched across from the wall.

Something wasn't right, and the alarms in my mind began going off. Genevieve said she dropped her off the day I left. There was one dirty outfit.

A cold dread slid through my veins as the truth stared me in the face.

Ophelia hadn't been in that room in *days*.

There was no way she would have left everything, which only left one alternative.

"Get me the access log for this room. Phone records as well. Send it to my office now."

"Yes, sir," Tomas said before heading out.

"Boss?" Michael asked.

"Get the CCTV footage of the hotel. Find her and follow her," I ordered before turning and heading back out. "I'm going to my office. Call me as soon as you find something."

"Yes, sir."

Damien was waiting for me out front, and minutes later we were stopped in front of the de Loughrey Tower. I wasn't dressed in my normal office attire, nor did I care as I blazed a trail to the elevator, ignoring everyone in my path.

Holly greeted me as the doors opened, her brow furrowed.

Ah—someone from the security team called her.

She took my hand and dragged me to my office. I let her. An unknown cold seeped into me, and it felt like I was shutting down. Until I found her, it felt as if the ice would work its way through my body until I was frozen solid.

"Anything?" I asked.

She shook her head.

I threw my head back, my fists clenched. Never again would I let her out of my sight. "Where is she, Holly?"

The unknown was suffocating. It wasn't only that she left, it was that she completely disappeared.

"Atticus," Genevieve called as she rushed in. Her eyes were watery. "She just wanted to take a break. She was in the hotel. I left her in the hotel!"

"What's going on?" Hamilton asked from the doorway, Rhys behind him.

"Ophelia is missing," I said in a monotone voice.

"What?" Rhys cried out.

"I don't know what happened, but there is no sign of her."

"Kidnapped?" Rhys asked. "We have a lot of enemies."

I turned to Genevieve. "How did you find out?"

"Jason got a notice from Michael."

"Damn it. We need some answers before this explodes all over the news." The pent-up emotions exploded out and I slammed my fist onto my desk. "Fuck!"

I needed to get a grip, but I didn't know how to process the hurricane growing inside me.

By the expressions of my family members standing in my office,

I needed to lock down my emotions before they left utter destruction in their wake.

"What the hell is going on?" Penelope asked as she stormed in. It seemed no one was showing my office any respect.

"What are you doing here?" I asked.

"Gen called," Penelope answered.

I looked around the room. "Why are all of you here?"

Penelope blinked at me. "Because we love you, Atticus, and Ophelia is special to you, which makes her special to us."

When did my siblings start caring about me? Especially caring enough they would drop everything to come to my side?

"Atticus, we have a problem." My office door swung open, startling all of us as Hugo barged in.

So little did I see the man that it took me a moment to recognize him: early fifties with greying brown hair, deep-set, brown eyes, nearly my height with a portly belly. Communication was always through the phone or email, therefore his appearance put me immediately on high alert, especially with Ophelia's missing presence.

"What happened?" I asked, the alarms going off in my mind again.

He stopped in front of my desk, huffing from exertion. "It's Milner." He slammed a piece of paper down in front of me.

I scanned over the document, my eyes going wide.

The document contained fragments of information that pointed to one thing—Lou, Ophelia's stepfather, was on the run.

"When?"

"He skipped bail. They served a warrant, but the house was cleaned out. The landlady said they were behind on rent and ran out sometime earlier this week."

I sat down in my chair and ran my fingers against my lips. Lou Milner had somehow made bail. It was a mystery, because the man had no assets, leading whomever lent the money to be out a million dollars when he failed to show up to court two days ago.

My stomach turned, and my chest clenched as every siren blared inside me. "Any leads on his whereabouts?"

"Every single one has come out to nothing. Amy Milner emptied out their accounts three days ago, and she's been withdrawing cash from her credit cards over the last few weeks. They're all maxed out. Cell phones aren't sending out signals. I've been using facial recognition, but we've had zero hits in the last two days."

"Where are the daughters?" I asked. "Are they still in New Haven?"

He nodded. "They are confirmed to still be with Amy Milner's sister in Connecticut. All of my information leads me to believe they have no idea what is going on, and do not know what kind of people their parents are."

"They know, just not the extent," I said, recalling Ophelia's frantic call to have them removed. For now, they seemed safest where they were, and we would keep it that way for now. Once Ophelia was located and Lou and Amy were dealt with, I would talk to Ophelia about what to do with her sisters for the future.

My thoughts moved back to Ophelia, and the sirens grew louder. "Find Milner. Now."

"What's wrong?" Rhys asked.

I clenched my fingers into a fist. "I don't know, but I have a feeling."

"Your feelings are often right," Penelope said.

"What is it?" Hamilton asked.

"Ophelia is missing. Her abusive fuck of a stepfather who tried to blackmail her is suddenly released on bail."

Everyone went still and a hiss of "fuck" was heard.

Hugo's head hung, and I was immediately out of my chair.

A crushing vise circled around my chest. Her stepfather was up to something, and I feared he would take the events of my doing out on her.

My phone went off, breaking the silence and gaining everyone's attention. Ice seeped deep into my bones as Michael's number flashed across the screen.

"Tell me," I said as I answered, wasting no time.

"Sir, we have a problem."

OPHELIA

Darkness and pain.

Those were the only two things I could sense. A throbbing in my head, the bite of something sharp against one side of my body, and the tingling sensation of one of my arms having gone to sleep.

Slowly, my eyes began to open, my head spinning as I tried to see anything, but there was nothing. The more aware I became, the more I began to notice my surroundings. The more I noticed the stiff and sore muscles. How long had I been out?

I tried to remember, to recall how I ended up in pain in a strange place, but my mind was still muddled. A groan left me and I tried to sit up, but when I moved to press against the ground, I found that my wrists were secured together in zip ties. The plastic scraped across my skin, and I hissed out.

Thankfully my legs weren't trapped, but that didn't stop the cold dread that began to crawl through me. A million questions filled me—how did I get here? What happened? And how long had I been out?

I retraced my steps as the fog cleared.

I'd been working on my computer when the phone rang.

Andrea.

She'd been frantic. When I moved to the hotel, I'd called Brooke and gave her the number there because I'd left my cell with Gen.

Andrea's whispered pleas filled my mind. "*Mom picked us up. She said she left Dad, that she was going to do better. She promised!*"

"*What happened? What's going on?*" I could hear someone in the background, and a shriek that was close but also far away.

"*He's hurting Brooke!*"

There was a tussle, and another shriek, this time from Andrea as she cried out, "No!"

The adrenaline pumped hard in my veins, gearing me up, frantic to know where they were so I could take them away.

"*Stop!*" *I cried out, my chest clenching. How could they?*

Harsh breaths came through the line, sending a chill down my spine.

"*You come take their place, and I'll stop.*"

"*You fucking asshole.*"

"*Ah-ah. Piss me off, and I'll take it out on little Drea,*" *he hissed, calling her by the nickname she hated.*

"*What do you want?*"

"*I want you here. Now. We'll talk, come to an understanding, and in exchange, I'll stop hurting your sisters.*"

"*They're your daughters, you sick fuck!*"

A scream rang out in the background.

"*Yeah, mine. You have an hour to get here before I start whipping 'em with my belt.*"

I flinched at that, remembering the welts left by the strap of leather.

"*Give me the address, and don't touch another fucking hair on their heads.*"

"*Glad I have your attention. When you leave that fancy hotel you're staying at, make sure you aren't followed.*"

Before I left, I'd tried to get ahold of Atticus, but the call had gone to voicemail. I didn't leave a message, and I regretted it the moment I stepped out of the hotel doors. He would notice the call, right?

Despite my unease about our relationship status, I'd long since realized that the only one in my life I could count on was him. No matter what, Atticus would help me. He would find me.

I grabbed a taxi to some run-down house in Jersey City. It took nearly the full hour. Mom answered the door, and I was barely through when I felt the prick of something at my neck.

Nothing like realizing what a total and complete monster your mother is, or any parent for that matter.

Mom had never been the loving, cooking and baking type. She was the cigarettes-and-booze type, just like Lou. Her style of raising was neglect. I cooked more for my sisters than she ever did, and I made sure to teach them to fend for themselves when I left.

I didn't worry about them, because I was the punching bag while they were the princesses. They were Lou's kids after all, while I was the thing he was forced to feed.

Eventually, it seemed they became more like Cinderella—slaves given no affection. No longer princesses.

With no windows, there was no light, and I had no way to tell how long I'd been stuck wherever I was. The basement? Or did they take me somewhere else?

Instead of cowering against the wall, I knew I had to get a better understanding of the space I was in. I stood and held my bound hands in front of me, shuffling slowly forward. My stomach clenched and my breathing became ragged, but inch by inch I continued. I drew in a shuddering breath when I found the comforting rigidity of a wall.

I continued on my slow path, following the wall, feeling for anything. Neither my feet nor my hands came across anything. After hitting a corner I made my way down the next wall, but it wasn't until the next wall that the surface changed. There was a bump with an edge, then a seam, followed by a wide expanse until the same bump was found.

Drawing my hands down, I ran them across what I now knew to be a door in search of a handle. Finally, protruding from the wood I gripped the rounded handle and turned it, but nothing happened. Despite the handle moving, neither pushing nor pulling made any movement.

"Fuck," I hissed.

Following the edge, I moved my hand up until I reached another bump, this one smaller and round. There was a slit for a key, and I leaned forward, my head slamming against the door.

There was no way out. No way for me to escape whatever hell I'd been dumped into.

I just wanted to get away. Take time to settle my mind and my heart without, as Gen said, de Loughrey influence. Now, all I wanted was to be locked up in that tower, because the fear was creeping in. Like long vines twisting and twirling, it soaked into my body.

"Atticus," I whimpered, tears filling my eyes. "Help me."

I slid down the wall, working on my breathing before I began hyperventilating. The silence was so great that the loudest thing was the whooshing of my blood. I didn't know how long I sat there completely defeated, but at some point the stress had me drifting off.

The sound of a latch releasing followed by footsteps echoing in the dark empty room had me on high alert. Blinding light filled the room, and I hissed as I covered my eyes.

"You stupid bitch," a gruff voice said. The brightness stung, and as I looked up, a familiar figure stood.

Lou.

He looked like he hadn't shaved in a few days. A grimy button-down shirt sat on his rounded shoulders, his beer belly protruding through the open placket exposing his trademark, dingy wife-beater.

"About time your lazy ass woke up."

"Where am I?" I asked.

"Doesn't fucking matter," he said, which neither confirmed nor denied if I'd been moved while out.

"How long have I been here?"

The door opened again and my mother walked in. A tiny spark of hope fought to light, but the fight quickly died. She was part of the plan and not on my side.

Never on my side.

She tossed a bottle of water at me, then a sandwich. "Those drugs were stronger than they said. You've been out for over a day."

A day? No wonder I was sore.

"And no one in that fucking family has even noticed you're gone. That's how little you mean to them."

No one? That didn't make sense. Atticus wouldn't…

I swallowed hard.

No matter my fears and doubts, there was one thing I was confident about—Atticus would come for me. He would search until he found me, no matter what.

Contract or not, I knew that truth. The goal was to hold on, to not lose hope in him while I waited.

He would come.

"Where are Andrea and Brooke?"

"We had 'em, but took 'em back to your Aunt's. Didn't want your prince to figure out too quickly."

At least they were away from him. For now.

"What do you want?" I ground out. The situation was extreme, even for them.

"I want that shithead fiancé of yours to pay, and I want to have him watch your fall from grace. What would he want with you when I'm done?"

A shiver rolled down my spine.

"First, I'm going to get your sisters again," Mom said.

The blood drained from my face. "What? You just said they were with Stacey."

The corner of her mouth twitched up and she sneered down at me. "Gotta keep appearances and keep my cunt sister from blabbing. Little traitor cried when I tied her up. She put up a fight. Only bringing them 'cause you might need some incentive to cooperate."

Lou took a set of keys out of his pocket and handed them over. "I'll handle the little bitch. You get the girls."

I scoffed, gaining their attention. "You really are the shittiest mother ever."

Her face twisted and she stomped forward, her arm swinging

back before her hand collided with my cheek. "You have always thought you were better than us. Always staring at me with those eyes just like your father's. But don't worry—Lou's gonna straighten you out."

My cheek stung, and I pressed the back of my hand against the warming skin.

They kissed, making my stomach turn, before she disappeared through the door and leaving me alone with him. His dark eyes narrowed in on me.

"Now, should I start with my fist, or…" he pulled something from his pocket and that familiar *schnick* sound hit my ears. Once upon a time that sound filled me with fear, and he used it to threaten me again and again.

"What the hell did I ever do to you? You're the fucking drunk that would fly off in a rage and hit me. You're doing it again now with Andrea and Brooke!"

"Shut up!" he roared as he raised his arm holding the knife.

A tremble vibrated in every muscle as I stared at his hand, wondering where he'd strike first. It took everything in me not to crumble at the situation, but I was stubborn enough I wasn't going to let him see my fear. Not ever again would I give him that power over me.

"This is all your fucking fault, bitch. I should have fucking put you down when your no-good father stopped breathing."

"Don't talk about my father like that." *That's it. Stay strong.*

"When he was gone, you were worthless. If he just woulda given custody to your mom so we could get the child support, but no, made me ram him with the car."

I froze, the blood falling from my face as I stared at him. The world seemed to turn on its axis, my stomach dropping as the ground went out from under me.

"What?"

He sneered at me. "Yeah, it was me. I hit your little bitch of a daddy. Asshole wasn't supposed to die, just take the hint to back off."

A lightning bolt broke through my chest. I was frozen as the dam inside me broke. For years, ever since Lou married my mom,

I wasn't allowed to talk about my dad. If I cried about missing my dad, Lou would get angry and push me against the wall or slap me.

It all made sense why.

"So what now?" I asked. What did he have in store for me?

"Now I gotta think about what I'm gonna do to you. We got some time. Think I'm gonna take some of this anger out of that pretty skin of yours."

I sat still, unmoving, trying to figure a way out of the situation. Running would result in him stabbing and possibly killing me. Staying would result in him probably killing me. Either way, not the greatest outcome for me. My bound wrists left me at a disadvantage. Otherwise, I could easily out maneuver him and lock his ass in the dark.

"What pissed you off so badly?" I asked. I'd never seen him so hyped up and began to wonder if he was on something.

I couldn't tell how long I'd been in there, so my tactic became stalling. Atticus had to notice I was missing by now, right? He would check in or return my phone call and when he couldn't get ahold of me, he'd have someone look for me.

"Some trumped-up charges were pinned on me. Think I can guess who tipped them off."

"It wasn't me."

"No, but it was that bastard you're engaged to," he snarled. "He's the reason the girls got taken away. Your momma's been miserable without them little shits."

After her act and what I remembered from living with them, plus what I'd heard from Brooke and Andrea, that was a lie. She probably just missed them doing everything so she could sit on her ass all day.

"If you hate them so much, you should have wrapped it up."

"Why you little…" He charged forward and grabbed at the hair at the back of my head, squeezing his fist around the strands as he pulled.

I cried out from the pain and reached back to loosen his grip.

"You're gonna do as I say, and if you don't, I'm gonna hurt you real bad."

"I don't think you're man enough."

His hand wrapped around my throat, squeezing hard, cutting off my air supply. "How 'bout now?"

"What does it matter? You already said nobody is looking for me. So, why all the dramatics? If he doesn't care enough, what are you going to do that will make him?"

Keep him talking, Ophelia. Find out all his secrets. Find out the truth.

Find a way back to Atticus.

"Were you always such an uppity bitch?"

"Yup." An annoying scratch in my mind broke open and my gaze snapped to him. "How did you know where I was?" He specifically mentioned making sure nobody followed me from the hotel I was staying at.

"Been tailin' you," he revealed. "Couldn't get near you in that heavily guarded tower, but then you went to that hotel. And I know those girls are your weakness."

He pushed me back down to the ground and headed toward the door. Fear shot through me when he flipped the switch, blacking out the room.

"About time you were good for something, and when the payout comes, your usefulness will be gone. Get me?"

He slammed the door and locked it, leaving me all alone in the bare room with his words ringing in my head. A blanket of dread settled on my shoulders, and it took everything in me to not sink into the fear.

Atticus would come for me.

He would come.

Just hold on.

FORTY-ONE

ATTICUS

Shortly after my near breakdown with still no notification on her whereabouts, a video link was texted to my phone from an unknown number. I immediately shared the screen with the TV mounted to the wall in my office so that all could see.

My body went numb as I watched the infrared video of Ophelia. All alone in the dark, tears slipping down her cheeks.

What tore at me and ramped up my thirst for blood was when she cried out for me. My name a whimper in the black, searching for comfort. I promised I'd keep her safe. I'd done everything in my power to avenge those who had wronged her, but my ego failed to think of retribution.

"Are we tracking where this came from?" I asked.

"The tech team is on it," Damien answered. It was minimal, keeping my anger from exploding.

Suddenly the lights flashed on and color filled the screen. She cringed against the flash of illumination, holding her hands up to cover her eyes, exposing raw skin and a sheen of blood from shallow nicks. It was then I noticed the zip ties cutting into her wrists.

Red filled my vision, blotting out everything else.

"Where?" I was going to fucking kill whoever had her.

"We're working on narrowing it at this moment."

She lowered her hands, her eyes still fighting to adjust. How long had she been trapped in the dark? Finally, I was able to get a good look at her condition, and every muscle tensed. The question wasn't simply how long had she been in the dark, but how long had she been in that room.

Dirt covered her clothes, her hair was matted, and debris coated her sweat-covered skin. Her beautiful face was littered with bruises and her lip was split.

"Say it," a low voice growled through the speakers.

I expected to see her beaten down, and while tears did stream down her cheeks, her jaw was locked and there was a hard set in her eyes as she glared up at someone.

"Go to hell."

A figure stepped into the line of the camera and a cry rang out as she fell back down to the ground. A fist grabbed at her hair, pulling, and she reached up to push them off as her lips curled back and her face twisted in pain.

A gasp sounded behind me along with a choked sob. Everyone in the room, all of my siblings, Rhys with his siblings, and security along with Holly stood powerless to the images before us.

In all my life, I'd never felt as helpless as I did at that moment. For all my money and power, I couldn't stop what was happening to the woman I loved. Stuck, forced to watch her be assaulted and unable to stop it.

The man that had her dragged her forward, closer to the camera, and held her by her throat, his other hand still fisted in her hair. "Do it!"

Her cheeks were red, tears pooling in her eyes, and blood dripped down her chin from the newly reopened split in her lip. The fear in her eyes, the pain, had me nearly doubled over, but I refused to look away. This was the penance for my pride, and I vowed that whoever had her would feel all that she felt a hundred times over.

"You son of a bitch, I said no," she hissed, a small smile on her lips as he roared with anger.

The smile faded as he threw her into the wall, her head slamming against the plaster. Her head lulled, but she tilted it back to look up at her captor.

"You won't win. I won't let you."

"You'll do it for Andrea, won't you? For Brooke? If you don't say it, I'll bring them down here and start in on them until you do."

Her face twisted in anguish. "You fucking bastard!"

"Say it!"

Her head drooped, her shoulders shaking. She looked up and into the camera. "The fucker wants a million dollars before he'll tell you where I am. Don't give it to him." A smirk lit up her face before her body jolted as a foot slammed into her stomach.

Again and again he kicked her until the camera fell over, leaving only a view of her delicate fingers blocking everything else.

"Get me her location now!" I yelled.

The grimy, overweight face of her stepfather filled the camera, his breath harsh from exertion.

I was going to kill him.

"You want her, de Loughrey? I'll give her back for a price. One million. The longer you wait, the less I can guarantee her condition when she's returned." There was a pause before a knife entered the picture. "For every hour I don't have my money, I'm gonna use this on a part of her. Wonder how many hours it would take before she dies of blood loss. Don't keep me waiting."

On the screen was a phone number and a bank account.

"I want him dead," I growled. Every muscle was so tight I was shaking in furious anger.

FORTY-TWO

OPHELIA

I drew in a sharp breath, a cough taking over that only made my stomach hurt worse. I'd forgotten how powerful Lou's kicks could be.

With no windows, I'd had no way to track how long I'd been there, but it had to be days. My body had grown weak, and it took every ounce of energy to keep my spirit up. They didn't give me food often, and a drink even less.

All of my body's energy was spent trying to repair itself from the damage inflicted every few hours.

The tang of rust hit my tongue, and I swiped at the cut in my lip. It had first broken open at least a day earlier. Brooke's tear-streaked face filled my mind, her cries for me as she pleaded with Lou to stop hurting me. He struck her in front of me, and I mustered all of my strength, tackling him to the ground.

I diverted his anger and became the outlet while Mom pulled her out of the room.

The latest round was the most brutal. Though I paid for my defiance, hope was renewed. That video was for Atticus. The end of suffering was in sight.

Lou underestimated Atticus, and soon the wicked king would rain hellfire down upon my captors. That, I could have faith in.

Faith in Atticus.

Faith in his destructive anger—that darkness that slept beneath the surface.

The door swung open, and I glared at the man. He turned to close it, his shirt lifting up, giving me just enough of a peek at a familiar silhouette.

The blood drained from my face at the revolver stuffed in his waistband.

So, that was how it was going to end. Lou's endgame.

My stomach turned, and a wave of nausea rolled over me.

Hurry.

"An hour's up," Lou said as he stomped into the room. The knife was back in his hand, and he waved it at me. "Where should I start?"

"How about your eyes?"

A grin spread on his face, sending a shiver down my spine.

"That's a great place." He squatted down in front of me and grabbed my face. "Your momma always hated your eyes. Think of how happy she'll be once I destroy them."

My eyes widened, and I struggled to release his grip. He moved the knife in closer and I pulled back, shifting my weight to press away from him.

"N-no!" I cried out.

I shut my eyes, sealing them tight as I pulled my arms up to protect me. The sharp edge of the blade hit my cheekbone.

His breath was harsh against my face. "Open your eyes."

"No," I hissed as the tip of the blade sliced into my skin.

The sudden slamming of the door banging against the wall startled us both. Lou turned his head ready to yell at my mom, but we both were frozen as we stared at the figure now in the room.

Relief flooded me, and tears slipped down my cheeks.

Atticus.

Our eyes met and there was a flash of pain in his expression that was quickly surpassed by anger.

Lou released me, backing up as he stared at Atticus.

My heart pounded in my chest, a sob erupting from me as happiness rushed in. He came. He made it.

"Well, well, well, if it isn't the fucking asshole who destroyed my life."

Atticus cautiously stepped toward me, his attention locked on Lou, who was blocking him from getting closer. "And I'll do it a thousand times again if you touch her one more time."

Lou looked behind him at me. "Bitch is still breathing, ain't she?"

Emotionally, I was frantically trying to hold myself together. Fear rocked me as elation raised me up. What if he got hurt? Lou was definitely in a vindictive mood, and I knew what he was hiding at his waist.

"She is, but you've hurt what's mine, and for that, you will not be breathing by the time the night is over," Atticus snarled.

"She that good of a whore? Should have been selling her body off long ago."

My stomach rolled again at that thought. I remembered his "friends," and I knew they were all as crooked and sleazy as him.

"You will refrain from speaking about my fiancée in such a manner."

I couldn't see Lou's expression, but I could see the tension in his shoulders.

"So fucking proper and shit. Just another jackass with a golden spoon in his mouth, money flowing from his momma's tit."

"Release her to me. Now."

Lou reached for me, grabbing hold of my hair and pulling me forward. I flinched and cried out, falling back to the ground when he let go. "Show me the motherfucking money, and I'll hand her over. But you seem to be empty handed, and my bank account is still empty, so hows about I just kill you both."

I was finally able to look at Atticus. The gleam in his eyes was murderous, but when he glanced at me, I saw pain flicker in their blue depths.

"And then what? I've ruined your life, and taking mine would ruin your future. Speaking of—where is your wife?"

"Went to fetch the girls again. We're takin' 'em with us."

Atticus smirked. "Are you certain of that?"

Lou's gaze narrowed. "What the fuck did you do?"

"What I had to." It almost felt like his aura increased, becoming larger and taking up more and more room, threatening to pull everything into its darkness. "You threaten me, I take from you. You take from me, I end you. There is no mercy and no second chances."

All of Lou's attention was focused on Atticus. I was weak, but I had to try to get away. There was just enough in me for one sudden burst. Pushing off the floor, I launched myself toward Atticus. Lou yelled out, and Atticus reached for me, catching me by my bound arms and pulling me tightly to his chest.

"You think you got the upper hand now 'cause he's here?" Lou sneered before locking onto Atticus again. "I ain't lettin' you take her. She's payback, 'cause I never did nothin' to you."

Atticus held me tightly to him. "You did to Ophelia. As my soon-to-be wife, she is an extension of myself. Ergo, you threatened me. You harmed me."

"He killed my father," I said, a tear sliding down my cheek. Would Lou take away the only other man I'd ever loved as well?

"I already suspected."

I looked up to him, but he wasn't taking his eyes off Lou. "You did?"

He nodded. "Hugo has been looking into it for a month." He looked back to Lou. "There is more than enough evidence to convict him."

The anger surged in Lou, and he reached behind him for the gun he was hiding. His arm rose, aiming the gun at us. Atticus pushed me behind him, shielding me. I gripped his arm, watching Lou.

What were we going to do now? I was a liability, slowing him down, and we couldn't run.

"You don't want to do this," Atticus said.

But Lou was past reasoning.

His dark eyes were trained on me. "Yeah, I do. Ending you both would feel so good after the shit you've put me through. Using your money to fuck with me. But I'd be satisfied if it was just her." Lou's lips twitched up. "If you don't want to die, move so I can end the bitch."

Atticus clenched his fist, not taking the bait Lou was throwing.

"I already told you—you're not going to touch her again."

The next second felt like an eternity as Atticus turned, his eyes meeting mine before he pushed on my arms, throwing me back away from him. I tripped and fell to the floor, tumbling before stopping against the wall. The commotion caused Lou to freeze in confusion, and Atticus took the opportunity to rush him.

I was no longer in the line of fire, but Atticus was. Years of sports and training made him faster and more agile than Lou, and he had Lou's arm up in the air.

The gun went off and a scream left me, terrified Atticus had been shot. They fell to the ground, both fighting for possession of the gun. Atticus straddled Lou, his weight holding Lou down as they struggled. The gun went off again and Atticus's arm whipped out, sending the gun flying across the room.

Then, a force I'd only seen once before took over Atticus. He pulled his arm back and slammed his fist into Lou's face with such force I swear I could hear bones crunching.

Over and over, he hit until Lou's struggles died down.

Atticus was breathing hard as he stood, his eyes still watching Lou while turning toward me. Blood dripped from his fist, but it wasn't the one he'd been hitting with.

Fear swept through me and I rushed forward, watching the adrenaline drain from Atticus. He started to drop, and I couldn't hold him. We fell to our knees, and tears filled my eyes as I cupped his face.

"Look at me," I cried.

He blinked, his eyes unfocused, and shook his head, trying to clear it. Red pooled around him, and a sob left me.

"Oph…elia," he struggled to say. His forehead pressed against mine, and he finally focused on me. "I love you."

Time moved in slow motion and terror ripped through me, slicing my heart in half watching his eyes roll back as all his weight collapsed down to the floor.

"Atticus!"

OPHELIA

Seconds later the room was rushed by men in suits, but my attention was focused on Atticus. They were simply a movement in my periphery as I fought the break happening inside. Someone took hold of my arms and pulled me off. I cried out, fighting against whoever had me as I was forced to watch them load Atticus onto a stretcher, a pool of blood beneath him.

Everything was in a strange combination of slow motion with fast-forward moments with the volume off. Suddenly, for the first time in days, my arms were freed from the zip ties and an arm swept under my legs, lifting me off my feet. When I looked up, Michael's familiar green eyes stared down at me. His mouth was moving, but I couldn't hear anything.

The bounce of each step up the stairs jostled my injuries, and pain began to seep back into my senses. The bright light shining in from large windows was blinding.

I cringed against the sun as we exited, people still flooding in. Black cars and SUVs parked up the street at both ends, and in a parking lot across the street a strobe-like effect was created on the ground by the large blades of one of the de Loughrey helicopters sitting in the center. They were loading Atticus in, and we were headed right for them.

We loaded in, but Michael kept me in his arms as the helicopter lifted off the ground seconds later. I couldn't keep my eyes off Atticus. I wanted to go to him, to throw myself at him, but they were working on him, putting a tourniquet high up on his arm.

My whole body shook as I was transfixed with each slight rise and fall of his chest.

We landed on the roof of a hospital minutes later, and then they were off, forcing me to watch Atticus disappear into the elevator. Michael carried me over to the elevator, and we got on with a guard.

We entered a floor of the hospital that appeared empty. I was seated into an awaiting wheelchair, the sudden loss of touch causing my body to flood with cold, and my teeth began chattering.

Someone approached us, but I continued to look down the hall, searching for him.

"I think she's in shock," Michael said, the first sound to penetrate since Atticus's last words.

Shock?

The doctor bent down in front of me, his brown eyes meeting mine, and I blinked. "Mrs. de Loughrey, we need to get you evaluated."

"Evans," I said, correcting him.

His eyes widened in surprise. "What?"

"We aren't married yet. It's Evans."

Everything came flooding back and a scream ripped from me, letting loose all of my suppressed anguish.

Footsteps sounded behind me, and suddenly Penelope was in front of me. She slipped her hand in mine and squeezed. It calmed my heart just knowing she was there, even though I didn't really know her.

"Can you tell me what happened?" the doctor asked.

I nodded. The shaking in my other hand stilled when warmth surrounded it. "We're coming," Genevieve said from my other side.

I glanced up at my two soon-to-be sisters-in-law and gripped their hands. "How?"

"We've been on high alert. We're here for you."

The doctor almost seemed like he wanted to argue, but then looked at the family and decided against it.

We entered into a single room and before I even sat on the bed, multiple photos were taken of my extensive injuries before my clothes were stripped and put into evidence bags. More photos were taken before I was poked, prodded, and scraped before the doctor was even able to examine me. I didn't even have the energy to be embarrassed standing in the middle of the room of half a dozen people with only my underwear on.

The doctor grimaced as he looked me over. My arms were covered in dried blood, and there was no way to tell if it was mine or Atticus's.

"Mostly not mine," I whispered.

"There is a shower in there. Why don't you get cleaned up so we can see what we're dealing with."

I nodded and, with the help of nurses, moved into the bathroom.

"Let me help," one of them said with a small smile.

I nodded before stepping into the warm spray. I cried out as raw skin was scrubbed and sealed wounds reopened. Once the torture was over, I stood under the spray trying to relax a little.

When I exited I felt a lot better, despite my weakened state, but was suddenly aware I no longer had any clothing.

"Jack brought this," Penelope said, holding out one of my bags I'd left at La Magnifique.

"Thank you," I said before digging in for some panties and a sports bra.

"You can get dressed once the examination is done," the doctor said, signaling for me to lie down.

More prodding was done and I cried out a few times, especially when he pushed on the developing bruises on my stomach from Lou's kicks. It wasn't the first time he'd done it, but he'd also never been that angry before.

After multiple tests, it was determined that the worst was a minor concussion. The kicks to my stomach left the area sore and painful, and contributed to my level of shock, but there was no internal bleeding. Everything else was superficial and only a few stitches were needed. I was bandaged up, given IV fluids and antibiotics, and allowed to leave my room.

"You should rest," Penelope said in protest as she and Genevieve helped me to pull on some yoga pants, a tank top, and a loose hoodie.

I shook my head. "I need to know."

Her brow furrowed and she grabbed the wheelchair, pushing it over. "You're going to sit here."

When we arrived in the waiting area, Hamilton and Rhys stood, their eyes wide as they looked me over.

"Anything?" I asked.

They shook their heads.

Every minute, the elevator pinged when a new family member arrived. As I looked around, I noted a lack of staff and other patients. In fact, the level wasn't laid out like any hospital I'd ever seen. For one, the waiting room was open to the rooms.

"It's the de Loughrey wing," Genevieve said, seeming to note my confusion.

"Wing?"

She nodded. "This section is for our family, and our family only."

With all that I knew, it shouldn't have surprised me.

I stared at the loops of the carpet, watching the expensively clad feet move back and forth against the tightly woven blue and grey. There were words, but nothing I could process. Raised voices and cries broke through, but still I couldn't make out what they were about.

My chest clenched and I let the numbness sink in, losing focus on everything around me. I stared down at my hands and the deep red that still stained the creases in my knuckles and around my cuticles.

What was taking them so long? The tears that had stayed away began sliding down my cheeks.

I tried to understand the reality of the past few days—the truths that were revealed—all in an effort to stave off the panic of not being beside him.

I didn't know where he'd been shot, only that there was a lot of blood.

Atticus had been shot.

A fresh wave of agony ripped through me, and I started to hyperventilate.

"Hey, hey," a familiar voice said as arms embraced me. "He's going to be okay. We have the best doctors taking care of him."

It was Penelope again, and I welcomed her warmth, but it did nothing to assuage my guilt.

"It's my fault."

"You're damn right it is!" Vera hissed, her shiny heels coming to a stop in front of me.

"Mother!" Penelope admonished.

"Michael is her bodyguard," Charles boomed out, gaining the attention of the whole room. "He should have been with her."

I froze. "What did you say?"

Charles sneered down at me. "You really are useless. Michael should have stayed beside you. That is his sole job."

"The other part."

"What other part?" Penelope asked.

"The bodyguard part."

Vera scoffed. "Did you really think my son would let you go out on your own without protection?"

I shook my head. "But he's a driver."

"All of our bodyguards are drivers," Vera clarified. "Are you so naive that you believed we ran around without security all the time? We are de Loughreys, Ophelia. We are always with security. The fact that you never noticed only proves how much you need them."

My stomach dropped as I tried to process what they were saying. I knew there was security, but I never saw them, so I never thought much about it. But often when Atticus and I were together, there was another man, Damien.

They fit so well into the background, I never noticed they were there.

"Mrs. de Loughrey?" a doctor called as he entered.

An entire room of heads snapped in his direction, and I stood as he approached. His eyes widened as he looked me over.

"How is he?" I asked. Penelope slipped her arms around my arm, helping to steady me. It calmed my heart just knowing she was there.

"He's doing well. The bullet passed through his bicep, barely missing the brachial artery and grazing his humerus. He was incredibly lucky. Millimeters and he would not have made it before the helicopter arrived here."

"All that blood?" I asked as fresh tears streamed down my cheeks.

He nodded. "Smaller arteries were severed, causing a lot of blood loss. He went into shock. We were able to stop the bleeding and give him a blood transfusion."

"When can we see him?" Vera asked.

"Soon." He gave a nod and walked away.

Relief flooded me and I looked to Penelope, her eyes brimming with unshed tears. She gave me a small smile. "He's too stubborn to die anyway."

Charles stepped forward and loomed over me, his jaw tight as he stared down at me with eyes full of contempt. "This is all your fault! If he hadn't met you, my son would not have been shot. You are unfit for this family. Leave. Now."

It was a shock to my system, his anger reminding me of Lou. If I hadn't backed down against Lou, there was no way I would let Charles push me. I glared back at him. "Never. I don't give a shit what you think of me, because you're nothing but a bully. You bully your children, your wife, and countless others, but you don't have that power over me. Only Atticus can remove me from his side."

His lip curled up in a snarl, and his arm swung back. I flinched, my arms instinctively raising to protect myself as they'd done for many years—and many times of late—but there was no impact. When I looked up, Silas held his uncle's wrist in his hand.

"If you strike her, there is nothing anyone can do for you when he finds out. You want to blame her for her circumstance without even noticing that one movement had her cowering and folding in on herself. What that man did was not her fault. She is a victim."

I stared at Silas, his blue eyes cold and dark as he glared at Charles. My interaction with the twins was mostly a glance from across a room, so I was shocked that he came to my aid. I only recognized him as Silas due to the length of his hair being longer than his brother's.

Charles yanked his arm from Silas's grip, and as he did, Silas moved to stand in front of me, his brother following suit, blocking me from Charles.

With a growl of rage Charles stormed out, the door banging in its frame.

Once he was gone, Silas turned toward me. "Are you all right?"

I looked up at him and nodded. "You're intuitive, Silas. Thank you," I said.

His hollow eyes stared back at me, his expression blank. "I observe. Besides, I saw the video feed. He didn't."

"Video feed? You saw it?"

He nodded. "Many of us were in Atticus's office after it was discovered you were missing, when the link came in."

"You showed great bravery," Atlas said.

"With all the attempted kidnappings and successful ones the family has dealt with, it was surprising to find it was your own family that betrayed you," Rhys said.

I froze as I stared at him. "Kidnappings? Multiple?"

"Did you finish the binder?" Genevieve asked as she stepped up next to me.

I nodded. "Yes, but I don't remember anything about that. It would have stood out." Even in all the de Loughrey books I'd purchased, only mentioned one from the thirties.

"I don't think she has access to the family files," Rhys said from behind me. "They have information her binder doesn't cover."

"Jack should have set it up," Hamilton said.

"Yeah, but if he or Atticus failed to tell her, it can't be helped," Georgiana said.

"Maybe Atticus wanted to shield her. To keep her completely to himself for as long as possible," Silas said.

Everyone looked to Silas.

"The dark prince speaks truth," Rhys said.

"Don't make me punch you," Atlas said, turning his bored expression to his brother.

The space around me was getting quite crowded, but for the first time I was seeing them in a new light. They were the same as any family, and they cared about each other, even if they weren't the best at expressing it.

"Come," Penelope said as Georgiana took my other hand. "You need to sit back down."

An hour later, the doctor returned and ushered us down the hall. When we reached his room what I now knew to be security flanked the door to Atticus's room and lined the halls. Some of the faces were familiar, but I noticed a lack of Michael and Damien.

The hallway was noisy, filled with more than a dozen de Loughreys.

It was a fight to get in the door, but whoever was pushing me made a path to the front.

Tears pooled in my eyes as I looked at him lying on the bed. His brow was scrunched, and he glared at everyone in the room.

"You're too noisy. Everyone but Ophelia, get out," Atticus yelled, his head falling back against the pillow.

There was an uproar of protest, but his steely gaze halted them, conveying that there was no room for argument. Once the door closed, our eyes met and I couldn't hold back the tears any longer.

"Why did you do that?" Now, I was the one near hysterics as I sobbed into my bandaged hands.

FORTY-FOUR

ATTICUS

My mind was still clouded and my body exhausted, but I still couldn't stand to see her cry like that.

"Come up," I said, holding out my arm, inviting her to take the space next to me.

She shook her head, her brow furrowed. "I don't want to hurt you."

"You're hurting my feelings and making me angry by not getting your ass next to mine right this instant."

She jumped and nodded before gingerly, standing up and shuffling toward the edge of the bed. Gauze wrappings peeked out from the cuff of her hoodie, and various other bandages and butterfly stitches dappled her swollen face. I scooted over a bit, cringing against the spike of pain in my left arm. Her tear-filled eyes stared at me as she climbed on.

"Don't think about it. Lie down. Now," I ground out.

Once she settled in my arms, I let out a sigh, my body relaxing. I leaned down, ignoring the jolt from the tug on my arm, and breathed her in. She was with me. She was safe. We were fine.

"Now tell me—why the fuck did you leave me?"

Her face scrunched up and her body gave a hard shake before she turned her face into my chest. Hot, wet tears fell upon my skin.

I reached up to rub circles on her back and pressed another kiss to the top of her head "There was no way in hell I was letting that insect harm you."

She lifted my head, sniffling. "I almost lost you."

"Don't cry. I can't stand to see you cry."

She cupped my cheek. "Don't do that again. Promise me."

"I can't," I said with a shake of my head. "If you are in danger, I will protect you."

"I'm sorry. I got scared."

"Elaborate. Scared of what?"

"We're just a contract."

"I know it was originally a business contract, but to me, it's become more than that. Am I not good enough? Am I not enough for you to fight for?" I asked. My voice was raw, exposed. I hated showing emotions, but between my injury and her distress, I was unable to keep it in. "Why did you leave?"

"Because the other night was real to me, and it was just another business deal for you."

"Everything is contractual to me, but that night wasn't."

"What was that stack of bills for other than paying me for my services?"

My eyes widened. "The money for your sisters?"

She stared up at me, her eyes wide in horror. Days before, she told me her sisters' tuition deposit for their new school was due and the school didn't take credit cards and she didn't have a checkbook.

"You didn't tell me you were going out of the country and then Jack handed me that envelope and I thought…I thought…"

The anger seeped out of me as understanding flooded in. From the beginning, despite our attraction, Ophelia didn't want to feel like she was selling her body to me—the whole reason for her clause in the contract. Handing her a stack of cash after sex with no explanation attached was bound to cause mixed signals.

"You thought something stupid, didn't you?"

She nodded in between sobs. "You left, and…and then, but you didn't say goodbye."

"Didn't say goodbye?" I tilted my head to look down at her. "Do you think me so cold to leave you like that?"

She nodded.

A groan left me. "Hmm, well, next time I'll make sure you're fully awake so you won't come to idiotic conclusions. Better yet, I'll just take you with me."

"What?"

I brushed the hair from her forehead, fully exposing her beautiful light brown eyes. "I very much said goodbye. I pressed my lips to yours, and you reached up and drew me closer. It was nearly impossible to pull myself away, but you were already asleep again before your head hit the pillow."

Her brow scrunched, and she shook her head. "I don't remember."

A sigh left me. "You are the most infuriating creature I have ever encountered. Fuck the contract—I just want you."

"What?"

"You heard me."

"Why?"

I paused and clenched my jaw. The words I was about to say I'd never said to a woman before. They weren't words that passed my lips often: foreign and weighty, and the verbal expression of the emotions I held for her.

"I'm in love with you, Ophelia. Utterly and all-consumingly in love with you to the point of madness."

"Really?"

"Truly."

"I love you, too." Another sob broke from her, but her expression wasn't filled with anguish, but rather a hypnotic glow with a blinding smile.

"What am I going to do with you?"

"What do you mean?"

"I'm completely wrapped around your finger, and you don't even notice. And you have a bad habit of running when you're scared. Stop."

Her fingers curled into a fist around the thin blanket covering me. "That's what I do. I run. I'm a runner."

"Stop running from me."

She met my gaze. "But you're the most dangerous thing to me."

"Why?"

"Because you can break me."

"That's the last thing I want to do. Talk to me, and tell me how you feel."

"How do you feel?" she asked.

"Overwhelmed, and besides the pain, I'm cycling between panic that is wearing off, euphoria of finding you unharmed, and the need to chain you to my bed so that you can never leave me again."

Her eyes widened. "Never leave you?"

"Never. Not in five years, and not in fifty." I cupped her cheek, making sure she was looking at me. "I mean it, Ophelia. I love you. I can no longer live without you beside me. And next time you can't find me and are worried, call until I answer."

"I'm sorry."

I shook my head. "What am I going to do with you?"

"You already asked that."

"Do you have an answer for me?" I asked.

She took her bottom lip between her teeth. "Love me forever?"

I ran my thumb against her bottom lip to soothe it, relishing the pink that spread across her cheeks. "I don't think that will be a problem."

I was certain I would never love anyone else but her.

FORTY-FIVE

OPHELIA

The flurry of events after Atticus was shot were a blur. Lou and my mom were both in jail awaiting trial for multiple offenses including false imprisonment and aggravated assault, not to mention the growing case for the murder of my father.

Between Lou's confession and the information Atticus's team uncovered, the answer to the question I'd asked from the moment the cops appeared at our door was answered. A selfish, greedy, evil man had taken away the person that meant the most to me. And he almost did it a second time.

I had hope that when the trials were done, they would both rot in jail for the rest of their lives. There was no good will left with my mother after I found out her involvement in addition to all that she had helped Lou with. My father's death was on her hands as well.

Rhys had tried to alleviate my anxiety by informing me that the first-degree kidnapping charge alone held a minimum twenty-five-year sentence, and that applied to both Mom and Lou. And that didn't even cover the list of other sins they were being charged with.

Brooke and Andrea were going to continue to stay with our aunt in New Haven, with financial help from Atticus and me. Their private high school and any college they wanted to attend was paid for. I also set aside two of our extra bedrooms for any time they wanted to visit or stay.

They didn't blame me for anything that had happened, only themselves for not telling me what was going on sooner, but I knew Lou had struck fear in them. Fear was a hard thing to break. Over the past few months, they'd overheard Mom and Lou talking, plotting, and even whispering, "We'll kill Ophelia if we have to."

Thankfully, Brooke and Andrea remained as sweet and innocent as I remembered, not seeming to take on some of their parents' vile traits, though they were showing signs of being the teenagers they were with their bickering. We had plans for them to come out the following week for a few days before the new school year began.

For now, we were taking a much needed break, mostly due to Atticus's injury but also my own. Cuts were still healing, and bruises were still visible, but faded more and more with each day.

Once Atticus was released from the hospital, we stayed at the Tower for a few days before moving out to the Hamptons house for a few weeks—the Asylum—to heal. Atticus's doctor told him he needed rest, and he wasn't going to get that in the city. A few other de Loughreys followed: a very pregnant Elizabeth and her family, Rhys, Georgiana, Hamilton, and Penelope. Though Georgiana's side had their own house, she stayed with us.

I had to admit I liked it when there were more people, because that also meant more security. Michael and Damien were always with us, of course, and Michael kept an eagle eye on me at all times. Guess I deserved that.

None of them stayed the entire time, coming and going as they pleased. Although we were outside the city, I couldn't get Atticus to completely shut off and relax. Even Holly had come out for work, bringing her partner Becca along with her, which only served to make me even more embarrassed about my jealous outburst weeks before.

Like all de Loughrey properties, it was huge, though small compared to Stronghold. My favorite part was sitting on the porch and listening to the waves crash on the shore. If only the water were warmer.

I sat on one of the plush lounge chairs on the covered porch as I stared at the list of invites for the wedding. I was thankful I wouldn't have to address all seven hundred myself as Vera had already hired a calligrapher.

Seven hundred.

I invited six—Aunt Stacey, Brooke, Andrea, Mitchell, my friend Dani from college, and my grandfather.

Atticus had his private investigator, Hugo, track him down, and I was happy to find that the last link to my father was still alive. I'd just gotten his address and telephone number the day before and was working up the courage to talk to him. Mom had brainwashed me that my father's family didn't want me and that had created an insecurity, but I had resolved to contact him by the weekend.

Long ago, before I was even in the picture, Vera had employed a wedding planner who was thankfully consulting me more about the wedding. Once I truly understood the scale of the event our ceremony would be, it didn't bother me at all. I just submitted ideas and was happy they were being considered. Less stress on me anyway.

And I was excited about it for the first time.

Why?

Because I'd stupidly fallen for the wicked king. And I couldn't be happier.

He loved me, too. He said it over and over again, and my heart was fit to bust.

We were in love and getting married. We were a legit couple planning a wedding, no longer simply carrying out the terms of our contract.

I moved my attention away from the never-ending list of names I didn't know, though half ended with de Loughrey, and moved back to my arch nemesis—the Binder of Doom. After two months and after skipping to the end that held the Code of Conduct and list of businesses the family ran, I'd finally finished.

In between mind-numbing years of information on my future husband, I'd gone through the family history and genealogical information, mixed in with other books I'd acquired. There was so much information, I wasn't sure I would ever remember it all.

My guiding light was the fact that I was learning about his life in a more organic way these days. The Binder of Doom couldn't tell me that he had the scariest side-eye I'd ever encountered, or that a smile was like winning the lottery.

The man was much more interesting than his history book.

I closed my computer and soaked in the soothing sound of the waves crashing on the shore. It was such a peaceful sound. And while for the most part, it was relaxing, there were still times of tension, especially when everyone was together at the dining room table.

Hours later, we all sat around the table. Atticus hissed as he grimaced in pain after trying to lift his arm up to cut his food.

"Here, let me," I said, reaching out with my utensils to help.

"I can do it myself," he growled.

At times his attitude ramped up, the wicked king leaking out. Coming across as weak and not having control were two things he hated.

I slumped back into my chair. "Fine, but you don't have to be so stubborn."

"See, this is what happens when you get involved with the help," Hamilton said with a sneer at dinner one night.

Of all the de Loughreys, Hamilton was the one I was getting the most tired of. The ruthless prince didn't mince words and was constantly expressing his opinion as bluntly as possible.

"What has your panties in a twist?" I asked, having had enough of his attitude.

"You're not good enough to be a de Loughrey."

"Watch your tongue, Hamilton," Atticus glared at his younger brother.

"I'm telling you, you're going to eat those words. And I'll be laughing the entire time," I said. I knew from experience the proudest men could be brought to their knees by the most innocuous of women.

His glare darkened. "That'll be a cold day in hell."

I grinned at him. "Better bring out that winter gear."

He threw his napkin down and abruptly stood before stomping off down the hall.

"I think you may have hit a nerve, Ophelia," Penelope said with a giggle.

"They bicker like brother and sister," Holly said, laughing.

Rhys shook his head. "They butt heads because Ophelia doesn't bow to him, reducing him to a child hurtling insults."

I started to laugh, then cringed as pain shot through my brain. A sigh left me and I pushed my plate forward, my appetite gone as the pain increased.

Atticus stared at me. "Are you okay?"

I shook my head. "Headache."

His lips formed a thin line. "They've been happening more since then."

I nodded in agreement. "The doctor said they'll lessen when everything regulates again."

After my initial retelling to the police where he was present, we didn't talk about my time locked in the basement. Atticus's anger was nearly unstoppable when the subject was brought up. He'd already worked hard from his hospital bed. It may have only been a few days, but all the beating combined with days of starvation and dehydration was proving hard to bounce back from.

"I'm going to go lie down," I said, pushing my chair back.

Atticus reached for my hand and pulled it to his lips. "I'll check on you shortly."

I nodded, then made my way up to our bedroom. It reminded me a lot of his room at Stronghold, full of navy blue, but instead of dark woods, they were painted white, giving it a lighter, more vacation-home-type feel.

The room was illuminated from the setting sun, and I crawled onto the bed and snuggled in. Every night, I couldn't help but touch him as I slept. Even if it was simply my hand resting against him, as long as I could feel him, I was okay.

He was safe.

I was safe.

We were safe.

FORTY-SIX

ATTICUS

There was an odd feeling in my chest. It was as if my body was lighter, and I found my mind wandering yet again.

Ophelia filled my every thought, distracting me from my work.

Is this what love is?

It had to be true, because after admitting it to her, it felt like a shackle around my heart released, leaving nothing but an all-consuming desire to possess every part of her.

No more barriers were in our way, and what was once just a marriage of convenience was now one of love. The only woman to ever have my heart.

The problem was that she'd completely infected my mind, and I'd wasted most of my limited day. After everything and we were released, I took Ophelia out to the Asylum. Her smile was missing, lost in all that happened, and I was determined to bring it back. It also got us away from the constant barrage of the press and the stress they created.

Somehow, they got wind of the kidnapping and my being shot, and they'd become relentless trying to get photographs. The incident was all over the news, and I'd even had to force the leakage of some information to keep them from spinning it however they pleased.

When a photo cropped up of Ophelia sitting on the veranda, we packed up and fled. It was better, less crowded, and we were finally able to relax some.

However, I was also determined to get some amount of work done. I barely took weekends off, making being forced to slow down excruciating. I didn't know *how* to relax.

Getting anything done was difficult, not only because of my doctor's orders to rest, but also due to my left arm being in a sling.

While Ophelia's injuries were superficial and she was healing quickly, my own would take a bit longer. The bullet had passed through my arm, barely missing vital arteries.

Even with one arm down, I was able to force her to relax, to make her writhe and blast away everything from her mind. Her flushed skin and tight nipples combined with her sounds was enough to drive any man mad.

"You are looking entirely too full of yourself. Stop it immediately," Rhys called out, pulling me from the memory of Ophelia's flushed face. Probably a good thing as next would be the auditory memory of her moaning.

"Excuse me?" He'd actually managed to catch me off guard. I seriously needed to get my focus back. I'd never found myself in such an absurd state.

Rhys sat down with a smirk on his face. "Gotta hand it to you, cousin. I doubted you when you said you'd have her pinned to your bed in less than six months. What I didn't expect was you falling in love with her in the process."

"Really?" Somewhere deep down, I'd always known. That was why I couldn't let her go, why I chose her.

His head tilted to the side as he scrutinized me. "Hmm. Well, perhaps. It was her after all. Your siren. She lured you in with ease."

"You think the last few months have been with ease?" I asked. Ease was not the word to cover the struggle, the walk through fire, we'd endured to get where we were.

"You haven't complained much." He blew out a breath. "Well, I suppose it was about time it happened to one of us. I'm certain our ancestors are rolling in their graves with ten…nine descendants in no hurry to marry and procreate."

It had been inconceivable to our grandfather that only one of his grandchildren had borne the next generation of heirs. Elizabeth was both praised and shunned by him as her children didn't bear the de Loughrey name.

"Before Ophelia, I felt that children were an obligation."

"That's because that was all you were seen as."

That was correct. I was an obligation to fill the role of successor. My being wasn't created out of love, and that was why I had such a difficult time with the concept of love.

Not anymore.

"It's hard to admit that I am not confident in my abilities to be a father, but that isn't enough to negate my desire to have children with her. I find I want and I am excited to see the perfect mixture of the both of us."

"Ophelia will make a great mother."

The image of her with a baby filled my mind, and I smiled. "Yes, she will." She demonstrated her devotion to family with her sisters. Her maternal instincts to protect were strong.

Her moans resonated in my mind and I internally cursed. I needed to heal and quickly, because I wasn't sure how much longer I could hold out from being buried inside her.

More than that, I wanted to take the first step to ensure she would always be mine, and that was making her my wife.

OPHELIA

Over a week had passed since we began staying in the Hamptons. As with every morning, I took a swim, keeping up with it to become stronger in the water, and exited the pool just as the sun was reaching its peak. I had to admit, the Asylum was quickly becoming a favorite of the many properties the family owned. True, I hadn't been to that many, but I loved being close to the city while feeling like I was far away. It was refreshing.

Rhys had come out again the night before, and he and Atticus had spent the morning locked in the office. It was difficult for Atticus to relinquish any of his responsibilities even for a short period of time, and I worried it was hindering his healing.

A physical therapist was coming soon, and I hoped it would help. Seeing Atticus in pain always made my guilt flare up.

I padded down the hall to our room in my cover-up, my hair a damp, wavy mess. A shower would be good, followed by some lunch, and then maybe I could pry Atticus away for some relaxing around the pool.

My eyes widened when I opened the door. Atticus was sitting on the end of the bed, his sling half off.

"What are you doing?" I screeched as I rushed forward.

"I hate this thing," he grumbled, grimacing as he stretched out his arm.

I took hold of his arm, checking over his wound. "It's starting to look better. The bruising is fading," I said.

"Get that look off your face," he growled.

I blinked at him, our eyes meeting.

"I can't fucking stand to see it. You have no guilt that needs assuaging." His other hand tugged on my arm until I was standing between his legs. "You did not do this. I will be fine. Healing just takes time." He reached up and lightly touched the last remnants of my own wounds. "Besides, I should shoulder the guilt. How many days did you suffer because I couldn't protect you?"

I cupped his face and pressed my lips to his. "You saved me. That's what matters. And you are not ever allowed to scare me like that again. Got it?"

"Yes, my dear."

I slapped at his chest. "You know I hate it when you call me that."

His bad mood faded away. "I think you secretly love it."

"Couldn't you find a better term of endearment?"

"What would you prefer? My Lia?"

I scrunched my nose at that one. "Mom called me Lia."

"Baby and other overly used filler names are out." He hummed as he thought it over. "My love?"

I pursed my lips. "Better."

"Darling?"

I shook my head.

"Waitress?"

I pulled back and glared at him, which made him throw his head back in laughter.

"You think you are so cute, and you are not at all," I said.

"My beautiful wife."

Heat rose in my cheeks. "You like calling me your wife."

His eyes sparkled. "I do."

"In a few months."

His brow furrowed as he stared out the window. "Do we have to wait that long?" He looked back toward me, our eyes locking. "Can't we just go to the courthouse one afternoon, and after I can call you that and it be true to your standing?"

"What about the wedding?" I asked.

"You didn't say no. There is hope. With regards to the wedding… my mother would slaughter me in my sleep if we didn't go through with it, but who is to say we can't marry legally and still have a ceremony months later?"

"Nothing, I suppose. She'll flip, though." Vera's angry face from the hospital flashed in my mind.

"I'm not afraid of her. Are you?"

"Deathly," I said, then let out a laugh.

"Well, if you won't marry me right this instant, which I'm going to guilt you on over the next five months, especially when my mother is driving you crazy, there is one thing I know we could do."

"And what's that?" I asked, curious as to what he was up to.

"A small bonfire."

I pulled back and looked down at him. "Bonfire?"

"I have our contract with me."

My eyes widened and my mouth dropped open. "Really?"

He nodded. "You love me. That was all I ever wanted."

My chest clenched, and my heart soared, a smile overtaking my face. "I do love you. Okay. Let's do that. Then we'll go get married."

His brow furrowed, and his lips twitched. "What?"

I shrugged. "Once that contract is burned, I can't exactly let you get away. Gotta nail it down. Seal the deal. Make you mine."

His forehead rested against mine. "I've been yours from the moment our eyes met."

My heart felt like it was going to explode if he kept talking to me like that. "Can we add the Binder of Doom?"

His expression dropped. "Have you read it?"

"Cover to boring-ass cover. I find talking to the real thing is a much better way to get to know you and your family." My brow scrunched. "Though maybe keep the family tree, property, and company lists." They would be good for reference.

"If you will become my wife today, I'll get the matches."

I was certain a manic expression grew on my face. "Give me ten to take a shower."

It was possibly the shortest shower of my life, the adrenaline of what we were about to do buzzing in my veins. I threw on a sundress and sandals while letting my hair air dry and applying some simple eyeliner and mascara.

"Is this okay?" I asked as I turned to him. It was definitely not a de Loughrey approved appearance, and so I was shocked by the warm smile that graced his face.

"Perfection." He reached out and took my hand and we descended to the first floor to look for Rhys. We found him in the office, sitting at one of the three desks inside the large room.

He looked up as we entered. "Why so excited?" he asked.

"Do you have that prenup on you?" Atticus asked. While it was the first I'd heard of it, I wasn't surprised. With a man of his status and wealth, it was a given.

His gaze snapped to us. "Dear cousin, you aren't thinking about going against Auntie Vera, are you? If you are, I will weep for you."

"Shut up and tell me yes or no."

"I do, but it hasn't been revised since my initial draft months ago." He turned his attention back to his computer, and a moment later turned the screen toward us.

As I looked over the document, which I knew was a necessity no matter what our original contract stated, I was overwhelmed. Even back in the beginning, when he didn't owe me anything past our contract, he had insured that I would be okay. That I wouldn't struggle and any children would be well taken care of. Even a place to live free of rent.

I nodded, fighting back the overwhelming emotions. "Print it. I'll sign it."

"Now?"

I smiled at him and nodded. "We're going on a field trip, want to come?"

Rhys's eyes widened as he looked to Atticus. "Now?"

He shrugged. "Why not?"

He blew out a breath. "Get Penelope in here. We need a witness."

Two hours later we walked out of the local courthouse as Atticus and Ophelia de Loughrey. Officially married.

My heart was so full, and I couldn't stop smiling. The Rock was more than just a very expensive ornament. It had meaning that bound the two of us together.

"Well, cousin, you finally got the girl," Rhys said with a smile.

Atticus tugged me to his side. "Yes, I did." He leaned down and pressed his lips to mine. "And I'm never letting her out of my sight again."

"Because she gets into trouble, right?"

"Correct."

"Hey!"

Everyone laughed, which was good after all the heaviness we'd been through.

"I'm going to work with Chef for a celebratory dinner," Penelope said as she headed down the hall.

"And I'm going to check the champagne and wine stock," Rhys said with a wink.

Georgiana let out a giggle as she looked to Hamilton, who was staring off grumpily. She wrapped her arms around his and pulled. "Come, Hamilton. I think the newlyweds need a little alone time."

Hamilton's face twisted and he glared at me. Did he have a brother complex or did he really just hate me?

"You can tell me all about Uncle's assistant."

Hamilton's eyes widened before narrowing. "What do you think you know?"

She beamed at him, then looked to me, giving a wink before tugging him outside.

"I wonder what that was all about," Atticus said as he watched them walk away.

"Maybe hell froze over?"

"Hmm. Well, no need to worry about him." He pulled me closer with his good arm. "I think it's best to consummate our marriage."

My skin prickled in anticipation at just the thought. "What about your arm?"

His lips ghosted up the column of my neck. "It's been far too long since I've been buried inside your pussy. As my wife, it is your duty to relieve me, is it not?"

"I don't want to shirk my duties." I grabbed his belt and pulled, directing us up the stairs. "That would be a bad start as your wife."

He chuckled and leaned down, a mischievous grin on his face. "I'd have to punish you."

"Well, you'll have to catch me first," I said, then ran up the stairs and down the hall.

"You have to be quicker than that," he growled as he smacked my ass.

A shriek of laughter left me and I picked up the pace, flinging the door open to our room. I stopped in the middle of the room, my body tense in anticipation, jumping when the door slammed shut.

His arm wrapped around my waist, and he pulled me into him.

"Caught you," he whispered against my ear, sending a delicious shiver down my spine.

Heat spread through me, and I turned to find his eyes dark and heavy.

"Get this fucking thing off me," he growled, pulling at his sling.

Once it was off we clawed at each other's clothes, frenzied in our need, our lips crashing together, his tongue brushing against mine sending heat and electric shocks to settle between my thighs.

"My wife," he whispered.

Skin against skin was filled with warmth and comfort, love and desire. Only with Atticus could I feel these things. We climbed onto the bed and I cupped his face, pulling his lips back down to mine.

He wrapped his arms around me, cringing as he froze.

"Your arm…"

He gripped my jaw, his eyes dark. "Don't worry about my arm.

Any note of pain, erase it, because I will ignore it for one reason—
your pleasure."

I pushed on his chest and he fell back down to the bed. "Then
we're doing this my way," I said as I straddled his hips.

With my hands flat on his chest, I rocked my hips against his
hard length, wetting it, teasing us both with the light friction. Each
time my clit brushed against his hard flesh, I got a little bit wetter
and needier.

His hands dug into my thighs, and a groan left him. "Ophelia,
it's been weeks. Stop fucking with me."

I bit down on my bottom lip as I smiled down at him. "So bossy."
I rose up and reached between us, lining him up before slowly sinking down on his cock.

His eyes rolled back, and his muscles tensed. I could tell that
as much as he enjoyed the view, he wanted to flip us so that he could
have control. Each roll of my hips elicited another groan.

I leaned forward, my nipples brushing against his chest. "There
was one last thing I forgot to tell you."

"What?" he asked, the strain coming through in his tone, the
thick cords of his neck standing out.

I brushed my lips against his and made sure his gaze didn't leave
mine. "I stopped taking my birth control."

It was like a switch was flipped. His pupils dilated, and suddenly I was thrown onto my back. His hips slammed against mine.

I stared up at him and the wild, needy desire that emanated
from him. With his good arm, he pinned my hands above my head
while his other arm kept my leg against him.

"Take my cock," he growled as he pulled back, then slammed
back in.

My vision blurred as shocks rocked my body. "Yes. I want it all."

"Who does this pussy belong to?"

"Y-you," I choked out.

His grip on my wrists tightened and his thrusts became more
forceful. "All for me. Your heart. Your body. Your orgasms. All mine."

"All yours." I squeezed my walls against his cock, causing him to curse against my ear. "Just as you are all mine."

"Everything that I am is yours."

My mind was going black, caught up in the system-overloading pleasure of each bottoming rock of his hips. Every muscle wound tighter as my body geared up, climbing higher and higher into euphoria.

"Look at me," Atticus said, his forceful tone cutting through the fog.

The deep, dark intensity of his blue eyes was too much and my back arched, a cry leaving me as my muscles snapped, shaking with each pulse of my orgasm.

"Always," I managed to whisper as I came down, shocks still rocking me.

He cursed and slammed his hips hard against me, a roar leaving me as I felt him twitch deep within. His breath came out in harsh pants and I watched as clarity returned to his eyes. Strength left him, and he relaxed beside me on the bed.

We were married. I was officially Ophelia de Loughrey, and madly in love with my husband.

A smile crept up on my face as I lay there, boneless, staring up at the ceiling as I felt Atticus's warmth beside me.

"How do you feel?" I asked.

"Indescribable." He patted his chest, rubbing at it with a curious look on his face.

"That feeling in your chest? That's called happiness."

He pulled my hand up to his lips and placed a kiss against my knuckle. "You make me feel this way. Only you, my beautiful wife."

A happy sigh left me, and I scooted closer to rest my head on his chest, the soothing beats of his heart beneath my ear.

For so long I'd been uncared for, unloved, with nobody to stand up for me.

Then a handsome king came and took my hand, and for the first time in a long time, I felt cherished.

It turns out, even wicked things can love.

OPHELIA

January

I stared at my reflection and bit down on my lip, unbelieving of the woman before me. It seemed like something I would be used to after all these months, but still, every time the de Loughrey stylists got ahold of me, I transformed into another person.

Today, the styling was a little different, and the dress white.

While Atticus and I had technically been married for five months, it was our wedding day.

"Lia! Lia!" Andrea called out as she ran into the dressing room, bounding as usual, her eyes wide as she looked at me. "You look just like a princess!"

I beamed at her. "Right?" I felt like my smile was going to break my face in half. I hoped Andrea would always stay so bright and cheery.

"You know she's going to tell everyone in school her sister's a princess now, right?" Brooke said, her expression pinched in annoyance.

"That's mean!" Andrea pouted.

Brooke rolled her eyes. "Oh, grow up!"

Andrea stomped her foot. "No, cause then I'll be mean like sissy."

"Girls, calm down," Aunt Stacey called from the doorway. She stepped up to me and smiled as she took my hand. "You look beautiful, Ophelia."

I squeezed her hand. "Thank you."

"Your dad would be proud of you. For all you did."

"Atticus is the one to thank." He prepared for Lou to be an issue long before he became one. The man was always two steps ahead of everyone.

"But it's because of you, and for you, that Atticus helped so much. Paul was the same. He loved you more than anything."

My eyes started to water, and I had to fan them to keep the tears back. Stacey had really liked my dad, and she'd helped him a lot when things started to crumble with my mom. As far as sides went, blood wasn't thicker than water, and her allegiance was with my father.

"I wish he was here," I said, my voice cracking.

"He is. In you, and in your grandfather."

I perked up at that. "Is he here?" After reconnecting with my grandfather on my dad's side, we had talked in some form nearly every day. That connection to my dad was the last piece my damaged heart needed to heal from the pain I'd had to bury for so long.

She nodded. "He's waiting to walk you down the aisle."

"Hey, Lia?" Brooke said, stopping by the door.

"Yes?"

Her brow scrunched and she chewed on her bottom lip. "Thanks for everything."

"Yeah, yeah! We love you, Lia!" Andrea said, popping back through on the other side of Brooke, her smile blinding.

"I love you both. Spring break we'll do something, okay?"

Brooke cracked a half smile, something I'd gladly take from my moody, hormonal teenage sister. "Can't wait."

The door closed behind them, and I was once again left alone. Which was weird—where did all my bridesmaids go?

Vera originally wanted ten bridesmaids, but I'd talked her down to Holly and Atticus's sisters. It gave a little more of an intimate feel having a small wedding party with such a huge guest list.

The door creaked and I expected to find someone from my bridal party, but instead the most handsome man in the world appeared.

"Atticus, what are you doing here?" I asked as he strode forward.

Once he reached me, he wrapped his arm around my waist, gripped my jaw, and pressed his lips to mine for a toe-tingling kiss.

"I stayed away all night. I'm not staying away any longer," he said when our lips parted.

"Breaking all the rules," I chided with a smile and a shake of my head.

"You're already my wife. Superstitions mean nothing at this point."

"Still, you're going to see me in a few minutes anyway."

"But then I'll have to share you with many other people." He raised my hand to his lips and placed a kiss, then nipped at my knuckle. "I need a calm before the impending storm. And I have something for you."

"What's that?"

He pulled his arm from around my waist, presenting a box. My brow scrunched as I stared at it, reading the name. My eyes widened and snapped to his.

"Oh, yes, I keep track of your cycle, my dear," he said with a grin.

I shook my head. "It's just the stress from the wedding," I argued. My period was three days late, but that sometimes happened. While I wasn't ready to pull out the pregnancy test, it seemed my husband was. "Fine, for you on our wedding day."

He smirked at me and held the box out. I snatched it from him and headed to the attached bathroom.

"Couldn't you have done this before I was trussed up like a Christmas turkey?" I asked as I tried to figure out how I was going to pee on a stick and not all over some part of my very expensive dress.

"Need a hand?" he asked from the doorway.

"I don't trust your hands."

"I think I'm insulted."

"You can be insulted. I just know what happens when you get your hands on me, and I swear to God if you mess up my hair, your mother will kill you."

He could only chuckle, but it was an honest threat. There would be hell to pay if we messed up Vera's big day. She eventually let our early courthouse marriage slide, but only after claiming we'd ruined everything.

Finally, I found a way to gather up my dress and hold it out of the way. With success, I managed to hit the target and finished, letting my dress fall back down without any issues except for the light sheen of sweat from wrestling with the twenty pounds of fabric.

By the time I was straightened, Atticus blocked the doorway while I washed my hands and we waited.

"You better act surprised when you see me," I warned him as I stepped forward and wrapped my arms around his waist.

"Your beauty always surprises me, so that won't be hard. Especially not on a day like today." He glanced down to the sink, and I watched a smile spread on his lips. "Even more so when I know you're carrying my child."

I snapped my eyes down, the word "pregnant" visible in capital letters.

"Whoa."

His lips trailed up the column of my neck, the sensation spreading goose bumps across my body. "I'm still an overachiever."

"How so?"

"I told Rhys I'd have you pinned to my bed in less than six months, and look at all I've accomplished in just over that."

We fell in love, we got married, and he knocked me up, all in the span of the last nine months.

"I love you," I said.

His gaze met mine and the once dispassionate gaze was lit with fire and passion. "Not as much as I love you." He cupped my face and pulled me toward him as his lips crashed down against mine.

"Atticus William, don't you dare mess up her hair!" Holly screeched from behind Atticus.

He groaned against my lips before pulling away. "I'll see you shortly, my love."

I bit down on my bottom lip, my heart skipping in my chest. Every time he called me that, I melted. I hated watching him walk away, but before he crossed through the door he turned back and gave me the most wistful smile I'd ever seen from him.

"Really, what was he thinking," Holly grumbled as she double checked my hair and makeup before attaching the veil to the crown atop my head. She smiled at me. "Can I blame him? I'm guessing it was positive, so I really can't."

"What was positive?" I asked before it hit me. "You bought the pregnancy test."

She beamed at me. "Atticus de Loughrey buy a pregnancy test?"

"Ludicrous, I know!"

"I know, due to a misunderstanding on your part, that we had a rocky beginning, but I want you to know how happy I am that Atticus has you. In nearly twenty years I'd never seen him happy. Then he met you. Thank you for loving him."

My lips thinned out, and I was fanning my eyes again. "Damn it, Holly."

She took hold of my hands and laughed, then tugged. "Come. Let's show the world who tamed the wicked king."

"I didn't really tame him."

"Hmm, maybe not for everyone else, but he's so cute when he's talking about you or to you or is with you."

"Don't let him hear you say he's cute."

"I'm not afraid of him. I hog-tied that lion and beat my friendship into him long ago."

I threw my head back in laughter. Their friendship was so strange to me, but I knew my ability to touch Atticus's heart was due to the groundwork she'd laid years before.

When we reached the doors leading into the hall, my grandfather stood awaiting us, his warm brown eyes the same as mine filled with tears.

"You look so beautiful, Ophelia," he said as I approached.

"Thank you."

Holly handed me my bouquet before excusing herself to join the procession as the first bridesmaid was already heading down the aisle.

"I'm so happy I could be here to see you like this," he said as we moved to get in line.

"Me, too."

"Ready?" he asked, his eyes twinkling.

I nodded and looped my arm into his. "Ready."

I blew out a breath as the music picked up and we began walking. The aisle was long, the space filled with over a thousand people, but there was only one that mattered to me.

Standing at the end with a wide smile that was all for me was my husband—my love, and the father of my child. He was the ruler of our family and king of my heart.

Five years with him? Five hundred wouldn't be enough.

We didn't need any more contracts or false affections or Binders of Doom.

I was his, and he was mine.

Together. Forever.

The End

acknowledgements

First to Ashley Jade and A. Zavarelli, who I bonded with at a convention in 2019. They were the first ones I shared my fledgling idea with and they gave me the courage to take on the Heartless Kingdom. Love you both! <3

Always to my boo. You're my person.

Danielle for helping me shape this world.

The Golden Ho's for pinging me awake to get me moving every morning.

To my readers—this is for you.

after all the words...

This book has been a hard wrought labor of love. Through family tragedy and a multi-month battle with pneumonia, and the holidays thrown into the mix, I was faced with so many obstacles.

The initial idea was spun from a stock photo I encountered while on a pic search. It ignited a billionaire family, set fire to eight different stories, and let rise the beginnings of my first intentional series. The Heartless Kingdom was born from that one flash. The titles gave birth to themselves. Soon I began to build their world, expand their empire, and find out just where each of them ruled.

American royalty.

American gods.

Atticus and Ophelia's story would be the hardest and longest. I knew from the beginning because they would be the foundation for the entire world. There are glimpses of all the other characters, tells about what their stories hold. Did you catch them?

Keep reading to find out.

Now…what is in store for Hamilton de Loughrey? Did you get a glimpse of the woman bound to make his cold heart beat? Maybe…. *wink*

about THE AUTHOR

K.I. Lynn is the USA Today Bestselling Author from The Bend Anthology and the Amazon Bestsellers, Breach and Becoming Mrs Lockwood. She spent her life in the arts, everything from music to painting and ceramics, then to writing. Characters have always run around in her head, acting out their stories, but it wasn't until later in life she would put them to pen. It would turn out to be the one thing she was really passionate about.

Since she began posting stories online, she's garnered acclaim for her diverse stories and hard hitting writing style. Two stories and characters are never the same, her brain moving through different ideas faster than she can write them down as it also plots its quest for world domination…or cheese. Whichever is easier to obtain… Usually it's cheese.

Website—www.kilynnauthor.com
Facebook—http://bit.ly/1qbp5tx
Twitter—https://twitter.com/KI_Lynn_
Instagram—https://www.instagram.com/k.i.lynn
Get my Newsletter—http://bit.ly/1U9NSoC

more books from
K.I. LYNN

Wicked Rule

I'm going to make her my queen.

One wedding.

One child.

Five years.

Ten million dollars.

Those are the terms of our contract.

My offer is sound, bold, and necessary. In order to gain my inheritance, I have to have a wife.

She thinks her clause will keep me from having her skin on mine.

She's very wrong.

The de Loughrey's rule the world, and I am their king. I get what I want, and what I want is her.

I'll have her beneath me no matter what.

Find out more here—books2read.com/WickedRule

Ruthless Rule

They call me the ruthless ruler…and they're not wrong.

In the boardroom and the bedroom I take no prisoners and when I'm done, it's all stop.

There's something about my father's new assistant and a chance encounter brings us closer than I ever expected. Once isn't enough, but for the first time in my life, I'm shot down.

Me.

A de Loughrey.

So I sweeten it with money. An indecent proposal that gives both of what we need.

When I learn her secrets I find the impossible bloom inside me.

I'm the ruthless ruler, but she has me by the heart.

Business is business, and when it's done, I don't know what will happen to the heart she holds.

I've met my ruthless match.

Find out more here—books2read.com/RuthlessRule

Off the Cuff

I spilled a cup of coffee on the President of Acquisitions.

He deserved it.

Not the brightest idea, but I'd had a bad day, and now he's getting back at me.

For nine weeks I'm to be his assistant, and there's nothing I can do about it.

It's punishment.

Every moment we're near each other it's a constant battle of wills, but I refuse to go down.

If only my fantasies didn't invade our arguments.

If only he wasn't so good looking.

Everything is off the cuff, including him pinning me to the wall.

Now he wants something else from me.

A date.

There's just one problem—he doesn't know I have a child.

Find out more here—books2read.com/ThatNightKILynn

That Night

I got pregnant on New Year's Eve.

That night was hands down the best night of my life. A magical night with the man of my dreams.

The aftermath changed everything.

After weeks of silence from him and a positive pregnancy test, it was safe to say I was in full out panic mode.

Until I walked into a conference room only to find Mr. Man-of-my-dreams-father-of-my-unborn-child at the head of the table.

Turns out the VP of finance isn't an old boring guy with white hair.

Two different cities.

A baby on the way.

An intense attraction.

And he's technically my boss.

Life just got even more complicated.

Find out more here—books2read.com/ThatNightKILynn

Domenico

The mafia never lets you go.

I thought I was safe, free, but I never expected to find myself
locked in a cage.

I'm in his territory. His prison.

The beast.

A fate worse than death awaits me if I can't get away, so when the
opportunity of salvation presents itself I grab it, even if I'm unsure
if I can trust the hand I'm holding.

The only way out is through, exposing secrets and spilling blood.

Things aren't how they appear. Nobody is what they seem.

Not even me.

Find out more here—books2read.com/AbductedKILynn

Forever and All The Afters

He promised me forever.

Then he boarded a plane for a college a thousand miles away and never returned. A decade later there's a ring on my finger with a new promise from a new love.

Just as my life falls into place, pretty as the pages of a magazine, my world is knocked over. The moment he touches me everything around me begins to crack, exposing all the lies I've told myself.

Every glance reminds me. Every touch ignites.

Things aren't how they used to be.

Love isn't easy.

Find out more here
books2read.com/ForeverAndAllTheAfters

Welcome to the Cameo Hotel

I get what I want.

When I walked through the door of the Cameo Hotel I didn't expect such a beauty to be working the front desk.

The effect she has on me is intense, and I make her life a living hell because of it.

I love her spirit, her internal defiance when completing the most inane task I assign her. My two week stay has turned into unending, just to be near her.

She's under my every command if she wants to keep me happy.

There's one last thing I want.

Her.

Find out more here
books2read.com/WelcomeToTheCameoHotel

Becoming Mrs. Lockwood

Every girl has dreams of meeting Prince Charming, or at least I know I did.

A fairy tale-like meeting of love at first site.

Real life and fairy tales are very different.

I'm just a small town Indiana girl that had a chance encounter with one of Hollywood's golden boys. You may think you know where this story goes—not even close.

Life is different. Marriage is hard. It's even worse when you're strangers.

Find out more here
books2read.com/BecomingMrsLockwood

Six

I had a one-night stand. It wasn't my first, but it would be my last.

A gun to the head.

A trained killer.

A deadly conspiracy.

Kidnapped and on the run, my life and death is in the hands of a sadist captor who happens to be my one-night stand. Armed with countless weapons, money, and new identities, the man I call Six drags me around the world.

The manhunt is on and Six is the next target. Can we find out who is killing off the Cleaners before they find us?

Two down, seven to go.

When it's all over he'll finish the job that dropped him into my life, and end it.

Stockholm Syndrome meets bucket list, and the question of what would you do to live before you died. The questions aren't always answered in black and white. Gray becomes the norm as my morals are tested.

Death is a tragedy, and I'll do anything to stay alive.

Are you ready for the last ride of your life? Six has a gun to your head—what would you do?

This isn't a love story.

It's a death story.

Find out more here—books2read.com/Six-KILynn
Check out the Trailer—https://youtu.be/fzpON3PadIA

Breach Book 1

His body was sin, his cock was sin, and I was a sinner.

To keep myself safe I hide in the world and let life move around
me.

My new partner, Nathan, isn't safe. Far from it.

The darkness coils around him, hidden by a shield created by a
blinding smile. But those who live in shadows see past the façade
we create.

Even in darkness, there is light. A spark that ignites, then explodes.

Every filthy word from his mouth, every possessive touch—I crave
them, need them. Violent and passionate and everything I need to
fill the void inside me, but one thing is missing.

He can never love me.

More than my heart is on the line, and I don't know if I'll survive
our breach.

Find out more here—books2read.com/Breach

The Executive

Business is king, and I have an empire to topple.

Ivy is my new assistant and a threat to me. She's my undoing. If ever I was to believe in a cosmic connection, it was the moment I met her.

For years I've had one goal—revenge. As CEO, I have crafted a strategic plan for business, but never a life beyond.

With one touch from her, the veil is lifted. Things are different, and every moment I'm near her, my world begins to change.

A wall of propriety keeps me from her. I need her as my pawn in this war, beside me in battle. Sharing the secrets of my enemies, and her desires in my bed. Her body to claim as mine.

Getting what I want has consequences.

Collateral damage is real.

In the game of crushing kings of men, I never planned on my heart being a sacrifice.

Find out more here—books2read.com/TheExecutive

Cocksure

Co-written with Olivia Kelley

A life altering lie, ten years, and one wild night later, the game has changed.

Niko

My life is great. I love my job, have awesome friends, and a great family.

Women love me, even if they know it's just for a night.

I always thought love at first sight was bullshit. Then she came storming into my life. She tore through my every rule, rocked my world, and knocked me on my ass.

There's only one problem…she lied.+

Turns out my best friend's little sister isn't so little anymore.

Everly

I stole a night with my fantasy. Lied to him.

After ten years of not seeing each other, Niko doesn't even recognize me.

So I take what I want from him, what I need from him. Without worry. Without consequence.

What I didn't count on was the lingering need for him.

Once the truth is out, the game changes. There are consequences.

I should have known nothing in my life is ever simple.

My brother is going to kill his best friend and I have nine months to figure out what I want.

Find out more here
books2read.com/Cocksure-Lynn-Kelley

Need Book 1

Co-written with N. Isabelle Blanco

I was Kira's from the first moment I saw her. Maybe it was love at first sight, but I was only ten.

She became my best friend.

My crush.

The girl I can't live without.

But I have to.

She was almost mine, but my father took away my chance.

Now she lives across the hall from me. Instead of the title of girlfriend, she's now my stepsister.

But that doesn't stop how I feel, how I want her. Thankfully, I'm off to college two hundred miles away, but even that doesn't help.

She's under my skin, all around me, and I watch her morph from a sexy teenager to an irresistible woman.

I can't take it anymore, I need her.

Is it possible to ever be happy without the one person you *need?*

"I'm Brayden, baby. The man you've been dreaming about your whole life. And I'm about to fucking show you why."

Part 1 of a 3 part series.

Find out more here—books2read.com/NeedSeries

www.ingramcontent.com/pod-product-compliance
Lightning Source LLC
Chambersburg PA
CBHW061211190726

48288CB00001B/136